Amar Alwitry is a Consultant Ophthalmic Surgeon working in the East Midlands. He was brought up in Jersey and is married with four children. He tries hard to balance the work of a good surgeon with being a good writer, good father and a good person.

Amar Alwitry

Emergence:
The Ideal World

TO MY
FAVOURITE
PATIENT !

Vanguard Press

VANGUARD PAPERBACK

© Copyright 2012
Amar Alwitry

The right of Amar Alwitry to be identified as author of
this work has been asserted by him in accordance with the
Copyright, Designs and Patents Act 1988.

A CIP catalogue record for this title is
available from the British Library.

ISBN 978 1 84386 921 4

*Vanguard Press is an imprint of
Pegasus Elliot MacKenzie Publishers Ltd.*
www.pegasuspublishers.com

First Published in 2012

**Vanguard Press
Sheraton House Castle Park
Cambridge England**

Printed & Bound in Great Britain

Acknowledgements

Many thanks to my good friends Justine McCullough and Jarrod Dunn for reading the proofs, and to my lovely sister, Ola, for unstinting support.

Dedicated to my darling angels, Max, Toby, Oscar and Safia, and to my gorgeous wife without whom I could not have done it.

Prologue

Anya picked up the flexisheet entitled: 'Giving up Your Child –
What to Expect', and dutifully read the opening paragraph.

'Every good parent wants what's best for their child...' it
began. The floppy piece of silicon shone with images of mature,
attractive couples looking respectable and dutiful, and taking
part in the sort of pursuits you could enjoy without children such
as trips into space and deep-sea exploration. At the centre of the
sheet was a huge picture of a man and woman in pressure-
resistant sea bubbles, floating deep underwater and looking
shocked and delighted as a huge-jawed deep-sea fish swam
towards them.

'How much longer do we have to wait?' Anya asked Tom,
who sat beside her in the relaxation room, holding their new-
born son in his arms.

Tom didn't answer, instead looking straight ahead at the
huge ceiling-to-floor sheet of water cascading down in front of
them. On it was projected 'Submergence Centre' in large, black
letters that swayed and moved with the flow.

'We've been here nearly –'

Anya was interrupted by the noise she'd been dreading:
hard, sensible footsteps from behind the sheet of water. With a
whoosh, the liquid stream swept apart like a curtain and into the
relaxation room marched Dr Yvonne Willis, head of
Submergence Relations, a tall, slender picture of good health
and breeding. Her clear, pale skin was blemish free, and her
shiny, thick auburn hair was cut into a neat bob that tapered up
at the back of her head. She wore a long white doctor's coat and

a sensible pair of work heels that gave her an extra few inches of height, but were guaranteed to be comfortable all day. Behind her, a personal assistant droid skimmed along on its anti-grav motor, the words: 'Submergence Centre' flowing over its smooth surfaces as it ran under the projection.

'Mr and Mrs Harrison?'

She looked from Anya to Thomas, and gave them both a warm smile.

Tom gave her a smile back that said: *Let's make the best of all this.*

'And this must be the new arrival.' Dr Willis peered into Tom's arms, and stared into the tiny, blinking eyes peering out from an all-weather baby grow.

'Nice to meet you, Dr Willis,' said Tom, reaching up to shake Yvonne's hand. 'We're ready when you are.'

'Good,' said Yvonne, taking a seat on her assistant droid. 'Well, do you have any questions? If you do, now's the time to ask.' She paused, tipping her head from left to right. 'No? OK, well we may as well get started. Come with me.'

They all stood up.

'You really are doing a wonderful thing,' Dr Willis said, as they walked towards the Submergence Centre. 'This is the best decision any parent can make.'

'What – you mean deciding *not* to be a parent?' whispered Anya. Tom glared at her and Anya looked at the floor and was silent. They followed Dr Willis and the floating PA droid through the inactive waterfall doorway, onto a wide bridge suspended from the ceiling by steel cables. It led to a complicated maze of floating platforms, bridges and droid bays, and before long Anya had no idea where they were.

'These are the research areas,' said Dr Willis, as they passed rooms built of thin, translucent screens, behind which the couple could see outlines of human beings moving around. They crossed another suspended bridge which sloped upwards slightly, and suddenly they could hear rain above them. Anya looked up to see a cobweb of monitoring equipment attached to the smooth ceiling.

'And this is the first incubation room,' said the doctor, as they reached the end of the bridge and a door rolled open automatically to reveal a room full of cots. Despite the fact there were at least twenty babies in the room, the only sounds were of nurses sweeping along by the beds, adjusting feeding systems and checking monitors. No crying. At least, not out loud.

There were several empty cots by the doorway, and Dr Willis pointed to one of them.

'Mr Harrison, if you'd put the baby in this cot here please. Thank you.'

Dutifully, Tom put the baby in the cot, and two nurses came forward and began fitting various pieces of equipment around the bed.

'OK. This is where we leave the staff to do their work.'

Dr Willis gestured towards the doorway, and as the couple walked back through it the opaque glass rolled shut behind them.

'I wouldn't look back if I were you,' said the doctor, as she led them over the bridge. 'Did you read the flexisheet? Onwards and upwards.'

Suddenly, a siren began to blare and the doctor's smile slid from her face. It wasn't a gentle 'peep peep' alarm, like an errant communication device, but a big, resounding alarm that started loudly and got louder and louder every second. A red light flashed around them, throwing brown shadows onto the doctor's face and giving her the appearance of a stressed clown. On the floor, big green arrows lit up, pointing away from the incubation room and towards the emergency exit.

Dr Willis turned and headed back over the bridge.

'Please excuse me,' she said, marching quickly towards the room full of cots. 'If the two of you could make your way to the emergency exit. I'll be needed. Just make your way to the exit please. Follow the exit projections.'

'What is it?' shouted Anya, but Dr Willis had already entered the incubation room, the door closing tightly behind her.

Tom took Anya's arm.

'Anya.'

She pushed him away and ran back over the bridge, reaching the incubation room within seconds and hammering on the door with her palms.

She could hear voices inside, some were shouting.

'Get the shocks. Why has no one got the shocks? He's code red.'

Then Dr Willis's voice:

'What's happening to him? Have we lost him?'

'Code red! Shock him again.'

Anya nearly screamed when someone gripped her arms tightly and pinned them to her sides. She turned and saw a big, red face and a blurred security uniform. The guard began to pull her, not unkindly, away from the door and back towards the bridge.

'Please! It's my son. It's my son. What's happening? What have they done to him?'

The guard pulled Anya, sobbing and staggering, back along the bridge to where Tom was waiting.

'We've got to go back.' Anya heard herself scream over the siren. 'Please, Tom.'

Tom's eyes were cloudy and his mouth was twitching and trembling.

'It's too *late*.'

Anya made a strange sighing sound, her legs crumpled and she fainted into Tom's arms. He half carried, half dragged her along the path of the green arrows and through the emergency exit into the pouring rain. The door closed with the finality of a death toll shutting off all sound.

Chapter One

It was a Saturday afternoon when the exam results came through: those insignificant-looking percentages that had the power to change Troy's life forever.

'For goodness sake, Troy, just open it,' said Sarah, sitting on a bar stool opposite and watching Troy bounce his data-disc from one hand to the other. 'You're driving me mad. Oh ratikins – Qigong is cancelled.' She nodded at the thinscreen on the wall, currently broadcasting a university news feed about campus transport times, society meetings and second-hand luggage droids for sale.

Troy banged the flashing data-disc down on the table.

'OK. Right. OK. Just give me one minute.'

Troy was usually a calm character, a trait that didn't sit well with his rangy, athlete's body and restless long limbs. But today, he was anything but calm. The winning smile that made him appear positively delighted with the world was noticeably absent, and his usually excellent posture had been replaced by an uncharacteristic slumped back, eyes fixed on the table. His sandy hair lay flat on his head, as if even it too was too nervous to sit up properly.

A server droid floated past and Troy ordered a long, fruit-syrup drink with a shot of clear spirit on the side – self-medication for the medical student. The droid paused momentarily, and Troy braced himself for the familiar public-service message he'd heard a hundred times before.

'Please enjoy alcohol in moderation,' said the droid, having already assessed Troy's speech patterns and decided he'd consumed over three times his recommended daily alcohol units. 'Why not try a soft drink? I have fresh fruit juices and vegetable water…'

Legislation insisted the drones broadcast their educational messages frequently, as studies showed this helped moderate alcohol consumption. Unfortunately, the positive results only applied to audiences sober enough to enjoy rational thought – an ability that rarely applied to patrons of university bars, especially on exam results day.

'…I have energy drinks. I have pseudo-alcohol preparations…'

Suchol had been hailed as a great breakthrough in its day, and continued to enjoy modest sales, especially since stocking it was a legal requirement for licensed premises. It cost around a third as much as its toxic big brother and contained a modified alcohol structure that delivered some of the euphoric effect without flooding the liver and kidneys with poison. It just wasn't the same.

'No thanks,' Troy said in a bored voice, and flashed his data-disc so the droid could collect payment from the sparse credits remaining in his account. He may have spent years studying how to heal the human body, but he wasn't about to be told he couldn't voluntarily wreck his own.

Sarah gave Troy a reproachful look when the drink arrived, but watched without comment as he downed the long cylinder of syrup and alcohol.

'You'll pass,' she told him, having heard him cry wolf over exam results one too many times. 'You always do. Remember the last time? "*I've definitely failed, Sarah, I'm not even joking.*" Remember? And then five minutes later you got brilliant results and had your whole future planned out. You'd even planned the apartment you were going to buy in the city. And the girl you were going to live with. Remember? Brown hair, blue eyes... the one you have those dreams about.'

'Hannah,' murmured Troy.

Sarah laughed her squeaky little laugh.

'I didn't realise she had a name.'

Troy had told Sarah about his 'Hannah' dreams last semester, and regretted doing so ever since. She mocked him mercilessly about his 'dream woman', but then he'd half expected her to. After all, how could she understand? How could he explain to anyone that Hannah, a figment of his unconscious imagination, sometimes felt like a real person – almost a friend?

'I remember all your amazing plans,' Sarah said, leaning forward and giving him a flirtatious smile. 'You were going to have two children and send them straight into the Academy. One happy, perfect family.'

'Did I say that?' Troy had nothing against the Academy, but he didn't remember ever consciously thinking about it for his own children. The Academy was essentially a boarding facility that offered 'perfect parenting' from birth, and had impressive success records for its inductees. It meant only seeing your children a few times a year, which Troy didn't particularly like the idea of. But then again, lots of parents saw plenty of their children and still failed them. Poor parenting was the cause of many of the medical emergency simulations he dealt with during his medical training: drug abuse cases, attempted suicides, injuries caused by violence. And if he was entirely honest, the idea of guaranteeing his children a 'perfect' childhood was appealing and something he'd never consciously ruled out – unless he failed his exams of course: the Academy didn't come cheap.

'So come on,' said Sarah, looking pointedly at the buzzing data-disc in Troy's hand. 'Let's have a look.'

But Troy still didn't quite have the courage to open the message. It was so strange to think all these years of study came down to one digital comm that would tell him whether he'd be welcomed into the medical profession with open arms, or branded a failure and cast into oblivion.

'I don't know, Sarah, some of them went really badly this time. Genetic re-sequencing and viral vectors... I don't even want to think about it. The gene insplicing simulation – however I programmed the viral-nanosegment it always missed out one or more nucleotides. I only removed the phenotypic abnormalities from the sim-patient two seconds before the assessment terminated. Luck, really.'

'Yeah, yeah. Heard it all before.' Sarah's gaze returned to the thinscreen. At the end of every year, Troy was sure he'd failed, and every year he passed with high marks.

'Socio-psychology went well though,' said Troy, considering another drink as a server droid scooted past. 'Even though, to be honest, I wasn't all that interested in it.'

'Fancy you being an expert on the human mind, Troy,' said Sarah. 'Should I be worried?'

Troy gave her his trademark charming grin: the one that got him out of trouble with girls, but also got him into it. As a matter of fact, it had got him into trouble with Sarah just last semester, but they were good friends and she hadn't held their brief series of one-night stands against him for long.

'Wait 'til next year,' said Troy. 'We're learning how to assess neurological flow directly and using electromagnetic currents to change thoughts and emotions. Then you should be worried.' He winked at her.

'Maybe you're studying the wrong degree,' Sarah mused, glancing at her data-disc and frowning. She was waiting for her mother to comm and ask how her exams had gone, but the call was late as always. 'I can imagine you as a socio-psychologist.'

Troy gave a spurt of laughter.

'What? Me, doing all that touchy feely stuff full time?'

Sarah blushed and Troy hurriedly changed the subject.

'I actually enjoyed nanosurgery. Good exam. We had to demonstrate how we'd pilot a nanodrone through the blood stream and remove specific cells. I wish I'd revised more, but… I think it went OK.'

Troy's data-disc gave another urgent buzz, and Sarah sighed and threw her hands in the air.

'Are you ready yet?'

'OK, OK.' Troy lifted his data-disc to eye level, then stopped. Over Sarah's shoulder he thought he saw someone familiar. A girl. She'd looked just like… Hannah. But that was ridiculous. He blinked and she was gone.

'What?' Sarah turned to follow Troy's stare.

'Nothing. Sorry.' Troy shook his head and refocused on his data-disc. Too little sleep, too much revision and drinking too much too quickly was clearly sending him over the edge. He'd felt very strange during the last few weeks. Nothing had happened exactly – he had no physical symptoms, nothing he could self-diagnose. But he'd felt very definitely as though something was pulling at him, stopping him make certain decisions and choices. A few times he'd wanted to do something reckless, like blow off revision and stay up all night playing VR games or ask out a girl he knew his friend liked, and something got in the way – a sort of psychological barrier that made him feel his choices weren't his own. 'Sorry. Open comm.'

There was a brief spinning strip of multicoloured light, which swept over Troy's hands and the table in front of him as the disc located a suitable projection site. Within a few seconds, the projector decided that the table, with its brown stains and collection of fingerprinted glasses, was its best bet and shone the exam-board comm, complete with date and time, on the uneven laminate surface.

Sarah was sitting upright now, watching him with interest.

'Well?'

As Troy struggled to focus on the collection of subject titles and percentages, he crossed his fingers under the table – an old superstition he'd read about in a history journal. The examinations had been hard, but although he knew full well he hadn't passed with flying colours, he felt reasonably confident that he'd scraped a pass. He was wrong.

'What is it?' said Sarah, seeing the colour drain from Troy's face. 'What's wrong?'

Troy couldn't bring himself to look her in the eye. He wanted to jump up and run away but he could not engage his legs.

'I've failed.'

Chapter Two

Troy stared at the projection, reading over the numbers again and again in case he'd misinterpreted them. But he hadn't. He tried to look away but his eyes remained locked to the letters and figures before him. His overall combination percentage totalled 39% – well below the figure he was expecting, and as if the percentage wasn't clear enough for him, the word 'FAIL' was projected faintly over the subject titles in blocky red letters. The letters seemed to bypass his eyes and imprint themselves directly onto his visual cortex.

The bar had become very quiet suddenly, and Troy's heart was whirring like an anti-grav drive. This couldn't be happening. It was as simple as that. There was some kind of mistake.

'Let me see.' Sarah pulled her stool around to sit next to him. 'Oh Troy.' Sarah was never one to dress up bad news. 'What are you going to do? You can't even do a retake.' University rules meant any students scoring under 40% were banned from retakes, even for final year exams.

Troy leaned back on his stool and stared at the ceiling. All those months of revision and years of studying. The money his parents had paid for his course and the plethora of expensive medical equipment and textbooks. Wasted. Every credit. A few minutes ago he'd been a trainee for one of the most eminent professions in the world. And now he was nothing. A failed student with no qualifications or career prospects.

'I can't believe it.' Troy read the results again, the words and numbers swimming over the bumpy table, the laminate warped by years of spilt drinks and bad behaviour. 'I... I didn't do *that* badly. It's a mistake.' He leant closer to the projection, trying to see some error, some blip, some clue that the numbers didn't relate to him, but a different Troy at a different university. But the results stared back at him, merciless and unchanging.

'It could be you studied the wrong things,' said Sarah, always ready with a half-full glass.

'I didn't, Sarah. You saw my mocks – I got nearly 80% in everything. It's the same syllabus they're testing, it... it just doesn't make sense.' He wanted to shout but amazingly his voice remained stable, belying the anger and frustration he felt.

To help make sense of things, Troy ordered another drink, before changing his mind and telling the server droid: 'Forget one drink. Bring us a full bottle of clear spirit for the table, and forget about the mixer. And no, I don't want Suchol, so don't bother asking.'

'Maybe we should have studied together,' said Sarah tentatively, as Troy decanted a healthy slug of alcohol into each of their glasses. Troy felt a pang of guilt. Sarah had asked him over and over again to partner her in the library, but he'd refused, knowing a lot of his revision time would be taken up reassuring her and helping her feel good about herself. It had been a selfish decision, one that he had regretted almost immediately. Perhaps this was his punishment.

Two bottles of clear spirit later, Troy wasn't feeling any better.

'I could be a droid manager,' he told Sarah, the glass in his hand weaving in mid-air before he brought it to his lips for yet another slurp. 'How about that? Hello Mum and Dad. You thought I was going to be a doctor. Guess what? I'm managing droids at FoodHanger.'

'You could take the course again somewhere else.' Sarah gave him a big, soft smile and for a moment Troy thought how pretty she looked, her blonde curls falling around her shoulders, and her round face happy and carefree thanks to half a bottle of clear spirit. With her lovely blue eyes and gentle intelligence she should have been irresistible. But the extra weight she carried around her face, shoulders and middle meant she never felt attractive, and was always just a little too keen around men she liked. Troy smiled back at her.

'You know I can't.' They both knew the odds of any other university taking him on were a thousand to one.

'Troy?'

Sarah was staring at him now. She leaned right over the table suddenly, her large, round eyes locked on his.

'I wish I could help you.'

She dropped her eyelids and moved in to kiss him.

Troy watched sleepily as Sarah's pale face came towards him. She smelt delicious as usual, and her face was immaculately made-up, not an eyelash out of place. He knew it was wrong, he knew he'd just be leading her on, but every muscle in his body wanted to lean forward and kiss her, to let things take their natural course and enjoy the comfort that came from sleeping together – until the next morning when he'd have to explain yet again that they'd never work as a couple.

He needed the comfort. The flow of alcohol entering his system caressed his recklessness and pushed his egocentric arguments to the fore. He wanted her. He wanted the release and would deal with the consequences thereafter.

'Sarah, I...' Troy put a palm against her shoulder and pushed her gently back into her seat. He felt guilty, especially when he registered her hurt expression, but the two of them didn't work together that way and he knew, even in his drunken

25

state, that venturing down that road only led to pain for her and guilt for him.

'Sorry, Sarah. Let's not get into all that again.'

It was probably the worst thing he could have said: clinical indifference was the last thing Sarah needed. She looked mortified.

'I'd better go,' she said, fumbling around for her data-disc and pulling herself off the stool. 'Sorry. See you. See you tomorrow.'

'Sarah…'

'No, it's OK. I should go. I've drunk too much.' Sarah pulled herself from the stool and walked her fast little walk across the bar and into the crowd that stood between her and the exit.

Troy knew she wanted him to run after her, but he also knew it would give her the wrong idea – false hope that they might one day be more than friends. She'd be fine in a few days, once her pride had managed to re-inflate itself, and they'd pick up where they left off. Once the temptation was removed Troy felt the familiar rush of endorphins reassuring him that he had done the right thing.

With no Sarah to tell him off for drinking so much, Troy hit the bottle even more heavily and even ordered a few side shots of methanol: a drink so potent it used to be toxic years ago, before a new food-science process based on hydrolysation lessened its poisonous effects.

After the methanol, there were only snatches of memories – trailers, rather than full movies. A few of Troy's course buddies approached him as he sat alone and watery eyed, gulping down clear spirit like it was fruit juice, but they left quickly when he made it clear he wanted to be alone.

Around 1a.m., the campus drug dealer, Daryl, sauntered over and sat himself in Sarah's vacant seat.

'Troy? It's Troy, isn't it?'

Troy nodded, trying to find the right words in his drunken brain to tell Daryl he wasn't, and would never be, a potential customer.

He knew plenty of students did drugs of course: you'd have to be blind not to notice the small black cylinders passing from hand to hand in dark corners of the campus bar, and the glazed expressions of students who pressed those cylinders into their necks every few hours. But the modern cocktail of designer drugs on offer these days were potentially more lethal than anything the human body had experienced before, and Troy knew too much about the fragility of life to risk using them.

Alcohol was one thing: granted, it was a drug and suppressed parts of the neurological system, but one's inherent flow of thoughts remained unchanged. It accentuated things, but didn't create new neurological pathways. The new wave of drugs to hit the streets over the last few decades did completely the opposite. They took the neurochemical balance of the human brain and completely rewired it. Thoughts and sensations that had not been present before materialised. Pathways of thinking that did not exist were artificially forced into being. Having trained in a hospital, Troy had seen some of the casualties firsthand.

'Life, eh?' Daryl looked around the bar and gestured towards the crowd. 'It's always up and down, you know? You never know what's around the corner.'

Troy didn't answer.

'How come you're sat on your own over here? You don't look like the type to be waiting for some girl to show up. More like the other way round, I'd say.' Daryl paused to see if he'd hit a nerve, and Troy rolled his eyes at the stupidity of the man. Didn't he know it was exam results day? You hardly needed a mind-reading kit to work out what was bothering him. He should get up and walk away but his common sense was being overridden.

Daryl scratched his stubbly chin and nodded at a girl in the crowd with glasses and short black hair who nodded back, then turned away as though she hadn't seen him.

'How's it going at this place? Studying hard?'

Troy flinched and Daryl knew he'd hit a homerun.

'What's up? Course not going well?'

In spite of himself, Troy raised his red eyes up from the frosted bottle of clear spirit and took in the fidgeting, restless man sat before him. Daryl didn't use his own products, but he lived in perpetual fear of being caught and arrested so he usually had the manic appearance of a drug user on a comedown. He was amiable enough, with his chubby, dimpled face and friendly manner, but his darting blue eyes revealed the paranoia below the surface and gave him a wolfish, predatory look.

'I failed,' said Troy, feeling too drunk to care who knew.

'Sorry to hear that. Really sorry. Honest.' Daryl's eyes did a lightning-quick circuit of their surroundings: Troy, table, bottle, Troy's hand on glass, Troy.

'I don't get it,' Troy murmured, suddenly deciding he didn't care if he got lured into conversation against his better judgement. 'I *studied*. I have no clue what I'm going to do. That's it. My life is over.'

Daryl's eyes flicked from left to right and back to Troy again.

'Do you want to know what you should do? You know, like good advice?'

'From you? I don't think so.' Troy was aware he sounded like a spoiled teenager, but he was beyond caring.

'No, not from me. From you.'

'What?' Troy gripped his glass and brought it clumsily to his mouth.

Daryl moved a clenched fist onto the table in front of them and slowly uncurled his fingers. In his palm lay a black cylinder, about the size of his thumb and covered in waves of grease.

'IQ. I've got twenty of them. See that girl over there?'

Daryl gestured to the girl with glasses he'd nodded at a moment ago. She appeared to be having an in-depth conversation with a mature student at the other side of the room.

'She just got 100% in her exams.' Daryl gave Troy a knowing look. 'And she met me before all of them.'

Troy had heard of IQ. It had been banned almost as soon as it was invented, but an impressive collection of scholars, political thinkers and novelists had admitted to using it. Indeed, some of the greatest intellectual works of the decade were said to have been created under its influence.

'It's a bit late for me,' said Troy. 'I've already failed.' But the cylinder glistened like diamonds, intriguing and desirable. He wanted badly to reach out and grab it, to grab hold of anything that would make him feel better. The temptation was almost irresistible.

'No, no.' Daryl smiled and withdrew his hand. 'Think about it. You'll know *everything*. What to do, how to make it all better... everything. You'll know how to hack into the university server and change the results. How about that?' Daryl slapped a palm down on the table. 'You can *rob* the university if you want to. You'll know everything you need to do it without getting caught. Get enough money to live in the city for a few years... whatever you want to do.'

'No one can know everything,' Troy slurred, shaking his head a little too emphatically.

'All right, not everything. But a lot more than you know now. It turns your whole mind around. New angles. New ways Answers. The old you failed. This is the key to a whole new improved you. The key to all the answers. Trust me.' He didn't want to talk to him anymore.

'If that were true,' Troy said slowly, trying to ignore the fact Daryl's face was going in and out of focus, 'you wouldn't have had to ask me twenty questions to work out why I'm sitting here on my own.'

'I'm not *on* the stuff,' said Daryl indignantly. 'If I was, you're right. I would have known. You can't do it *all* the time, you'd go lose your mind.'

Troy drew himself up taller on the table and leaned forward, fixing Daryl with what he hoped was a serious stare.

'You know I've seen patients after they've been on that stuff.' Troy paused to check Daryl was listening, and was rewarded by an inquisitive nod.

'Your brain...' Troy waved an unsteady hand around his head. '... it's not meant to cope with all that extra strain. It burns it out. You can fuse your neuronal synapses beyond repair. Seriously.'

'That's after years.' Daryl gave his best smile, all gums and dimples. 'You just have to make sure you take it...' Daryl paused as he struggled to find the word. '...rec-cree-ationally.'

Troy put both his elbows on the table and leaned even closer to Daryl.

'Look. I've seen *sixteen-year-olds* who've burned out on the stuff the first time they've taken it. Some people, fine... some people, they're a vegetable. No electrochemical induction can help them. I've sat with mothers... fathers... they've terminated their own children.'

'All right, all right.' Daryl's eyes slid left and right, aware that Troy's raised voice could give away his current activity. 'It's here if you need it.'

Because Daryl always thought of himself as a 'life facilitator' rather than a 'pushy drug dealer', he stuck his hand in his pocket and walked his bouncy walk across the bar to talk to a first-year student.

Troy watched Daryl meander away, and was considering another shot of methanol when he saw her again. Hannah. Or rather, a girl who looked just like her, on the other side of the room, holding a drink and moving a little to the music as she pushed through the crowd. This was ludicrous: it couldn't actually *be* Hannah – she was a figment of Troy's imagination. But the girl bore an uncanny resemblance, not just in the way she looked, but also in her expression and the way she moved.

Troy smacked his skull with the palm of his hand and shook his head vigorously. But the girl was still there, moving between the assorted drunken students, occasionally allowing Troy a tantalising glimpse of her petite, clear face with its plump cheeks and pointy nose. He thought back to the many dreams he'd had about Hannah over the years: sometimes she floated around in the air, hardly real at all and little more than a fleeting traces of her eyes and tiny mouth in mid-air, a swoosh of rich brown hair and a tantalising glimpse of a beautiful figure; other times she was full and real, a gorgeous guest at a cocktail party in a long, red dress or a companion on a deep-sea dive. But always her voice was the same: full of intelligence and half laughing, as though they shared a secret joke. His friends all thought it slightly odd that he dreamed in such intense detail about someone he'd never met, but it didn't feel strange to him at all. However, seeing a dream person in the middle of a real bar certainly *did* feel strange.

OK, time to think rationally. Troy had drunk enough intoxicating brain-suppressing, short-term-memory-erasing liquid to give an elephant amnesia. He was seeing things. But whether he was imagining it or not, there was no getting away from the fact that he could see a girl who looked just like Hannah, perfectly clearly and as real as the table in front of him.

Troy got to his feet. As he stumbled forwards, his legs struggled to hold him and the swaying, colourful group of people, drinking, shouting and gesticulating, became an immediate blur. Pushing through the crowd, his drink-addled brain took snap shots: a short girl giggling and shrieking and holding an energy drink; a pool of sticky liquid on the floor of the bar; a tall guy with very pale skin and dark hair talking earnestly to a university lecturer. The more he pushed through, the more lost he became and he couldn't see her anywhere. Through his mental fog he felt a stab of relief like a man suddenly spared a necessary but unwholesome task. It was just his imagination after all reality and dream were distinct.

'The results aren't true.'

The words were whispered in his ear, light and full of humour.

He turned around and saw a beautiful pointy nose and a delicate, pale profile framed with brown hair.

'They're not true,' the voice said again, this time in his other ear. 'Remember your aeropod test?'

'Hannah?'

But there was no one there – at least, not anymore. He whirled around and saw a male and female deep in drunken conversation and a vastly overweight man with yellowy, almost white hair, knocking back clear spirit directly from the bottle. There was no one else nearby. Whoever had spoken to him had vanished into thin air.

But the voice had been so clear – clear as can be.

Troy went back through the crowd, looking all around but seeing no one except the same old students he'd met throughout the year, and Daryl bobbing up and down, selling what he could. Whoever had spoken to him had gone, but the voice had imprinted itself within his mind.

Chapter Three

Troy woke to find himself in his own bed, fully clothed and in a blinding amount of pain. His head hurt, his back hurt, his stomach hurt. His bladder positively throbbed. He had vague recollections of the journey home, but the images were jumbled, fleeting and surreal as if the memories were implanted artificially. Indistinct images floated around his brain: a flashback of a police sentinel drone spearing him in its lights, asking him if he needed assistance and scanning his data-disc for his address and identification, its metallic and featureless face blank and non-judgmental. He couldn't remember his reply, but he remembered being escorted to the end of his road and dumped outside his apartment, a synthetic apology ringing in his ears as the sentinel rushed off, presumably to attend an emergency elsewhere.

Theoretically, he should be delighted to have made it home in one piece, but his brain was still soaking in its ethanol stew and refused to link thoughts with emotions.

Troy decided to close his mouth and allow his sandpaper-dry tongue much-needed shelter from the synthetically dehumidified atmosphere of his room. While he waited for saliva to resuscitate his oral cavity, he decided he'd better get up and rehydrate himself somehow and, if he could manage it, refresh his teeth to rid himself of the nauseating taste of stale spirit. Half way through he decided that standing was incompatible with the current state of his physiology and that horizontal was much more appropriate. Yet he made it to his feet.

As he stumbled to the bathroom a thought struck him. Or rather, a memory. A voice. Last night... *remember your aeropod test?* Who had he been talking to?

He remembered the test very well indeed, mainly because he'd failed and got himself in a lot of debt at the same time. It happened years ago, long before university. Troy had pleaded with his parents to pay for an aeropod test, but they'd refused, insisting he save up the money he earned managing droids at the local food warehouse and buy the test himself. They'd always tried to impress upon him the value of money and annoyingly they had always been right.

But Troy had been too impatient and used his father's credit details to obtain a betting contract with an insurance broker, who offered him a loan gamble to pay for the test – with 10/1 odds. If he passed the test, he won the loan outright and didn't have to make any repayments, but if he failed he had to pay back ten times what he'd borrowed. The chances of a seventeen-year-old male passing his aeropod test first time were improbable to say the least. He knew he shouldn't and yet he still went for it. He was filled with foreboding from the start.

As it happened Troy was a safe, sensible driver and passed the test with flying colours – or so he thought. But the results came back a clear fail, and he'd lost his bet thus forced to pay back ten times what he'd borrowed. His father had been quite happy about it to say the least, he recalled.

As Troy leaned into the refresher and let it caress his teeth and gums, he remembered that feeling – the feeling he'd had when he was seventeen – that he *should* have succeeded. He'd felt certain of it. At the time he thought perhaps some unseen hand had written a fail note for him just to teach him a lesson. In fact, he'd suspected the insurance broker had had a hand in things. But there was no proof.

As the refresher blew hot steam into his pores and exfoliated his face and neck, an uneasy thought occurred to him. What if something, or someone *was* failing him on purpose? Ridiculous thought. Troy dismissed it. Conspiracy theories were ridiculous.

But he couldn't dismiss the feelings of utter despair, hopelessness and failure that enveloped his whole being like a cold, damp blanket as he remembered why he'd drunk so much last night.

I've failed. I'll never be a doctor. My life is over.

Then another thought occurred to him.

Hannah.

Suddenly he remembered seeing her, and the words whispered into his ears, so clear and so real. His head began to throb. It had to have been some drunken trick of his imagination and, even if it wasn't, seeing an imaginary girl in a bar was really the least of his concerns. He was far more worried about the fact he'd failed his exams, was no longer eligible for his life-long career ambition and had nothing – no plan, no explanation for his failure and no clue as to how to make everything all right again.

Except there was a way. Troy felt sick thinking about it and his brain throbbed in protest, but there was no denying the fact that a tiny chink of light shone through the big pile of rubble he was buried under. He couldn't remove the image from his mind's eye. Flashes and after-images of a little clack cylinder.In the bedroom, Troy's data-disc lay on the bedside table, flashing with unanswered messages from friends he should have met up with last night. As he picked up the data-disc his hand was shaking, partly due to his hangover, but mainly because of the person he was going to contact. His brain rebelled despite its stupor. Remorse and fear flowed through him as if injected directly into his veins. He tried to stop his hand reaching for it. He didn't know the comm ID but his disc automatically obtained ID's from unlocked discs in his proximity. There it was. The ID and the time stamp. The details of the comm were missing but he knew who it would be.

'I don't usually pay home visits,' said Daryl, perching uneasily on Troy's sofa and looking around his modest student apartment. 'Don't you share with anyone? I thought you were a student.'

'Some students share,' said Troy, already regretting the decision to invite Daryl to the apartment, rather than meet him at the bar. Daryl's agitation and restlessness compounded Troy's already stretched nerves.

Daryl pulled out a credit collector.

'It'll go through as a stationery order. Anyone who looks will think you've bought data sheets or something.'

Troy nodded, his mind elsewhere. In addition to his medical experience, he'd heard lots of stories about IQ and they weren't the kind you read to children at bedtime. Some people became deranged, thinking they were superheroes and beating themselves up with metal poles; others went missing and turned up years later roaming the streets without a clue who they were... and so on. The newsfeeds about drug casualties were endless. He knew it was bad. He'd seen the problems. He'd experienced the consequences first hand. What was he doing?

Troy watched Daryl's eyes flicker all around the apartment.

'Are there any... side effects?' Troy said, although forming the words were a struggle. He knew very well there were.

'Side effects?' Daryl thought about this for a moment. 'You mean like getting a headache?'

Troy nodded.

'Just don't take any tests or anything like that tomorrow – you won't know what's going on.' Daryl's left leg began to jiggle. 'When I used to use, I remember one time, I remember you wouldn't believe it. I was buying a drink and they gave me a choice of something. Toppings or something. Anyway, two things, right? Two toppings. And I just couldn't get my head around it. I kept asking them to say it again. They threw me out in the end...' Daryl shook his head, smiling at the memory, his face alive with amusement for a second. He looked like a cheerful toddler.

'OK.' He had taken Troy's data-disc and completed the credit transaction. 'You want me to do it for you?' Daryl pulled a black cylinder from his shoe and waved it near Troy's neck.

Troy head forced into a nod, only a curt drop of the chin.

'OK.' *Shit*. His mind screamed in protest.

Daryl leaned forwards and pressed the black cylinder into Troy's skin, where it deployed with a hiss. As Daryl leant forward, arm extended Troy could see his own hand moving up and pushing Daryl's away. But it was already hazy and translucent. A ghost moving towards him, Daryl's hand and the black cylinder seemed to pass through Troy's arm and make contact with his neck. Troy's neck began to tingle where the transdermal injector had been, and then the tingle changed to a mild burning sensation that remained localised for a few seconds. Suddenly in one heartbeat the wave of burning expanded to encompass every part of his body. His breath quickened and as he breathed in he felt his chest was about to explode from the lungfulls of air he was inhaling. He could not stop the flow. Colours inverted. Black appeared white.

Daryl got to his feet and pushed the cylinder into an inside pocket.

'Why the hell did you ask me here to waste my time," Daryl murmured. Shooting Troy an angry glance as he turned on his heel and left.

'Mmm.' Troy's teeth had suddenly decided to lock together so words were impossible. He sensed a white space in his brain, like a bubble that was getting bigger and bigger and bigger. Elation flooded through him but he felt blunted as if he were simply an observer. The walls of the apartment disappeared and the world opened up to him. When he looked up, his vision unimpaired by the limitations of physiology, he could see all the way through the many ceilings above him and to the sky overhead. The smoke from the vents outside the window curled and moved in rhythm to his heartbeat. He felt like he controlled it all.

Why did I fail?

He asked himself the question: himself, Troy. And just like that he knew all the answers – at least, everything it was possible for him to know, given the raw visual, audio and sensory data he'd accumulated over the years. The drug must have opened up his ability to remember and make links between experiences, so he could understand much more now than he ever had done before. Technically, he was now a genius. If he were to take an IQ test, as pioneers of this drug had done in the past, it would be off the scale. IQ was supposed to be fixed from birth. This broke all the rules. There was no way to measure the intellectual abilities he would possess for the next few hours. Great things had been done on this drug. Great things and terrible things. It opened the large fraction of the mind which went unused.

You didn't fail. It sounded like a voice which bypassed his ears and went straight into his brain.

The answer came back to him immediately, but there was more, much more, to know and understand.

Then why?

Troy's vision filled with light: instantaneously blinding light. And his ears were assaulted by a stream of alien noises. Vague voices and sirens. Indistinct and unclear, but loud and building to a crescendo. Suddenly he was lying flat, although he was certain he hadn't been a moment ago. His hands clutched at

38

something in mid-air and he heard unfamiliar voices. Lots of them.

'Code Red. He's Code Red. Get Harris.'

Other voices shouted, but there were no words that Troy could discriminate. The voices seemed to be coming from all around him.

'He's in neurofibrillation. Cortical stimulant is reading it's shockable!' a female voice shouted, much louder than the others and more anxious.

Troy's hands were forced down to his sides, and the light began fading to dark. He felt like he was sinking, and black water lapped his face and eyes as he went deeper. A brief wave of light dazzled him but was gone in an instant leaving blackness.

'We're losing him. Where's Harris?' The voice was distant, with a curious echo.

'Cortical stimulant is go for third shock,' said another voice on his right, loud but muffled. He tried to turn his head towards the voice but couldn't.

Through the din, a quiet voice penetrated Troy's consciousness like the finality of a death knell:

'Don't bother. He's gone.' Cold blackness and emptiness was all encompassing.

Suddenly, the light came back in one great rush. It was so bright he felt if he wasn't lying down it would have knocked him over like a physical blow. And then he realised – he'd opened his eyes. The light was coming from illuminated ceiling tiles overhead: pure white and constant, like hospital light. Shadows moved around in his peripheral vision, and then gradually they turned into faces that loomed over him. He didn't recognise any of them. They looked shocked and horrified.

Arms held him down and instinctively he tried to struggle. The voices continued shouting, activity flowing all around him in a frenzy. He couldn't see his apartment. Everything was wrong. Fear rushed through him, layered with confusion.

An authoritative voice said:

'Well sedate him, for goodness sake.'

Troy redoubled his struggles, but was helpless against the arms that held him down. He felt a cold prick on the right side of his neck and the sound of a jet of fluid entering his bloodstream. A few moments later his ears registered another low hiss as the drug invaded his nervous system and interrupted his cerebral pathways. His arms failed him: leaden, useless. His consciousness slipped back into a now warm lake of darkness and everything went black.

There were a few mumbled words which he couldn't quite decipher – one word registered – emergence.

Chapter Four

Consciousness came back slowly. When Troy finally managed to pull his eyelids open he could see nothing but white: white walls, white floor, a sealed white door opposite him and bright white light coming from the ceiling tiles. He was on a hospital bed, of that much he was certain, but there were no floating trolleys of medical equipment, no data terminals, no medidrones. The only objects in the room were his bed, a service droid resting on its pedestal beside him, and a white gel chair in the corner.

Troy knew hospitals and hospital procedures. He should be hooked up to monitors continually assessing his biosigns, and there should be a medidrone ready to scan him the second he regained consciousness. But there were no scanning droids anywhere. There was nothing in the room to monitor Troy, except for a small AV sensor in the corner: a standard security measure in public buildings.

He reached for his data-disc, expecting it to be in the pocket of the trousers he'd put on that morning, but discovered he was wearing something completely unfamiliar: light green billowy cargo trousers and a loose green cotton top, similar to the scrubs he used to wear in the university operating theatres. His data-disc was nowhere to be seen. Silence was total.

Suddenly, an irrational thought occurred to him: he was dead. But that was ridiculous. He could feel and he could think.

A more logical explanation was that he'd had some sort of bad psychological reaction to IQ and now he'd been brought to this anonymous room to recover. And yet...

Suddenly, around the bare, white room echoed a noise, faint at first, but it growing steadily louder until it consolidated to the unmistakable sound of approaching footsteps. Someone was coming. Troy sat up, his heart hammering as the entrance in front of him slid open with a hiss, and a large shadow fell over his bed.

There in the doorway stood a broad figure – a middle-aged man, probably in his late fifties, with striped grey and black hair that receded from his temples. He wore a smart blue pin-striped suit that was deftly tailored around his powerful frame, but his eyes were his most striking feature: deep-set, staring blue and crowned by thick, bushy eyebrows.

'Hello Troy.' The voice boomed from the giant frame: a deep, resonant sound that oozed authority and confidence.

Without waiting for a response the man entered the room, letting the door slide shut behind him, and took a seat on the gel chair in the corner, which sunk to accommodate his great bulk. Seeing the bewildered expression on Troy's face, the man smiled, a benevolent smile that belied his hard, square face.

'It's a real pleasure to meet you,' he said, taking his data-disc from his pocket and bouncing it lightly in his palm. 'I apologise for keeping you waiting so long, but you've created quite a stir. I've been fighting off a whole list of people who want to see you. My name is Professor Shaw. I'm Chairman of the Institute. I'm sure you have lots of questions, but please be patient: everything will be answered in due course.'

Shaw was clearly an authoritative man, and powerful, yet despite this his voice was rich and kind.

'What Institute?'

'Would you like something to eat?' asked the Professor, ignoring Troy's question, and instead gesturing to the service droid which had silently entered behind him. 'You must be hungry.'

'Starving.'

'Allow me.' The Professor stood up and tapped the droid, which quickly whirred to life and spat a square, brown package and wooden fork onto its extending arms. Shaw passed the package to Troy, who took it grudgingly, then cracked the lid and waited a moment while the exothermic chemical reaction warmed the food within.

Steam and the aroma of a roasted vegetable dish rose tantalisingly from the container. Troy peeled back the lid to discover a creamy soya-cheese and miniature-vegetable bake: a perfect mix of protein and nutrients. At university, he ordered exactly the same meal from the Foodhanger on campus at least once a week, remembering his mother's words about miniature vegetables and their high nutrient content.

Knives of fear stabbed his chest: did his family know where he was, or what he'd done? He silently prayed his mother and father would never find out he'd taken IQ and hoped they weren't in the vicinity, but at the same time all of a sudden he longed for familiar things: his family and friends, his own bed. But hunger took precedent over homesickness, and he dug into the meal. The food tingled as it slid down his gullet, and felt strange when it reached his stomach – almost nauseating – as if his insides weren't used its weight. *How long have I been here?* thought Troy. *It feels like I haven't eaten in weeks.*

'I have to tell you a lot of things,' said Shaw, gripping his data-disc tightly and taking a deep intake of breath that made his chest double in size. 'Some of them you will find hard to believe and some may distress you. Forgive me if I am tactless in some of the things I say, but this is the first time I've personally had to deal with a situation like this.' He paused for a moment, then pointed his data-disc at the bare wall and clicked. The word

'Submergence' was projected onto the white surface, rippling like water.

'You are unique, Troy,' Shaw continued. 'You represent a great dilemma to this Institute and to me personally. For an Institute which relies so heavily on protocols and programs your presence has caused much consternation. We have no protocol or precedent to dictate how we deal with you. But I will explain all of that in due course. Neither of us will be served by hastiness. I promise I will answer all of your questions, but please be patient.'

'At least tell me where I am,' Troy asked. 'Does anyone know I'm here?'

'You are now on the twenty-second floor of the Harborough Psychodevelopment Institute,' said Shaw, smoothly, 'an Institute of which I am Chairman and Chief Physician. This is not a hospital, although of course in many ways we share many of the same functions as a medical facility. We do care for people here, a great many people, but we do not care for sick people. In fact, the opposite.'

'So I'm not sick?' Troy felt utterly confused and helpless. What was going on? Was he in a psychiatric facility? A test centre? Or was this all some strange hallucination induced by IQ? His brain throbbed from thinking over all the possibilities.

'Before we discuss you and your wellbeing, we need to talk about some history,' said Shaw, clicking his data-disc again.

An AV-still flashed onto the wall, and Troy's throat tightened around half-chewed vegetables as he took in the giant image. He set his fork down on the service droid and pushed his meal to one side.

The projection showed an extremely overweight mother hooked up to a virtual reality, or VR, simulator, while a blue baby, clearly dead, lay on a gel pillow a few metres away from her. Years ago, when VR first became widespread, society panicked about these sorts of scenarios: neglectful mothers, so addicted to VR they lost touch with reality and failed to care for their children. But the panic had proved ill-founded, and VR was now generally believed to enhance family relations, rather than hinder them.

'This isn't history,' said Troy, cheese and vegetables churning in his stomach. 'This is what people *thought* might happen after VR. But there were never any major negative consequences – why are you showing this to me? Why am I here?' He threw the food container on the bed and glared at the Professor. 'Just tell me what's going on.'

'I am. But it will take some time. This is the history you never learned,' said Shaw, waving his huge hand at the AV still. 'One hundred years ago, society was on the brink of collapse. Crime rates were high and the incidences of personality disorder were rocketing. VR scenarios and interactive AVs ravaged mankind like a virus, sapping its will to survive and thrive. Psychologists throughout the world strove to find a solution for society's ailments and then one brilliant individual, Dr Harold Anderson,' a gleam entered the Professor's eyes and a wistful smile crossed his face, 'discovered the solution.'

'I've never heard of anyone called Anderson,' Troy protested. 'And one hundred years ago, we signed The Psychiatrists' Treaty and personality disorders were practically non-existent. What are you *talking* about?' The Professor didn't look like a mad man, but that was the only explanation Troy could come up with as to why he was spouting such nonsense.

The Professor extended his hands in a placating gesture, 'Please Troy. Just bear with me. Everything will become clear.' He paused, as if willing Troy to try and interrupt again. But Troy was far too confused to speak. If the Professor was mad, Troy decided, the man was certainly totally convinced about his own delusions. There was nothing about Shaw's manner that suggested he was concocting a wild story. When Troy said nothing, Shaw continued.

'Dr Anderson was the foremost socio-psychologist in the history of mankind.'

Shaw clicked his data-disc and a new image appeared: adults fighting in the street with laser whips and projectile weapons.

'This is society as it was after VR: violent, apathetic and on the verge of collapse. Not some dramatic financial collapse, no great war, no devastating plague, nothing tangible, no earth-shattering collapse in the true sense of the word, but a collapse nonetheless. A more insidious creeping type of deterioration was occurring under everyone's noses. Everyone saw it and many recognised it, but it went ignored. When finally all the signs were analysed scientifically it was clear that society and mankind as a whole were in trouble. They tried to ignore it but eventually they could not. Now...' The Professor's blue eyes bore into Troy like a laser drill. 'You're wondering what this has to do with you. The answers are coming, I promise. You are a clever young man; I can see that from your data. You know about the process of evolution and its inherent basis on survival of the fittest. Evolution was regressing, or to be more precise, working in reverse. Rather than progressing and facilitating advancement of the species, a turning point was reached. All the indices by which we attempt to measure the state of society had dramatically turned for the worse. IQs were getting deteriorating, obesity and illness were spreading like a plague. Things were bad and getting worse.'

As Shaw spoke, he flicked through increasingly more violent and disturbing images: two hugely obese children force-feeding a third, a group of teenagers with black cylinders hung around their necks sleeping on a busy highway in broad daylight, and scene after scene of violent and bloody outbreaks in city centres.

'For years governments and religious groups tried to change society, but their strategies always failed. Why? Because they were dealing with the most uncooperative subjects in the history of the world: humans, mankind, us. We were at fault. We were the disease. Without changing us, society stood no chance of changing its course.'

Troy shook his head. What was Shaw talking about? Nothing made sense. This was all an IQ hallucination, it had to be. He pinched his arm hard, but felt a pain real enough for him to know he definitely wasn't dreaming.

Shaw clicked the data-disc again, and the wall went blank.

'But all of this so far is just talk,' Shaw said, slipping his data-disc back into his pocket. 'Why should you believe anything unless you see with your own eyes what I'm trying to explain? Come with me.'

Shaw walked to the doorway and hit the pressure opener. The door slid open.

Troy felt simultaneously angry and afraid.

'Where are we going? I'm not going anywhere until you tell me what's going on.' His head began to throb again. Nothing, *nothing* made sense, unless... what if he'd stumbled into IQ psychosis and was lying like a vegetable somewhere with his friends and family around him, whilst his mind played out this weird dream scenario? He shuddered at the thought: *here lies Troy, brain dead in his twenties thanks to one stupid experiment with a dangerous substance.* He had known it was wrong. Every experience in his life had taught him that it was wrong and now he was paying the consequences.

'That's exactly what I'm trying to do,' said the Professor. 'You have nothing to be scared of Troy, but we've got lots to talk about today, so let's get moving.'

He moved away from the entrance then, and Troy saw that what he'd expected to be a hospital corridor was in fact a transparent bridge, suspended from the ceiling by heavy-duty steel wires. Over the bridge was almost a mini-city of suspended bridges and smooth-sided opaque boxes that looked like giant ice cubes with holographic plaques projected over their entrances. Troy's university had some complex architectural arrangements around the medical training areas, but nothing like this.

What is this place? Troy stumbled forward and stared at the vast collection of bridges and boxes. He looked back at the room behind him with its basic furniture and decided if he was going to get any answers, it made more sense to follow the Professor. Leaving the relative safety of the bedroom and stepping out into this vast and confusing new world was unsettling, but still he followed Shaw out of the room and they began crossing the bridge. He decided that there were basically two answers to what was going on: either the he was mad, or the Professor was. If the Professor was some lunatic academic who'd kidnapped Troy for a bizarre experiment, it made sense to play along for the time being and then find a way to escape.

'The Institute is a very special place,' said Shaw, as the bridge swayed slightly under his weight. Halfway across, the Professor stopped and gripped the steel balustrade, staring down at the many bridges and platforms below.

'What makes a man, Troy?'

Troy shrugged, resisting the urge to say: *sanity,* but the Professor didn't seem to need an answer.

'What makes you? What makes me who I am? There are two factors Troy – only two that dictate what I am, what I do and how I behave. Genetics and environment. A simple equation. Your genetics, your DNA, the fusion of your parents make you what you physically are. They give you your looks and they dictate the lay of your brain neurons and their integrations. This may seem like a lot, but the impact of this pales into virtual insignificance when compared to the other life-shaping factor. Your environment.'

Troy knew all of this. He had debated the nature versus nurture issue endlessly, with his friends, his parents and even with himself. Why the Professor was talking about this classic ethics debate now, he had no idea. He had heard it all before. Maybe not exactly word for word but he had heard the concepts many times before. It was a standard text. A basic concept. Maybe Troy was part of some sort of experiment about how environment affects psychiatric wellbeing?

'It is what makes you what you are,' Shaw continued. 'In your short life, you've been moulded by your experiences: the good and the bad. Those experiences have moulded you into the fine young man I see before me today. The love of your family, the closeness of friends like Sarah. You are what they all made you.'

He turned and walked down the remainder of the bridge, with Troy hurrying to catch up.

'How do you know about Sarah? Have you been spying on me?' Anger threatened to overwhelm him, and he wanted to grab hold of the big man, shake him, demand answers. This was no hallucination, Troy decided. Everything felt far too real: the gentle sway of the bridge underneath him, the cool air swirling around and the faint smell of cleaning chemicals. The Professor must have been watching him, waiting for a moment of weakness, a time when Troy's psychical and psychological defences were low, and then somehow knocked him unconscious and taken him to this building. Maybe the IQ he'd taken wasn't real IQ after all – maybe the whole thing was a set-up to kidnap him and make him part of some strange experiment.

'How?' The Professor answered, without turning around. He stepped off the bridge and into an open paternoster-style elevator, linked to the bridge by a metal platform. 'Because she's here Troy, in each and every one of us. She was my best friend, your best friend, everyone's best friend,' *what?* 'but I will explain that to you in moments. Do you understand everything I have told you so far?'

49

Troy climbed in the elevator beside him. The anger hadn't left him, and indeed seemed to be growing with every second. He was on the verge of exploding. He didn't know how he managed to contain himself.

'*What* have you told me so far? Some fabricated history and a pre-school ethics debate about nature and nurture.' Troy was fuming. He tried hard to steady his breathing, knowing it was probably prudent to appear calm, and his chest burned with the effort. How dare this place hold him without his permission. How *dare* they!

'Please,' said Shaw, as the elevator began to ascend. 'Allow me to continue, to explain further. We all know how formative your childhood years are. Any wrong turn or mishap can cause life to diverge down an unwanted route. Real life is fraught with dangers and risks of adverse events, events which can result in serious psychological compromise. Such a random life can severely affect psychosocial development. One traumatising event or one unheralded turn in your life's path may destroy the potential you have.'

The elevator slid to a halt, and Troy and the Professor stepped out.

'This way Troy. We're going to the Submergence facility.'

Chapter Five

'The what?' asked Troy, but the Professor didn't answer.

They crossed another suspended bridge and arrived outside a huge opaque cube with a pressure pad entrance. As they walked, Troy looked around, considering how he might escape from this man and leave this building. But all around he saw a maze of bridges and opaque boxes, none of which seemed to link up in any logical way. He looked down, but all he saw were more bridges: no exit that he could discern. If he ran, he feared he'd end up more lost than he was already and be apprehended very quickly.

'I'm about to show you something very special,' said Shaw, making no move to hit the pad and open the door. 'Only a handful of people ever get to witness this spectacle. But first, let me finish telling you about Dr Anderson, and his vision. He believed we needed to take and protect humanity during its most formative years and nurture it, protect it and thus ensure that those adverse events do not limit the potential of our future generations.

'He had a vision where all the indecision and risk was taken out of life. He had a vision where we take a forming human identity and gently direct it down a safe route to maximise its potential. His vision is now a reality. Biotechnology has allowed us a route into the individual's brain. Electromagnetic and positron neural interfaces are a part of life and allow us to input sensory images and experiences retrogradely, directly into the human brain via its own spinal cord.'

He could hear the enthusiasm in the Professor's voice. The conviction and the joy the words held for him were clear. He'd clearly given this lecture many times before and yet still gleaned satisfaction from it.

'We've done that for years,' Troy objected. 'What about VR? And educational simulators?' *You're a mad man,* he added silently. *But somehow, you're a madman with a lot of expensive-looking equipment at your disposal.*

'Yes, but in those scenarios the individuals know their experiences are virtual. I'm talking about the ability to fool the brain. To give it a life of artificial experiences it can't tell apart from real ones. We use this ability, Troy, to give growing individuals the lives which they deserve. We use this to take babies through their early life without risk of mishap and with all the benefits of life without the risks.' He turned to face him, eyes alight. 'We take children through their lives without the chance of accident, without the risk of psychological damage. We give them what we know and, more importantly, can *guarantee* an ideal childhood. We give the new generation of humanity a perfect childhood and adolescence, thus giving them the best chance to fulfil their potential.'

The Professor paused, allowing Troy to let this bit of information sink in. When he resumed, his voice was slower and more considered. 'Troy, this is what we have done for you. Your parents brought you to us as a baby, just like other parents bring their offspring to a place like this. They had a choice of Institutes, but chose ours because of our track record of positive adaptation and low pre-Emergence rates. They left you in our care, along with nine other babies that month. In total we took 176 babies into our care that year. Since that time you have been engaged in a psychosocial neurosomatic development program.'

Troy went white.

52

'What? A *what?*'

'A neurosomatic development program. An artificial childhood, in layman's terms.'

Troy shook his head, fighting a strange urge to laugh. He ran his hands through his hair over and over again. 'You're not making any sense at all, Professor. I really think it's time to contact the authorities now. My parents will be looking for me, and –'

'It will inevitably come as a shock to you,' Shaw interrupted. 'There is no easy way to say this, but you have been asleep here with us for all of your life so far and have undergone 231 chapters of our Program. We have put all of your experiences directly into your cerebral cortex. We have given you the life you have led up until twenty-one hours ago. We have nurtured not only your mind, but also your body in all that time. But something went wrong in your case. Your body rejected the Program before the final chapters could be instilled – thus, you haven't been readied for Emergence. You have no understanding of the Submergence Program, and therefore will struggle to accept the concept of it.'

The urge to laugh became overwhelming and Troy let it out – a loud, booming laugh that echoed around the chasm of the Institute.

'This is rubbish, absolute rubbish! You really are crazy. Contact the authorities and have me sent back home. Whoever you are, it's illegal to hold people against their will, no matter what academic circles you move in.' He paused. 'Look, if this is about taking IQ – if this is some sort of punishment I've learned my lesson, I promise.'

'I assure you it's nothing of the sort,' said Shaw. 'Although your reaction to taking that particular substance is certainly related to you being here. The chapter was supposed to teach you remorse and regret and to cement the aversion to drugs and any form of artificial cerebral augmentation. You had an excessive reaction to the scenario which in itself does you credit but it was an anomalous response and overloaded the neurointegration pathways. We believe that's why you Emerged too soon.'

'So you're saying... none of my life has been real until now? That's seriously what you're saying? And you expect me to believe you? That's absolute bullshit.' Shaw flinched involuntarily.

'Your swearing shows me how upsetting this is for you. You don't need to believe me,' said Shaw. 'You're about to see it for yourself. I'm taking you to one of the incubator rooms, so you can see some Submerged patients, and watch what usually happens when Emergence – or entering reality for the first time – takes place. I'm sorry to say you didn't receive the usual support an Emerger should expect. We were so busy saving your life, there wasn't time for your counsellor to ease you into reality.'

'What counsellor?' Troy's brain hurt. Absolutely nothing made sense. Dreams had merged with reality, fact with fiction. He felt like a lost space pod no longer communicating with the control room on earth, floating in blackness with no port of reality to cling to. There was nothing here that was familiar, no object or person that could confirm anything about his previous existence.

His brain finally rebelled against the scene he was facing. 'Rubbish, it's all rubbish, this is some sort of hoax, some game.' Troy's voice reached a crescendo. 'I have rights. Let me go.' He pushed his way out and Shaw stumbled backwards to the floor.

'Let me go.' Troy searched feverishly for an exit. He had to get out he had to flee. All rationality left his mind. He was in the midst of a nightmare.

Professor Harris stayed on the floor and made placating gestures with his hands. 'Please Troy I know this is hard...'

'You know nothing! Let me out of here. Stay away from me, let me out, I want to see my parents right NOW!' he screamed.

The Professor put his hands down, anxiety written over his face.

The room was spinning and reality was squeezing the breath from Troy's body. The walls were not static. They were closing in on him. Space was disappearing. The only thing that remained solid was Shaw's figure sitting on the floor before him regarding him with unreadable eyes.

Shaw still looked concerned, consternation creasing his forehead into a frown, but he made no move to get up. Troy noticed his eyes flick to look over his left shoulder. A slight nod, barely perceptible. It took him too long to react. He heard the gush of air behind him and spun too late to stop two pairs of strong arms grabbing him like clamps of steel. He had just enough time to glimpse two large men in white uniforms before a sharp prick invaded the left side of his neck. He tried to struggle and kick out but the arms that held him would brook no resistance. His ears heard the torrential flow of his own blood coursing through them. His vision swam as a heaviness climbed up his body and rapidly darkness claimed him.

Chapter Six

No. He awoke suddenly, the transition from sleep to wakening artificially abrupt. He was unsure what the dream had been, the memory of it fading all the faster as he reached for it. He opened his eyes and looked around. He was back in the same white room again.

The interview... Professor Shaw... How long ago was that? His sleep was drug induced he had no doubt, however, he was certain that he had not dreamed the earlier events. His mind recoiled sharply when he attempted to think about the information he was given yesterday. Had it been yesterday? He had no concept of time. He felt a hollow empty feeling within the pit of his stomach. Had all the facts been right? It all seemed so far-fetched. Better to accept that he was insane than accept that everything in his life until now had been all part of some ridiculous virtual reality experiment.

None of it could be true. Of course not. His rational brain was right. It was all some misunderstanding. His illness must be far more complicated than he could understand. Some game was at play he had no doubt. He had heard of broadcasts back in the zeros where they used to mess with people's minds. They used to create scenarios and then AV record the poor victims reactions and behaviour. This "reality TV" phase had passed rapidly as the public had realised the impropriety of ritually humiliating and embarrassing people for public amusement. If he was part of such a resurgence in AV programming he would not be impressed. His parents would never cooperate. He knew that. There had to be some sensible explanation. This whole experience was not entertaining in any way. It couldn't be the case but it was the only logical rationalization he could bring his beleaguered cerebrum to accept.

He sat up and looked around again. A vertical perspective of the room did little to ease his concern. He looked up at the AV sensor keenly aware that anonymous viewers were scrutinising him from the safe vantage of some recording room somewhere within the building where he now sat.

He stood, fearful of vertigo, and only then realised the pressure sensation within his lower stomach was far keener than he had first imagined. Once again his priorities rapidly changed to matters of bodily housekeeping. He had no idea how long it had been since he'd relieved himself. He looked around for toilet facilities. Barely imperceptible on the wall closest to the bed was a small touch pad. He took a few steps towards it and pressed it gently with his thumb. A door materialised and slid virtually silently aside. A light sparked within the room beyond revealing a small fully tiled toilet and shower room. Once more the room had the feeling of sterile cleanliness associated with a hospital setting.

A brief examination revealed no visible sensors much to Troy's relief. He walked in and pressed an identical touch pad on the inside of the room. The door slid silently shut sealing Troy in, away from hostile prying eyes for the first time since this ordeal had begun. Even the aching within his bladder was ignored for a moment while he relished the privacy and safety of seclusion. The reality within that small room was completely under his control and he savoured the autonomy. Once more he listened carefully for any sounds that may give away any new clues with regards to his surroundings. He was again greeted by virtual total silence. He thought he could detect the same gentle hum of machinery or air conditioning devices in the distance but no other sounds were distinguishable.

After utilising the facilities and gratefully relieving his bladder he washed his hands welcoming the peace and tranquillity of this temporary haven from uncertainty. *What reality was this* was the question he really needed answering. The automatic flow of water soothed him so he left it running for a minute. He closed his eyes hoping that he would awaken back in his room nursing the after effects of the IQ. He opened his eyes and, of course, the world had not conformed to his desperate wish.

Taking a big breath he again touched the contact and the door sleekly slid to one side. The lights within the bathroom dimmed as if encouraging his quick departure. He stepped out and looked around fearful that in his temporary absence the room had been invaded. Thankfully the room remained empty and silent. The door shut silently behind him.

He only now noticed a tray resting upon a shelf on the far wall with several unmarked food containers and some metal cutlery. His stomach jarred as he realised exactly how hungry he was. Had he been more than twenty-four hours without food? His pangs of hunger would certainly support that hypothesis. He had no idea how long ago he had faced the Professor.

He cracked the lid on one of the packages and the food rapidly warmed within. Steam and the aroma of a pasta dish rose tantalisingly from the container. He peeled back the rest of the lid saw that there was indeed a creamy pasta sauce with an accompaniment of roasted potatoes and vegetables within. Every Monday evening when he was at home he had been given this exact same meal. Reminiscing filled him with a longing for home. He just wanted to get out of this place and go home. He needed answers and he needed a way out.

Perhaps this was a psychiatric institute and he was mad. He didn't think he was mad and yet if he were indeed deranged would he know it? His thought processes still worked normally, he was sure of that. He knew you could have insight into psychosis but could he survive within this imposed pathological world of insanity without dipping deeper into madness?

He rapidly resolved to cooperate until the opportunity arose to either formulate an escape plan or contact his parents or even the legal authorities. He had watched enough AVs to know that he had rights. He could not be held without his will and without legal representation. Again the thought recurred: unless of course he was insane. Unless of course he had some form of brain injury or cerebral tumour as he suspected and he was now mentally unstable. Perhaps they had had to excise a large portion of his brain and he was now not who he used to be. He must have had some sort of operation. He couldn't remember anything from the moment that cylinder was placed against his neck. The next moment he'd awoken on the table with everyone running around and restraining him. Nothing in between. Nothing at all. He had a vague memory of a medipod but was not sure if he was imagining it.

Amnesia would fit with the clinical picture. He had a headache due to his raised intracranial pressure secondary to the tumour or a chronic subdural haematoma. But why hadn't the medidrone scans picked it up? It should have been crystal clear. It couldn't be a haemorrhage, it was more likely to be a tumour, probably something benign. He passed out because the IQ interacted with the tumour. He had had it resected and now he had some retrograde amnesia. Scars... He would have scars after the surgery. Even modern microneurosurgery using cutting lasers would leave a small scar.

He ran to the bathroom and pressed the contact again, squeezing through the door while it was still sliding open. The lights sprang up and filled the room with renewed illumination. The mirror on the wall was oval and plain. Rummaging through his hair with his fingers he searched avidly for any evidence of any scars or anything to suggest that his hair had been shaved. All his visible scalp was clear. He obviously could not assess the back of his head but felt every inch methodically. Even the best surgery left some sort of scar. He was a medic, he knew this. Basic wound healing – a whole damn hour in lectures spent on it. Nothing. He flattened his hair back down with some water and went to sit on the bed once more. He would not lie down. He dare not risk sleep claiming him again. He had to maintain volition.

A chime sounded and he looked up over to the door in anticipation. He expected the door to open unbidden and yet it remained firmly closed. A few seconds passed and the chime rang out once more reverberating across the empty room. At least they were treating him like a human being now and asking for his permission to enter. He stood and walked to the door keenly aware that opening the door or calling out may be constituted as a welcome. He did not want to display any form of welcome to anyone or anything until he found out what was going on and why he was being held here.

A third ring and not even Troy's righteous indignation could justify ignoring it again. He steadied himself mentally and pressed the door contact.

The door slid to the side and the realisation that the events of the day before were not a complete figment of his imagination hit him like a blow. Professor Shaw stood before him with a smile fixed to his face. He looked identical to how he had done previously. Looking beyond him over his shoulder he could see two orderlies in white jackets standing to either side, their eyes staring at the walls. The Professor noticed Troy's gaze and smiled. 'They're just here as a precaution, hopefully we won't need them eh.'

'Troy, you've had a bit of time to rest and, I hope, absorb all the information I threw at you yesterday.' So, it was a whole day ago.

Shaw checked his watch. 'I need to show you something. We were going to see it yesterday but we got waylaid as you know. The second wave of Emergence is scheduled for ten minutes' time and all the counsellors are, of course, there already. I want you to see what we do so you can understand the wonder of it.

'You will cooperate won't you Troy?' Troy nodded in resignation. 'Let's go.'

Rapidly they once again reached the cavernous space traversed by innumerable suspended walkways. Somewhere along the way their escort of orderlies had vanished. Clearly they sensed his internal defeat. Troy had hardly noticed. His thoughts were still disconnected. He felt he was walking on autopilot. Shaw stopped and turned to him placing a hand on his arm. 'One thing I should ask you, though, is to be very quiet. This is a miraculous and confusing time for the Emergers. Please make no noise and do not try and talk to them. The immediate post-Emergence period is very sensitive and all communication is handled by trained counsellors.'

They came to a plain-looking door. Shaw hit the pressure pad, and the door whooshed open to reveal a large airy room with calming scenes of landscapes and fish projected on three of the four walls. There were no windows, but the ceiling tiles projected enough light to make the room feel bright, almost sunny. It would have been an attractive room, even pleasant, if it hadn't contained approximately thirty transparent-barred cages, all facing inwards towards a central control station manned by three white-clad nurses. Each cage had a figure inside it, some walking or moving around on a four-way auto-road – the kind Troy used to play on in VR arcades as a kid. Others lay on white beds at the side of the cages. All of their heads were obscured by an arch of gleaming black equipment.

'Who... what are they doing?' asked Troy.

'They are Submerged,' said the professor. 'They are experiencing a simulation of an idealised upbringing, just like you did – before you turned Code Black. Every Institute has a few Code Blacks each year. Deaths, to put it crudely. Submerger survival rates are much, much higher than those of non-submerged children and young adults, but no system is perfect. You, Troy, are an even rarer statistic. You're a Code Black survivor. We haven't had one of those for over thirty years.'

Troy felt like he'd just swallowed a heavy weight and was struggling to walk with it. He didn't believe it, any of it, but... seeing this room and the people in cages, how could anyone manufacture something like this? It was unreal. Troy noticed that above each cage a string of indicator lights glowed green. The closest cages were quiet, with a single nurse moving quietly between them, checking the figures systematically. In contrast, the ten or so cages at the other end of the room were being watched much more actively. Each of these cages had at least three people around them, some dressed in white uniforms, others in more casual clothes.

'Life counsellors and specialist Emergence doctors,' said Shaw, nodding towards the far cages. 'They're getting ready for Emergence. Which should happen any second.'

Suddenly, the lights above the far cages flashed amber.

'Yes – here we go.'

He tried to look away and not participate in this theatre but failed. It all meant nothing to him. He could not allow himself to partake in the game.

As soon as the lights changed, the life counsellors and doctors moved inside the cages, unhooking helmets from the figures inside, settling them on their beds and removing tubes from arms and legs.

Medidrones whirred to life and helped restrain flailing limbs, but the caged individuals didn't struggle for long and gradually began to sit up, staring with blinking eyes, each with a bewildered look on their face.

Shaw motioned for Troy to follow him towards the far cages, putting a finger to his lips as he did so. Too stunned to feel anything anymore, Troy allowed himself to be led, dumbly, by the Professor.

As they came closer, Troy noticed the cage bars weren't made of a hard, mineral glass, as he'd imagined, but aquaglass: a cushiony water-based substance usually used for children's playpens. Some of the counsellors had begun talking to the cage inhabitants, and as Troy and the Professor approached, he heard a female counsellor say:

'Welcome to your Emergence, Alan.'

She was addressing a man who now sat upright on the bed in his cage.

'Congratulations,' she continued. 'Don't worry, my name's Susan, it's all OK, you've come through fine.' Then she cleared her throat and said: 'Welcome to this new world we have made for you, we have given you all that we can up until now. Thank us not, but help us build a better society.'

Around the room the message was being echoed to all the upright figures on their beds. A smiling nurse bobbed in and out of the cages, disconnecting what appeared to be an intravenous access system from the newly awakened figures.

Troy couldn't think. He could hardly breathe. It *couldn't* be true. It wasn't possible. But... it all looked so real. He tried to imagine himself inside one of those cages, hooked up to all this equipment since... since *birth*. No... it wasn't possible.

Some of the Emergers met Troy's eyes with glances full of curiosity. They were all smiling. They appeared at ease. There was no confusion, only awe and wonder at the world they were finally a real part of.

'This is how it was meant to be for you,' said Shaw, putting a strong arm around Troy's shoulder. 'How easy it is if you complete the full Program. No denial, no heartache, no pain.'

Each Emerger was being lead out a door at the back of the room, with their counsellor by their side, guiding them.

'But it can't be…' Troy spluttered.

'It is.' Shaw nodded sagely. 'It is true. You are one of the privileged ones. There are many thousands of people who aren't able to Submerge. Thousands who live in slums, in poverty – the world Emerged individuals left behind. Your parents, in particular, made many sacrifices to give you a Submerged childhood.'

Troy felt Shaw's hand on his back urging him to follow the stream of figures leaving the room. He glanced back at the caged figures that remained. All looked peaceful, their faces almost hidden by the arch enclosing them, green lights twinkling above their heads. Each had a series of tubes projecting from them and running into the ceiling: an intravenous drip feeding system. The same drip-feeding system had presumably been used to feed him for his whole life. With a sickening jolt, Troy thought of the vegetable bake he'd eaten… had it been his first ever real meal?

But it just *couldn't* be true. A throbbing began in Troy's temples and spread behind his eyes. His mother, his father… they didn't exist. That was what Shaw was saying. Nothing about his life so far had really existed. He was experiencing life for the very first time.

As the new Emergers filed through the doorway, Troy noticed how much like a family they seemed, hugging each other, smiling, chatting as if they'd known each other for years. He felt sick to see them, so happy and so relaxed. It just wasn't right, none of this was right. Maybe he was just going mad – that now seemed a much more palatable explanation than some horrific idea about waking up for the first time from a fake childhood.

'We're going through to see our parents,' the Professor told Troy, his voice laden with emotion. 'They're a program, of course. A simulation, but a very good one. The pride of the Program, as a matter of fact. They're the main reason why you and your Emergence brothers and sisters will be such fine, upstanding citizens. You'll only see them every month or so from now on, but they'll never die – you won't suffer the heartbreak most non-Emergers suffer.'

Troy shook his head. *No.* Not his parents – not the two people who'd loved him, cared for him, given him unconditional devotion. He couldn't bear the idea of it: his parents a computer program. No words could express the feelings of loss and betrayal that threatened to overwhelm Troy. *This can't be happening.*

They were drifting into what was essentially a 'standing' lecture theatre with a huge thin-screen on the wall and no chairs: just like at university. Troy remembered feeling quite excited about the prospect of 'standing' lecture theatres before he started university; they were statistically proven to help attendees learn more, with the added benefit of lightly toning legs and improving circulation. Of course, after a week of standing he cursed the bad luck of having such a 'progressive' university, not to mention his aching legs. Now he longed for such unimportant concerns.

If what Shaw was saying was true, his university had never really existed. Troy thought about the day he failed his exams, and his sense of disbelief and unreality. He had felt very strongly that something wasn't right that day. That there were forces at work constructing what was going on, at odds with what *should* have been going on. But was this the explanation? A manufactured upbringing?

This was all a dream – an IQ hallucination. It had to be. Or some practical joke. Perhaps he was on that VR practical joke show, *Is This Your Life?* where they VR-fed people a fake scenario and AV'd their responses for laughs?

Technically, a fake upbringing was possible, of course. Battery-farm animals and the terminally ill were given simulated realities for humane reasons, to help improve their existence, so there was no reason why an entire human being's existence couldn't be simulated from birth. The human body was really only a computer taking in all sorts of sensory stimulus and interpreting it in a way that allowed it to survive. Computers weren't all that difficult to fool. He had volunteered at a hospice. He'd seen terminal patients given VR scenarios of peace and happiness to ease their final hours. He had even connected patients himself and had approved as the smile dissolved onto their faces when they relaxed into blissful falsity.

But what about human rights? A person's right to choose their own existence? What sort of society would allow that right to be overridden?

Eager, relaxed people crowded around Troy in front of the thinscreen, and Shaw moved to the back, leaving Troy at the centre of the room, shifting uneasily from one foot to the other. No one stood too close to him: it was as if they knew he wasn't really one of them.

Suddenly, two faces lit up the screen and a hush fell over the theatre.

Chapter Seven

Troy stared at the faces. They were about the size of a person, and smiling: gentle, familiar smiles that made him feel loved and sick and confused all at once. His parents. *His* parents. This couldn't be happening. But there they were: his mother with her cropped bright blonde hair, long face and very white teeth – the teeth she was so proud of and refreshed three times a day. His father's face floated next to hers, his almost-grey hair cut very short against his scalp, and his bright blue eyes looking fondly out at the mass of enraptured faces.

'Hello children,' they said in unison.

Troy knew what was coming – it was like an imminent eruption from a volcano. He fought it off for a few seconds, but the reflex was involuntary and with a retch he expunged his stomach contents of half-digested vegetables onto the swirling floor at his feet. Time seemed to slow for a moment and as acid filled his mouth, he mustered enough energy to raise his head and look around. His bleary eyes struggled to focus and bring his surroundings into some semblance of recognition. At his feet, he was dimly aware of a cleaning droid speeding across the floor and then absorbing and incinerating the mess at his feet, but all he could focus on was his parents' faces.

Tears prickled under his eyes and began flowing freely down his cheeks. Everyone else in the room was crying too.

'You're all exceptional people,' said the woman on the screen, 'and I'm so proud of the life you've led so far. I know many of you will be wondering about Annabelle, whether you'll see her again... why life's lessons had to be so cruel so early on.'

Annabelle. Troy's sister. The tears came even thicker then, and he noticed many of the people in the room, the Emergers, he supposed he should call them, were clinging to each other for support, some looking wretched, others looking sad but accepting. Had they all experienced the same thing? Had everyone in the room lost a little sister called Annabelle, just like Troy had?

Troy remembered Annabelle's first nosebleed. She'd been seven at the time and a healthy child, so the family dismissed it as nothing serious. They'd even laughed about it. Annabelle was often laughing. She had one of those perpetually happy temperaments. But a week later, her nose had bled again and Troy's mother took her for a medidrone check at the local medical centre.

After a perfunctory scan, the medidrone had sped off rapidly, reassuring them in its metallic static voice that their queries would be answered by the doctor, who arrived a moment later and carried out several other manual scans, his forehead persistently creased in deepening furrows. Then Annabelle had been podded directly to a paediatric haematology unit in Scotland: a grey building surrounded by stubby little heather bushes and besieged by parents holding up their data-discs, begging for credits to fund life-saving treatments for their children. Troy knew his family were lucky: he had many friends at school who couldn't afford the more complex medical treatments and suffered short-sightedness, flat feet and sometimes more life-threatening conditions as a result.

After specialist medidrones swarmed over Annabelle for almost an hour, it was discovered she had a virulent form of monoblastic leukaemia. It wasn't good news, but at least it wasn't life threatening – if, like Troy's family, you could afford the treatment. Not everyone was so lucky. Troy remembered a girl in room next door who had not been so lucky. He remembered his mother's words telling him how he had to be thankful for everything he had. The same mother who was now on the screen in front of him, betraying him by offering her love to everyone in the room.

Within a few hours Annabelle was rushed for a bone marrow transplant and had her entire circulatory system drained while she was in cryogenic stasis, and replaced by synthahaem and white blood-cell concentrate.

Annabelle had recovered well at first, and within only a few days the family had been able to take her home. That was where she'd collapsed three days later, to be found by Troy, grey and shaking on the bathroom floor, after the home CCU summoned her for dinner and she hadn't responded.

She died quietly in the medipod on the way to hospital, holding her mother's hand. The doctors said she'd had a rare reaction to the cryogenic stasis: her new bone marrow had failed totally and catastrophically, with her spleen rapidly eating up all her red blood cells in a matter of hours so she could get no oxygen around to her organs. It was a very rare occurrence, a one in ten million chance, they quoted. No one was to blame. The doctors had told them the risk, but one in ten million was so rare as to be virtually impossible. You couldn't get much better odds than that, unless you were the one who got it of course. For you the odds were one in one and it wasn't such a sensible bet.

After the initial shock, numbness and disbelief, the whole family got used to living with a gaping Annabelle-shaped hole inside them. They became bigger, kinder, more empathetic people – they needed to grow in order to cope with the pain. They raised funds for children with leukaemia, knowing that what happened to Annabelle was rare, and wanting to save other families the pain they were suffering. The memory of Annabelle always stirred a fire of anguish – but that same fire had fused the family together as an indestructible alloy.

Annabelle's death made us… me, a better person, Troy thought. *It made me kinder and more caring. It was real!*

'With the greatest pain,' said the woman's voice, as if she could read his thoughts, 'comes the greatest lessons. Losing Annabelle was a unique lesson for all of you. You won't see her here in post-Emergence but she is still in all of our hearts ready to offer us love and support when we need. You are lucky. You have entered a world of excitement and opportunity where you have so much to learn and give.'

'We've given you all the best experiences we can,' said his father, 'and we know you'll become fine citizens, able to give freely to others and help build a better society.'

There it was, that phrase again: *build a better society*. With a jolt, Troy realised it was the sort of thing his father always said to him. '*Every citizen should go to university. It means building a better society.*' And during his teenage years… '*You should experiment and try life on for size, Troy, but always remember you're here to build a better society.*'

Shaw was telling the truth. The realisation hit Troy like an industrial shuttlepod. Everything made sense. The pieces fitted together so neatly it was impossible to deny the validity of what he'd seen and heard. His upbringing had been manufactured. It was all true, or rather – nothing had been true until now. The nausea rose up again, but this time only reached chest level before it faded and was replaced by hot tears. Troy wiped them away so fiercely his cheeks burned red. It was all a lie. All of it. Annabelle had never existed. The people on the screen, his so-called parents, were an invention. A computer program. And they had no more a personal link to him than the cleaning droid that had just swept up his vomit. His anger remained subdued, probably an after effect of the drugs he had received. He wanted to hate and he wanted to rave once more.

'But although you lost a sister,' his mother's voice boomed, 'look around you. You've gained a whole family – brothers and sisters who'll be with you for the rest of your life. Because my children, you've had the *same* childhood, the same parents, the same experiences. So you are all brothers and sisters. We are so, so proud of you all.'

Emergers looked affectionately at one another, hands were held and arms went around shoulders.

Troy looked at the happy, healthy faces around him. *Everyone in here has had the same upbringing as me, the same parents. So we're family.* He tried to digest the thought, but found he couldn't. He didn't believe it. *I need time, time by myself to think, to get some answers.* His head pounded harder than ever, and within that pounding Troy made a decision: he had to get out of here. He had to get out of this place and find out what was going on outside, in the real world. Slowly, he began to take tiny sidesteps towards the sealed door leading back out into the Emergence room, but then he changed his mind: there were lots of nurses that way – it would be better to try the exit on the other side of the theatre: he could see the white outline of a doorway through the crowd.

As he sidestepped through groups of Emergers holding hands, leaning on each other for support, Troy turned to see if Shaw was watching him, but the Professor was apparently captivated by the two figures on the screen. It wasn't surprising really: his mother and father were, had been, amazing people. They'd always got on well, always been the best of friends and model parents. Odd snags of memory poked at Troy's consciousness as his parents' voices filled the theatre: his mother bringing him a glass of vegetable juice and a cassette of subliminal learning chips when he was ill in bed with a cold... eating freeze-dried ice-cream in zero gravity with his father while they toured the moon… he already missed them so much. If he accepted what Shaw was saying, it meant he had no parents and never had done. No one had really ever loved him, it had all been manufactured. The thought made his throat swell: how could this place, this system, take that away from him – his right to real-life parents?

Troy shuffled past a pretty girl with very straight, blonde hair, her arm around a short, cherub-faced boy, and reached the exit, trying to block the soothing tones of his mother and father, and more importantly his emotional responses to them. The shimmering pink pressure pad that would open the door hovered in his peripheral vision. All he had to do was press the pad and then slip out the exit. Easy.

He risked a glance at the room of young, healthy-looking people, all wearing identical loose green outfits. Suddenly he was angry. His life, all their lives, had been taken away from them. And in the other room were more sorry individuals experiencing an identikit upbringing while these doctors and scientists swanned around pretending to know what was best for everyone. The Submerged were like lab droids, being force-fed an existence they had no choice about whatsoever. The pain hit him then, the pain of what he had lost. It was worse than losing Annabelle. He had lost everything: his whole life. He had to get out of here. He had to run.

Troy reached out and pushed the pressure pad, breathing in sharply at the loud hiss. A few people near him flinched, but no one turned around, so Troy slid through the exit, not looking at anything but the thinscreen, even as he edged over the threshold. Despite himself, cherishing the comfort of those figures before him.

Gradually the thinscreen voices faded, and Troy slowly turned around, exhaling. There was nobody in sight out here, no sentinel droids, doctors, nurses: everything was as slow and calm as a biological tree farm.

He was standing on a platform that forked into two bridges, the left one leading to a square laboratory block suspended in mid-air, and the other connecting to a huge wood-clad cylinder, perhaps a kilometre in length, that ran from the floor of the Institute right up to the ceiling. The cylinder had many small windows set into it, and around fifty bridges meeting its round sides over the many different levels of the building. It could have been an office block, but there was something not quite right about that: the size of the windows was wrong somehow, and too many of them were frosted.

'It's the accommodation cylinder,' said a familiar voice, and Troy's teeth clenched together and nipping the side of his tongue. He turned to see Shaw's strong face, eyes narrowed, gazing out at the multi-windowed cylinder as if it were a beautiful space shuttle or underwater cruise ship.

'This is where everyone else will go after the pre-integration lecture,' said Shaw, throwing his arm around Troy's shoulder like a harness. 'But it's too soon for you. You're not ready to be integrated just yet. There are procedures, programs that need to happen. Come with me.'

Shaw steered Troy to the left fork, over the bridge and away from the accommodation cylinder.

'You've got nothing to worry about, Troy,' said Shaw, although it was more of an instruction than a reassurance. 'I know why it got too much for you in there – it's perfectly understandable. We knew it would be, as a matter of fact, but we'd assumed you'd manage the whole lecture before... well, before things became difficult. But that's OK. Now, there's someone I'd like you to meet. Someone very important to your reintegration and wellbeing.'

Shaw wasn't holding Troy, exactly, but under the weight of that great arm Troy found himself unable to go anywhere other than where Shaw steered him – which was across the left-hand bridge and into the square, hanging block with 'L1 Submergence Monitoring Laboratory', projected over its doorway.

Chapter Eight

Inside the laboratory looked like a typical tired old public sector lab, with old-fashioned admin droids sitting on pedestals and a wall of forty dusty thinscreens, each projecting different changing images. Below the screens were rows of clunky datadroids clicking away as they recorded streams of data, and in the corner was a simple testing area, with a VR helmet hung above a frayed lounge chair. What the lab lacked was people: it was completely empty, save for the rattling droids crunching their numbers.

'The lady I'd like you to meet is dealing with test subjects upstairs,' said Shaw, scrolling through his data-disc for a contact code, then holding the shiny pebble to his mouth and speaking. 'He's here. Yes. I'll meet you back in area 114.'

With that Shaw took his heavy arm from Troy's shoulder and moved towards the exit.

'She's on her way. I'll be back later to take you to the integration party.'

Shaw left, and Troy stood in the centre of the lab, his body tense, waiting for an opportunity to run. As datadroids clicked away below the thinscreens, the moving images caught his eye, and he noticed one of them showed the top of a bar table with a bottle of clear spirit on it. As the feed panned up, Sarah's face filled the screen, lovely and soft and full of concern. Sarah: nothing more than a VR invention. It hit him like a wrong note on a piano – if all this were real, he would never see her, or his friends and family again. So why was she being broadcast on a screen in this laboratory? Were they trying to torture him?

As a lump grew in his throat, there was a whirring sound from the far wall of the laboratory. A section of the ceiling began to float down, slowly revealing a woman in low heels and a bright red, skin-tight business suit, standing on a moving platform. The platform settled to the ground and the woman's whole body came into view – pale, pointy face with deeply intelligent green eyes, red bobbed hair that tapered around her neck, and holographic badge shining blue on her lapel that said: 'Dr Yvonne Willis, Head of Non-standard Submergence.' She was smiling.

'Hello Troy,' she announced as she stepped off the platform and advanced towards him, sturdy hand reaching out to shake his. 'Good to meet you. Please – take a seat.' She gestured towards the chair lounger in the testing area.

'I'm fine standing.'

'Suit yourself. As long as you're comfortable.' Willis leaned against a table that ran the length of the lab. 'You'll be seeing a lot of this room in the next few days,' she said, her eyes darting back and forth over the thinscreens. 'It's where I do all my research.'

'What research?'

'There are twenty monitoring rooms in the building,' said Willis, frowning at one of the thinscreens. 'They all have their research and monitoring specialisms. This particular lab monitors individuals with a high default complex, or L1s as we call them. Rebels, in other words.' She gave Troy a conspiratorial smile. 'L1s are my research area.'

'What's that got to do with me?' asked Troy, noticing the screen that had held Sarah now panned around a bar – *his* university bar. His old life was up on the screen.

'Because I'm a Code Black expert,' said Willis, 'and you're a Code Black survivor. I assume Shaw has already shown you his little slide show?'

Troy nodded.

'Then he'll have told you a little about Code Black already. But let me give you a bit more detail. You, Troy, like a very, very small percentage of L1s, suffered a psychological imbalance that led to premature Emergence, or Code Black. Technically, you shouldn't have survived. The human mind generally can't cope with Emerging, unless it's been prepared for it. That's what the last Submergence chapters are all about. Preparation.' Dr Willis looked right at Troy, lines appearing around her narrow eyes. 'I understand how you're feeling Troy, believe me, I do. Accepting this new reality, without being eased into it... it's very, very difficult. You'll have all sorts of problems adapting. You'll feel anger, a deep sense of loss... confusion. Integrating with other Emergers will certainly be difficult at first: it will be hard for you to understand how they can accept Submergence so readily.'

'I can't imagine anything, any "chapters" that would make me accept what's going on,' said Troy. 'I'm not even sure I believe it. In fact I don't, I don't really believe it.'

'You'd be surprised,' said Willis. 'The last chapters really are a triumph of the Program. They don't just help us get used to the idea of Submergence and mediate the shock – they help us feel grateful for being Submerged. We have, after all, been given a wonderful opportunity. A perfect start in life.'

Troy blew air through his nose.

'There's nothing a VR program could give me that would make me feel grateful for this... this...' Troy threw his hands up in the air, but in the absence of a better word, he settled for: 'situation.'

Willis gave a gentle smile.

'You would say that. You're an L1, like me. We have the hardest time accepting the new reality, but we do accept it eventually. Those of us who survive.'

'So I'm an L1?'

'Certainly. All Code Blacks are L1s. That's why we monitor L1s so carefully.' Willis nodded towards the thinscreens and pointed at the one showing the university bar. 'I remember that day like it was yesterday. We used to sit alone in that corner and watch the world go by observing the people as they went about their lives.' When Troy flashed anger and then confusion, she added: 'The screens show monitoring feeds from Submerged patients – effectively the Program which we all lived. Our lives in pictures. Whenever I get lonely I look at the screens and remember the beautiful life we all shared.' She waved her hand at the screen and immediately it changed to a myriad of graphs and tables of numbers. She paused a moment her gaze fixed on the screen and then turned to him. 'I know you have questions. Your cerebral engrams show an above average level of curiosity. I'll try and answer everything for you I promise.'

'So everyone has exactly the same life,' said Troy, his voice flat. 'You, me... everyone.'

'Not exactly the same,' said Willis, seeming not to notice Troy's. Her eyes once again on the screens. 'There are mild variances but we will all have broadly similar experiences, yes. It is how we learn. It is how we become the people we are. It is the cement for our broad all-encompassing family.'

On the next screen, the images wheeled around even more uncertainly and the memory hit Troy like a shot of clear spirit: his last journey home from the university bar. The thinscreen showed a police sentinel drone approaching – the same sentinel Troy remembered spearing him in its lights that night and scanning his data-disc for ID and address, its metallic face blank and non-judgemental.

'Not a great night,' said Willis. 'Or a great morning for that matter.' She shook her head, smiling. 'We can give a human being a completely artificial upbringing, and yet we can't cure something as simple as a hangover. Post-emergence hangovers are just as bad so we have to prepare you. Thankfully people rarely drink to excess. Another benefit of our Program.'

Troy nodded. Lots of his medical student friends injected analgesics and alcohol chelators to mop up any residual alcohol in their bloodstreams before they went to sleep, but Troy never had. He felt that if he'd done the crime, he should do the time. People had dealt with alcohol for many years without the aid of injections, and he was strong enough to take the pain without using borderline illegal medications. They'd been a thriving underground trade among medical students, he remembered, and Daryl was always trying to push analgesics, alongside his other more potent products.

The AV camera wobbled back and forth as whoever was living out the Submergence scenario tried to stumble up the three small, yet troublesome steps into the university apartment block and then fell against a front door – *his* front door. Wood filled the screen for a moment, and then the AV moved down to the key-card slot, and a key card waved uncertainly above it before sliding in and releasing the lock mechanism. Troy felt homesick again. He'd give anything, *anything,* to wake up in his own bed at university and find this was all a dream. He wanted to melt into the thinscreen before him. To be back there himself.

His old front door: it seemed a million miles away now. He remembered being told by the estate agent that the key card feature was a great period detail, and highly sought after, but not being able to walk up to your own front door and be instantly recognised by an Auto-secure turned out to be incredibly frustrating. What he wouldn't give to feel that frustration now. For such small things to seem important.

Now the AV wobbled around inside the flat, and Troy's insides turned in a knot as the CCU system illuminated furniture and possessions, some familiar, some alien. His work desk was still there with data chips scattered across it to remind him of the weeks of continual revision he'd just undergone, but his life-size skeleton hologram no longer hovered in the far corner. He used to talk to the skeleton like it was a friend – had they all done so? They must have done. He remembered he'd been studying the anatomy of the eye just before his exams, so the hologram had looked slightly comical, with an enormous bulging right eye, magnified so he could clearly see around the orbit.

On the thinscreen, a hand reached out to the hypojet dispenser on the wall, and with a shock Troy saw it was a female hand: slim and pale, with three pierced fingernails. So it was a woman living this scenario at present. But presumably not everyone was trained as a doctor, hence the lack of Mr Bones in the corner. Troy always thought he'd been interested in biology at an early age, always attending after-school biology clubs and spending an inordinate amount of time on his biology projects, but now, if he were to believe what he was being told, everything was in question.

'How was medicine chosen for me?' he asked, aware that posing such a question was in many ways an act of acceptance about what he was being told. 'How did the system know... I mean, why did it think I should be a doctor?'

'It didn't,' said Willis. 'Submergence is both a passive and reactive system. It feeds you positive scenarios, but also gives you new scenarios depending on your responses. Do you remember your careers advisory algorithm?'

Troy remembered it very well. The school's central net had on five consecutive occasions told him that he was ideally suited to be a doctor, and everyone said you couldn't get much more damming evidence than that. Indeed, medical schools accessed such data on a regular basis to gauge future demand for places.

'Everything was like a conveyor belt after that,' Troy murmured. 'Higher-level assessments, submitting my note of interest for a medical school placement... whenever anyone asked what I wanted to do, I always said medicine. But I always felt it was like a rollercoaster I couldn't get off. It went forward, but I wasn't controlling it.'

Willis nodded.

'That's because you're an L1. The other types have less trouble believing their futures are determined for them. Ironically, the last chapters of Submergence are the most important for L1s, and yet this is exactly the time they're prone to Code Black. There's a link somewhere – I've spent my life looking for it, and of course that link makes you very important. In my opinion, Code Black survivors hold the key to explaining the entire Code Black phenomena and eradicating Submergence fatalities.'

The thinscreen they'd been watching had now turned black, but on the screen next to it a morning scenario was being played out. Troy could see a column of neon light projecting from a data-disc sat on a bedside table, displaying the current time, alarm time and current location in glowing figures on the wall. The AV then panned around an apartment, Troy's apartment save for a few details, with his cheap domestic droid doing its slow cleaning routine around the flat and his even-cheaper luggage droid in the corner – the one that could barely get off the ground, and always made an irritating whirring noise that turned heads.

He'd always meant to get around to replacing both of them, but he supposed nothing like that mattered anymore. If only he'd appreciated at the time how little he really had to worry about. With a heaviness in his stomach, he realised once again that it all made sense. He believed it, he really did. He believed Submergence was real. All his life, he'd had a sense of something amiss, something not quite right or real – things not adding up. The exam failure, the driving test, the sense of a psychological barrier that prevented him from taking risks… not to mention that all his experiences in this place, the Institute, felt so, so *real.* The food sliding down his gullet, the pain when he'd pinched his arm, the feeling of air on his skin and in his lungs, all of it.

The deep, gnawing sense of loss enveloped him again, coupled with a heavy sense of responsibility. For the first time in his life, he was entirely culpable for everything that happened to him. But he was still aware he wanted to get out, to get away and see the real world. If his whole life so far had been manufactured by other people, it was time to start really living.

His anger surfaced like a bolt of magma overflowing. "With all due respect, I don't believe it and I don't believe you. I can't believe you. You're telling me that I've been in The Matrix all my life. I guess that makes me bloody Morpheus or even better Neo."

Yvonne smiled patiently, not rising to the challenge in his voice, but did not respond.

'How can I accept that you dictated my life?' his voice was once more steady. 'How could I have not known that all my actions were programmed?'

Yvonne's eyes lit up and she leant forward towards him with a smile. 'An excellent question Troy, really excellent. You do not disappoint.

'Choice Troy, what is choice? I'm sounding like Morpheus now! Please sit Troy.' Two chairs rose silently from the floor and they both sat.

'Troy, you probably have nothing but contempt for it at the moment, but the Program's sole purpose is to make you and all of us better people. Yes you're right it was a Matrix-type system. That is why we created The Matrix AV; that is why we created *The Truman Show* AV; that is why you watched *Utopia* about a hundred times. Can you deny that Truman turned out as

81

a good individual after immersion in his controlled environment? He escaped in the end and the world loved him for what he had become'

It was all artificial! He yearned to scream at her.

'Those AVs were specifically designed to adapt you to what you are experiencing now. If you hadn't Emerged so soon you would have seen many more AVs to prepare you. Our Program gives us the experiences that benefit us but all the time it makes sure we are safe. It is like a hand always protecting and cushioning us.'

Troy shook his head over and over. His mind was reeling once more. It was so beyond imagining that he truly did not know where his emotions lay.

'Think on this Troy. You've been standing in a lecture theatre many times. I know that because *we* gave you those experiences. No wait Troy. In a silent lecture, did you ever feel like shouting out just to see what the reaction would be? We cannot be certain but your engram readings indicate that you were experiencing urges like that. Have you ever been sitting in a pod travelling up the M1 motorway and thought what it must be like to rip out the controls and force it to swerve into the central force field? Have you ever felt like jumping out in front of a transit pod to see what it would feel like? To test whether the central controller would stop it in time? Those are "death wish" phenomena. What stops you from doing that? We do, the Program does.

'However low you feel, however unstable you are, we protect you. The Program makes sure you cannot do anything that could create harm. You've watched *Sliding Doors*. It teaches you that one moment can change your life. One wrong turn can lead you down a dark alley. Remember the time when you were fourteen years old when you got into that fight with your dad about going to that big rock concert? Remember running away and meeting that group of youths, remember them trying to talk us into breaking into that pod with them? We were angry and upset and irrational. Had we actually gone with them rather than walk away we would have been caught with them. Had it been real we would have ended up in a juvenile rehabilitation institute, never gone to mainstream school, our permanent record would have been flagged, we would have never been able to go to university and so on. We were young and immature. How could we be expected to make a mature sensible decision? We could not.'

'How the hell did you know about that,' Troy said to himself, his voice only just audible. Despite himself his brain provided the answer for him.

Ignoring him Yvonne continued, 'We could see that we wanted to go. Our neural kinetics, like 83% of our peers, showed that we really wanted to go. We were young and foolish and we were certain that looking back now we realise what a disaster it would have been if we had gone with them. How easy it would have been to just go and watch, but we would have been caught. That is what we call a divergence point, or some people casually call it a *Sliding Door* scenario. A point in your life where things could go either way. One bad apparently innocuous decision could send your life spiralling down a route to disaster.'

Troy wanted her to stop talking now. He felt beleaguered and battered by the constant attrition of information being thrown at him. He was losing.

'Let's take an example, let us say we are at school and we plan a prank, we get a balloon and fill it with water, we throw it out of the window at a fellow pupil, it hits him and soaks him. Ha ha, very funny at age thirteen. No harm done. But he is startled by the water and jumps back flailing his arms out, a ten-year-old girl walking behind him is shoved into the street. A transport pod is coming and its safety systems do not have time to react. She is hit and dies. I am not making this up; we have records indicating that such events have taken place in the past.

Bad luck, undoubtedly. Not intended, inevitably. Not fair, certainly. But you would be guilty of involuntary manslaughter.'

'I know, I know, I get the point,' Troy muttered his head remaining down turned.

'Well you're a fine young man, you could have handled it very well and despite having a criminal record and being required to go to a dedicated schooling facility and subsequently being thrust into an environment surrounded by other young people with social problems, some of them real pre-meditated criminals, you could have been fine. Alternatively, you could have been aggrieved by the unfairness of life, you could have rebelled even more, and with your newfound friends you could have got into more trouble. You can see where I'm going with this,' said Yvonne.

Troy's head lifted, 'I get it, I get it,' his voice thick with defeat.

And yet Yvonne continued as if she could not stop. 'Your childhood is the most vulnerable time in your life. Looking back to your earlier years you can, I'm sure, agree you had no idea about the implications of the decisions you made. You were nowhere near mature enough to understand what you were doing.

'Let's simplify it even further, accidents and mischance may occur at any time. You are walking along a corridor and come to a T-junction, you look right and left, identical corridors. Which way do you turn, right or left? You toss a credit in your head. You turn right. You walk down the right corridor and the roof collapses on top of you and kills you. Your last thoughts are "I should have taken the left turn". How were you to know? You couldn't have foreseen it. Bad luck indeed but now your life is gone and the things you could have achieved will never be,' her voice became pleading and intense as if the strength of her words would somehow force their way into Troy's understanding. 'We protect you from all of these things. You were safe and you still are safe.'

She stopped talking, looking intently at Troy's bowed head. Troy looked up at Yvonne and noticed her flinch at the depth of confusion and despair she saw in his reddened eyes.

The silence was interrupted eventually by a gentle voice. 'Troy I'm going to leave you now, you've got a lot to think about. The orderlies will take you back to your room. Food will be brought to you. You'll be back here this afternoon.'

Chapter Nine

He was back in Yvonne's laboratory again sitting once more in front of her. The thinscreens on the walls were portraying other scenes of his life. He avoided looking at them.

'You've had some breathing space. Do you have any questions Troy?'

He had reflected on her words and on Professor Shaw's lecture. It was all too far-fetched. None of it made sense. He wanted to close his eyes and make it all go away. He wanted to run and keep on running until he reached a reality he could understand. He was the chosen one who survived. He felt like an actor in a poorly conceived film. At least Keanu Reeves had been a hero, he was only a victim. Questions failed to materialise in his head, his cognitive processes overloaded by conflicting emotions.

He formulated words slowly and laboriously. 'What about choice? You started to answer me but then you spoke about something else. You're trying to tell me that everything I experienced was part of a computer program. So how were you controlling my thoughts?'

She smiled as if congratulating him. 'A good question Troy. We were not controlling your thoughts. Your thoughts were your own. The Program simply inputs tactile, vocal, visual, and other sensory experiences to you. You see with your eyes but that is of no relevance, you perceive with your mind.'

Again Troy's thought processes rallied. 'Hang on a minute. If my brain was my own and my thoughts my own, how can this whole thing possibly work?' He was surprised by his own insight. His brain was overloaded and yet it seemed to still manage logical constructs.

'We do not brainwash you. We give you experiences which you may have had in real life and we leave your psychosocial development to you. That is the beauty Troy. You are still you.' Exuberance was clear in her voice like religious zeal. 'After experiencing the things you experience we leave the interpretation up to you. Had you been in the real world you may have experienced the type of childhood you did if you were very fortunate indeed. It is more likely that you would have not. We gave you the gift of guaranteeing your experience.

'For example, a year before you Emerged we went through a traumatic experience. That section is called Chapter 293, Section 82. It is the culmination of the experiences which we hope will give you an appreciation for the law and the danger of transgressing beyond it. It also teaches you about loyalty. Looking at Jack as he lay in pain was a real experience because you did experience it, just like I did. We did not brainwash you Troy. We did not put the awe and the fear and the guilt into your mind. We hope you felt those things because it is what the individual who we know you to be would feel when exposed to those events. We hope you understood the dangers. Can you deny that you have these feelings? Can you deny the revulsion for those individuals who did that to him? Search yourself, are such feelings wrong? How could it possibly be bad?'

Despite himself, he found that what she said was true. Part of his being, the part that was partitioned from the violence and anger he felt, was pleased that Jack had not actually been injured. Was the pain he had experienced worth it for this lesson? But at least Jack hadn't actually suffered. He

87

consciously searched his emotions for evidence of any change. Did what he now knew change the way he felt about the law? He could still picture Jack's pain illuminated by the lights of the policepods and medidrones. The emotions it generated were only slightly suppressed by the storm of other thoughts oscillating in Troy's mind.

At length, he managed to form the words to speak, his voice uncertain. 'But it didn't happen. It was a lie. You put me through that for nothing. Jack didn't take a dart to defend me. He didn't try to save me because he didn't exist.'

Just the slightest nod came from Yvonne as she answered his assertions. 'The means may be difficult to accept in your current state of mind but the ends do justify them. Jack would use his body to shield you because he is your friend. Now I am your friend and I would do what Jack had done for you. Why would I do it for you? Because Jack once did it for me too. Jack saved us all and he has a special place in here,' she touched her heart with the palm of her hand. She scrutinised Troy's face.

'I see you smirk,' she continued, 'Maybe you could be sceptical in the world we created for you but in this real world we *are* all brothers and sisters. We have no drug problem because of the work we do in this Institute. Why am I so confident in the brotherhood and sisterhood of our lives? Why are the people outside these walls so good? It is because each of them has been through the Program and each of them was moved by what they experienced. Each of them Emerged and each has accepted the honour of what we have given them. They are true because we gave them the chance to find the best in themselves.'

She paused, her hands in front of her beseeching, 'A formative experience like that in the real world could have cost you your life or the life of a friend. We gave you the respect and understanding you now have at no cost. No one died and yet you have the same appreciation for life and law. Regardless of the

88

means are you a better person for it, yes or no?' Only silence answered her. 'Troy?'

Her words seemed inherently logical. He felt like he was being led by a rope in a circle around the same issue. His thoughts were being forced through hoops. His mind kept on rallying, trying to escape these bonds but always he was pulled back to face the inevitable. 'Yes I guess so,' he muttered sullenly.

'I know this is hard for you. These issues are dealt with at great length in the last twelve chapters of our Program. Of your Program, the one intended for you. The one you have left too soon. You unfortunately have to come to terms with them yourself with only my inarticulate ramblings to help you.' She smiled a vacant smile at her own humour. It was intended as a soft gentle smile, designed to placate.

'It still doesn't answer my question. What if I hadn't taken the IQ? What if I decided against opening my results? What if I had walked away? You claim my thoughts are my own so explain that. If you take away choice you *are* brainwashing people.' His eyes blazed, his rage stirring once more.

'Troy, entire semesters are devoted to this very topic and you want me to answer and explain in a few minutes.' She shook her head fractionally. 'What is choice? Back to my old analogy of the corridor with the T-junction. Turn right or left? How do you make that decision? You will tell me that you analyse the pros and cons of each way and then make the decision based on those factors. But what makes your final decision? What is the link between making the decision to go right and actually doing it? Do you stand for a moment and say to yourself "I'm going right" and then turn to face right and move your right leg forward and then your left? No. It is unfortunately not so consciously structured. You think right or left and then go right. That is your decision and the time lag is milliseconds while you make that choice.'

Yvonne paused and whetted her lips before continuing, 'We make that decision for you, and, incidentally, it just so happens to always be the right decision, and you do it. Your brain does not rebel because you intuitively assume that it was your decision, and indeed why should you not? If you did it you must have chosen to do it. If you had stood at the door to that alleyway and had decided in your head that you did not want to go out there at all. Of you had felt that Sarah wasn't worth it and indeed you were adamant that you would not go to her rescue. If you had been so determined not to go and then suddenly you found yourself walking through that door, how would you react? You would not react at all but assume that the other half of your brain had decided to go and confront events after all. Do you see Troy?'

She paused waiting for some recognition or acknowledgement but received none from Troy. 'It's the same scenario with speech. All your conversation was dictated by the Program. The words that you heard coming from your lips were chosen by us for you. You said things we wished you to say but by saying them your brain presumes that that is indeed what you were thinking and what you actually believe. Why would you think otherwise? There is no other explanation. When you are talking to me now, do you say in your head, "I am going to say this and that" and then speak? No you do not. It just comes out. It is one of the major routes of psychodevelopment we use. If you say something you assume you thought it and by assuming you thought it you alter your thoughts about it. A classic "which came first the chicken or the egg scenario?" If you say you dislike the colour blue you assume it is true because why would you say it if it wasn't what was in your head. We call this a Korkovsky loop.'

'I dreamt about Jack and those thugs for two whole weeks, the same dream, reliving it over and over again,' muttered Troy in a low voice shaking his head. 'Why would you force me to relive it over and over again? I got the message the first time.'

'Ah Troy, we cannot control your dreams. Although we rest you down and close your eyes in the world we create for you, as I have said previously, we have no control over your thoughts, only your subliminally conscious decision making. For you, sleep is where you lie down and close your eyes. Your brain is still working, thinking about your day, imagining things that may be. We can send you into true REM sleep with simple drugs but we try and avoid that if we can. Your sleep and your dreams are your own.'

They sat in deafening silence for what seemed like an eternity. Neither of them meeting the other's gaze.

'So what happens now, Dr Willis?' asked Troy.

'Please,' said Willis, leaning back in her chair. 'I told you please call me Yvonne. And that's a very good question. Shaw brought you to me so I could assess you and make recommendations for reintegration. You're such a rare statistic, you need specialist assessment: no Program exists that works for all Code Black survivors.' Yvonne's eyes darted away from the screens and to the floor. 'Each of you needs to be assessed individually, but there's no guaranteed method of reintegrating you. You're likely to always carry some feelings of loss, even if you're successfully Re-submerged and come through the other side.'

'Re-submerged?'

'Yes. You missed the last chapters of your Submergence, so one solution is to Re-submerge you and let you finish the Program. It's an option that's been proven to work in our AI scenarios.'

'I don't want to be Re-submerged,' said Troy.

Dr Willis nodded, her eyes flitting between Troy and the thinscreens.

'I've spent my whole life studying L1s and Code Blacks,' she said, pausing as two data droids rattled particularly loudly. 'And I'll be the first to admit we're far from finding perfect solutions. We keep trying, but... my point is, we're not going to Re-submerge you until we've tried to reintegrate you naturally. Before we do anything, I'd like you to attend the Emergence party this evening. See how you feel amongst the other Emergers, and Hannah, of course.'

Hannah. His heart quickened. 'I wanted to ask about her,' said Troy. 'She was... I saw her when I was Submerged. Why?'

'That's part of Emergence – gradually merging our reality with yours.'

'So I get used to the idea of my life counsellor.' Troy filled in the rest for her. 'And when I finally meet her, it's not such a shock.'

'You are intuitive. Already you've got the building blocks for acceptance and understanding within you. She's more than your councillor,' said Yvonne, her thin eyebrows shooting up. 'Didn't Shaw tell you? Life councillors are chosen to match your personality. Around 90% of people experience deep and lasting friendships with their life councillors, but you're one of the lucky ones. The system found you a double-positive match. A love match, in other words. Anyway – that's the next step. You'll get to know Hannah tonight, and we'll take things from there.'

Troy nodded, although he had no intention of staying for long at any Emergence party. The first chance he got, he was breaking out of the Institute – but there was no harm in meeting Hannah first.

Chapter Ten

'Welcome to Sky Restaurant.' The shiny door droid discreetly scanned Troy's fingerprint with a white laser, and confirmed an ID match with the temporary data-disc the institute had provided him and its internal guest-list database. 'Good evening, Troy Harrison. You are part of the Emergence party. You are the twentieth guest to arrive. Please proceed to the bar area where drinks are being served before dinner.' An arrow glowed on the wall opposite, leading Troy along a sumptuously carpeted corridor, lined with floor-to-ceiling windows that offered spectacular views of a pink and orange sunset outside. The restaurant was around a mile from the ground, housed in a leisure complex on the roof of the Institute.

Sky Restaurant was a good name for it, Troy thought, watching wisps of clouds drift past the windows. Before taking a bullet-elevator to the restaurant, Troy had read a flexisheet about the Institute's Sky Leisure Complex, which consisted of four pointed towers, interlinked by transparent walkways. He'd read everything he could get his hands on that afternoon, partly to learn as much as he could about what was going on and partly to take his mind off the storm of emotions that took it in turns to thunder around his body: anger, loss, fear, denial. The information he'd accessed agreed with everything the Professor and Yvonne had told him. The theories were all there in print. The logic inescapable. The progression from theory, to action to consequence all played out in the scientific texts. However, his access had been restricted to texts that the institute approved.

All four towers of the complex extended a mile from the ground, and appeared to sit on a cushion of clouds that obscured the Institute below. When there were clouds the height of the restaurant floor could be altered so that it appeared to rest just above them on a cushion of white. But today there weren't too many, and Troy could see far into the distance, the black spikes of London skyscrapers jutting through thinning vapour towards the fading sun.

Earlier that afternoon, Shaw had taken Troy to the accommodation block, where Troy had been given his own apartment, new data-disc and a wardrobe of clothes – from which he'd been asked to select an outfit for the Emergence party that evening. He'd been impressed, in a hollow sort of way, to see several files of clothes available, and after viewing holo-images of himself wearing a few different smart-casual outfits, he'd chosen a one-piece suit. The wardrobe had then whirred, puffed with steam and delivered him his warm, pressed garment a few seconds later: a garment he now wore.

Troy was reluctant to admit it, but while he was changing thoughts of escape had temporarily been replaced by a very different desire: a desire to look good when he met Hannah. He hated the idea that the Submergence system should be able to accurately select a 'love match' for him, but at the same time he was intrigued and excited. Every time he'd dreamed about Hannah during Submergence, he'd been desperate to meet her in real life, although until now he had thought it would forever be impossible. Now, he finally would. He had to remember that it was all synthetic and false but, unbidden, a portion of his mind was querying why that should matter.

As he headed down the bright, beautiful corridor towards the restaurant, Troy could see ant-like figures of people on the walkways between the towers, some journeying to another part of the complex, others presumably enjoying the fresh air and dazzling sunset view. He was in the west tower, where the Sky Restaurant sat just under the top point, a big rotating dome of panoramic glass, like a huge, transparent mushroom cap. The flexisheet assured Troy that like all mega-tall buildings, an external force field supported the framework, so there was no danger of strong winds swaying or cracking the structure.

At the restaurant entrance, the carpeted floor turned into a hard thinscreen that simulated orangey-blue sky and clouds passing under his feet. It was a little disconcerting. The decorative floor covered the entire dining area, running right under the chairs and tables, through to the bar, and giving everything the appearance of floating on thin air. Troy nearly stumbled when he first trod on it, but as he began to walk a thin, swaying wooden platform flashed up, plank by plank, under his feet, which in many ways felt more precarious than walking on sky.

Troy was so focused on the floor, he didn't notice Hannah at first. But when he looked up and saw her in the restaurant bar, surrounded by Emergers, he couldn't help but stare. She was so dazzlingly beautiful, so much more so in real life than in his dreams, and she was smiling and waving at him like they were old friends. She was a dream come true, cloned from his subconscious and into his reality. Another nail in the coffin of his denial.

'Troy!' She grinned as he approached, her deep, piercing blue eyes framed perfectly by sleek, shiny black hair that hung down to her shoulders.

Troy found himself scanning up her body like some erotic hologram: perfect ankles attached to perfect calves and perfect thighs, barely hidden by her shimmering chameleon-fabric dress that gripped her slim figure. It was amazing: she was real, and she was really here, standing right in front of him. Every slight movement Hannah made changed the colour of her dress, and a veritable kaleidoscope fluctuated over her body, accentuating the curve of her breast and the slenderness of her waist.

After a moment, Hannah coughed, and Troy realised he'd been blatantly looking her up and down and hadn't even said hello. Blood rushed to his cheeks, but Hannah was still grinning.

'Great dress, isn't it? It was an Emergence present.'

'I think you're incredibly beautiful.' The words leapt from his mouth before he could stop them, but he still spoke slowly and deliberately.

Immediately Hannah's face melted into a broad smile and she reached for his left arm, encircling it with hers.

'Typical L1, always ready with the chat-up lines.'

'I'm not –'

'Don't worry. I'm just teasing you. Now, as your guidance counsellor, it's important I help you integrate, so the first thing I'm going to do is get you a drink.'

They made their way through the crowd, and past two thinscreens showing multicoloured fish swimming in a bubbling stream. Each screen had a holoprojector above it, which simulated fish leaping from one thinscreen and splashing down into the other.

'Almost everyone's drinking soft drinks,' Troy commented, feeling the need to make conversation, but it was true: hardly any of the Emergers appeared to be drinking alcohol. Most clutched fruit waters, but looked as comfortable and relaxed as if they were downing glasses of wine.

'What do you want?' asked Hannah, peering over the counter, trying to spot a serving droid. 'I knew this would happen. All the servers are circulating. Let's go… oh, too late.'

A gentle, tinkling sound like musical running water flowed around the bar's sound system, signifying a guest announcement.

'Emergence party,' said a soothing female voice, 'please take your seats for dinner.'

Server drones sped forwards to escort the Emergers through to the dining room, pulling chairs back, arranging napkins on laps and filling water glasses.

'Come on,' said Hannah, who still had hold of Troy's arm. 'We're on table Cirrus, right by the panorama.' She led Troy back over the now pale grey floor, which mimicked the descending dusk outside. As they moved out of the bar area, a courteous gleaming server drone showed them to their table, which was an intimate hovering square right by the window, conspicuously set for two diners, in contrast to the other tables that seated ten or twenty guests.

'Just the two of us,' said Troy, feeling his voice crackle. He was nervous. Hannah was so soft and kind, but her beauty made him feel intimidated – especially since it now appeared they were having a one-on-one dinner date, which wasn't what he'd expected at all.

They both took a seat, smiling shyly at each other, the gentle whir of the seat servos adjusting to the weight of their bodies beneath them. As the cushions moulded around their posteriors, Troy found himself unable to look Hannah in the eye. Did she know they were supposed to be romantically compatible?

'So,' said Hannah, taking her napkin and folding the corner over and over. 'What's it like?'

'What's what like?'

'*You* know. Being special. A Code Black survivor. It must feel pretty amazing.'

'No. Confusing.' *Awful,* he wanted to add. *I hate this place so much, I hate them all – they've taken my life away from me.*

'Oh.' Hannah blushed, and Troy realised she was probably as nervous as he was. 'I hadn't thought of it that way. Confusing. Of course it is. Sorry. I can be a real Johnny Sampson sometimes.'

Troy stared at her. Johnny Sampson had been one of his friends at primary school, and was someone who consistently failed to engage his brain before he spoke. Troy had always been very fond of Johnny, but whenever anyone spoke without thinking he always thought of his tactless friend and smiled to himself. Tactlessness equals Johnny. The words of his mother on the thinscreen came back to him: *you're all family.* He supposed that was one way to look at it. He'd lost everyone he'd ever loved and who had ever loved him, but he'd gained a whole load of people who'd shared an almost identical upbringing. Somehow, the trade-off didn't seem worth it.

And another realisation occurred to Troy: every person he had ever met up until now had been created to teach him something. Johnny had been engineered to help him think before he spoke: a lesson for the entrapped juvenile psyche, in a class no-one had a choice but to attend. He'd read how they used post-Emergence psychometric tests to feedback and fine tune the Program. Further perfecting their perfect childhood.

Two short bleeps pulled Troy from his thoughts: a serving drone was lowering plates onto the air conveyor at the corner of the table and covered dishes floated towards them. Once the platters had settled in front of Troy and Hannah, the clear domes over each dish evaporated and luscious food smells floated around the table.

A thick piece of steaming steak greeted both of them, appropriately reared and slaughtered of course – Troy didn't doubt the pedigree of the establishment, so saw no reason to ask their server about the living conditions of the cattle. Not that he would anyway, he had far more important things to worry about. A second server loaded their plates with bright green asparagus stalks and refreshed their drinks.

'I can only imagine what you're going through,' said Hannah, picking up her electric steak knife. 'Normal Emergence is enough of a strain. Some people can't handle it, even with all the care we're given.'

'Really?' Troy was starving, but what Hannah had just said was much more interesting than his food. 'Other people have trouble?'

Hannah didn't look up.

'Yes. We call them...' She paused. '*Demergers*.' She struggled to say the word – as if it had a bad taste. 'They're the biggest tragedy of the system. People who've had all the breaks, all the luck... and just throw it all away.'

'Who are they? Are there any Demergers here? At the Institute?'

Hannah flinched slightly.

'Troy, there are some things you'll get used to. One of them is that we don't usually mention Demergers in polite society.'

'Why not?'

'We just don't Troy. We have something perfect here. We have been given a gift and we strive continually to make the gift more perfect. These people live among us and pretend to be part of our family but all the while they begrudge that which made them what they are. It's like Sarah or Suki or Jack turning around and betraying you.'

Troy cut into his steak, wondering why, if 'Demergers' were such an inappropriate topic, Hannah had brought them up. The pieces of meat tasted and felt divine in his mouth. It was so strange, living for the first time. Troy didn't think he'd ever get used to it, all the questions and strange experiences and sensations.

When they'd finished their main course, Hannah gave a tired smile and put her hand over Troy's.

'Sorry. I shouldn't have mentioned... you know. Let's forget it and order dessert.'

Troy smiled back. Her hand felt great over his. Every girl who'd touched him up until this point hadn't existed, she'd been nothing more than a simulation of warmth and pressure on his muscles, but that unsettling thought didn't take away from the fact that Hannah felt terrific.

'Good idea.' He leaned forward and tapped the centre console, feeling the warmth of Hannah's tiny hand as their plates floated to the centre of the table and lowered out of sight.

As holo-projections of desserts rose up from around the centre console and floated in mid-air, Troy tried to ignore the fact Hannah was still touching him, and focus on selecting his next course. The sticky toffee pudding looked particularly appealing with holographic toffee sauce perpetually flowing over the top of the succulent-looking cake. In fact, it looked so appealing that Troy wanted to lean forward and take a bite of the glistening holographic image that rotated before him.

'Everything looks delicious,' Troy announced, jabbing a finger at the pudding. Hannah stroked the air in front of the fruit salad. Their eyes met through the holo-projections and suddenly, as Hannah's deep blue eyes gazed back at him, everything went quiet: the chattering voices and hiss of drinks being refreshed around the restaurant became muted and far away. But the sharp tinkle of a metallic object hitting crystal cut through the silence and echoed throughout the restaurant.

'The great Emergence toast,' Hannah whispered, snatching her hand away from Troy's. Across the restaurant, Troy saw Shaw's huge frame rise up and loom over the seated diners.

'Ladies and gentleman.' His voice was as loud and clear as if he were speaking through the restaurant's audio system. 'We are here to give thanks to everything the Institute has given us, but also to welcome a very special addition to our extended family. A miracle of the Submergence system.'

Troy looked at Hannah, panic sweeping across his face.

'He doesn't mean *me,* does he?' Troy hissed. The last thing he wanted was to be exonerated in public as a success of the system: proof of its miraculous powers. The anger was back again, the quiet simmering rage that Troy had felt since the moment Shaw had come to visit him. *I hate this place, I hate everything about it. This is wrong, they've taken my life from me.* Hannah didn't say anything, and the next moment Shaw's great shoulders swung towards Troy and Hannah's corner table. He held aloft a glass of orange juice in salute.

'To Troy – our miracle. Welcome and happy Emergence.'

'Happy Emergence,' repeated the crowd, and a gentle cheer flowed around the restaurant.

Troy gripped the table, the veins in his neck standing out, and Hannah, noticing, took his hand again and held it softly.

'You want to get out of here?'

'I can't think of anything I'd like more.'

Chapter Eleven

They finished dessert, and Hannah linked her arm through Troy's and led him across the restaurant, both ignoring the curious glances that followed them. As they walked Troy caught Shaw's eyes. He nodded fractionally and smiled as if offering his blessing. Troy wanted to run over and throw a glass of water into his smug face but instead he kept his head down, held onto Hannah and kept walking. Now night had fallen, the floor had changed into a bright image of the Grand Canyon, with a narrow stream running many metres below. Troy once more had difficulty finding his footing as he stumbled beside Hannah, but finally they reached the carpeted corridor outside: a firm floor for Troy, and blissfully out of sight of the Emergence party.

'So where are we going?' Troy dropped his arm and took Hannah's hand, and she squeezed her thumb against his palm – an accepting gesture that made Troy's heart hammer like a bathroom refresher on deep exfoliate mode. It was a gesture so pleasantly familiar it was paradoxically painful. A gesture that Sarah had made to him countless times to reassure him. It was their private code. A secret they had shared as best friends. The anger and confusion lessened slightly every time she touched him and it felt good.

'Out. You'll see.'

They took the elevator down a few floors, through a heavy-duty electric door and then suddenly a soft, cool breeze stroked

Troy's face. *Outside*. They were outside in the still night air, walking along one of the great bridges that cut through the sky and joined the four towers into one huge leisure complex. The air, the stars… it was all so… *new. This must be the first time,* Troy thought, *I've ever been outside. Like Truman leaving the set.*

Under his feet, Troy felt something so joyous that words temporarily caught in his throat: soft grass, grown along the length of the bridge, grey in the moonlight, but still beautiful, nonetheless. He looked up and saw the clean white lines and turrets of the structure around him rising into the sky, and, high above, the clear immeasurable beauty of endless sky. A few grey clouds blew across the blackness, and the moon, the *moon* – it hung low in the sky, familiar but dazzling, fresh and brand new. Troy didn't think he'd ever seen anything so beautiful. For a brief moment his thoughts were not of deceit and programs and brainwashing. All he could feel was joy: joy at being alive.

After a few moments, Hannah spoke.

'Let's sit on the grass Troy.'

They both slid to the ground and, now they were alone, all the anger and feelings of exposure Troy had felt in the restaurant seemed to melt away.

'Does everyone do medicine?' he asked Hannah, putting his palms flat on the grass and enjoying the damp, slightly tickly sensation.

Hannah smiled, a radiant smile that lit up her whole face, clearly not disconcerted by the banal question.

'Of course everyone doesn't do medicine. Submergence – it's a variable program. They measure our psychometric parameters. Hasn't someone explained all this to you?'

Troy shrugged.

'Dr Willis said something about my careers algorithm.'

'Oh.' Hannah picked a strand of grass and twiddled it in her fingers. 'It's a bit more than that. We're given a series of tasks.

103

Test tasks – but you don't know they're tests at the time. Our cerebral activity is measured when we go through them. Remember when we were seven and we found the young girl in the park? Remember her arm and how we looked after her? That was a test task. Your cerebral activity would have shown a heightened level of neurokinetic activity during that time. They use all those sorts of things to work out what career paths we should take – it's not all about our careers algorithm. I was terrified through the whole experience and hated every second. It didn't take an analytical algorithm to work out I wasn't up to medicine.'

Troy leaned back against the bridge and gazed up. He could see the pale, circular outline of a solar generator station, one of the twenty-two in geosynchronous orbit around the earth, connected by vast cables to the surface miles below.

'At primary school,' said Troy, 'I had a best friend.'

'Davey,' said Hannah, and Troy felt mildly sick. Of course – she knew everything about his childhood, just as he knew everything about hers. They'd had, to all intents and purposes, the same life. They were brother and sister, a relationship he would share with everyone else he would ever meet from now on. In fact they were probably even closer than brother and sister. Siblings had distinct experiences whereas they had had the same life. They were emotional and psychological clones. It wasn't a comfortable thought, that total strangers would know every intimate detail about his upbringing, and he felt the rage again, the awful uncontrollable anger that made him want to tear up the grass and smash the high windows of the towers around them. But he looked at Hannah and felt calm again reassert itself.

'He had that model,' said Troy, pointing to the curves of the solar station high above them, and Hannah nodded and rolled her eyes.

'Yes – he'd go on and on about it when all I wanted to do was go outside and play. *Did you know, Hannah, that eleven of the twenty-two solar stations are always bathed in sunlight? Here – these are their connection points on Earth. They power the whole globe: free fuel for all, without cost to mother nature...*'

They both smiled at the memory, and Troy lifted his arm and put it around Hannah's shoulder. She felt small and soft against his chest.

'He went on about history too, didn't he?' said Troy, and Hannah laughed. Davey was always pulling out his history holograms and talking through the sad history of mankind: how people had sucked the life out of the earth's core before being forced to turn to alternative sources.

Troy could hear Davey's theatrical voice like it was yesterday as he read out information from his various flexisheets and holobooks. *'The oilfields dried up first, forcing the change from gasoline-powered vehicles to electrical. Then the last of the 'dirty' fuels, gas, coal and so on, were extinguished. But luckily, the sun had not turned its back on mankind. Troy, you don't look impressed – this is important.'* He could picture his face right now – the diligence and excitement about his topic shining through.

Had all that been a test too? If Troy's cerebral engrams had registered a fascination in the many different power sources, solar, geothermal, hydroelectric and wave power, would he have been steered down a different career path?

'Tell me what you *felt* when you found the girl in the park,' asked Troy, looking into Hannah's bright eyes.

'As I said, I was terrified,' she said, not meeting his gaze. 'I kept looking at that broken arm and felt like being sick. I remember my thoughts vividly. I still helped her and got her home, even though I didn't really want to my body just acted for me, but I hated every second. I did socio-psychology at university until my Emergence. Then I was given the choice – did I want to continue with it and become a life counsellor? I decided I did.'

'So now I can choose whether to carry on with medicine or not?' Troy asked.

'It's a free world.' Hannah pressed her weight against his chest, and he felt the warmth of her bare arms through his cotton top. 'You can choose whatever you want to do. But we've been helped in the right direction. Imagine – getting to our age and having no idea what you're good at. Where your talents lie. Everyone in the world used to suffer it.' Her voice trembled. 'We're *so* lucky.'

Troy's fingertips began massaging Hannah's arm. She felt amazing. Everything felt amazing. So he had choice, at least. His life was real. He could walk and talk with his own body. He was free. Free? If he was free now then by definition he was not free before. If he was not free he was a prisoner, a captive. It had to be wrong. It had to be a violation of his rights. The Program had taught him about human rights and freedom and yet that very Program broke all of those rules. His breathing quickened as a wave of anger threatened to overwhelm him. He was inwardly amazed at the ability of his emotions.

Did the system make the choices for them? Troy knew the answer before he'd even finished mentally posing the question. Yes, the system had made his choices. So many times he'd wanted to do something, thought about doing it but ended up doing something totally different: always the *right* thing as it turned out. So he'd been pushed into his choices up until now, they hadn't been his own. Presumably this had been to condition him, to teach him which routes to take. Had it worked? He wasn't sure, but then as he'd been told by Yvonne, he wasn't like the other Emergers.

'Hey.' Hannah got to her knees, recognising the change in Troy's temperament. She turned to him, placing a hand on his chest. 'What are you thinking about? It's OK. Really. Whatever it is, everything's going to be OK.'

Almost instantly, Troy felt at ease. Hannah was so gentle. He really felt he could open up to her: she reminded him of his sister and Sarah rolled into one. Were all Emergers so perfect? So fantastic?

Troy felt himself lean forward and stroke dark hair from her cheek.

'I'm not such a tragic case, you know,' he whispered, leaning towards her.

A caretaker drone floated by, and Hannah smiled shyly and pulled her face out of Troy's palm.

'Maybe... this is too soon. For you,' she said delicately. 'You've still got so much to learn...'

Troy nodded and remained silent. Despite the strong rush of feelings that spun around his body whenever he looked at Hannah, he had to remember she had been chosen for him by the Institute. *Chosen for him.* That was how much his life was still being controlled, even after he'd exited the system. But he had to admit, the system had chosen perfectly. They knew his tastes, knew his physical and emotional preferences. They'd given him the perfect route into the system: an attractive, seductive intelligent female to lure him into his new life. And he had no doubt Hannah was clever. Gentle, yes. Sweet, definitely. But beneath it all burned a bright intelligence, of that Troy was sure.

'OK – well, let's call it a night,' said Troy, getting to his feet and helping Hannah up, regret surging through him.

'Really?'

'Yes. I've got lots to think about.'

'Can we at least sync discs?' Hannah produced her datadisc from some mysterious place by her hip, and waved it at him.

'Sure. Why not?' said Troy, but he knew full well why not. Getting to know Hannah was dangerous. He needed to live his own life, to get away, make his own choices – and she was a beautiful silk rope winding tighter around him the more they were together, keeping him tied to the Institute.

As Troy made his way back to his apartment, he found he couldn't focus on getting away from the Institute. All he could think about was missing the opportunity to give Hannah a goodnight kiss. *First thing tomorrow*, he assured himself, *I'm getting out of here, by whatever force necessary.*

The yellow light flickered over Troy's eyelids, growing steadily whiter and whiter until it was so bright as to be impossible to ignore. *Morning already,* Troy thought, peeling his eyes open. He rolled towards his data-disc, which sat on the bedside table emitting rapid bursts of light – a routine designed to stimulate his eyes through his closed eyelids at precise intervals, affecting the occipital visual cortex itself, and by secondary stimulation, the pineal gland of wakefulness. The result: immediate abolition of melatonin levels and instant alertness, with no drowsy legacy of sleep.

It took a few moments before reality came crashing down on him, and the lingering feelings of anger and grief that gripped his stomach and windpipe reasserted themselves. In one great rush, Troy remembered everything, all that he had lost and the confusing, awful reality he now found himself in. It wasn't a dream: he was in an apartment the Institute had given him, experiencing what was only his second ever day living a real life.

Ending the morning light sequence with a click of his fingers, Troy pulled himself from the gel mattress and stood, alert, enjoying the stillness of the apartment. He was alone, which meant one thing: the possibility of leaving the Institute.

'Windows,' he barked, and three holo-projections appeared around the room showing daytime city scenes that looked real enough to step into. Really, Troy thought, this new apartment was the same as the one he had at university. His old flat may have had 'real' windows, but of course they'd been no more real than the holo-projections currently glowing on the walls. The layout was the same and the décor neater and more modern but otherwise it was almost identical.

Troy scanned his wardrobe files, requesting only utilitarian clothes to view, and eventually settling on a green outfit very similar to the one he'd worn yesterday. He had no idea what security measures the Institute had in place – perhaps he could simply walk out, no questions asked – but he sensed leaving would be more problematic than that, and that practical, unobtrusive garments would be the most beneficial thing to wear.

After dressing and using the refresher, Troy headed to the galley kitchen and pulled a breakfast pack of syntho-eggs and grilled tomatoes from the vacuum unit, hurriedly cracking open the lid. He barely waited for the food to heat before he began forking it into his mouth, eager to finish and get going. But as he pushed the last tomato into his mouth, a chime sounded and a door AV visual appeared above the vacuum unit, showing the image of a visitor outside. The half-chewed food felt heavy in his stomach: Yvonne Willis stood at his front door.

Coughing and wiping his mouth, Troy dropped the food container in the waste compactor and reluctantly went to open the door manually, not wanting to shout 'open' and allow Yvonne to walk straight in.

'Good morning Troy.'

'What are you doing here?' asked Troy, barely able to contain his annoyance. Were they checking up on him? They had no right.

Dr Willis, today dressed in a black skin-tight interviewer's suit, looked much more tired than she had the day before. Tired and older. Looking at her now, Troy thought she looked around 60 years old. Aside from the lines around her eyes and blueish bags underneath them, her auburn hair momentarily flickered to a mixture of pale red and grey, suggesting she had a little helping hand from a hair care drone that needed recharging. She was smiling, but there was something slightly off about the angle of her jaw. She looked nervous.

'I'm here to take you for tests,' said Yvonne, hiking the smile higher up her face. 'Code Black tests at my lab.'

It was an obviously rehearsed monologue, and left no room for questions or choices on Troy's part: he was going for tests, whether he liked it or not.

Chapter Twelve

'Everything is already set up and waiting for you,' said Willis, turning her back on Troy and heading towards the paternoster shaft that ran through the core of the accommodation cylinder. Troy's apartment was on the 121st level, far above the laboratory he'd visited yesterday. He'd yet to meet any of his floor neighbours – ten front doors greeted him when he stepped out of his apartment, arranged in a semicircle around the paternoster shaft in the middle.

'You've had breakfast, haven't you?' she called, as Troy came to join her by the paternoster. It wasn't really a question.

She took his arm, a friendly gesture Emerged people seemed to favour, and guided him onto a moving platform, which descended at speed.

'What sort of tests?' Troy asked, as apartment doors and empty connection levels flashed before them. 'I don't want any tests, I just want to be left alone. Haven't I been through enough?'

'I'm primarily a psychologist,' said Yvonne, as if he hadn't spoken. 'So the tests will be mainly psychological. It's my belief that psychology is the key to the entire Code Black phenomena.' She relaxed her grip on his arm. 'When we... when Code Black is understood, we'll save so many lives. So many.'

Despite himself, Troy felt himself warming to Yvonne. She seemed to genuinely want to help people. But then again she was a psychologist, he reminded himself, and trained to win people's trust.

'Did you sleep well?' she asked, as they reached the level that housed her laboratory. They both stepped off the paternoster.

'Bad dreams,' said Troy, trying to squash down some of the harrowing images that had troubled him during the night, 'about my parents.' He'd dreamed his parents, his Submergence parents, had been decapitated.

'Really?' Yvonne stopped, her sensible low-heeled brown shoes planting themselves firmly on the rubbery ground. 'Most people don't have many dreams when they Emerge – or much less vivid ones, anyway. Vivid dreams are a side effect of the Submergence system. We all miss our parents.' She paused. 'You haven't asked about your genetic parents yet. Aren't you curious about them?'

'I… hadn't thought about it,' said Troy. 'I suppose I assumed I didn't have any.'

Willis gave a girlish laugh. She had probably been quite attractive in her younger years, but decades of hard work and study had obviously taken its toll and her skin was loose and lined.

'Did you think you were grown here, or something? OK – some people call us the London Baby Grow centre, but we don't grow the biological specimens. You were conceived and born, just like children have been for centuries.'

'So I've got real parents? Where are they?'

'Your parents? Your mother is…' Willis's brow furrowed, '…we're no longer able to contact her. But your father knows about your recovery and sends his love and best wishes. I've personally spoken to him, and he's asked you to remain calm and cooperate with us as best you can. When the time is right, you'll be reunited, I promise.'

The Institute, calling the shots yet again, thought Troy angrily. *What if I want to meet my father now, why can't I make the choices for myself?*

They crossed the bridge and reached the lab, Troy unable to string thoughts together. His father... his mother... total strangers.

'Let me tell you about Code Black,' said Yvonne, as they entered the laboratory and she gestured for Troy to take a seat in the reclining test chair in the corner. Troy remained standing, and Yvonne frowned.

'I've spent my life trying to understand it,' she said, approaching the line of data drones and scanning their screens. 'At it's most basic level, it's very simple. You went Code Black because your cerebrum was rejecting all of the input transducer signals being sent at you. Excessive neurotransmitter feedbacks were generated causing localised cerebral vasoconstriction and independent thought. Essentially you were fighting and rejecting our neuro-integration equipment.'

'But why? Why did I fight it? What's different about me?'

'That's what I've spent my life trying to find out.' Yvonne walked to the test chair. 'Please, Troy. Take a seat.' When he didn't move, Yvonne sighed. 'I didn't want to be explicit about this, but these tests aren't voluntary. Your data is extremely valuable to us here at the Institute, and of course society as a whole. All Emergers have a duty to make life better for everyone. If you can help make the Program better then you must. You feel it in your core I know you do. Anything we learn from you could save lives. If you don't submit voluntarily, I'm afraid I have to use secure droids and submission personnel. Let's not make this unpleasant.'

Troy took a surreptitious look at the ceiling. Sure enough, secure droids loomed in the corners, their restraining straps dangling down like streamers. Reluctantly, he sat in the chair and swung his legs onto the upholstery so he was partially reclining, although his body was tense. *No matter what it takes, I'm going to get out of here.*

'This isn't right,' he said. 'You shouldn't force people to take tests.' But when he looked up at Yvonne, he realised she was as unhappy about the situation as he was. There was no point arguing – she was clearly being manipulated by unseen hands.

'OK,' she said gently. 'Let me just call up your data.' She went to a holo-filing projection on the wall and began pointing at various words until the wall filled with text. 'Here we are. Your Submergence medical history.'

Troy craned his neck to see the data.

'Like most Code Blacks,' said Yvonne, tapping her foot, 'your trace indicated serious rejection episodes during Submergence – five in your case. We call these Code Reds. You've had twelve. A record. You have your first when you were just a baby. Code Yellows too: minor reactions, not uncommon or serious, although you've had quite a few of them. We treat these easily with sedative or psychotropic medication. Usually, all that's required is a slight alteration of the oscillatory potential of the afferent impulses.'

'You monitor everyone's brain scans the whole time they're Submerged?' said Troy, impressed, in spite of himself. 'That's a lot of work.'

'Of course,' said Yvonne, sounding slightly offended. 'We're one of the leading Submergence centres in the country – we take safety very seriously. Neurokinetics are constantly monitored, both by computer and manual observation.'

'So what happens when people Code Red?' Curiosity was beginning to overtake feelings of anger, and Troy found himself wanting to know everything he could about Submergence.

'A Code Red is treated very seriously,' said Yvonne. 'It suggests a severe dysfunction and a possible terminal neuro-rejection episode. Our recovery rate to Final Emergence after a

114

single Code Red is more than 85%, a figure more than comparable to those of our brother and sister Institutes. But after two Code Reds the recovery rate falls to less than 35%. After three Reds recovery is unheard of and progression to Code Black is virtually inevitable, despite all our efforts. So we take serious interventional methods: new Submergence scenarios are created, bespoke Programs designed... let me see.' She waved her hand so the text scrolled downwards. 'Ah. Your first Code Red was in 2282 – your very first year on the neuro-integrator device. In fact... your first *day* by the looks of things. Now that's unusual. Why wasn't that picked up on before?' She waved her hand again and said thoughtfully: 'You were a late baby. One-year-old before you were linked in. Some tests show later babies are more prone to rejection syndrome, but my research hasn't found that to be true.'

'They must have been monsters,' said Troy. 'My parents. To leave a new-born baby.' It was devastating, he realised, to know he'd been dumped on the Institute's doorstep as a child, to be rejected so utterly by the people who were supposed to care for him. Didn't they know they had a responsibility?

Yvonne shook her head.

'Quite the contrary. It takes very special, very good people to understand what's best for their children and let Submergence take charge. So many parents fail their children. Their failures become society's failure as a whole. But our success rates speak for themselves: submerged babies are happy babies. That's one of our slogans.'

'If they were such good people, what would have been wrong with them bringing me up? Two good parents – that's what a happy upbringing is all about, isn't it?'

Yvonne shook her head, and walked over to Troy, reaching for the shiny, black helmet suspended above his head.

'Before Submergence, plenty of children had two loving parents. Nine times out of ten they turned out to be fine upstanding members of society – an asset to us. The better the childhood the more stable the person. But some parents just don't bring their children up properly. Come on Troy, imagine you had a child. Remember when we found the little boy in the Jersey Mall. You can't tell me that you didn't feel protective and parental towards him? We all did. How could we resist those big eyes looking up at us with simultaneous fear and trust. In fact I could access your data and show you your engram readings to prove it to you. When you become a father would you not want the very best childhood for your offspring? If you couldn't give them the best would you not seek it elsewhere for them?'

Yvonne pulled the helmet down, fitting it over Troy's eyes. He gritted his teeth, wanting to leap out of the chair. But he knew if Yvonne thought he was being co-operative, it would be easier to escape later. He let cool darkness wash over him, and Yvonne's voice suddenly sounded louder and more important.

'But there were still exceptions,' said Yvonne, adjusting the gel cushioning around Troy's forehead and vacuum-sealing the helmet, which exerted a gentle pressure around his skull. 'What some parents believe to be good for their children isn't always correct. A child can have material wealth, but if he or she doesn't have the right collection of experiences, the right psychological input from parents, they can still develop Psychosocial Anomalous Behaviour Traits or even full-blown PSDD: PsychoSocial Dysfunction Disorder.

'And of course children with abusive or violent parents, attending run-down schools, experiencing early exposure to drugs and violent behaviour – I could go on but I think you get the point – a child exposed to this frankly doesn't have a chance. Nine out of ten of those children will grow up with severe PSDD. One hundred years ago these people were responsible for 98.2% of all crime and 99.8% of all documented instances of antisocial behaviour. These people were a drain on society! Evolution reversed. Survival of the fittest meant that the brave,

116

the clever, the healthy reproduced and moved mankind forward. Suddenly the fittest and cleverest restricted their reproduction and instead the less desirable elements of society multiplied at exponential rates.'

Troy was surprised by the sudden vehemence in Willis's voice. It unsettled him, especially now he was unable to see her face.

There were some clicking sounds and an image of two little girls playing in a school yard appeared in the front of the helmet. One was bashing a toy pod on the floor, a horrified teacher rushing towards her in the background, while the other was smiling and deep in concentration, building an intricate and impressive model of the solar system using an antigrav model kit. It was like watching an AV, and unlike Submergence, Troy was aware of his separateness from the pictures – something he was glad about.

'OK Troy,' said Yvonne. 'These children are the same age and attend the same school, but you can see their behaviours are very different. The reason is upbringing. Why have these children had such different upbringings?'

'I don't know,' said Troy. 'Fate? Just luck, I suppose. Children can't choose their parents.'

'Exactly right.' Yvonne was triumphant. 'Fate and luck. Being born into the right family and the right circumstances is luck. Why should a child born to emotionally healthy parents have all the chances, while the child born to unstable parents have no chance at all? This is the inequality the Institute deals with. Years ago, we had two options. First we could improve schools, improve housing, improve jobs, improve wages, make life as pleasant as possible for everyone. We have been trying this for centuries and it doesn't work. Why doesn't it work? Because the very people we were trying to prevent from coming into being, those with psychosocial anomalous behaviour traits or PSDD, were the ones already eroding society from within and propagating sociologic decline.'

Troy heard Yvonne cough delicately, and sensed she was standing by the data droids, presumably watching his neurological data.

'The second option was to give each and every child the perfect upbringing,' she continued, and now Troy could hear her moving around the lab in her soft shoes. The volume of her voice rose and fell as she moved nearer and further away. 'Make sure they were safe, make sure they had exposure to those things essential for growing up, but always within the constraints of safety and control. Educate them and foster within them all the traits that make an ideal man or woman, an ideal member of society. Take them through the most formative and risky parts of their life caring for them and protecting them from any unpleasantness that may exist within the outside world.'

'Is this a test?' asked Troy. 'Or are you trying to convince me how wonderful the system is?'

'Certainly it's a test. I'm measuring your neurological responses while we discuss basic ethics and the Submergence Program. This is a standard L1 test: what are your reactions to conformity? To the idea of trusting a system to do what's best for you. It's something you've been tested for your whole life, but now you've Emerged we're really getting the raw data.' There was a bleep and a click and another picture appeared. It took Troy a moment to realise it was a group of rather edgy individuals he'd met at a rock concert as a teenager.

'Fascinating,' Yvonne whispered. 'Do you remember, Troy, when we were thirteen and a group of delinquents asked us to come and watch them steal a cruising pod?'

Troy tried to nod against the weight of the helmet. He remembered his father had turned up just before he was about to leave with the group, and he'd been podded home. At least, he'd *thought* he was going to leave with them. But if the system made his choices for him, probably he would always have ended up going home no matter what happened.

'We could see that you wanted to go. Your neural kinetics, like 83% of L1s, showed that you really wanted to go. You were young and foolish and I am certain that looking back now you realise what a disaster it would have been if you had gone with them. How easy it would have been to just go and watch, but you would have been caught.'

'It was on the news,' said Troy, remembering the very next day, news of the group being caught and prosecuted. It was only then he'd realised what a lucky escape he'd had. But of course, that escape had been manufactured, as had the news itself he reminded himself.

'Your childhood is the most vulnerable time in your life,' said Yvonne. 'Looking back to your earlier years you can, I'm sure, agree you had no idea about the implications of the decisions you made. You were nowhere near mature enough to understand what you were doing. Now. Let's move on.'

A far more unsettling image flashed inside the helmet. Sarah, Suki and Jack – his best friends at university.

'*Very* interesting,' Yvonne muttered.

'My friends,' said Troy. It was so sad to see them. He felt like his insides had been torn out knowing he'd never see them again.

'*Our* friends,' Yvonne corrected. 'I had the same friends. I loved them as well, and I still do. They were designed to give you the best possible start in life. A triumph of the system.'

Troy's hands had balled into tight, sharp fists. He knew the neuro-monitor would be going crazy, essentially telling Yvonne that he was struggling to deal with things, but he didn't care.

'Don't you see the beauty of it?' asked Yvonne. 'We all had the same friends, so in effect we're all friends as well. We're like family.'

A fake family, Troy thought. *Synthesised lives, moulded and bent without consent.*

'What gives you the right to dictate what I am and what I become?' said Troy, trying to wrestle the helmet from his head. 'What gives you the right to fill my brain with what you want? What gives you the right to make a mockery of everything I have lived through and seen, a mockery of everything I am?'

'Because we have a duty to society,' said Yvonne. 'A duty to mankind. A duty to you and all our fragile charges. We are the caretakers. The Program is the ideal parent, always there, always protecting, always teaching, never too strict, never too lax. Troy, entire semesters are devoted to this very topic: understanding takes time.'

'What about choice,' said Troy, still lamely struggling to remove the helmet. 'Submergence is brainwashing. Surely? How can you say it's a good thing? How can you think it's right?'

'Submergence doesn't control your thoughts. We've been through this before, Troy.' Yvonne sounded horrified. 'No, your thoughts are your own. We only control the outcomes. The Program inputs tactile, vocal, visual, and other sensory experiences and makes sure you're steered on the right path. We give you experiences and leave your psychosocial development to you. But you are *conditioned* by the outcomes to a certain extent, that's part of Program. It controls to an extent what you do so you're steered on the path that's been planned for you.

'Think of all the formative experiences you've been given – your sister dying, one of your best friends suffering a severe disability. All of it was designed to give you respect and understanding, but without the death and pain it would cause if you were to live it for real. Aren't you a better person? Regardless of the means, are you a better person for it, yes or no?'

There was a long pause.

120

'But you're killing people,' said Troy, eventually. 'You told me yourself: Code Black is fatal.'

'Without Submergence, death rates from accidents and infection are much higher. We lose one in 1567 subjects to Code Black – not bad odds considering the alternative. It's a known risk among parents, but don't you see? With the data you give us, we may be able to eradicate it entirely. You're a breakthrough... we haven't had a Code Black survivor in thirty years.'

'There are other Code Black survivors?' Troy's eyes sprung open and he tried to sit up, but the helmet was too heavy. The picture of his friends' smiling faces still hung in the air, a reminder of what he'd lost.

'Two others. Thirty years ago the system wasn't as good as it is now. A sad side effect of our technological improvements is that since we have perfected the neuromodulation no one survives a Code Black anymore. There were only two.'

'Who? Are they here? Can I meet them?'

'There were... difficulties with the other patients,' she said, and he felt her near his shoulder again. There was a clicking sound and the image of his friends faded to black. 'One of them rebelled severely against the Institute and its teachings. As a test patient... well, it just didn't work.'

Troy felt the helmet pull slightly to the left, and with a hiss the vacuum was released and Yvonne lifted the black dome from his head. It was a relief to see the laboratory again, but Troy wondered what data Yvonne had gleaned from the test he'd just undergone – if it really was a test. It could just have been a lecture with pictures, part of his reintegration. If it was, it hadn't worked.

'So... can I talk to them?' Troy swung his legs from the recline position. 'Where are they? Do they live here?'

Yvonne's chin wobbled slightly, but she quickly regained control.

'No. The first patient was lost. Gone. Probably to the underwater slums, where all the severe Demergers end up, and most of the non-emerged too, scraping together an existence, fighting, stealing...'

'What about the other patient?' Troy rubbed his eyes.

'The other patient was successfully reintegrated,' said Yvonne, pushing the helmet back into its anti-grav field. 'She works here, at the Institute, but we learned very little from her. She was slotted back into the last Submergence chapters without being tested. They didn't realise, you see... the other patient. They thought they had two patients, so they could re-Submerge one and comparatively test the other. They didn't know the other patient would disappear, would leave us.'

There was a scraping sound above them. A loud, unsettling noise that made Troy's shoulders tense and set his teeth on edge. Slowly, secure droids floated down into each corner of the room.

'Troy,' said Yvonne, leaning forward and touching his arm. 'It's time to go back to the Submergence suite now. For the last of the tests.' She gave a high, false laugh. 'Everything's ever so quick these days. Thirty years ago, the Code Black tests took around two years to complete. Now we can do everything in a matter of hours.' She paused. 'After the tests we'll put you into re-Submergence as soon as possible. Ideally within the next four hours.'

Troy leapt from the chair, but the secure droids were too quick for him, approaching at speed and lashing him to their cold bodies with soft, white straps.

'You can't do it, Yvonne,' Troy shouted. 'This is wrong. I don't want to be re-Submerged.'

She turned her back, seemingly unable to look at him.

'You need the last chapters,' she whispered. 'I'm sorry.' She pointed to a data droid and raised its screen to show Troy a series of numbers, presumably gathered while he'd been sitting under the test helmet. 'Your negative L1 aspects are far too high. You're a danger, Troy, to yourself and society. You need the last chapters. After the tests you must be re-Submerged. I'm sorry Troy. You have all the foundations to be a perfect addition to our society but this whole experience has introduced variances to your personality which may be damaging to you. I stroke we are doing this for you.' Her voice broke then. 'I really have no choice.'

Chapter Thirteen

The hard surface of the secure droid dug into Troy's back as it floated him out of the laboratory and over the suspended bridge. Troy watched the stainless steel cables drift past, their twisted surfaces as taut and strong as the woven restraints binding his arms and torso. Then stoking his mounting horror, he recognised he was being carried back through the empty lecture theatre and into the Submergence suite.

Troy could hear Yvonne's quick little steps behind him as she directed the secure droid with a thumb controller, and he caught a glimpse of the side of her tired face, mouth drawn down.

'Dr Willis?' he said, as they travelled into the human zoo of caged bodies. 'You said you were taking me for tests.' The Submerged were peaceful, moving or sleeping in their own little worlds, undisturbed by the rhythmic bleeps from the monitoring stations, or the two nurses sweeping between the cages, checking vital signs.

'That's correct,' said Yvonne.

Troy felt himself being steered towards an empty cage set back from the others. Like the other cages, it contained an advanced suite of VR furniture: four-way auto-road, narrow bed, black VR dome suspended from the ceiling, drip feeds and what appeared to be some sort of suction device. Around these objects were monitoring screens and data-feeds, blank but humming and ready to compute. Stark wires and VR equipment hung from the ceiling.

'Take me back,' said Troy, the eerie stillness suppressing his urge to shout.

'I promise you, Troy, you're not going into Submergence just yet,' said Yvonne, stepping out of the way to let the secure droid float Troy into the cage. 'You're going into test Submergence first.' It felt warmer inside the cage, and as the droid lashed Troy to the white gel bed he wondered if the temperature matched whatever weather was simulated by the Submergence Program. He guessed it must be a sunny day.

'So why test me here?' said Troy, as the droid disconnected itself from the restraining belts and floated out of the cage. 'I don't believe you, let me go. Let me GO!'

'We have the facilities here,' said Yvonne, entering the cage and closing the door behind her. 'The test bears a resemblance to Submergence – of course it does. Try to think of it like a VR game. Did you know Submergence was originally developed by the gaming industry?'

Troy tried to shake his head, but found he couldn't.

'It always seems,' said Yvonne, tapping a monitor, 'that the greatest scientific advances never come as a direct result of scientific research. It's the funding, I suppose. The leisure industry and the military can invest when other organisations can't.'

Troy got the feeling Yvonne was chatting away to keep her mind off what she was doing. But he was still intrigued, despite the rage and fear that boiled inside him.

'Yes,' said Yvonne, as if replying to his unasked question, reaching over Troy's head and checking a receiver. 'AV gaming developers are forever trying to improve the realism of their games. They developed the first body-sensitive suit. We've got one of those old suits in the tech history department – it squeezes and tightens in response to the VR simulation, would

125

you believe. The height of technology at the time.' She gave a little laugh. 'And the first full visual field was developed around about the same time – 180 degree vision. Of course the visual projectors were very cumbersome at first. They had to go around the whole eye. But then the industry developed micro-projector contact lenses. It's highly advanced technology, even now. The lenses require a tracking system to monitor eye position 20,000 times per second. For years there was some ghosting of images if people looked left and right too quickly, but then the military invested trillions and true natural sight was born.'

Troy pushed his shoulders back and forth under the soft restraints, but he was locked tight.

'We'll loosen the restraints when you're under,' Yvonne said matter-of-factly, pulling Troy's eyelids back and placing VR lenses over his eyeballs. A milky film clouded his vision, but he could still see his surroundings: Yvonne, tall and formal, checking monitors around the cage and hooking her own data monitors into them, and the secure droid outside the cage, its plastic surface completely blank.

There was a soft chugging sound and suddenly Troy could feel warm air on the back of his neck. Then something hard rolled back and forth over the bare skin.

Troy fought under the restraints.

'Please try to relax,' said Yvonne, kneeling down by Troy's bed. 'It's just the spinal neuro-integrator and skin sensor. It detects muscle activity and stimulates the muscles. We map the spinal column, so we can identify which muscles are moving and then create muscle impulses. We can even use it to stop muscle atrophy if a subject isn't exercising.'

Troy was impressed, in spite of himself. He knew all the science. He'd been taught modified versions of it and had watched numerous docustreams about similar issues.

'Of course, we create both nervous and sensory impulses,' Yvonne went on. 'Part of the spine neuro-integrator's job is to create a small, localised magnetic field that stimulates single nerves. So we can create sensory perceptions, like hot, cold, taste, pain... And of course it emits a nullifying magnetic field too, so any impulses transmitted by the brain are arrested and reality is completely replaced with simulation. It's remarkable, when you think about it.'

Troy tried to pick at the restraints with his fingers, but the cloth was so thick he thought it would take a laser cutter to get through it.

'I'm going to place you in one of your former life chapters,' said Yvonne, taking a black VR dome covered with tiny monitoring leads from the antigrav field on the ceiling and lowering it onto his head. The hiss and tug of the vacuum seal felt familiar, but this helmet was different from the last one; it covered not only his eyes, but his ears and nose too, and was weightless – almost certainly supported by a force field.

'We won't need to put you on intravenous feed,' Yvonne continued. 'Usually, we pass semi-solid food directly into the stomach during Submergence. No solid waste – everything is completely absorbed. We simply stimulate the bladder and suction the liquid waste away. But you won't be under long enough to need nutritional support.'

Already, Troy's senses were confused and diluted. He was in total blackness, defused slightly by the milky film of the VR receivers, and his skin felt alive and tingly.

When probing rubbery arms moved around his ears, locating his ear canals and sliding into them, he was rendered totally deaf and the outside world was shut out. He could do nothing now except wait for the feed to start.

It didn't take long. A second later the translucent sheen over his eyes vanished, and a rushing sound pounded his eardrums, like a cruising pod taking off. White light replaced dark, followed by a beautiful spectrum of colours that spun and settled into a plain white ceiling above him.

Troy turned his head left and right. He was lying on a gel bed, and under his fingers he could feel a woven thermal sheet. He tried to sit up and discovered he was no longer restrained. Of course not. They didn't need to restrain him now he was VR'd: he had absolutely no sense of what was real and what wasn't. Escape was impossible. Still, at least in this virtual world he could move freely, and he did so, sitting up and letting his senses pick up all the fake data being fed to him.

What greeted him was a three-dimensional world so realistic, so tangible, that Troy felt almost breathless with the beauty of it. Everything was achingly real, familiar and perfectly detailed: the crumpled, slightly stained clothes on the floor, projections of little space pods on the wall and the electric muscle-building equipment he'd played with as a teenager. He was back in his old bedroom. The one he'd slept in as a child.

This isn't real. How could they have done this to him? Simulate his whole upbringing and leave him with these aching feelings of loss and homesickness. *Remember it's not real,* Troy thought. *Don't get sucked in. Fight it.*

He could hear the faint echo of his parents' voices somewhere nearby, which sent his heart racing.

They're not real, they're not my real parents.

Troy reached up to see if he could feel the VR dome around his head, but with the neuro-integrator on his spine he could feel nothing. Only soft hair and an even softer chin.

'OK Troy.' It was Yvonne's voice, but since he couldn't see her, it felt like she was inside his head: an uninvited mind guest. 'The idea is to take you though one of the scenarios that made you Code Yellow. Then, depending on your reaction, we'll take you into a Code Red scenario. I want to keep you aware, I don't want to lose you in the Program, so I'll be talking to you throughout. This might be a bit of a shock for you, but I've taken you back to a scenario that happened to your twelve-year-old self. This is just after your twentieth Code Yellow and your second Code Red.'

There was a knock on the door – a gentle thud, thud that sounded much more real than Yvonne's voice. Troy swallowed deeply. Suddenly the memory came rushing back to him, and he knew exactly why his parents were at the door and why he was sitting in his bedroom.

'Darling, will you let us in?' His mother's voice, soft and muffled. She was right outside.

And then his father's:

'Can we come in, Troy?'

It was like it all happened yesterday. Yvonne had taken him back to the day his mother and father had argued for hours in the kitchen, while he'd hidden upstairs. He remembered locking himself in his bedroom and staring at the ceiling for what felt like forever until they came and apologised. *What perfect parents*. And they had been. They rarely fought, but on the few occasions they did, they'd explain to Troy exactly what they were rowing about and then the whole family would make up.

Troy looked down at his body. His legs were like skinny posts, bony knees poking up under thin cotton trousers and the backs of his hands were smooth and hair free. Stumbling to the mirror, he stared at the boyish, twelve-year-old version of himself staring back, blue eyes full of confusion, lean face taut and stressed.

'Stay with me Troy.' That was Yvonne again. 'We're getting lots of Code Yellow data – lots of blips. Good. Very good.'

There was a crackle and she was gone again.

'Please Troy.' His mother's voice was more insistent. Any minute now, his father would override the door control and the pair of them would come in, take him in their arms and tell him they loved him over and over. He remembered it all so well.

Troy went to the door and opened it, feeling a pang of something, maybe nostalgia or loss, as his parents' worried faces looked in from the hallway. He wanted to lash out at both of them, to shout and scream, to bellow at them: *you're not real.* As computer simulations, the two of them were perfect in every detail: his father's deep-pored skin, the grooves around his nose and dimple in his chin; his mother's light, almost white blonde hair. He wanted to hold onto them and never let them go.

'Can we come in?' asked his father again, looking tired but happy. 'We'll tell you all about it.'

'It's OK,' Troy found himself saying, momentarily surprised by the highness of his voice. It sounded like the squeak on the faulty waste incinerator downstairs. He hadn't chosen to speak, the system had chosen for him. 'I know you still love me.'

His mother gave him a fond smile. 'You've been up here crying… we saw on the monitoring system.'

Troy knew what was going to happen next. Despite the rage and confusion, despite knowing the people he was seeing weren't real, were nothing more than computer programs, he moved forward and embraced them both. He willed his legs to stop moving and yet they were out of his control and he was nothing more than a spectator in his own cerebral prison. He wanted to be real. He wanted to link into their embrace. He wanted to be back there and be safe.

But Troy knew he had to fight. He willed it with every nerve in his body: free choice. He wanted to hold them and let them comfort him. A part of him wanted to ignore the truth and just submerge himself again. So what if it wasn't real. It was his. They would take the pain away. But he couldn't. He shouted his betrayal into their faces but no sound came from his mouth.

And then Yvonne's voice.

'Troy! Troy, you're approaching Code Red... you're surpassing... don't challenge the Program or you'll go into shock.'

I'm causing conflicts with the Program, thought Troy, as his father reached to touch his shoulder, *because I'm not doing what's expected.* He looked at the veins standing out on his father's hand, and the blunt-cut white fingernails – all so intricately detailed. *It's not real. He's not real. He's a computer program.* Troy reached out and touched his father's arm, which was warm and soft. Warm. It was a simply a sensory stimulation. *I have to fight it... I have to.* He shouted a voiceless scream again.

Suddenly there was a blinding flash of white light, and Troy's head exploded with pain.

'We can't lose him!' he heard Yvonne shout. He felt curious sensations: a compression on his arm and a chill, then a cold rush of air.

'Set eleven.' Yvonne's voice was clearly verging on panic. Troy wondered if the warning lights above his cage were flashing amber, or even red. He touched his head and, although he couldn't feel the VR dome, he tried to press and pull at thin air, watching his parents' faces distort in front of him, then disintegrate into pixelated dust.

Chapter Fourteen

'He's approaching Code Black. Code Black!' The woman was shouting now, and Troy felt more compressions on his arms: odd sensations that felt like muscle spasms.

'The scans confirm neuro-disintegration,' said another voice, another female. 'Confirmed. Test patient is Code Red.'

Troy continued to feel around in mid-air. He was sure he was touching wires and transducers, but without any sensory or visual perceptions, it was like feeling around in a dark cave.

'Follow the protocol. IV methyl-hydroxy-ket. Full dose,' the second voice said. 'How long?'

'Just literally this second,' Yvonne stammered. 'We can't lose him. He's the Code Black survivor. It shouldn't be possible. He's not even properly neurointegrated.'

Troy pulled at the air more frantically now, desperate to find some sort of release or connection with reality. The VR sensory data was so powerful... he began feeling behind his neck, trying to disconnect the device reading his spine.

'He's agitated,' came the second female voice. 'Still no response, neuro indices dropping. Connection almost lost. Code Red worsening... we're heading towards Black.'

'No!' Yvonne's voice was almost hysterical. 'We need to get him out of the VR. This can't be happening.'

'I disagree. Get the neurostim charged and shock him. Otherwise you'll lose your test data.'

'Stop!' Yvonne no longer sounded hysterical: she was very, very angry. 'Move! Now. Out of the way. He's fibrillating. We need to get him out of the test system, data or no data. Troy? Troy can you hear me?'

Troy murmured Yvonne's name and felt his skull expand as the pressure was released from the VR dome. Probes withdrew from his ears and he could hear everything around him: bleeps and clicks of machines, raised voices.

When Yvonne lifted up the helmet he saw the Submergence floor had descended into chaos, with teams of medical staff charging around, frantically scanning the monitoring equipment by his cage, rushing back and forth with trolleys and barking orders.

As soon as the helmet was clear of his head, Troy felt for the VR receivers in his eyes and ripped them out. He found he was already standing, his feet planted on a motionless four-way auto-road, spongy and grey, and the receivers clung damply to his fingers for a moment before he flicked them onto the clean, white floor. Yvonne and another woman, short with thick dark hair cut into a scientist's fringe, were in the cage with him, and the cage door was open.

Troy shouldered his way past a startled Yvonne, taking a quick, sorry glance back as she fell against the wall monitors, clinging to the shorter woman in an attempt to stay upright.

He ran out onto the bare, squeaky white floor of the Submergence suite, pushing past startled medical staff and running between the cages, the silent figures inside totally oblivious to the escaped prisoner. His elbows knocked the rubbery bars as he headed towards the exit, and he hammered the door release frantically, looking over his shoulder as the door rolled opened. No one seemed to be pursuing him, but he knew it wouldn't be long.

As Troy squeezed through the half-open exit, something else dawned on him: escape wasn't enough. He needed answers.

He needed to know why he'd survived Code Black, and what had happened to the other survivors. If he escaped without finding out, he'd be just as lost outside as he was here at the Institute. And answers almost certainly lay in the last place he wanted to be: Yvonne's lab.

Troy leaned against the long desk inside the laboratory taking deep breaths, watching the AV screens of Submerged patients on the far wall. Getting into the lab had been easy: no door codes, nothing to secure the room. He guessed few people tried to break in. In this perfect society they trusted everyone.

On the ceiling were three secure droids, inanimate and placid, their restrainers reaching towards him like handshakes. He shuddered, wondering if the other Code Black survivors had been forcibly restrained in the same room thirty years ago. Had one of the survivors submitted willingly and the other fought back? Or had they both been held against their will?

On one of the walls was a library projection and Troy went to it, reading the shiny red subject titles: L1 Infant Behaviour, Psychological Profiles, Code Black Research, Genetic Research... Troy pointed to the Psychological Profiles tag and followed a chain of title links, but the text sections were all locked.

There was a low drumming sound from outside of the laboratory, and Troy tilted his head to listen. People were coming. Maybe the top level of the lab had more data, and going up a level had the added advantage of moving him out of immediate eyeshot.

He went to the hovering platform, the one Yvonne had descended on yesterday, and felt it click as he stood on it, alerting the grav mechanism to release and let the platform float upwards.

The second level was calm, still and mercifully empty: a room of blank walls and empty stainless steel tables. Along one wall were three semicircular white desks fitted into the walls, each with their own metre-high thinscreen and green gel stool. The stools looked as if the gel filling had seen better days, and two of the thinscreens were dented and scratched, but generally the room looked clean and hygienic: a scientist's place of work. One of the thinscreens had power, glowing a pale silver, and a pair of well-used interface goggles and gloves lay on the desk next to it. *The Ethernet.* Troy hadn't been allowed access to it at the apartment, and it had felt like being without a limb. Now he realised he'd just stumbled upon an ideal source of data-discovery – perhaps even better than Yvonne's research.

He picked up the goggles and slipped the rough gloves eagerly onto his hands.

'Activate.'

Immediately, an image lit up the huge screen: a large pair of pink hands holding a smiling baby in their palms. The words 'London Psychodevelopment Institute' danced below the picture in twinkling yellow and black letters. Below that was written: 'Submerged babies are happy babies.'

'Interface.'

The image changed to a screen saver which Troy presumed must be Yvonne's: it showed Willis sitting on a beach simulation with a glass of pink juice in her hand, her arm around a dark-haired woman who shared her pointy nose and chin. A relative, maybe. Over the screen saver were three options: Touch, Voice and VR.

Troy paused. Voice was certainly easiest, but it could often be slow, especially if facilities weren't top of the range. Touch was faster, but he didn't know the system and it would take precious moments to adjust to someone else's settings.

He selected VR and watched as buttons and icons surrounded him, the familiar cockpit imagery floating behind it as a backdrop. It was identical to the interface system he'd used for the majority of his teenage years, but he pushed through the stab of nostalgia, the pain of what he'd lost, and pressed the Ethernet icon, watching the 3D projections around him surge forward and transform into a search library, complete with the virtual search master, an middle-aged bearded man with black glasses and old-fashioned fibre-pen at the ready.

'Search words, Code Black survivor, subsets all.'

The search master stirred up a silent whirlwind of books, which surrounded Troy, spinning rapidly, before settling into twelve piles – each labelled in glowing typeface. One of the piles said: Troy Harrison. It was a humble stack in comparison to the others, but it was too intriguing to resist. With a wave of his hand, Troy laid out the pile of virtual papers, his eyes darting along the heavily inked titles at the top. One document was an Institute news feed, presumably aimed at academic staff, spreading the good news of Troy's miraculous Code Black survival. There was even a quote from "Code Black expert", Yvonne Willis.

Another set of papers was headed: 'Genetic Relations', which presumably meant family.

Troy heard dull thuds under his feet: people, or maybe droids, entering the lab below. But he had to read on. He spread out the next pile of papers, his gloved hands shaking, and read the first one which appeared to be a visa-style list of his relatives.

Father: Mac Harrison. Occupation: Hydro-maintenance engineer.

Mother:

Sibs: None.

The blankness of the mother field was conspicuous. Troy pointed at it to drill down for more information, but an error message flew up.

'Data error: file removed. Consult keeper of genetic database.'

The thuds and sharp notes of voices below grew louder: Troy could hear movement right beneath him now, and the more disturbing sound of the platform humming as it was called down a level. He ripped off the goggles and saw the platform descending, leaving a shining hole of light. There was nowhere to hide. The upstairs lab was filled with clean silver tables for lab work, wires dangling from the ceiling, a few lockers in the corner and trolleys loaded with equipment: electricity boxes, test helmets and neuro-monitoring clips. In this clean, functional workspace, no thought had been given to a runaway Emerger who wanted to slip out of sight.

Troy stood, body tense, still looking desperately around for another exit or some sort of hiding place. But it was no good. He was trapped.

Slowly, two people appeared out of the light hole in the floor: Yvonne Willis and someone Troy didn't recognise. It was a man with very pale blond hair, a day's worth of grey stubble and a rounded nose that made him look slightly cartoonish. He didn't look like a scientist.

'Troy.' Yvonne shook her head, a half smile appearing when she saw him. 'We followed you on the security AVs, thank goodness. Thank goodness. I was worried you'd hurt yourself, or you were in the midst of a psychotic episode... anyway. You're here. I'd like to introduce you to someone. Someone I think, we all think, can help you.' She turned to the man next to her, who gave an uneasy jump as the platform settled with a click into the floor. The man gave a shy smile, showing two front teeth whiter than the others, probably a result of cheap tooth transplants, but other than that he had a wholesome appearance, dressed in a checked cotton shirt and utilitarian slacks.

'Troy,' said Yvonne, 'I'd like you to meet Mac Harrison.'

The colour drained from Troy's face as the name clanged like an alarm bell in his brain.

'Your father.'

Chapter Fifteen

Troy stared at the man, whose eyes glittered with tears under the white lights.

'Look at you,' the man said, shaking his head in disbelief. There was genuine tenderness in his voice. 'I would never have believed... my boy. You're a fine young man, that you are.' He stepped forward, arms outstretched, and took Troy in a clumsy embrace. Troy stood stiff as a traffic droid until the man let go, stepped back and wiped his eyes. He felt nothing towards this man, this stranger, who'd abandoned him as a baby – nothing but anger and contempt.

'To think...' Mac looked from Troy to Yvonne, his eyes still glistening. 'A boy of mine... a doctor.'

'He hasn't finished his training yet,' said Yvonne with a little smile. 'But we're hoping, with your help, he'll come to accept that re-Submerging is the best thing for him.' She turned to Troy. 'This is Mac Harrison,' she said. 'Your biological father, and a hydro-maintenance engineer on the North London thermo plant.' Yvonne paused for a moment and looked uncomfortable. 'Which is of course a very worthwhile and useful profession,' she finished.

Mac gave a mighty cough and shook his head. 'It's a dead-end job for non-Emergers, that's what it is. And I wouldn't wish it on anyone.'

Yvonne turned slightly pink as he continued to cough.

'Your father made a great deal of sacrifices to ensure you'd be accepted on the Submergence Program,' she said, 'and naturally he's as worried about you as the rest of us.'

Troy stared at the man in front of him, noticing the line of fat around his middle, his see-through skin and slightly bloodshot eyes. He had to admit the man's nose, face shape and colouring were similar to his own, but it was hard, even impossible, to simply accept that this stranger was his father. Even if Yvonne carried out a DNA match right there and then, he wouldn't be able to accept it on an emotional level. For years he'd been brought up by another man, a lean, fit, well-respected hospital surgeon who had the physical build of an athlete and positively glowed with good health. To suddenly be confronted with the knowledge that this paunchy stranger was his true father, the only father that existed for him in reality... Troy wasn't sure he'd ever be able to believe it. He felt wretchedly lonely all of a sudden. Lonely and tired. The emotional rollercoaster of the last few days was enough to send a sane man crazy, and he wasn't at all sure he hadn't already been sent a little bit over the edge already.

'The Program was written to give you the best possible childhood,' said Yvonne, as if reading his mind. 'Your Submergence father looked different, *was* different, for good reason. Mac didn't have the benefits of the Submergence Program. We had to create a simulation of an educated, healthy person to become your male role model, but Mac really deserves all the praise for your upbringing. It was down to his sacrifices and hard work that you were funded through Submergence.'

'I'd do it all over again, son,' said Mac, looking earnestly at Troy. 'You deserve the very best – I'd do anything for you, anything. It's been a hard life for me, but I'm hoping for you things will be different. A better life, isn't that right Yvonne?'

Something caught Troy's eye: the hovering platform was descending, presumably on some auto-program, and alarmingly two secure droids had floated up from the ground floor, filling the empty hole and blocking access to the platform controls and any chances of escape.

'Troy.' Yvonne reached out and touched his arm. 'We realise we've been taking things too quickly, far too quickly. We've decided there are things you need to see, to understand, before any of us should think about the last chapters. That's why Mac is here. Most Submergers don't meet their parents until much later on – things work better that way. Most parents are Emergers anyway so they understand. But in your case, we think Mac as an NE is the ideal person to take you out into the real world and explain to you why finishing Submergence really is the best thing. Will you do that Troy? Will you go with Mac on a visit outside the Institute? It should only take an hour or so, and we think it will give you some real perspective.'

Troy glanced again at the secure droids.

'Doesn't look like I have a choice, does it?' He spoke slowly and contemptuously. 'Tell me something Yvonne, when are you going to drop the act? When are you going to stop pretending you have my best interests at heart? You, the Institute, Professor Shaw, you've taken away everything. Everything.'

Yvonne and Mac exchanged uncomfortable glances.

'If you agree to go with Mac,' said Yvonne, 'it will then be your choice as to whether or not you undergo the last Submergence chapters. We want you to realise for yourself why taking the last chapters is for your own good.'

'Seriously?' Troy couldn't believe what he was hearing. Only minutes ago he'd been forcibly restrained and dragged down to the Submergence suite. 'If I go with Mac, you're telling me I can choose whether or not to take the last chapters?'

'Yes,' said Yvonne, although her expression was uneasy. 'It'll be your choice. But we do hope you make the right one.'

'How do I know I can trust you? You've destroyed me, everything I ever thought I had is gone, an illusion.'

'You don't know,' said Yvonne. 'But you'll have to try.'

Troy's face was glued to the pod window as he and Mac floated through the Institute grav field and out onto the streets of central London. They were squashed uncomfortably together on the back seat, and Troy could hear Mac's wheezy chest and shortness of breath; he guessed, given Mac's occupation, that he was most likely suffering from a pneumoconiosis: a disease that had been completely preventable for centuries.

The streets and buildings outside the pod were familiar, but the scene though the window was nonetheless a twisted version of reality as far as Troy was concerned. But not necessarily twisted in a bad way. Everyone on the street was healthy, smiling and happy. There were no homeless people lying in heaps on street corners, or VR arcades with grey-faced addicts sitting beneath wired helmets. There was no litter, and maintenance and courtesy drones were omnipresent, hovering up and down the pavement. There were no overweight people – of course there wouldn't be: most of society was programmed to be healthy and fat-averse. Was it a good thing? He wasn't sure.

'It's good to finally meet you, son,' said Mac tentatively, putting a heavy hand on Troy's shoulder. 'Or I should say, good to finally be met? You won't remember me visiting you in your Submergence suite – not too often, they don't encourage it. But I did come from time to time. And of course I spent many months with you as a very young baby, and what a beautiful young baby you were, so strong and healthy.'

The hand felt totally alien and strange and Troy was half tempted to throw it off. He couldn't yet quite believe that this man, this stranger, was his father. In truth, he had much more in common with the fake father who was nothing more than a computer simulation: a fact that hit him with a nauseating jolt.

And also, Troy couldn't forget that Mac, biological father or not, held the same beliefs as Yvonne – that he should be fitted like a cog into the great machine of society. Neither seemed concerned that he'd had his whole childhood and life so far falsified.

'I still…' Troy put a hand to his forehead as he searched for the right words. '…don't you think… I mean, Submergence has taken my life away from me.'

'No.' Mac shook his head and let his hand drop down. 'It's given you a better life. You'll see. When we're out near the wastelands. You'll see I did what any good parent would have done.' The pod continued along the calm, clean streets, sweeping along white roads with floating markers down the middle.

'Doesn't a good parent bring up their child?' said Troy angrily, his eyes searching Mac's for any sign of regret or sorrow for what he'd put his son through.

'It's the best life I could have given you.' Mac coughed hard into his hand. 'Me and your mother… if our parents had known what being Submerged would mean in this day and age they would have done the same for us. The Emerged get the best of everything. Us Non-Emergers, the few of us that are left up here away from the slums, have to fight for the crumbs. I mean, my parents weren't rich people – nor am I. But they would have found a way, just like I found a way for you.' Mac shook his head and smiled sadly. 'Who would have known Submergence would take off so quickly – when I was a boy there were still protests against it. I wasn't alive when they did the first human tests, but they had to be done in secret.' Mac tapped his nose. 'Illegally. They condemn it now, but everyone knows if they hadn't been done, we wouldn't have the world we have today. No crime. No social disorder, except in the Non-Emerger districts. It was the military who were behind the secret tests – they think now babies were brought over from China, orphans

142

obviously. Did you learn about Chinese orphans in Submergence?'

'Yes.' Troy thought about the docustreams showing Chinese girl babies wrapped in dirty blankets, cared for by rented mothers as they were shipped around the world. But his history lessons said the babies were adopted by willing parents: it said nothing of forcing them into an artificial upbringing.

'Did they tell you about VR centres?'

'Not in Submergence,' said Troy, noticing a group of twenty or so women jogging together around the streets. For a moment, he thought one of them was Hannah and felt a rush of excitement, but then the woman turned around and he saw she was much too old. 'I was shown... images. After I Code Blacked and came around.'

'The Artificial Reality centres used to be everywhere,' said Mac, watching food hangers and virtual shops rush by. 'Hundreds of thousands of VR addicts, plugged into VR centres all over the country. Seven out of ten citizens had VR habits, begging and stealing credits, doing anything to fix themselves up another few hours of fake reality. There were zillions of fantasies: emperor for a day, front line soldier, adult ARs of course – nothing designed to help society, only serve one man's needs.'

'Shaw told me things got bad,' said Troy.

'Bad isn't the half of it,' said Mac. 'But the whole phenomenon paved the way for Submergence. It gave us the technology and the requirement. We needed something to lift us all back into the light. People couldn't be bothered to work because they could live like kings in the virtual world. They couldn't be bothered to love because they could sleep with the sexiest women, whole groups of them. After they began stimulating the senses with VR, hot, cold, touch, and use taste fibres on the tongue, people didn't feel they needed to eat when they were hooked up. Some of them would go days... thousands died on the VR machines. My parents told me awful, awful stories. They were never sure about Submergence, coming from that part of history. Didn't trust VR, but now we know different. We know Submerged people make a better society – for everyone.'

'Wasn't it hard to give me up?' said Troy, the scene outside the window growing sparser and more suburban 'Giving up your son to strangers? How could you do it?'

Mac shook his head. 'The only thing that worried me was Code Black: it's every parent's worst nightmare. I remember the newsfeed about the first Code Black – I was just a child back then. It brought out all the old anti-Submergence groups, parents screaming and crying, telling the world they'd paid their life savings to give their child a better life, only to have that life snatched away. It was in one of the last printed newspapers, before they switched to pure newsnet reporting.' Mac's eyes crinkled at the memory, then his face drooped. 'But by the time we had you, the world had got used to the idea of a few Code Blacks. Statistically, children still have a much better chance of survival if they're Submerged. These days, it would be harder for parents *not* to Submerge their kids if they have the means. It's so much safer to have a Submerged upbringing, believe me. Society now… it's incomparable to how it was. Things are just so much better. When people are brought up right, a happy society just slots into place. It works Troy, Submergence works.'

'But I was Code Red as a baby,' said Troy. 'I heard Yvonne–'

'I know you did,' Mac interrupted softly. 'It was the worst day of my life – I've never felt so scared. It sent your mother… she never quite recovered. But you survived, that's the important thing.'

The buildings grew lower outside the pod windows, only ten or twenty storeys high now, old-fashioned buildings with no need for grav fields to hold them in place. White roads gave way to old grey tarmac tracks, the kind used by automobiles years ago. Troy could see one of the huge solar cables that held a fifty-mile-long solar panel up near the sun, swaying gently in the distance: ugly, black and twisted. In his Submerged world, Troy knew solar cables were always housed in the worst districts, the poorest neighbourhoods, but he'd assumed, given the images of a perfect society he'd just witnessed, that slum housing areas didn't exist in the Emerged reality. After hearing Mac talk, he decided they probably did: for the Non-Emerged.

'Here.' Mac reached in his pocket and brought out his comms device. 'I've got something to show you.' He spoke into it: 'Search North and South pole, Troy baby.' A miniature holographic image of Mac, many years younger, appeared. He was standing next to a brown-haired woman with a very young baby in her arms. The woman's face was just out of focus. 'We couldn't put you in until you were three months old at the earliest – the system can't cope with very young babies – so we had a few months with you, your mother and I. In fact your mother wouldn't let you go until you were one. That's how much she loved you. We decided, since you wouldn't be seeing the real world for twenty odd years, that we'd take you on a whirlwind trip to the North and South pole: two poles in a day. It was one of those package things – your mother hated it, she always hated that sort of thing, but I think you liked it. We saw one pole in perpetual darkness and one in daylight: you liked the daylight one best.'

Troy leaned closer, looking hard at the picture of his mother. Under the blur he got the impression that she looked tired and unhappy, with dark circles under her eyes, and Troy noticed she had a permanent hologram photo-stated on her cheek: a pink tiger, strangely clear.

'We made that trip in three hours,' Mac continued, 'but it was still a rushed day. The supersonic transports were late, and we nearly missed the Aurora Borealis, but we saw it in the end.

They showed us historical shots while we were there – it used to be much brighter, the Aurora Borealis, apparently, but pollution has worn down the electromagnetic effects of the earth's gravitational field. We sat through a whole docustream about it.'

There was nothing outside the pod now but old tarmac roads and the buildings lining them were decidedly neglected, some empty or abandoned, others massively overcrowded with clunky old droids hanging out washing on tiny balconies. For the first time he saw security drones stationed at the street corners. On the horizon, gigantic thermal drills were hammering down into the Earth.

'That's where we're headed,' said Mac, pointing towards the drills, which Troy now saw were part of a huge thermo plant that spanned for miles across the horizon. 'My workplace – has been for the last twenty years.' As the pod came closer, Troy saw the barren, burnt sandpits surrounding the drills and the air above the plant, black with smoke and red with sparks of lava. 'My job is to keep the water running and keep everything cool,' said Mac, as the pod approached the plant. 'It's hard, hot work, low pay, no benefits. Just take your credits and don't complain. We're cheaper than droids, those of us who haven't Emerged: we break down less in the heat, eighty years of good service and no new parts needed.'

The pod stopped at the edge of the sandpits, and Troy saw the plumes of smoke escaping from the drill holes and heard hot pebbles of lava spraying out and bouncing off the pod roof. Even through the triple-glazed, plastipolymer windows, with tinted carbon-based gas continually circulating around their cavities, Troy could smell and taste the thick fumes. And yet he could see men working around the drills without air masks, accustomed to the smoke that was no doubt ruining their lungs.

'I remember the first docu-advertisement for Submergence,' said Mac, smiling at the noisy drills lasering away rock. 'It gave lots of facts and figures about Submerged people: their IQs are in the top 1% of the population, psychometrics say they're super well adjusted, they're more honest and trustworthy, and of course big companies snap them up as employees. It really is an amazing thing Troy, amazing. A genius idea. No one would have thought a century ago that it was possible, but here we are, living proof. Give children the perfect upbringing and you get the perfect society. You said something about Professor Shaw earlier – have you met him?'

Troy nodded.

'Shaw was one of the first, you know. The first of the Submerged babies. A model citizen now by all accounts, very clever, very successful, still fit and well at ninety-eight: what parent wouldn't want that for their child?' A lava pebble bounced off the windscreen, leaving a black burn mark. 'And then of course there's the prejudice. Years ago, Submergence was for the elite. We laugh about that now: it's so mainstream that us Non-Emergers are in the minority. Very much in the minority. We're looked down on, and of course when it comes to jobs, well, we take what we're given. We're too much of an unknown quantity for employers. Most judges are Emergers, most CEOs of companies... courts have ruled that employers can discriminate, and what Non-Emerger fancies their chance in court against an Emerger? We're discriminated against left, right and centre. The worst jobs, worst homes... but at least our children can escape, if we work hard enough.'

The pod's temperature was becoming sweltering despite the pods environmental unit's best efforts, and as Mac rolled up his sleeves, Troy noticed his arms were covered in little round scars.

'Lava,' said Mac, nodding at the puffy marks. 'There isn't a day goes by when I don't get burned. My lungs are packing up because of the smoke, and you lose friends in this job – people fall down the lava holes and that's that: not a nice way to go. Open.' The pod doors lifted up and the body of the cab was immediately filled with choking fumes.

Troy pulled up his shirt up to cover his mouth and followed Mac out of the cab, his eyes stinging, partly from the hot air and partly from tears that threatened to spill down his cheeks. Mac sounded like such a good man, such a hard worker, and yet he'd abandoned him. Troy didn't think he could forgive him for that – the anger just wouldn't leave him. There was no cover for miles around, nowhere to hide if he tried to make an escape, although perhaps the decaying tower blocks in the distance would provide some cover if he could reach them. But as Troy stood by Mac's side under the thick clouds of smoke, he realised he didn't want to run away, at least not yet. There was something very kind and genuine about Mac, and there was so much more he wanted to ask, about his mother and Code Black. Mac seemed to trust him, too – it didn't seem fair to break that trust by running away.

'C'mon kid, I'll show you my station.' Mac began stumbling across the uneven sands, dodging spitting lava and waving away clouds of smoke. Troy followed, the soft, sporty shoes he'd chosen to wear that day absorbing the heat of the ground through their thin soles.

'Where's my mother?' asked Troy, struggling to keep up. 'Do you live together? Is she still… alive?'

Mac stopped and turned around, the smoke momentarily lifting above their heads. 'It's probably best not to think about her. She's… I haven't seen her in years. We never saw eye to eye about Submergence – she always hated the idea – and after you went Code Red that was the end of things between us. I don't know where she is now.'

'She didn't agree with it?' asked Troy. 'She didn't agree with Submergence?' A flutter of hope: someone, there was *someone,* who wasn't pro-Submergence and that someone was his own mother.

Mac was walking away from him now, taking huffy, short breaths. 'At first she did,' he called over his shoulder. 'Or she wasn't against it, anyway. But as we got nearer to giving you up, she… she didn't deal with it very well. She waited 'till you were almost a year old. She took it right to the day. After five minutes of giving you up we ran into your first problem. Things were never the same between us after that. She blamed me, and I could never do anything right.' He carried on walking.

Good. Troy felt oddly cheered by the idea of his mother leaving his father. *Serves him right for abandoning me.* He thought of his Submergence parents, the parents he'd known all his life. They'd been so hopelessly in love, so happily married: presumably designed that way to offer him the best possible role models in life. If he'd been brought up by Mac, a maintenance engineer and single parent, what sort of person would he have become? Would he have had the confidence to train as a doctor? Would he have made it to university? And if the prejudice against Non-Submerged people was true, what prospects would he have had anyway? He had to stop these thoughts. They led inexorably to acceptance so he had to stall them. His head hurt again and he tried to quell the barrage of thoughts fighting for attention.

Mac headed towards one of the largest laser drills, which was blasting away thousands of miles of rock below the ground. From the hole, red-hot lava sprayed out, and men ran back and forth, hosing the sparks with cold water.

'That's my station,' he said, hands on hips, watching the men holding the powerful hoses, coughing hard as sweat poured down their faces. 'This is the sort of work you'll do now Troy – it's all that's left for those of us who aren't Submerged. You haven't finished the Program so that's what you are: an NE – Non-emerger. An unknown. That's how they think of us: unpredictable. And who knows – maybe they're right.' Mac gave an almighty cough and instinctively Troy went to him and put a hand on his back. Mac nodded to signal he was OK, then Troy stood awkwardly, not knowing what to do next. He hadn't meant to pat Mac on the back. The intimacy was too much and now his emotions were reeling from it.

'I saved up from the age of twelve to give you a better life,' Mac said, wiping his eyes and standing tall. 'My parents couldn't do it for me, but I scrimped and saved and sold and well before you were even conceived or I'd even met your mother, years and years of hard work later I had enough to put my first child through Submergence. It was all I've ever wanted: to give my child a decent life.' Mac turned to Troy then, his blue eyes filled with love and concern. 'Don't throw it all away, son. If you don't complete the Program, you'll be just like the rest of us at this end of town: broke, ill, no future. Please. I live amongst NEs. I know them. People who haven't been through the system. Who haven't had its benefits. They are violent and you cannot trust them. You have no idea what damage has been done to them in their childhood. For the sake of everything I've been through, take the chance that's being offered. This is a golden opportunity, truly. Submergence makes our world a better place. Complete the last phase. Please.'

Chapter Sixteen

The pod carried them back to the Institute in silence, with Troy ignoring all Mac's polite attempts at conversation. His head was such a jumble of thoughts he couldn't manage even the most basic small talk, and he hoped Mac understood. Troy didn't doubt Mac was a decent man. He'd clearly worked hard all his life, and if what he was saying was true, Troy owed him a massive debt of gratitude. But there were still so many things he wanted to understand, like why his mother hadn't wanted him Submerged and why he'd survived Code Black. If he were re-Submerged, he might never find the answers. And the fact he'd been abandoned and tricked: that was something he still couldn't accept. To have his life taken away without permission, it was just wrong, whichever way he looked at it.

As they neared the Institute, Mac said: 'Have you made your choice?'

Troy watched the mile-tall Institute tower get wider and wider until it filled the windscreen. 'Maybe,' he said, not wanting to give Mac an answer either way. 'But listen, Yvonne said one of the Code Black survivors was successfully re-Submerged and one wasn't. I should meet a survivor before I make any decision, meet someone like me.' The words sounded more ominous then he'd meant them too, but he was finding it hard to disguise his outrage. They were *still* trying to control him, he realised. When would they realise he wanted to live his own life?

'Code Black survivors?' Mac frowned. 'It's just a fluke – there's nothing in it, son. People don't survive, you got lucky. Don't get me wrong, it's a miracle. But miracles don't need to be questioned.'

'Yvonne said one of the Code Black survivors works at the Institute,' said Troy, noticing Mac had begun to squeeze his hands tightly together. 'It shouldn't be too hard to arrange a meeting with whoever it is.'

'If you meet the Code Black survivor at the Institute, will you agree to be re-Submerged?' asked Mac, his knuckles turning white.

'I… I don't know,' Troy admitted, finding no better way to answer the question. The smoke from the thermo plant still tickled his throat. 'Maybe,' he added, just in case Mac realised just how opposed he still was to the whole Submergence concept. Genius it may be, but Troy couldn't help the way he felt.

'I'll take you to the other Code Black survivor,' said Mac, taking a sideways glance at Troy's safety belt, 'as soon as we get back to the Institute.'

'Really?' Troy asked, as the pod approached the towering Institute. 'You'll take me to see a Code Black survivor. But… how? Have you met him? How do you know who he is? How could you know them?"

Mac didn't answer. Instead he glanced again at Troy's safety harness, and eventually said:

'Let's just say I have connections.'

'So – the Code Black survivor,' said Troy, as he and Mac took an open elevator up to the higher levels of the Institute. 'The one at the Institute – does everyone know about him? Have you actually met him?' The elevator came to a stop at its programmed floor, and Troy felt a shudder of uncertainty. He recognised the level: it was the one that housed Yvonne's laboratory and the Submergence suite.

'Wait – where are we going? You said we were going to meet the Code Black survivor.'

Mac rested a hand on Troy's shoulder and steered him towards the bridge that led to Yvonne's laboratory.

'I am,' he said, although his hand had become heavier and was now propelling Troy forward. They crossed the bridge, and Mac guided Troy through the door of the laboratory.

'Why are we going in here? What's going on?'

'Please, son,' said Mac, steering him inside. 'Please trust me.' The door whooshed firmly shut behind them.

'Hello Troy.' Yvonne Willis sat on a stool in the corner of the lab, her electro-dyed hair flickering much more rapidly than before. It was clear she'd been waiting for them.

Troy turned to Mac, his face flushed with anger. 'Trust you? I don't know you.' The words came out before he could stop them. 'So what – you donated some DNA years ago, then left me for my whole life to be brought up by a machine. We might look the same, but my real parents were computer simulations. They were a bunch of programmers and socio-psychologists.' He shrugged Mac's hand off his shoulder, only then noticing the secure droids hanging in the corner of the lab were active, humming softly and ready for immediate mobilisation.

Troy swallowed hard: how could he have been so stupid? All Mac wanted was for him to complete his final chapters. He wasn't taking him to meet the Code Black survivor at all; it had just been a clever way to get him back to the Institute.

'I'm going to leave you with Yvonne,' said Mac, patting Troy lightly on the shoulder. 'I'll see you soon.' The lab door opened and closed, and Mac was gone.

'Take a seat, Troy.' Yvonne gestured to a gel stool opposite her. 'Mac commed me – it seems we've got some things to talk about.'

Troy didn't move.

'I told Mac,' he said, jabbing his finger, 'I won't be re-Submerged until I meet the other Code Black survivor. If you put me back in Submergence, I'll force the Program into Code Black again. You know I can do it.'

'No you won't.' Yvonne crossed her thin arms across her chest. 'We've worked with your data, your algorithms, since we last had you Submerged – we have information now that allows us to work the Program around you. It will no longer be possible for you to Code Black, voluntarily or otherwise.'

'But you promised!' Troy's voice rose to an outraged bellow. 'My choice, you said. Re-Submergence or not, it's up to me. You're all Emergers – honesty, integrity and truth should be ingrained into you.'

'That is true. You are betraying your understanding. Indeed it is still up to you,' said Yvonne. 'Mac told me you'd like to meet the Code Black survivor who works here, at the Institute. After that, will you agree to be re-Submerged?'

Troy hesitated. He badly wanted to meet a survivor, but he also wanted to find the missing survivor, the one who wasn't re-Submerged, and also he wanted to meet his mother. How easy would it be to find two missing people in a world he knew nothing about? Probably impossible. If the Institute couldn't track down the missing survivor, what chance did he have? He could still taste the choking thermo-plant fumes in his throat, and his eyes were sore from the blistering heat of the drill holes. Mac had worked hard his whole life so Troy could have a chance to escape a life of hard manual labour, and Troy was so close, just a few chapters away from being an Emerger.

Troy's head ached. He felt like he was being psychologically pummelled by steams of thoughts pushing him in completely different directions. Now he'd seen the life in store for him as a non-Emerger, all thoughts of escape were twisted and broken. He was so angry at everything and everyone. There was no way out.

'OK,' said Troy, letting out a deep breath. 'Yes, I'll be re-Submerged.' At least he'd get to see the Code Black survivor and maybe understand more about why he'd been thrown out of the system.

'That's marvellous news, Troy,' said Yvonne, uncrossing her arms and gesturing to the stool in front of her. 'Then won't you please take a seat and I'll introduce you to the Code Black survivor?'

Troy sat on the stool, but Yvonne made no move to retrieve her comms device.

'Are you going to call them?' asked Troy.

'I don't need to call anyone,' said Yvonne, leaning back on her stool. 'The Code Black survivor is right here in front of you. It's me.'

'*You're* the Code Black survivor?' Troy leapt from his stool. 'Why didn't you tell me? Why didn't you say something earlier?'

Yvonne remained almost motionless, cool and calm as always.

'I'm a Code Black specialist,' she said. 'Didn't it occur to you that if there was a Code Black survivor in the Institute, they'd be working, at the very least, extremely closely with me?' She frowned as she noticed something on a monitor, and waved her hand over a few command sensors. 'Not that my experience means I'm a bank of knowledge on the subject, but I'm the best they have. Code Black remains very much a mystery. However, I'll certainly tell you as much as I can about what I remember.'

'I'd like to hear it,' said Troy, taking a seat on the stool again.

'Not here.' The secure droids above Yvonne's head floated down and flanked her on either side. 'At the Submergence suite.'

'Are they really necessary?' asked Troy, looking over his shoulder at the two faceless droids, who were whirring along behind him. He and Yvonne were entering the eerily still Submergence suite, which was an unsettling experience in itself, without two metal bouncers tagging along.

'The restrainers?' Yvonne trod gently over the rubbery floor, fixing her gaze on the see-throughy cages of people up ahead. 'It's Institute protocol: potentially disruptive visitors, meaning NEs in truth, must be accompanied by secure droids when visiting restricted areas.'

'Potentially disruptive?'

'Potentially disruptive. And please keep your voice down – people are working.'

Troy saw medical staff in white uniforms creeping around the Submergence cages, and realised that before long he'd be right back in one of those cells, hooked up to an artificial life once again. He envied the docile people inside the cages who knew nothing of the pain and loss he was suffering and probably never would. He had to admit, if he'd Emerged without any feelings of loss then Submergence would have benefited him hugely. He'd be trained as a doctor and programmed to be a healthy, happy individual – an asset to society.

'How long before I'm… you know,' said Troy, as Yvonne stopped by one of the cages. Inside, a pale-blonde girl ran frantically on a four-way, the top of her head obscured by a VR dome.

'Re-Submerge? We should do it as quickly as possible,' Yvonne said softly. 'But I won't break my promise. I do mean to tell you about my Code Black experience. This is Subject 5434.' She pointed a slender finger at the blonde girl in the cage, who was becoming increasingly agitated, running and pushing at thin air. 'If you notice the screen above her head, you'll see her movements aren't matching the visual input we're giving her.'

Troy noticed a monitor in the girl's cage displayed peaceful images of woodlands about a mile down the road from his home – presumably the environment she was currently interacting with. He still thought of it as home. The image was static, meaning it didn't make sense for the girl to be running or pushing at anything: by all accounts she should be standing very still. Outside her cage, an amber light flashed.

'Subject 5434 has had three Code Reds this year,' said Yvonne, 'and in all probability, will Code Black soon. Her parents have been informed, they've made the necessary arrangements… it's very sad, very sad indeed.' She put her hands to the flexible bars and watched the distressed figure begin to run in circles. 'Now we have your data, we're one step closer to preventing Code Blacks. And of course, your re-Submergence data will be extremely useful too. It's such a tragedy, Troy, to lose these young people, many of them so close to Emerging.'

The girl was now scratching at her face and arms.

'Take her out of the simulation,' shouted Troy, utterly bewildered by Yvonne's coldness and inaction. 'Look at her – take her out! Why are you leaving her to Code Black?'

Yvonne shook her head. 'You don't understand. During Submergence the spine's own neural impulses are inhibited. Only selected impulses such as breathing and heart control are allowed through. Her brain is now completely dependent on the external input – to disconnect immediately would be to kill her. Disconnection requires a gradual weaning of the impulses allowing the spine to take over its normal function. Otherwise, her breathing will fail and the heart will go into fibrillation. Even if we artificially operated her lungs and heart, sudden cessation of neural-integration input will send her brain into neural shock and kill her instantly.'

157

Yvonne stepped back from the cage, looking away as subject 5434 began to sob and brush invisible objects from her arms and legs. 'That's the dilemma we face here: a catch twenty-two to use an old-fashioned term – we're dammed if we do, dammed if we don't. Take the subject out of Submergence and we kill her, leave her in and she'll almost certainly die – but at least we'll obtain data that might help us prevent future incidents.'

'A lot of good that data's done you so far,' said Troy. 'Only three Code Black survivors.'

'Yes.' Yvonne looked down at the spongy floor. 'It's a poor record. Our aim is not to improve survival per se but to perfect the Program to a degree whereby we eradicate Code Black entirely. We're dedicated to improving it. But we're not here to debate the Institute's Code Black record. You wanted to know more about me, about my Code Black experiences.'

'Yes.' Troy nodded. 'Yes, very much.'

'Well – my experiences, and I happen to know yours too, were nothing like this subject's. You'll notice subject 5435 is distressed, anxious. Her reality isn't matching the visual, audio and sensory data we're giving her – her imagination is taking over, inventing new scenarios, which of course will be traumatic, since her body knows her physical experiences aren't matching up. We believe this experience feels like a living nightmare – that's what Code Red survivors have reported – although of course the only person who knows for certain, in this instance, is subject 5434. But she's releasing cortisol, the stress hormone, in abundance so we can guess her experiences are unlikely to be pleasant.' Yvonne turned to Troy, the low lighting shadowing the lines on her face. 'You and I, Troy, experienced something quite different.'

'Did we?'

'Yes. Before we Code Blacked, OK, our experiences weren't pleasant: you took a banned substance, and I... it's embarrassing, but I'll tell you. I cheated in my exams and got caught. Both major, slightly traumatic events, but the Program puts us all through traumatic things like this all the time to make sure we change and grow. Not such a big deal. In fact, our experiences weren't nearly so traumatic as what 5434 is going through. At least the Program's stimuli matched our mental experiences. So why did we Code Black? Well, the answer is that we weren't supposed to experience what we did. You weren't supposed to take IQ and I wasn't supposed to cheat. Somehow we tricked the system into giving those experiences to us, but the Program couldn't keep up and 'crashed', to use a techy term.'

'We tricked the system?' Troy looked at her with amazement.

'Look at subject 5434.' The girl in the cage was now whirling her arms around as though being attacked, yet the screen in front of her still showed the tranquil woodland scene where she was approaching the lake. Troy had swum in it nearly every summer. 'Her imagination is rebelling. Look at the screen. The system is trying to give her the right experience, but her imagination is working independently. The Program is an intuitive one: it adapts to the user to a certain extent, so it can be changed – but core experiences should play out regardless. What we need to understand is why you and I were able to add new core experiences to our Programs, to bend the system as it were.'

Troy nodded, understanding for the first time why the Institute were so keen to test him, and just how valuable he was. They must have been devastated to lose the other survivor – all that valuable data lost.

'So were any tests carried out on the other Code Black survivor?' he asked. 'Any at all?'

Yvonne shook her head. 'None. The Institute was naïve back them. They re-Submerged me without my consent.' She

159

held up her hands. 'No, no. It was the best thing. They were right to do it – otherwise I would have expressed misgivings, perhaps run away and never been re-Submerged. Anyway, the other subject, the other Code Black survivor – they assumed... they'd never dealt with a Code Black survivor who hadn't been re-Submerged. After my re-Submergence I underwent tests quite happily, and they assumed that's how all of us would be. So they tried to test the other survivor before she was re-Submerged, without the necessary security. No one thought for a moment she'd try to escape, but she did. And with her, precious data that could have saved thousands of lives.'

'Did you meet her?' asked Troy. 'Did you get to know her at all – before she ran away?'

'I knew her very well,' said Yvonne, her lip trembling ever so slightly. 'She was my sister.'

Chapter Seventeen

'What? Your sister? *Your* sister?'

'Shussh!' Yvonne put a finger to her lips and motioned towards the patients in cages. 'Yes, my biological sister. I met her several times... things were difficult, but I thought we shared a common goal. I never thought for a moment... well, Emerging ahead of schedule does funny things to people.'

'So where is she now?'

'I told you before. I imagine she lives in the underwater slums or some other Demerger waste tip – somewhere her kind aren't looked down upon, living the sort of life no civilised person would wish on anyone.'

'Don't you want to find her? Don't you miss her?'

Yvonne's usually expressionless face was weary. 'Of course I miss her. I had two sisters. Annabel our sister and my bio sister. I miss... I miss her potential. I don't miss the difficult young woman who Emerged too soon and couldn't accept her new reality. She was... there were problems. That's the trouble with NEs – they're unpredictable. You can't blame employers for preferring Submerged individuals. I wouldn't hire an NE, knowing what I know.'

Yvonne looked at Subject 5434 and smiled nodding as she settled. Reassured she turned her back completely on the girl and took Troy's arm.

'Let me show you your Submergence cube,' she said, walking them towards the back of the room where several cages stood empty. 'You'll be very comfortable. It's relaxing, being re-Submerged – all that worry, all those questions, everything is simply taken away from you, and when you Emerge again you'll be fully trained with great prospects, ready for life in the real world.'

Troy looked around at the caged people, trapped, programmed, without free choice. He knew that if he were re-Submerged he could meet all his own friends again, his parents, and his insides felt soft at the thought. He looked at the happy staff and Yvonne's face, full of belief and righteousness. It all seemed so perfect. But the rage at what he had lost, had stolen from him, was still there too, simmering like hot lava.

Yvonne led Troy to an empty cage, which looked surprisingly light and spacious now he wasn't entering it strapped to a secure droid. But it still felt like a prison, and Troy thought things were moving too quickly. Wrong, it just felt *wrong*.

'Wait – I've still got more questions… there are a few more things –'

'Troy, you'll always have more questions.' The weariness had now crept into Yvonne's voice, too. 'There's always one more thing you'd like to do or ask. There's never a good time to be re-Submerged, trust me.'

'Tell me what happens when I'm put back under,' Troy asked. 'What will I experience? How can you guarantee that the last chapters will make me accept everything? You won't wipe my memory, will you?' He began to panic, remembering the last time he'd been re-Submerged whilst held down by secure droids. This wasn't right. Yvonne had restrained him before, who was to say he could trust her now?

Yvonne smiled. 'No, Troy, certainly not. That would defeat the purpose of the system. The whole idea is that you accept the idea of being Submerged – after all, you have to live your whole life surrounded by many other Submerged individuals. If we wiped your memory, you'd find a lot of conversations in the real world very confusing. You will realise that this is right because it is. You are part of something beautiful.'

'I still think this is too soon,' said Troy, taking a glance at the exit, which was several metres away, guarded by the secure droids who'd accompanied him earlier. 'I'm not sure I'm ready...'

Yvonne shook her head. 'Typical of a non-Emerger. You gave us your word that you'd be re-Submerged after you spoke to a survivor. I kept my promise to you, if you remember – I'm afraid you must keep your side of the bargain.'

'So you're saying I don't have the right to change my mind?'

'That's exactly what I'm saying.'

I knew it, thought Troy. *I knew I couldn't trust you. Choice! That's a good one. You've never given me a choice, this whole time.*

'Please understand.' Yvonne's voice had dropped to a whisper. 'This isn't *my* choice, Troy. I'm a doctor. I would never force a patient to do something against their will. But the Institute... I feel they know what's best. They know what's best for all of us.'

'The Institute! Give it a rest, Yvonne. *You* don't sound sure.'

'Who is sure? No one is sure. But we have facts and figures to tell us what is most likely the best way to do things. To tell you the truth, I have had doubts in the past. Perhaps no one should be Submerged. Perhaps society should have figured its own way out of a mess, without having to falsify our entire upbringing. Yes – things are ordered, peaceful, yes... but parents... they have a responsibility...' Yvonne gave her head a little shake and smoothed down her hair. 'Anyway. I'm rambling. The point is, Troy, statistically re-Submergence is the best thing for you, and statistics are all we have to go on.'

'So tell me this,' said Troy, intrigued by Yvonne's confession, 'if re-Submergence is so effective, if it will make me completely contented and happy and accepting, why aren't you 100% behind it?'

Yvonne rubbed her temples.

'I… I'm 99% behind it. That's good enough. Re-Submergence was the right thing for me. It straightened me out, helped me think clearly. Without it, I wouldn't have a career here at the Institute, I wouldn't have a lovely place to live, trustworthy friends… I'd probably be shelling peas in a factory somewhere, unhealthy, ill…' Yvonne broke off, and looked back at Subject 5434 a few metres away. 'It's for the best.'

'At least tell me more about it,' said Troy, 'so I'm prepared and… not afraid,' It was only when he said the words out loud, he realised how afraid of re-Submergence he really was.

'I can't.' Willis shook her head emphatically. 'All I can tell you is you'll receive certain story lines – experiences that will lead to your understanding and acceptance of the Submergence Program. I can't tell you what those story lines are: that would have dire psychological consequences. While you're in Submergence, you'll soon forget you ever Emerged too soon – you'll feel once again that your Submerged reality is your actual reality.'

'Like brainwashing. I just… I just don't get it, Yvonne. I don't understand how *any* storyline could convince me, just like that, to believe in Submergence, to erase 99% of my doubts.'

'Troy. Please.' Yvonne was rubbing her temples. 'I can't risk telling you how it works. Don't you understand it's for your own good? Yes – if I had my choice perhaps I would explain things to you… perhaps I'd even risk you experiencing life for yourself from now on, in the real world. But *we* can't. The

Institute and I, together we can't. It poses too great a risk to your psychological wellbeing.'

'It's got to be religion. Is that how you do it?' Troy asked, deciding if he couldn't stop the inevitable, he could at least stall for time. He'd learned plenty about religion at school, or should he say, in Submergence, and could talk about it for hours. Maybe the Program corrupted faith to further acceptance.

Yvonne shook her head. 'We're a Unifaith society, just like you learned during Submergence. You won't learn anything new about religion when you're re-Submerged – everything you learned about the three faiths and the Holy Meeting was correct, although the programmers changed the timelines a little – they wanted us to experience the before and after: living with the conflicting three major faiths, and then a unified Unifaith planet.'

Before and after. Troy remembered his first day at school, aged five, a few years before the Holy Meeting had taken place. He'd arrived at the school playdome wearing a red T-shirt, the unofficial colour of Judaism, and, although his parents weren't strong supporters of any particular faith, he'd been asked to change his shirt to prevent potential scuffles with his new classmates.

Presumably the playdome scenario had been manufactured to teach him about the benefits of Unity – and it had worked: he, like everyone else, had celebrated on the day the Holy Meeting had been completed. No more conflict between the three major religions, which had caused untold hardship and pain for countless generations. For centuries, each religion had supposedly preached understanding and tolerance for the other religions, yet failed to deliver on those promises and pledges, usually in a spectacular fashion. More violence, pain and hardship had occurred due to divisions of religion than any other cause in the history of mankind. So philosophers and scholars from the big three had sat down together in a momentous Holy

Meeting in Jerusalem, the most holy of cities, and for three months they had deliberated and discussed their views and beliefs in closed sitting. They had agreed to leave all animosity and pre-conception outside the meeting hall, but initially the discussions had been heated as millennia of differences inevitably surfaced in a torrent of emotion. Finally, only silence could be heard at the doors of the conclave. When the attendees finally emerged, none of them ever spoke again and it was thought they had uttered words so profound and created such healing amongst the peoples of man that they could not pollute their work by further words. A new scripture was released which joined all the beliefs: a new framework for a good and fruitful life, based upon one God and his three peoples made one.

Troy and his classmates were told that an amalgam had formed incorporating the ethos of all three religions, and was appropriately called Unity. He'd had the benefits and beliefs of Unity drummed into him throughout his later school years and sincerely believed in the goodness the new faith seeded amongst all levels of human society. In his Submergence lifetime, he had seen the people of all the previously divided faiths turn and embrace each other as brothers and sisters. He had also seen the history streams of the violence and hatred that had occurred before Unity. But how could he trust beliefs based on fabricated storylines?

'The last storylines are way beyond a faith-based model of persuasion,' Yvonne said, and as she spoke the secure droids came closer and flanked her. 'They're much cleverer than that, much more subtle. They work on your own beliefs and experiences – you convince yourself in the end that Submergence is best for everyone. The beauty is that it is true. Clever, isn't it? Who better to convince you, than you? Move into the cube, please Troy.'

Troy understood that his time was up.

'Wait.' He held up his hand, searching for something, anything to stall, to give him more time. He needed to think, to get away from these people and be alone. He wanted to get off the rollercoaster and make his own decisions for a change, and felt like a wild animal backed into a corner. Maybe he did want to be re-Submerged, but not by force, and not yet. A pressing in his bladder alerted him to a potential delaying tactic. 'May I use the water facility first?' He looked at the ground. 'I'm guessing it's going to take a while to get me hooked up again, and I'll be a little uncomfortable.'

Yvonne rolled her eyes.

'Really, Troy. What do you take us for? Of course you can visit the water facility. The secure droids will have to accompany you, of course. Procedure. You understand.'

'Fine.' Troy had expected as much.

'Straight ahead on the far wall. There's a couple of meds up there – if you get lost they'll show you the way.'

The water facility was cool and calming, with hygienic water constantly washing basins and waste receptacles, but Troy's thoughts were in turmoil as the automatic door to the Submergence suite closed behind him. He'd hoped five minutes to himself would give him time to think, but he felt as capable of logical thought as the table-top philosophy drone his parents used to bring out at parties. He knew he didn't want to be Submerged immediately, but equally a second escape didn't seem likely with two secure droids waiting outside, not to mention Yvonne and the team of medical staff.

He splashed scented water on his cheeks and examined his taut, stressed face in the mirror, realising that for most of his life, every time he'd looked in a mirror he'd been viewing a computer simulation: an amalgamation of shots taken by a facial scanner.

As lukewarm water ran down his face, there was a clicking sound in the corner and a panel raised up to reveal a chemical-carrier droid, which scooted out onto the hard, resin floor and made its way towards the basins. It hovered underneath one of the white bowls and began refilling barrels of germ-killing chemicals, emitting a regular whistling sound as it worked – an addition designed to reassure water room users that they were in the presence of artificial life. His vision focussed on the empty compartment within the body of the droid, a thought struck Troy like a pod-smashed bird falling from the sky: *If that droid could get in here, it means there must be a way for it to get out again. Which means there might be a way for me to get out.*

Troy scanned the wall panel through which the carrier droid had arrived, and saw it was still open. He dropped to his knees to look at it more closely, willing there to be a turbo-lift inside that could boost him to the upper levels and away – but there was nothing, only an empty shaft, plunging perilously down to the ground around thirty storeys below. The droid itself must have powerful antigrav motors, Troy realised, so the only way up or down would be on or in the chemical carrier itself.

Across the room, the droid continued to fill the tub beneath the basin, its side panel showing red chemical fluid dropping lower and lower as its cavity emptied. By the time it pulled back its hose, only a thin layer of chemicals remained inside its drum. So… there was room for him inside the droid, if he didn't mind some minor chemical burns and lung irritation.

From his crouched position, Troy glanced at the door, then back at the droid, which was now sealing up the tub. It had no alarms on it, no audio or video monitors – it was an auto-programmed maintenance droid that was presumably now going to return to chemical storage and refill itself. Troy looked at the door again. If, *if,* he managed to escape, what then? A life on the run? Social isolation? It didn't matter – at least he'd be living, and at least he'd be away from the Institute, the organisation that had stolen his life from him.

He couldn't do it. It was far too risky but it seemed he had no choice.

Keeping his eyes fixed on the door, Troy held the droid steady, its motors whining as he un-clicked its lid and climbed into the reeking barrel of swirling red liquid. He folded his head down and out of the way, letting the droid auto-close the lid and prayed there was enough oxygen in the drum to last until he reached the refill area.

Chapter Eighteen

After what felt like hours in the darkness, bouncing around inside the droid's drum like a basketball, caustic chemicals sloshing all over his legs, Troy heard and felt the carrier come to stop in a room that hummed with electronic activity. He pushed at the lid above him, but it was held fast, and suddenly there was a disconcerting sound: a spinning, clicking noise followed by rushing liquid. Around Troy's feet, liquid chemicals began charging into the drum and he coughed and spluttered as fumes filled his nostrils and lungs.

'Help!' He banged at the top of the drum, but the lid wouldn't budge. 'Help!' But within the sealed chemical droid nothing, no human attendant or audio alarm, could hear him.

Chemicals began splashing around his torso, and he took great gasping breaths, feeling around with his foot until he found where the liquid was rushing in. Panic was beginning to overwhelm him – he knew he was only moments away from suffocation, and desperately pushed with his foot, trying to plug up the hole, spitting splashes of chemicals from his mouth.

Within seconds the chemicals had reached his shoulders, and he gasped and coughed, jamming harder with his foot. *Please, please...* The liquid didn't seem to be flowing into the drum as fast with his foot in the way, but he knew, even if he didn't drown, the fumes would kill him unless he got out quickly.

He had almost drowned once before. He had been playing by a lake having ignored the warning signs and had fallen in. He had become entangled in the roots of the plants by the shore. He remembered vividly the fear he felt as he struggled to reach the surface. The images came unbidden into his head. The murky water was all around him and flooding his consciousness. He remembered his lungs burning surrounded by the white noise of rushing water churning around him as he struggled. He remembered suddenly feeling at peace as the water stilled. The water around him gained a brilliant clarity. The blue light filtering from the surface of the lake danced around him illuminating him in a beautiful ballet. He would never forget that blue. He had been rescued by a passer-by but now there was no one to rescue him. He had been protected by the Program but now that protection was gone.

Around his foot, the opening was beginning to tremble, and Troy pushed with more force, willing the liquid to retreat, until suddenly there was a grinding, cutting, squeaking sound. An explosion of hot chemicals and plastic surged up Troy's neck and chin, and for a moment he thought this was it: his time had come. But suddenly, cool oxygen flowed all around and Troy saw he was sitting in the ruptured shell of the carrier droid, red chemicals running all over the floor around him.

Dumbstruck, Troy scrabbled over jagged plastic and metal, coughing and pulling himself to his feet, looking back at the ripped body of the carrier droid. He looked around to discover he was in some sort of store room, stacked high with barrels of chemicals. A filler droid was beside him, beeping an alarm sequence, and Troy knew it wouldn't be long before human staff came to deal with the explosion. Seeing a door in the far corner, he ran to it and pushed through, finding himself in a bare maintenance corridor with a staircase at the end. The sign above the staircase said: 'To Aerodrome'. *The Aerodrome,* thought

Troy, thinking of the space shuttles and trips to Mars. *What better way to get out of the Institute than in a space ship?*

'The whole geostationary platform network was designed by the first round of Emergers,' the wiry-haired middle-aged woman beside Troy told her younger compatriots, as they walked towards a waiting shuttle. 'It's genius. An engineering triumph. Another example of how the Institute is boosting the lives of all. Take this launch platform, for example. It's on top of the Institute, one of London's tallest buildings, so the energy cost of launching transporters is minimal. So there's an energy saving, plus minimal pollution because of the fusion generators. And under the launch platforms there are massive recycling and purifying systems, so pollutants are continually filtered from the atmosphere.'

None of the girls paid any attention to Troy, who walked nonchalantly alongside them, slightly damp, smelling of chemicals and trying to look inconspicuous. He had sneaked out of a maintenance door into the main thoroughfare of the aerodrome and immediately melted into the crowds. Despite the hustle of the many people traversing the area there was an overlay of clam and purpose. Happiness and contentment seemed to pervade the atmosphere and although people looked busy they seemed to walk round with a perpetual semi-smile on their faces. While Troy worried that they would look at him suspiciously. He was only met with smiles. He had managed to dry himself with some paper towels he had found in a maintenance closet but the smell of the chemicals was still strong.

It was easy for him to join the group of girls who were heading to the launch bays. They all chatted freely to each other and many held hands. Troy was able to determine that they were part of a group who had Emerged two months earlier and were still undergoing their orientation and settlement trips.

Occasionally they glanced at him but the only query sent his way was in the form of a smile which he responded to with a smile in return. They were on an observational mission into London but they were going to go extra-planetary first. Up into low orbit and then back down to the London Central Hub. It would be perfect. He could get onto the shuttle and be far away into the hustle and bustle of London before the Institute would know.

He kept close to them as they walked along the vast Aerodrome launch platform. With its eight launch pads connected by rigid cables, like legs on a giant spider.

'Of course, it was also the very same group of people,' Troy heard the lady continue, as the group of twenty or so young men and women neared a gleaming shuttle open for boarding, 'who discovered a way around using fusion energy to break the Earth's gravitational pull, and –' The firing of jets interrupted her, and she and her friend smiled at each other. 'Launch time,' she said, and began climbing the metallic rungs up into the space shuttle. Troy stuck close to two of the girls, not being able to resist a quick glance over his shoulder to check there were no security personnel or droids around. He knew the Institute was a vast place, almost certainly housing tens of thousands of people at any one time, but he also knew that they were one happy family. Surrounded by Emergers the need for security was minimal so there were no checks.

Once inside the comfortable interior of the shuttle, Troy tried to relax as safety nets extended from the ceiling and tightened around him, and excited young adults clambered to sit with friends, winding their arms and legs under nets. There was a low rumble as the shuttle boosters kicked in and pulled the craft away from the launch platform.

Although space flight was relatively cheap and easy according to Troy's Submerged upbringing, he still found the idea of it awe-inspiring – to think humans had the ability to

173

leave the planet at will. The pull of acceleration took Troy's breath away as the shuttle shot up spaceward, the movement far from smooth at first, but Troy was eagerly anticipating the weightlessness he knew would come. He had always wanted to travel into space. Although it was an everyday affair for the majority of people, it still struck Troy as astounding how man could break beyond the limited confines of the earth and stretch his hand out towards the stars.

'Oh look!' the girl beside him said, as the effects of gravity began to lessen, 'The Mars Transit Station. We've always wanted to go to Mars, haven't we?'

Troy looked over and saw the majestic gleaming structure that was the orbiting station where Mars shuttle began their journeys. Troy had dreamed of visiting some of the Mars colonies once he left medical school: he guessed every Emerger had the same dream, and worse, they all knew it of each other. The thought unsettled him. All of them, every Emerger in this group, all knew intimately what had happened in his life, from the laughter to the tears. But they also had an extra chapter of experiences, something else shared, that had made them accept, be happy and contented. What happened to everyone in the last sections of the Program? He wished he knew. Was his curiosity enough to wish he was back in the system?

As the shuttle began to drift over the Earth, Troy noticed the other passengers rapidly making audio notes on their comms devices, so he pretended to do the same, looking covertly around to check no one noticed he was speaking into an empty hand. It felt odd not having his own comms device, almost like he was missing a limb. He had left the data-disc the institute had given him back in the locker as it would have been too easy to trace. Troy tried not to dwell on it – after all, the upside was it made him relatively free.

He looked out of the window at the stars, feeling peaceful for the first time in days, knowing, at least for the time he was in this shuttle, no one could get to him. But just as his body began to relax, he saw her, sitting a few rows in front of him: Hannah. It couldn't be coincidence, it was too convenient. His heart quickened as he looked around again. Had they found him already? His eyes returned to her. She was even more beautiful than he remembered, wearing a silver costume that was disappointingly nowhere near as figure hugging as the chameleon dress she'd worn the night before. Her hair was swept back in a clip making her face appear slender, and accentuating the sharp angle of her nose, a feature that divided her symmetrical beauty and tantalisingly pulled the observer's gaze to her sparkling blue eyes. He stared for too long, drinking in her face and body, until his observations were interrupted by a synthetic voice:

'Two minutes to landing.'

The shuttle began to descend, and Troy braced himself for the rush towards Earth, already feeling gravity tug all around him. Anxiety clung to him as tightly as the safety net, not just due to the fast descent, but because of what was waiting for him on the ground. Leaving the Institute had been easy, but Central London Aerodrome would be a different matter – there may be other checks. Wherever there was a possibility of NE presence inevitably the security protocols would be more stringent.

As the shuttle raced downwards through the clouds, Troy could see the central tower of the London Aerodrome extending into the skies, surrounded by flat rings of pod lanes and loading bays. Gleaming aerodynamic pods rested on landing pads, ready for engineers to look them over, while taxi-pods jostled along the surrounding lanes and down towards the underground pod stacking facility that packed pods together vertically for optimum space saving.

He remembered when he'd first arrived at University in central London how amazed he'd been by the big city. He'd spent the whole of his first taxi-pod journey with his face pressed against the thin windows, having switched all the thinscreens to external views so he was surrounded on all sides by the sights and sounds of London. It was awe-inspiring seeing the grandeur and sheer size of the buildings, although in Troy's version of the past – his Submergence past – the Institute tower, which despite its distance still dominated the horizon like a giant church spire, hadn't existed.

At its heart, the Aerodrome consisted of a centripetal launch platform: a huge spinning cylinder that generated enough force to lessen the affects of gravity and allow effortless, atmosphere-friendly launches. It was a triumph of practical design, using the most energy efficient techniques to generate power, whilst offering enhanced safety for passengers. Troy remembered learning about it in one of his Submergence history classes: *the engineering success of the century,* it had been called.

He felt a pulling at his chest as the shuttle rapidly slowed down, and moments later landed gently on one of the landing pads.

'No, Darla will be taking that section. I'm just here as back-up…' It was Hannah's voice, clear and intelligent, and Troy instinctively hunched over to disguise himself, bowing his head as he listened to her excited chatter about the amazing science utilised to construct the Aerodrome, and how some of the greatest Emerged minds in history had taken part in its construction.

The coarse ropes of the tough safety net that lay tightly over Troy's legs and chest became light suddenly, and Troy stretched his arms out as the net was sucked upwards onto the roof of the shuttle. Everyone around him got to their feet, stretching their legs and clicking their stiff necks back and forth.

A hissing sound signalled the vacuum release of the door, and as light shone into the cabin Troy saw shuttle drones speeding up to the craft and attaching a ladder for passengers to climb down. A few metres away from them, Troy watched the air wobble as the magnetic field around the landing pad – a safety measure to forcefully repel any people or objects that came near the dangers of a landing craft – was switched off, allowing the passengers to pass through and towards the security gate.

In his increasingly anxious state, Troy had an odd memory: he and his best friend from school, Arnie Deacon, throwing stones and dirt at one of the national hover-rail tracks, which had been surrounded by a similar magnetic field. The hover rail system was quite a new development back then, and most children, Troy included, were fascinated by everything about it: the fast, silver trains speeding through the green countryside; the special loading system that talked directly to luggage druids; the fact that the entire country was now accessible in under an hour and, most amazing of all, the magnetic force field that covered the tracks.

Because the hover trains were propelled by magnetic force, the whole hovertrack was surrounded by a negative electro-magnetic force field which had the beneficial side effect of propelling mass objects away from the tracks. Thus, anything with sufficient weight to it: a stone, a bird, a human being, was pushed away from the tracks without any harm coming to them, but dust and light rain could penetrate the field.

Troy and Arnie had some great times sitting by an unguarded stretch of train track in their home town, hurling themselves at the magnetic field and being forcefully repelled, and then testing out different weights of stone and grit: which piece would go through and which would bounce away? It was terrific fun, and when they ran out of games to play with the force field, they simply sat and enjoyed watching birds fly into it and bounce away, usually minimally bruised and ruffled, but more obviously, just confused.

However, despite the new hover tracks being publicised as 'extremely safe', an unfortunate incident had occurred just outside Troy's hometown of Ekington: an incident that scared Troy and Arnie away from the hovertracks and bought them back, instead, to the safety of the play bubble a few roads away from Troy's house. A group of teenage boys and girls playing by the tracks had managed to collectively breach the field by forcing an iron bar through, which had subsequently flown straight onto the magnetic track and held fast, pulling a teenage boy with it. Trapped inside the magnetic field, the boy couldn't escape the oncoming train, charging at 250kph along the track. He was killed, and the first two carriages of the train derailed, although the rest were, fortunately, clamped down to the tracks by the emergency systems. When the emergency drones arrived at the scene they found forty-eight dead and fourteen seriously injured. Most were train passengers, but the derailed train, which flown out of the force field, also killed all but one of the teenagers who'd been messing around by the tracks. The surviving teenager, Toby McDouglas, had minimal physical injuries, but psychological scars that would last him the rest of his life: by a cruel twist of fate, his father had been a passenger on the train and been killed instantly.

Troy remembered the news feeds vividly: Toby had faced charges in the Juvenile Justice Courts and was found guilty of murder before being bound over into a Juvenile Re-adjustment Institute for five years of psychotherapy.

There had been an enquiry after the sentencing, and Toby's mind and experiences had been dissected by psychotherapists. Experts concluded that Toby's parents, despite one of them being a victim of the train crash, were to blame for the incident. Their parenting had been inadequate, the experts decided, and without their negligence the incident would never had occurred. Toby's mother was taken into custody and sentenced to several years of psychological mentorship. It all fitted perfectly. Another lesson.

As thoughts of Toby and childhood receded, Troy noticed the passengers either side of him had long since got up and exited the craft, and with alarm he realised he was the last person on the shuttle. He climbed down the exit ladder as quickly as possible and hurried to catch up with the crowd, who were now making their way into the terminal building.

That was the year, thought Troy, still unable to completely shake thoughts of Toby McDouglas, *the courts ruled that parents of criminal offenders were responsible for a third of their offspring's offences, and sentenced them accordingly.* The idea was to deter bad parenting. It didn't work of course: the social and economic differentiators between families remained the biggest determinants of criminal offending. But then again, he'd been fed a computerised version of the world's legislation and consequences. So far, reality did seem to match up with the fake Submergence reality he'd experienced, but who was to say whether the political newsfeeds during Submergence matched reality, or manufactured it? The victors wrote the history and so far it was clear that the Institute was all powerful.

Chapter Nineteen

Troy approached the security area, still keeping his head bowed and looking out for Hannah, who he kept catching glances of amid the crowd – just like the night before he went Code Black, when he'd seen snatches of her face, her body, among the students drinking at the bar. But now of course, the scene was entirely different and far less relaxed: security drones were scanning data discs and more worryingly, a few human security personnel lounged in the background in case of any complications. Had the Institute registered his details with the city's AI? If they had, it was more than likely all the major transport hubs in the city would be looking out for him. But he had a hunch they wouldn't have realised he'd left the Institute just yet.

As the checking drones scanned the travellers Troy found his gaze wandering to the arrivals area past the security zone. He could see slidewalks ferrying people towards friends and relatives; men and women hugging and smiling at one another; people laughing together – there was no pushing or shoving, no tension or raised voices. It was a utopian scene by all accounts: almost too good to be true. And yet no children were there to enjoy the atmosphere. No children were there to revel in the joy of it all, or benefit from the safety and camaraderie that was so evident around him.

'Sir.' The electronic voice of a security drone made Troy jump. Its black shell, electronically coloured with a bright yellow stripe, floated towards him. 'Please move along, sir. Thank you, sir. No congregating in the security zone.' It waited patiently for Troy to move towards the queue. 'Thank you sir. You will be waiting approximately three minutes.' The drone floated away, leaving Troy waiting anxiously in a line of ten people, fully aware that he had no data-disc or ID confirmation and that he was moments away from being security checked.

Suddenly, Troy felt a hand on his shoulder.

'Troy?'

He turned around slowly, his shoulder tense. Hannah stood behind him, her pale face concerned.

'What are you doing here?' she said.

'Erm...' Troy knew, even though he'd had more pressing things to do than check a mirror, that he looked somewhat wild and dishevelled after his chemical drone experience, and that his hair was almost certainly matted with chemicals and sitting in stiff spikes and waves around his head. And he still reeked of cleaning fluids. But even if Hannah didn't notice, and Troy was sure, by her worried eye movements up and down his body, that she already had, he realised he couldn't lie to her.

'I escaped,' he said, matter of factly, peering over her shoulder at the queue of people trotting through customs. No one was paying any attention to Troy and Hannah's exchange. 'I couldn't do it, Hannah – the last chapters. There are things... there's another Code Black survivor. One who escaped. I need to find out what happened to her – decide for myself whether to re-Submerge based on the facts, not what some doctor in a lab coat tells me.'

'I know,' Hannah said, nodding. 'Everyone knows about the other Code Black survivor. The Institute have been trying to find her for decades.'

Troy shrugged. 'She won't want to be found by the Institute. But maybe I'll stand a better chance.'

'And what if you do find her?' asked Hannah, gripping Troy's arm as they inched towards the security drone. There were eight people ahead of them now, but the drone seemed to be operating at alarming speed, checking people through in a matter of seconds. 'What then?'

The two of them took another tentative step forward as more people were checked through.

'I hadn't thought that far ahead,' Troy admitted. 'But I need to see the real world, Hannah. I haven't seen anything – I just need to… before they… I've never seen a real thunderstorm. Never tasted real seafood or…' He felt Hannah's soft arm against his and knew there were other things he wanted to do, plenty of them, before he was forced back into artificial existence again.

'And just what exactly,' Hannah hissed, 'do you intend to do in the real world? You're a Non-Emerger – an NE. Do you know what sort of life you have to look forward to? Do you want to live near the methane pits, work at the thermo plant and drink cloudy spirit all day? Or maybe you'd prefer a trip to the underwater slums so you can deal IQ or whatever other genetic enhancers you can get your hands on, until one day you're caught and have your personality altered and memory erased?'

'Yes.' Troy shook free of Hannah's arm. There was only one person in front of them now, and Troy didn't want Hannah associated with him when he was hauled off by security.

'Yes?'

'Yes – the underwater slums. That's where I want to go.'

'*Why* in the name of Unity would you want to go there? Have you ever *seen* the slums, Troy – do you know what goes on down there?'

'Do you?'

182

Hannah was silent then. She looked at the ground. 'I've never been there. But I've heard –'

'We've both heard lots of things. But what have we seen, really *seen*, with our own eyes?'

Hannah blushed, then flinched as a customs drone announced a 'check through error' particularly loudly. The young man being checked in front of them fumbled to restart his data-disc, clearly embarrassed.

'Listen, you're not going to get through customs,' said Hannah. 'If you haven't completed Submergence, your data disc won't let you into the centre of London unless you've been police checked.'

'That's not a problem because I don't have the data-disc.'

'You don't... oh for goodness sakes.' Hannah looked left and right, then deep into Troy's eyes. 'Troy, I don't know what's got into me. Maybe I do believe in destiny, and "best matches"... oh – forget I said that. But listen, I'll help you get through customs. And I'll go with you to the underground slums. You're right. I haven't seen anything. Maybe it's time I did.'

'How will you –'

'Excuse me!' Hannah shouted, grabbing Troy's arm and pulling him up to the security drone, waving her hand at one of the orange-vested security personnel. 'Hey! Over here – yes, I need some help.'

The woman in security uniform adjusted her orange bib and smiled at the attractive young lady before her.

'Yes, sweetheart. How may I help you today?'

Even airport security are polite, thought Troy.

'Oh – we've got a bit of a problem.' Hannah gave the woman a look, then nodded towards Troy. 'This newly Emerged idiot here has left his data-disc back at the Institute, and the group are booked in for a very important sightseeing tour around the Aerodrome today.'

The woman nodded sympathetically.

'Young people, eh?' she said, seemingly oblivious to the fact that Hannah was also a young person. 'The system brings them up best it can, but… they still develop little faults of their own.' She smiled warmly at Troy. 'Young man, that data-disc should be glued to you. *Glued.* We've all had it drummed into us, haven't we? Remember Jeremy Adams? Carli Singh?'

Troy hoped the woman didn't notice that his mouth had involuntarily dropped open. It was very strange to have a perfect stranger mention two of your school friends as though she'd been in the same class as you. And of course she had been, in a way. The great Submergence school of learning. He would never get used to it.

'Erm, yes,' Troy stammered. 'It was really stupid of me.'

Both Hannah and the woman nodded and rolled their eyes, and then the woman approached the security drone and swept her security pass along the scanner on its body.

'Grant day permit – you'll be flying home this evening, right?' the woman asked Hannah, who seemed to have decided that Troy was too incompetent to talk to directly.

'Yes – for the day,' Hannah said quickly.

'Be sure not to lose it,' the security woman called, as Troy and Hannah hurried out into the arrivals area.

'Thanks,' said Troy, as they blended into the arrivals crowd, jumping quickly onto walkways out of the building, neither sure if in a few moments they wouldn't be chased by security personnel. 'I can't believe how trusting everyone is. That would never have happened –' Troy stopped himself saying *in Submergence*. Is this what happened to everyone, he wondered: they gradually came to accept Submergence as a normal, albeit separate, part of their background?

Hannah looked strained. 'They wouldn't expect an Emerger to lie. I can't believe I actually lied for you. I feel dirty.'

The arrivals area led straight out onto Oxford Street: London's pod-free shopping zone, crammed with people charging up and down the slidewalks, and Troy felt a sense of huge sense of relief as they exited the drome building and joined the throng of shoppers.

'Our parents took us here when we were really young, do you remember?' said Hannah.

Our parents. The words were an emotional bullet. Troy knew rationally he shouldn't have any feelings for his 'parents' – the two 'ideal' computer programs that had brought him up. They weren't real: he knew that. Not only weren't they real, but they weren't his. They belonged to every other Emerger, including Hannah. But the memories of them were so strong and vivid, and so fond. He couldn't help loving them – the feeling was still there, even if his thoughts were bitter and angry.

He remembered how much his parents looked forward to him coming home from university for the holidays – he'd never been in any doubt about how much they loved and wanted him. His mother was particularly anxious to have him back in the comforting confines of the family nest, always sending pointless comms to check when his train was due in, or what he'd like for supper when he got back.

'I remember the trip,' said Troy. 'Mum had just quit work to look after my – our – little sister.'

Hannah nodded.

'Our Annabelle. Mum used to take her to the crèche at the university…'

'…where she taught World Ethics,' finished Troy. 'But then she gave it up, even though she loved it. And she never complained. Having a Mum at home was great… I suppose that's the way they planned it. Getting off the school shuttle pod and seeing Mum there waiting for me, asking about my day, helping me talk through any problems. Keeping her comms device on all the time in case I needed to comm with anything.

She was perfect. I always used to tell my friends how perfect she was, how she'd always seem to know when something was wrong and be able to fix it. I thought every child thought that way about their parents, but… I guess not all parents are perfect computer programs.'

Hannah sighed. 'I miss them too.'

'I didn't say –'

'You didn't have to. Of course you miss them. We all do – but you can still see them. You'll never have the pain of seeing them die, or growing old and ill. You can see them whenever you want, ask their advice – the Program will always be there. It's a bit like going to a Unity Temple, we all do it. When you're feeling low, you go and talk to the 'parent program' and get a bit of perspective on life.'

'When I started university,' said Troy, 'I realised more than ever how much Mum and Dad did for me – how much I'd relied on them and how easy they made my life. They encouraged me, and cushioned me when I fell. They let me experiment and try things for myself, but they kept me safe too.'

'Remember Mum and the Kid's Foundation?' said Hannah, jumping expertly into a gap on one of the crowded slideways and pulled Troy on behind her. 'How Dad always used to joke that he was out earning all that money, and she'd go and give it away without a second thought?'

Troy laughed despite himself.

'He'd say they may as well set up a regular transfer account to the charity, so we could send our money there directly and save the convoluted journey between credit accounts. But she was amazing, wasn't she?' Troy let himself feel it – feel the love and wonder he'd always had for his mother. She'd been inexhaustible – always having enough energy for his father, the children and anyone else who'd needed it. There were times when her tales of good deeds did become a bit preachy, and he supposed, if there was any error in the programming, that had been it: his parents had been a little bit too perfect.

In fact, his whole family life had been just a little bit too perfect: he could see that now. Every day, they'd set aside half an hour or so to talk about their day and any problems any of them had. How he'd missed those family meetings when he went away to university. Of course, he and his sister had rowed quite a bit during family time, but he presumed this had been to teach him about debate and arbitration, since his parents always managed to intervene and make each of them see the other's side of the argument.

'You have no idea where the underwater slums are, do you?' Hannah whispered as the walkways took them west, towards the kilometre-high Nike building on the corner of Oxford Street and Regent Street. It was all completely familiar. He had to hand it to the Submergence programmers: they'd done an exceptional job of copying reality.

Troy knew, if his Submergence history classes matched reality, that this area of Central London used to be crowded with buildings, but that the area had been thinned to make way for the Aerodrome, and thousands of shops and restaurants now utilised sky-high architecture, which used force fields to construct kilometre-high buildings, their top floors accessed by super-charged elevators.

Since 60% of the population worked from home using the Ethernet, work buildings had been dwindling for years in the Central London area, so a clearing had long been overdue. And now the morning rush-hour crowds ceased to plague the city centre, taxi-pods were free to pick up tourists and shoppers and take them to their destination in double-quick time – making them every bit as cost-effective as the old underground tube system, which was gradually being dismantled. Several hovering black cabs waited in the centre of the walkways and Hannah grabbed Troy's hand and pulled him towards one of the sleek, black vehicles.

187

Chapter Twenty

The door opened with a hydraulic whoosh as the heavily conditioned air of the cab was released and the voice of the auto-driver welcomed him with a slightly over-enthusiastic synthetic greeting.

'Good day to you! I see you have...' a pause, '...NO luggage drones.'

'We need to get to a hovertrain station,' Hannah explained, as they climbed in the back, and she told the automated dashboard to take them to Victoria station. The door closed, insulating them against the bustle of shoppers outside.

'I only detect ONE data-disc,' the taxi-pod announced, and there was a vibrating sound as Hannah's device vibrated while the cab connected with it. 'I will take credits from HANNAH GRACE.' Hannah passed her data-disc forward, and allowed it to be docked in the dashboard. Once it was in place, the auto-driver pulled out and into traffic. The onboard central controller linked directly into Hannah's disc, accessing the travel itinerary she'd programmed as she and Troy were leaving the Aerodrome. After detecting her rail booking, matching it with its train timetable database, and recognising that Hannah and Troy's train was leaving imminently, it automatically accelerated, although the speed increase was imperceptible to either passenger.

They both sat back in the comfortable seats as the navigational system directed the pod at rapid speed along the near-empty pod lanes.

'You say I've never seen the slums,' said Hannah quietly. 'And you're right. But I have heard about them – more than you have. And they're dangerous.'

'You're three minutes from your destination,' the autopilot informed them, as they approached the towering silver structure of Victoria Hover Station on the banks of the Thames.

The hovertrain shot through West London in a matter of minutes, past the crumbling antique of Buckingham Palace, preserved from further decay under a vacuum dome, and out into the stained, narrow streets of the lower-class suburbs. 'This used to be the wealthy part of London, didn't it?' said Hannah conversationally, as the train whooshed along. 'Before we needed bigger streets. It's weird to think that. Now it's all the low earners who live here – people who don't mind walking everywhere.'

Troy nodded. 'How far out are the slums?'

'A fair way,' Hannah admitted. 'We'll have to walk a few miles. No public transport will go near them – not even taxi-pods.'

They dismounted at the terminal station, hanging back to let all the passengers with luggage drones, stored in a separate baggage carriage, be reunited with their belongings.

'I had a luggage drone at university,' said Troy. 'Christmas present from Mum and Dad. I suppose every Emerger did. Same parents, same experiences...'

Hannah laughed.

'Not exactly the same experiences. There's still a difference between the sexes – I'm sure my romantic experiences were different from yours. Sarah and I didn't get quite as physical and you guys did and I have a sneaky suspicion that you and Sanjay didn't get quite as close as he and I did.'

Troy couldn't help blushing. He was amazed at how comfortable Hannah felt talking about these intimate issues.

Hannah continued, unperturbed, 'But yes, I was given a luggage drone for Christmas. A really rubbish second-hand one. Sound familiar?'

Now it was Troy's turn to laugh.

'Old beaten up! It could detect movement all right – whenever you didn't want it to. And it didn't compact things properly, so everything was forever springing out the top. I remember whenever I took it to the train station, people would walk out of their way to avoid my old, chugging luggage drone scraping along the ground. The trip with Victoria –' He stopped himself. It didn't seem right talking about Victoria in front of Hannah, even though Victoria had been nothing more than a simulation.

'Go on, you can tell me.'

'No, it's OK.'

'Don't be silly Troy, I went on the same romantic trip with a delightful chap called Victor,' said Hannah, teasingly.

Only three drones had dropped out of the storage carriage, and now they'd located their owners, Troy and Hannah made their way out of the station. Hannah shielded her eyes from the bright sun overhead as she pointed towards the dark blue of the sea in the distance. 'That's it. Or at least, a way down into it.'

'Let's go,' said Troy.

Despite the proximity to the sea there were seagulls. The high cliffs that once stood proud and defiant to the sea had collapsed long ago as the sea level rose and their resilience was defeated by ever higher waves. Now nothing remained of their grandeur but broken rocks and piles of rubbish and detritus. The smell of the sea was clouded by the stench of decay.

'I can't believe people can live close to this stench,' said Hannah, as she and Troy walked along the desolate, cracked-concrete streets under the warm sun, the rubbish-piled shoreline growing larger with every step. 'You must be thirsty, here, drink this.' She took a thumb-sized bottle of water concentrate from her bag and handed it to Troy stretching the bottle so it filled with liquid. Troy realised he had not had a drink of anything for ages and gratefully took three large gulps to quench his thirst.

Troy squinted into the distance. 'That's the English Channel isn't it?'

'Yes, in the midst of all of this rubbish the slums begin. At least, that's the rumour. There's an official entrance about two miles down the coast, but that's manned by police drones through day and night, and they monitor closely who goes in and out. People, the Non-Submerged, who live in the slums – the police need to know their whereabouts at all times. It's prejudice really: if you're a Non-Submerged, you're a criminal, or a potential criminal. That's basically the way they look at it. There is a permanent help post outside there where any NE can seek help to leave the slums but most of them don't want to take it up or are too scared to.'

They moved closer to the steaming mountains of rubbish lining the shore, rotting at an alarming speed thanks to the decomposition vapour being routinely sprayed on the piles by hovering waste droids.

'We're looking for a waste exit pipe,' said Hannah, picking her way across the bottom slops of the rubbish, moving nearer to the dirty waves lapping against the shore. 'For the slums. They shoot out their rubbish through a big pipe, and – '

'What is this place Hannah?' Troy asked

'As the sea levels rose the land was eaten away. Tunnels and underwater spaces were built for people to live in. At the time it was feared that the ice caps would melt fully because of human beings polluting the air and we would all have to live

191

under water. It was an experimental network of underwater caverns and conduits.' Hannah continued to ferret around the piles of debris as she spoke. 'It was deemed a great success but then Emergence changed everything for us and the waters stopped advancing. The undersea city was abandoned and the NEs moved in and made it their own.'

'You should leave,' said Troy suddenly, unsettled by the fact Hannah, in her beautiful, figure-hugging silver all-in-one, was picking across used drug cylinders and rubbery bottles of cloudy spirit.

'I know I should,' said Hannah, irritated, looking at Troy over her shoulder. 'But we're in this together. Aren't we? The Submergence Program says so – we're 98.5% genetically and intellectually suited – the best match for both of us. More importantly we have been through so much together through Submergence. The point is Troy that I would do this for any Emerger as they are my family. That is the whole point of this. So we're in it together.'

'Is that really what you believe? That a program can decide who you're best suited to?'

Hannah faltered, no longer looking for the waste pipe. 'I didn't. I didn't believe it – no one does until they meet their match. And then everyone feels the same thing: the Program got it right. It's destiny. We're right together.'

'So what do you feel?'

Hannah blushed. 'I feel... I really don't know.'

Troy smiled, probably his first genuine smile since he'd woken from Submergence, and he went towards Hannah, put his arms around her and kissed her. She responded so beautifully Troy forgot momentarily where they were, the fact they were both fugitives, about to break into a dangerous zone full of subversive individuals and surrounded by filth. After a moment, they stopped kissing and gazed at each other.

'I'm happy you're with me,' said Troy, 'but I have no idea what to expect. Do you?'

'I do,' said Hannah, suddenly pulling free of his embrace and moving forward. 'Psychopaths,' she shouted over her shoulder. 'Drug addicts, genetic mutations... but look Troy, I've found it!' She stopped and pointed proudly to a dark grey ring lurking unobtrusively amongst the rubbish like a huge antique tractor tyre.

Troy reached her in five large strides. 'So what, we go down it?'

A metallic charging sound rumbled beneath them, and Troy and Hannah both quickly stepped backwards. Suddenly kilos of rubbish erupted from the pipe, shooting into the air and raining down on the waste mountain behind them.

'Now we do,' said Hannah, watching the various weights of rubbish float and plummet to the ground.

'OK,' said Troy. 'But let me go first. If it's OK and I reach the bottom, I'll call up for you.'

He could see she was about to object and so he immediately jumped into the velvet darkness before she could stop him.

Chapter Twenty-One

As Troy slid down the slimy insides of the pipe, praying another rubbish explosion wasn't imminent, the air became warmer and thicker, until it was almost impossible to breathe. Heat radiated through his legs as the friction of the pipe built up, and as he neared the bottom, he could hear and feel a drumming sound radiating through the metal.

The air changed suddenly, becoming less dense but smelling more of decay, and he landed in a bruised heap on a damp resin floor strewn with sticky rotting brown matter. He held a hand over his mouth and his nose: the smell was so awful – putrid and oddly familiar. Of course, his knowledge of real smells was limited. Technically, he'd only been smelling real odours for a few days. This smell was something he'd experienced in Submergence. He searched his memory banks, or rather the artificial programs that had been inserted into his memory banks, and found the link: the dead monkey on his trip to the Amazon rainforest nature reserve.

That trip had been a present from his parents after he'd received his higher-level examination results, and he'd asked along a girl he'd been smitten with at the time: Victoria – the girl he hadn't wanted to tell Hannah about. It was still strange to think she was nothing more than a computer program; that her existence, like everything else in Submergence, was specifically designed to teach him a lesson about something.

The two of them had met in the last year of school. Both attended single-sex establishments, but meeting in affiliated shared lessons and sharing a molecular microscope in biology. The relationship had ended abruptly when she had accepted a place at the Australasian Central Exobiology Institute. Troy had been keen to continue their relationship as she would only be a simple transport journey away, but she had been adamant that they should have a clean break. She had refused his comms thereafter and put a block on his access to her apartment block. It had hurt terribly, but he had got over it in the end. His friends had all rallied around and got him through the heartache. How many times had he heard that what didn't kill him would make him stronger? It didn't help at the time. The madness that was love, or was it lust – he still couldn't tell – controlled his waking mind. But in the end the adage was right. He was stronger. He did survive and although for years he still had emotions, which threatened to surface when he reminisced, he felt that he could learn from them.

It had been a whirlwind romance, a flurry of hormones – he'd always known that – and yet he still had a strange feeling inside when he remembered her, still felt that fondness. If reality was based on a person's memories and feelings, who was to say his past had been fake? It felt as real to him as what was happening right now.

Troy pulled himself up out of the sticky floor goo, and looked around the brown walls of the waste unit. He could see a man-sized rubber valve in one of the walls, which presumably was used to push rubbish into the unit, but no other exit. Deciding that he wouldn't call to Hannah until he'd ventured through the valve, he forced himself against the black rubber, feeling frighteningly suffocated as he pushed and shoved his way through, until eventually his head poked through the other side and he gasped not clean, but cleaner air.

Pulling himself all the way through, Troy fell onto a collection of hard metal wires running along the floor, his shoulder connecting painfully with the sharp edges. The drumming sound he'd heard in the pipe was louder now, and Troy realised it wasn't machinery working, as he'd first assumed, but music: loud nightclub-style music.

He was in a dark and dingy corridor with rounded walls and a clear ceiling panel running above him, showing the grey-green waters of the Channel swirling overhead. Along the walls, round, porthole-style doors were fitted, and music pounded from what he now realised were audio panels fitted at various points along the corridor. In addition, he could hear other sounds: clicking, whirring, clanging sounds like old-fashioned machinery being operated. The smell of pressed humanity and sweat was tangible, despite the dilapidated environmental control systems chugging away overhead.

Suddenly there were clanging noises from the waste room, and a scrambling sound.

'*Hello?*' Troy heard Hannah yell over the deafening music, and then saw her pale face poking through the rubber valve. She coughed as she breathed the overly warm air, and choked as she tried to breathe oxygen into her lungs.

'The air's not good here,' Troy told her, taking her hand and pulling her through the valve. 'I wasn't going to call you until I knew it was safe.' He looked around, strongly reminded of one of the seedier nightclubs he'd visited with friends while at university. Everything about the grimy hallway, from the thrumming music to the smell of sweat and spilt clear spirit, reminded him of the downmarket drinking and dancing venue, *Rish,* he used to visit as a student.

Troy remembered the small black cylinders passed from hand to hand in the dark corners of that club – the security drones seeming to purposely avert their sensors. And 'drum heads', touching the black containers of substance to their skins.

Some looked fearful. Others were more eager, desperate even – long-time users, anticipation printed across their visage. But most had the haunted ghostlike expressions of those deep in despair, who had only one outlet possible to fool themselves into believing their lives had worth. Troy had seen, or thought he'd seen, the long-term consequences of drug use: brain activity declining, sometimes minimally, sometimes severely and permanently. Patients terminated by their own parents after it became clear their vegetative state would last forever. He knew about the high penalties and psycho-modification sentences handed out to drug users. His thoughts were interrupted by the sound of shifting metal. He looked up to see two oval shadows lifting up from the junk metal strewn on the floor. As they rotated two red lights spun into view and locked onto them. The sentinel drones reached their operational elevation and then stopped hovering ominously. Both Hannah and Troy froze in panic.

There was another sound behind them and one of the doors in the corridor swung open. An agitated, young man, tall but hunched over as though he had stomach cramps, peered out into the hallway, looking left and right. As the door rolled open further behind him, the clicking, whirring noises got louder, and the sounds of angry, hostile voices could be heard. Troy stood in front of Hannah as the man spotted the pair, and Troy thought: *I recognise you,* as the man gritted his white teeth together, his nostrils flaring and eyes widening.

'Oi!' the man yelled over the din of the music. 'Who are you, what you doing here?' He bounced up and down slightly as he gripped the doorway, and reached down to his calf, pulling something from a holster strapped to his leg. His clothes were grey and tight across the thighs and chest, and stained all over with white powdery marks.

Troy stepped forward.

'Daryl?' said Troy, putting a hand to his ear. 'Is that you?'

'What is this?' the man replied, continuing to bounce up and down. 'Who are you? How do you know my name?'

Troy shook his head. 'I... we've met. During Submergence?'

'*What?*' Daryl shook his head. 'You met me in *what?* Sub-mer-gence?' He said the word like it disgusted him. 'If you're an Emerger, what in Unity are you doing down here? And more to the point, how would we ever have met?'

'I told you,' said Troy, hoping his voice sounded calm. 'I met you while I was Submerged. Don't ask me how – but I know you. You were younger and healthier but it was you!'

Daryl spat, but eyes remaining wild and confused.

'Who *are* you?' Daryl said again, this time holding up the object he'd removed from his calf: a projectile weapon with a smooth, silver barrel. Troy had only seen a gun once before when Jack had been shot. Behind him he heard Hannah gasp. Daryl's long fingers were draped casually around the trigger.

'OK, OK!' Troy held his hands up. 'Listen, we don't know where we are... we came in through the rubbish dump. We're looking for... *I'm* looking for answers. I'm a Code Black survivor.'

Daryl lowered the gun, stepped forward and quietly closed the door behind him, putting a finger to his lips.

'A Code Black survivor? *You* are?'

Troy nodded, and Hannah said: 'He is.'

'Weird.' Daryl let the weapon drop to his side. 'So... what do you want to know? Tell you what.' He leaned back to the door again, putting his ear against the metal surface and listening for a moment, before pulling away. 'Come with me.' At a silent command one of the drones settled back into the rubbish while the other took up a position behind them.

198

Chapter Twenty-Two

Daryl led Troy and Hannah into a stim room at the end of the corridor: the sort of room ordinarily found in a nightclub, and used by clubbers who had drunk too much and needed to sit in an acoustic neutralising field that minimised the volume of the music. The ionised air caused Hannah's hair to stand on end, and the air tasted electric, but the oxygenated atmosphere was wonderful. The room was blissfully quiet and filled with soft, although clearly well-used, seat bags and cushions – old furniture from years ago, clearly still put to good use in the slum areas.

'Sit down,' Daryl ordered, and Troy and Hannah both perched on a soft, tired-looking sofa that clearly had once been beige in colour, but was now greeny brown and slightly damp. 'You really have no idea where you are?'

'I know,' said Hannah, not meeting Daryl's eye. 'It's a black cylinder factory. I could hear the machinery… it sounds like the genetic production we do back at the Institute. And… well, where else would have a stim room?' When Troy looked at her blankly, she added: 'For the fumes. Whoever works here will need a break from the fumes, or they'll become psychotic.' She glanced at Daryl.

'You say you're a Code Black survivor. Even I know no one survives a Code Black,' said Daryl, his expression aggressive and distrustful. 'We'll see about that.'

He looked down at an old data disc in his hand, accessing it manually with stubby grimy fingers. He glanced up repeatedly spearing Troy with piercing hostile eyes.

'All right,' said Daryl eventually, when he'd read the data. 'I can't believe it, a Code Black survivor after all these years. Those Institute bastards must've wet their pants.' He let out a high-pitched laugh, his face momentarily alive. 'Oh my life, there is someone who is definitely going to want to see you.'

'We're here of our own accord so we need to be guaranteed our safety,' said Hannah suddenly, her voice frail and shaky.

Daryl smiled at her, a full smile which softened his wild eyes a little.

'Don't worry, I won't let anyone hurt you. You're *beaut*iful. Isn't she?' Daryl turned to Troy. 'She's *beaut*iful. But listen: this place –' He jabbed a thumb at the wall. 'What goes on behind there… they won't like you being here. Is she a Code Black survivor too?'

Hannah shook her head.

'You're still something special though,' he said softly.

'So who are *you?*' Hannah snapped. 'You've asked us enough questions – why don't you tell us who you are?'

Daryl looked uncomfortable. 'I don't work here – I'm just here on a pick-up. I just happened to be here when the alert came in from the drone. I was sent to check it out and I'm glad I did. Right place. Right time. Maybe my luck's changing.' He leant forward, looking at Troy. 'So what the hell are you doing here?'

'We… I want to find a Code Black survivor. The one that escaped, and –'

Troy stopped talking as Daryl laughed out loud.

'You're joking, right?' he spluttered. 'That's where you want to go – to find a Code Black survivor? *The* Code Black survivor, I should say.'

Troy nodded.

'Well, that's pretty lucky, cause that's where I was gonna take you, anyway. She will be *happeee* to see you, take it from me. She'll be happy with me too. This'll settle a debt. Come on then – here you go, my Unity,' he said, reaching towards Hannah, 'let me help you up.' Hannah reluctantly let Daryl take her hand, but pulled away as soon as she'd got to her feet.

Daryl led the two of them along a series of flat-floored corridors with rounded ceilings and walls. Along the floor, Troy noticed the remains of old electric tracks – the sort used to power freight vehicles. The silvered lines of wire were broken and corroded in many places. At each turn in the corridor, a grubby piece of red fabric with strategic holes cut into it hung down, completely blocking the path, and Daryl would peer through the holes before urging Troy and Hannah under the cloth and forward.

'Security,' Daryl explained, as they reached the fifth piece of fabric. 'Bet you haven't seen anything like this before, have you?' He addressed his comment to Hannah. 'It's not like this in Emerger land, is it? No checky checky up there – everyone trusts each other. Down here, we don't even trust our own family.'

After five minutes of twists and turns, they found themselves in a much larger tunnel than the others, at the end of which Troy could see three scruffy, overweight women lounging against the tunnel walls, projectile weapons (rather dated ones) dangling from their hands. The end of the tunnel wasn't fabric covered like the others: instead six large, triangular metal scales formed a hexagonal barrier that clearly required electronic intervention to open it. The sentinel drone behind them turned and flew away down the corridor, its antigrav motor straining sending a reverberation down the tunnel.

The three women jumped to alert at the sound and pointed guns at Daryl, Troy and Hannah as they approached. Troy tried to push Hannah behind him.

201

'All right, all right,' said Daryl, ambling forward hands empty before him.

'Who are they?' The taller of the three women, who had a fat, baby-like face that belied her angry expression, lounged back even further against the wall, her mean eyes darting back and forth between Troy and Hannah.

'There's some credits in it if you let us through,' whispered Daryl. 'Come on Tamsin, you know I'm good for it.'

The woman laughed, but the two other women, who shared similar fleshy noses and perturbing bottom lips, clearly sisters, were more interested in Daryl's suggestion. The larger of the two, whose greasy black hair was tied in a tight ponytail at the back of her head, stepped forward, her rolls of fat wobbling.

'How much?'

Tamsin turned and smacked the woman in the face with the butt of her weapon, and she fell to the floor unconscious, her stomach smacking on the damp ground. Pulling herself up tall, Tamsin waved her weapon at the third woman, who looked contemptuously at her, but made no effort to move forward.

'You know what will happen to me if I take bribes?' Tamsin said.

'No one has to find out,' said Daryl, beginning his agitated bouncing again and looking from left to right. He was about to say something else, when a sound cut him off: the sickly, wet sizzling sound of someone being hit at point-blank range with a projectile laser.

Tamsin's mouth fell open and her knees gave way under her as a dark circle of blood appeared at her stomach, the burnt edges sizzling and steaming. Behind her, the third woman held her projectile weapon pointed at Tamsin's back, the end white with heat from the laser that had just passed through it.

Troy turned to the side and vomited onto the floor, sickened to his core by what he had just witnessed. He was dimly aware of Hannah in his peripheral vision down on her hands and knees retching.

'So we have some Emergers here do we? Oh so sensitive. How sweet,' she turned her attention back to Daryl, 'How many credits are we talking about?' she asked. Now Tamsin had fallen to the ground, the woman's weapon pointed directly at Daryl.

Daryl put his hands up. 'Jumeira. Listen, we can't have trouble in here.'

'How many credits?' Jumeira asked again.

'Fifty.'

'Ha!' Jumeira held the gun up higher and took aim.

'All right, all right. I'll give you half of whatever Noir puts my way. OK?'

'And why would Noir put anything your way?'

'Because.' Daryl tried hard to control his bouncing, but only succeeded in moving his shoulders up and down instead of the souls of his feet. 'She is an Emerger pure and true but he... h*e* is a Code Black survivor.'

Jumeira's eyes widened.

'No shit!'

Daryl nodded.

'OK.' Jumeira lowered her weapon, holding it against her expansive stomach. 'Give me fifty now and I'll come with you to Noir's sector.'

'I don't have fifty on me...'

Jumeira held the projectile out again. 'Don't play around, Daryl. Just give me the credits.'

'Maybe I do... on second thoughts, I *do* have fifty spare.' His face broke into an embarrassed grin, and he pulled out his disc and synced with Jumeira's, who checked her own device carefully before deciding Daryl had indeed transferred the funds. Then she nodded replacing her weapon in its holster and held her disc out to the wall sensor.

'Open. Come on you guys.'

Troy helped Hannah back to her feet. Her eyes were full of horror and tears streamed down her cheeks. She could not take her eyes from the body crumpled on the floor.

The metal plates covering the exit ground and sprung apart with a dreadful screeching noise, and the sounds and smells of hundreds of human bodies floated around the now-open tunnel exit.

Troy stepped towards the end of the tunnel, hugging the wall as he passed Tamsin's crumpled form, and peered over the edge. Many metres below, a closely packed crowd of people barged past each other, shouting and fighting, on what appeared to be a huge landing strip lined with tunnel entrances. It was a vast space, maybe three kilometres square, and many times bigger than anything he'd seen at the Institute. If the smell and air quality was anything to go by, the whole area was very poorly ventilated with hardly any temperature regulation.

Troy looked up in wonder at the curved, transparent roof that covered the space, clearly sticky with human condensation and pollutants, and partially concealing the outline of a shuttle opening.

'This place used to be a storage facility,' Hannah whispered her voice weak, coming up beside him. Her tears had dried and her shoulders were now held back as she marshalled her inner strength, 'It was designed so water shuttles could float down with goods for storage. Then drones would take goods down the tunnels to cold storage bays. Then the businesses moved away and these people moved in like parasites.'

Swooping near to the ceiling, or hanging upside-down by their claws over tunnel entrances, were vicious looking seagulls with patchy feathers. Every few seconds, a bird would flap down into the crowd below to try and scavenge some food.

As Troy watched the crowds of people surge in and out of tunnels, shouting and shoving, he suddenly thought of his arrival at Central London Aerodrome, and how different that scene had been. Here, there was no love, no kindness. He watched people fighting for service at the various vendors, men pushing small children out of the way to force their credits on the unit holder and snatch their goods. It was obvious that this society, if you could call it that, was held together by a thread. It was a seething group of angry, distrustful people, on the verge of riot at any time. Tinged with the smell of human sweat, greasy food and damp, was the distinct aroma of cloudy spirit – the low-grade alcoholic drink that was a by-product of the clear-spirit distillation process and well-known to contain dangerous pollutants and congeners.

Hannah joined him looking down at the press of people below. 'Our socio-psychology teacher would have a field day looking at this,' whispered Hannah, and Troy turned to stare at her.

'You're talking socio-psychology when we're up to our necks?' retorted Troy.

Hannah ignored him. 'Knowing how people's minds work is incredibly important to running a civilised, ordered society. It's much easier to forgive someone if you know their motivations. It is also one of the pillars of Emergence – understanding.'

Troy felt pain as Daryl slapped a palm hard against his shoulder.

'Listen. I'm going down first,' said Daryl. 'You two in the middle. Jumeira follows. Right?' Without waiting for an answer, Daryl turned and climbed onto the rubber ladder that hung from the edge of the tunnel and descended many metres down into the swarming crowd. 'But you two had better stay close. I'm serious. Or I'll shoot you,' he said as his head disappeared.

Chapter Twenty-Three

'Keep your eyes on the ladder!' Jumeira barked, her bulk shaking the ladder back and forth.

Once they were in the crowd, Daryl gripped Troy's arm and held the barrel of his gun raised against him, and Jumeira did the same with Hannah. Hannah's clothes marked her out amongst the populace. Even his scruffy clothes which were still stiff with dried chemical cleaner were smarter than the clothes many of the people around him wore. They pushed forward, stepping over rotten food and bird excrement, Troy continually looking over his shoulder to see if Hannah was OK. She kept giving him a look as if to say, *Now do you see? Do you see why Submergence is necessary?* And truly, he was beginning to see the benefits of the Submergence system. If it could eradicate the kinds of behaviours he was seeing, maybe it wasn't such a bad thing. Perhaps the feelings Troy was experiencing, of a life robbed, weren't as bad as feeling no love for the people around you, of living in a society without hope or dignity. There was no family here. No brotherhood of shared experience. No trust. But surely there had to be a better way than manufacturing people's upbringing? Surely parents, with the correct help, could bring up children that would create a good and worthy society?

A scream rang out from their left, but no one seemed to react.

As they moved into a thinner section of the crowd, Troy and Hannah were able to walk side by side, and Hannah was clearly anxious to speak.

'Don't blame these people for how they behave,' she whispered, glancing at Jumeira behind her. 'Their parents failed them. History is full of people whose parents failed them. Society's monsters are mankind's failures. People with loving, supportive parents, with good families, plenty of credits – they're an asset to society. But our failures – those who don't have caring parents, or any parents at all, for them life will always be a struggle. Nature and nurture Troy. To hope those sorts of people become an asset, well, the odds aren't good.' Troy couldn't understand how she could recite an institute lecture at a time line this.

There were no direction signs anywhere, but Daryl and Jumeira both seemed to know where they were heading as they hurried Troy and Hannah past second-hand drone units and the putrid smell of pay-per-use toilet facilities. After a difficult, slow journey through the crowd, they reached a large tunnel entrance set far back into the wall which was barred by criss-cross white laser beams.

'Every one of these people,' Hannah whispered to Troy, as Daryl spoke into an intercom outside the laser-sealed tunnel, 'should have had the same chances we had. They deserve a perfect upbringing too. We're the lucky ones, Troy. We live with prosperity, love, hope. These people down here...' The lasers vanished suddenly, and Troy and Hannah were shoved into the low-lit tunnel, the crowd noises fading away as they walked further into the gloom. '...they just don't have a chance.' Hannah sounded on the verge of tears. 'How can anything, any business, any idea, grow down here? Without any trust or love? Where no one helps anyone except themselves? We grow because we have others, Troy.' Hannah straightened her shoulders. 'Without others we're nothing.'

Daryl snorted as they moved into the gloom of the tunnel, and smirked at Jumeira. '*Without others we're nothing,*' he repeated in a falsetto voice, and they both giggled. 'Listen.' He turned to Hannah. 'You're born alone, you die alone. When it comes down to it, we'd all save our own skin – that's just how human beings are made. Your shitty lectures won't change reality. People are just people.'

'If they don't have a loving family,' said Hannah.

Daryl rolled his eyes and he spat on the floor.

'Emergers. Think they've got the answers to everything. Try living down here for a day or two – let's see how compassionate you are at the end of it.'

A dented carrier droid scooted past them, causing Hannah to jump and Daryl to exclaim: 'Holy shit!' as it charged forward, appearing to be carrying some food items and flasks of water. 'We're nearly there,' said Daryl, pointing out a shaded patch against the wall further along, into which the droid scooted and disappeared.

'This is where the Code Black survivor is?' asked Troy, as they approached, and it became clear the dark shadow was actually a jagged entrance cut into the tunnel wall. 'Does anyone care about her down here? Is she important?'

'Yeah, 'course she's important. She got out of the system, didn't she? And now she dedicates her life to the cause. She gets a lot of respect.'

'The cause?'

'You know, blowing the whole stinking Submergence Program to pieces.'

'Why would you want to do that?' asked Hannah, clearly upset even by the thought of it.

'Why? Come off it – who'd want a life down here? We want what you've got up there. But we don't have a chance, do we? Not unless we get rid of Submergence.'

'You're all welcome to join us. We care about you all. We want to help you,' Hannah said, her voice pleading.

Daryl spat on the floor yet again, holding his weapon threateningly before him.

'If she's important, why isn't there any security?' asked Troy keen to diffuse the disputation. 'The factory had three guards – surely this woman, if she's important, wouldn't she have guards?'

Daryl's gaze left Hannah and he laughed, clutching his gun tighter.

'She's got more security than all of us put together.' He jabbed his weapon up at the ceiling.

Troy and Hannah looked up, then exchanged horrified glances. The ceiling was teeming with restrainer droids, lining the entire roof of the tunnel like giant robotic bats with grimy dangling cloth arms. Most of them looked old and battered, and had certainly seen better days, but each and every one had a red light gleaming at its centre to show it was operational and alert.

'They're B100s,' said Hannah, alarmed. 'They're illegal. You can't…. Please! It's dangerous to even be around these droids – they're unstable. They've had their programs altered. They're aggressive. They've got no fail safes.'

'I've commed through already,' said Daryl, taking an uneasy glance above him. 'I don't like walking under them either, but they won't do anything unless we mess around.'

As they reached the jagged edges of the entrance way, steam hissed and puffed out, blocking the view of what lay ahead. Someone – certainly a human and not a droid, since the job was so inexpertly done – had cut into the tunnel wall to create an offshoot: a cocoon-shaped room the size of a small public-transport shuttle. Rather than having solid walls like the tunnel they stood in, the room was made of a soft, clear substance and looked like a large balloon waving around under water.

Around the sides of the entrance, where the soft sides of the room had been improperly attached, water dripped and pooled.

The fibrous balloon itself was the strangest thing Troy had ever encountered. He could see without touching it that it was soft and billowy; it swam under the sea, its soft walls breathing in and out as the dirty water swayed around it, and it had a certain firmness. A shadowy figure was just visible in the steam. Suddenly Troy and Hannah were pushed forward into the soft cavity, the floor wobbling under their feet like a water bed.

'Security,' Daryl whispered to Troy, nodding at the woman who stood inside the floating space. 'Just play it cool.' In a louder voice he said to Jumeira: 'Do you still need to hang around, or what? Look – she's seen us.'

The woman inside the balloon, a muscular woman with long, blonde hair and thin lips, stepped forward, waving away steam and pointing a weapon at Daryl, then Troy. She held the weapon with a prosthetic arm, which Troy's medical training told him was probably a T430 or T431: a model now decades out of date with rubber skin instead of silicon and very slow internal motors.

'Lane.' Daryl held his hands up to show he wasn't armed. 'It's me.'

'She got your comm,' Lane told Daryl, her eyes darting around the group. 'Jumeira, she's not happy with you – she knows you abandoned your post.'

Jumeira went white. 'How does she... will I...?'

The woman shrugged. 'How should I know? You were stupid to leave, that's all I know. The longer it's left unguarded, the worse it'll be for you. If anything happens... if Institute Security get in...'

Jumeira went even whiter, 'Fucking IS,' she muttered as she turned to leave.

At the back of the billowy room were two dark-metal doorways with keycode locks and through the murky, green water outside the clear walls Troy could see the outline of further underwater rooms and passages tunnelling into the distance.

'What is this place?' Troy asked Daryl, pushing his foot tentatively against the floor and feeling the light wobble of water once again.

'What, this?' Daryl looked around. 'It's, you know, a secure comb. Like a passageway, but its untraceable. They can't track what goes on – them up there.' He jerked a thumb towards the undulating ceiling. ''Cause of the walls.'

'There are sound trackers along all the old storage holds,' said Lane.

'That's nonsense,' said Hannah, her voice indignant. 'They don't put *trackers* down here – that's totally paranoid. Why would we? Whenever we hold conferences with you, you all say you want to be self-policing.' She coughed and added quietly: '*And now I know why.*'

'Daryl,' Lane tapped her weapon. 'Please don't tell me you've brought an angelic *Emerger* who works for the Institute down here. What are you playing at?'

'No… listen, Lane. She's with him, and…' Daryl paused and then said: 'Oh Unity,' and put his head in his hands. 'Noir's not going to like this, is she?'

'I'll take the Emerger to the secure pen,' said Lane.

She grabbed Hannah's arm and led her towards one of the dark entrances, while Daryl held tightly to Troy, whispering: '*Leave it, leave it – just play along and it'll all turn out all right.*' Hannah tried to make herself as tall as possible, but she was still tiny in comparison to the well-built guard standing beside her. As she was taken through one of the doors at the back of the room, Troy shook himself free of Daryl and ran to her just as the door sealed tightly in front of him. He banged it in frustration until Daryl came and put a hand on his shoulder.

'Seriously. She'll be all right. But we can't take her in to see Noir – that's a bad idea. Taking an Emerger to see *the* Code Black survivor! Come off it. Emergers shouldn't even *see* this place: it's totally illegal. Who's to say she won't go right back up to the surface and have IS onto us? Listen, just play along with everything until you meet her royal highness.'

Troy had felt edgy and alert from the moment he'd landed in the underground storage hold, but now a heavy layer of nausea settled over his stomach. Logic told him that if Hannah shouldn't have seen this strange adjunct to the underwater town, they weren't going to let her go. But she hadn't seen much of it, and the Code Black survivor – Noir, or whatever her name was – didn't know about Hannah or what she'd seen. He let Daryl take his arm and guide him forwards towards the other entrance, whilst Lane typed in a code that opened the door.

Chapter Twenty-Four

As the black sheet of toughened metal rolled open, Troy took an involuntary step back: the air rushing out was humid, heavy and unpleasant smelling, like a warm cave that had been used to cook and burn meat. It was dark inside, very dark, with only low amber-coloured floor lights that cast eerie orange waves over the walls and floor, but, unlike the undulating room outside, this room felt solid, probably made of metal like the tunnels outside, Troy decided. He could make out the flashing lights of a service droid sitting dormant in one corner, but other than that everything and everyone else in the room was obscured in shadow – and there was definitely someone in the room, Troy could hear irregular, raspy breathing.

'Erm... I've got him here,' Daryl called into the blackness, clearly just as unsettled by the dark room as Troy was. Behind them, they heard the door pull closed.

'*Well.*' It was a woman's voice, not warm, but rich and intelligent. It sounded oddly familiar, and Troy struggled to think where he might have heard it before. A Submergence dream? No – it felt like *before* that, if that were possible, as though it had always been embedded in his mind, just waiting to be remembered. 'Come forward. Both of you. I'm delighted, just delighted to see you.' Troy moved tentatively to the centre of the dark room, no longer sensing Daryl beside him but feeling his hair sway slightly as he walked under an air purifier overhead. The ground was solid but uneven, as though it were made of lots of different metal sections bolted together, and moving over it in darkness amid the dim lights was extremely unsettling, especially since Troy couldn't see where the voice was coming from.

'Goodness, you look so *normal*.' The voice was nearer now, but it popped and fizzed around the room like a firecracker, leaving Troy no clearer as to its whereabouts. 'I never thought I'd see another one – yes, I can see you, don't worry – I haven't lost my senses. Let me introduce myself. I'm Noir, and you are?'

There was a pause as Troy wondered whether she was talking to him or Daryl.

'Troy,' Troy ventured. 'I'm a Code –'

'It's quite amazing how adaptable the human body is,' Noir interrupted. 'When we first built this place, I was as blind in it as you are, but now I can see clearly. To me, this room is completely illuminated. You're... yes I can see the difference now I'm looking at you more closely. You're no Emerger, but you're no NE either.'

A face leaned forward out of the darkness, pale and pointy with light eyes – Troy couldn't see what colour – and orangey brown hair similar to Yvonne Willis's but much darker. Although Troy could see the curves of the woman's cheekbones and dramatic set of her dark eyebrows, most of her face was still obscured in shadow and the image of the floating white forehead was very unsettling in the humid, shadowy room. It was a very odd experience seeing even the outline of her face. Just like her voice, it felt familiar somehow, although in a dark, ghostly way as though someone had taken a childhood memory of the fairground and painted in phantom clowns and pools of blood.

'This is a security measure.' A ghostly white hand suddenly flashed in mid-air as Noir gestured to the space around them. 'Darkness. It takes months to build up a tolerance to amnilighting. Without a tolerance, all you can see are those tiny circles of orange light you're so fixated with. But for those of us who've lived with this lighting for some time, it's as illuminating as regular light. Infrared goggles and all the clever gadgets Institute Security have are useless in here. To me, it's as bright in here as the floating passage outside. Brilliant, isn't it? It was developed by a Demerger, a physics graduate. He created it for the army soon after he Emerged, but then learned more than he should have done about the Institute and ended up joining us underwater. They don't know we have an amni-cell down here, and as long as that remains the case they have no way of infiltrating us in a hurry. Please, take a seat.'

There was a whirring sound and Troy flinched as a server drone gently touched the back of his calves. He reached behind him and felt a gel cushion resting on the drone's solid top, so tentatively sat down. Beside him, Troy heard Daryl's clothing crumple and assumed he'd taken the instruction literally and sat down on the ground.

The wall flickered and for a moment Troy thought Noir had activated some sort of lighting, but then flat colours, mildly backlit, appeared and he realised it was an AV feed being broadcast onto the wall.

'Listen, I came to you because –'

'I know why you came.' The words hung in the air for a moment, before Noir said: 'For answers. Why? Why me? Why did I survive?'

'Yes.' Troy blinked in the darkness. 'Yes, that's right. But not just –'

'I certainly have answers for you,' she said. 'When Daryl told me he was bringing you here… I can't tell you how pleased I was. We found out about you as soon as you Code Blacked, of course – the Institute likes to think it keeps its secrets, but we still have our ways of finding out what goes on. I know you were re-Submerged and Code Blacked again, and I know they introduced you to your perfect match. That's her, I take it? The girl you brought with you? What's her name?'

'Hannah.' As soon as he said the words, Troy felt like the woman had stolen something from him. He swallowed, hoping there would be nothing more asked about Hannah. Did Noir know she'd seen her security measures, or that she was being held nearby?

As if to answer his question, Noir said: 'Yes, I know Lane is guarding her. She's safe, don't worry.'

Troy felt a little relieved, but still wished Hannah was within eyeshot.

'We would have tried to steal you,' Noir continued, 'if you'd have stayed put. So imagine how pleased I was when I heard you'd made it down here all on your own.' She clapped her hands together. 'Finally! We'll be able to move forward, to progress, make some changes. Things badly need to change down here Troy – you must have seen for yourself already the poverty, the cold and damp, the drugs. Have you noticed how warm it is in here?'

'Yes,' said Troy, noticing for the first time sweat beading on his forehead.

'That's my privilege,' said Noir, 'As the Demerger Dominant. My privilege is a warm room to carry out our covert operations. Can you imagine if that were the case in Emerger London? Imagine the outcry if heat were a luxury! Anyway, I imagine the Institute talked to you about history, about how awful society was before Emergence came along.'

'Sort of,' said Troy, thinking back to Shaw's lecture about a society addicted to VR, rife with crime and social disorder. 'Hannah said something about a history refresher –'

'We have different information we show people down here,' said Noir. 'The real history behind the Institute. The story they don't tell you. History is written by the winners, isn't that what they say? The Institute omit everything they don't want people to know about them and brainwash Emergers with history refreshers that feed them only the information they choose. Information that conveniently forgets whole parts of history. But… later. There's time for that later. How many years was it?' The odd question lingered in the air, alongside the heat and strange aromas. 'Well?' Noir's voice was impatient.

'How many years was what?' asked Troy.

'Submergence. How many years?'

'I was… you mean how many years was I Submerged?'

'*Yes.*' The voice sounded tired.

'More than twenty.'

The face disappeared into shadows again. 'So it's true: we're getting worse at it. I was eighteen. Yvonne was sixteen. You were held down for much longer.'

There was a clicking sound and an AV still flashed up suddenly projected into the air in front of him, showing a frozen picture of two red-headed teenagers sitting together on an English beach. Troy's stomach tightened.

'You and… Doctor Willis?' he heard himself say, staring at the image.

'Yes. You've met my sister, haven't you? She took you to be re-Submerged, I know that much, but you Code Blacked again. I don't know what else she told you, but she's quite the expert on Code Black these days, isn't she? Works for the Institute and all the rest of it. We were two years apart in the Program. I was two years ahead of her and yet we Code Blacked within two hours of each other. Coincidence? I think not. Did she not tell you about me?' Noir's face came forward again, and for the first time Troy noticed she was wearing some sort of helmet – a helmet unnervingly similar to the one he'd been forced into during re-Submergence. He couldn't see it well, but orange light reflected off its dark surface and he could make out the outline of wires springing from its sides.

'She told me her sister was the other Code Black survivor,' Troy said slowly, trying to work out why Noir would wear such a strange device. 'She said she didn't know where you were… that nobody did. How did you know? That I was re-Submerged?'

Noir laughed. 'We know a lot about what goes on at the Institute. It's our job. If we're ever to have a free society, a *really* free society, the Institute is the key. So we make it our mission to keep on top of what goes on there. Tell me about the time you spent with my sister. I haven't seen her for a while – a few months perhaps.'

'You saw Dr Willis a few months ago?' Troy's mind was racing. 'But she said –'

'Yes, yes. She's not going to make it public, is she? Her visits here. Actually, she rarely visits in person, but we keep in touch. She's quite the do-gooder, always trying to win me round, persuade me to come back. So tell me – what happened when you met her?'

'I… yes, Dr Willis needed me for tests,' said Troy. 'They tried to re-Submerge me by force but I fought against the Program and they had to take me out. Dr Willis, she wasn't happy about any of it I don't think, using force, but… she was playing along with what the Institute wanted.'

'Watch the screen,' said Noir.

Obligingly, Troy focused on the flickering wall image which now started to move. Seeing Dr Willis again was oddly reassuring – even watching this young, skinny version of her was like seeing a family member in a crowd of strangers.

'What is this?' Troy asked. 'Some old family AV feed or something?'

'Hardly. Memories. These are my memories.'

Troy saw a white hand tap the helmet as if suggesting that's where the memories were coming from, and Troy thought the device must be some sort of neural transmitter.

As he studied the AV, he saw a young Yvonne and what he assumed to be Noir sitting on the beach within an antigrav windbreaker, its four silver anchors lying around them and projecting a strong field that rebuffed the wind and sand. Yvonne had a few adolescent spots on her cheeks and looked as serious as ever, whereas the girl beside her seemed more relaxed and healthy – happier, even. Since Troy could only see fragments of Noir's real face in the amni-cell, he took the opportunity to take a good look at this youthful, well-lit projection of her. The AV showed an attractive woman, and although he assumed Noir's hair would be greying by now, he doubted her strong jaw and high cheekbones would be much changed by age.

Behind the two girls, green-topped cliffs cut into the sea and fly-surfers attempted dangerous-looking stunts in the blue water, circled by hovering safety droids. A picnic lay on the sand between the sisters. Yvonne began tearing apart bread, layering it with salad.

Troy heard seagulls and sighs of wind, and realised sounds were being projected from somewhere behind him. Suddenly, Yvonne's voice, young and earnest, could be heard:

'How long did it take to walk from the train terminus?'

'Ten minutes,' an eighteen-year-old Noir replied, sweeping her hands across the sand. 'Don't worry – we won't miss it. Lucky the rain's cleared up – the countryside looks amazing.' As if on cue, a rainbow appeared over the green cliffs in the background and both girls stared at it.

'Our first real rainbow,' said Noir. Under the rainbow, green fields extending for miles in all directions, with only a few transporters criss-crossing silently across the sky to ruin the view. Farming drones moved methodically through the fields, tending the crops with meticulous precision and dedication, but people never thought of farming drones as eyesores: like the solar cables, they were useful, life-giving devices. 'You feel like my sister,' Noir said, turning to Yvonne and smiling. 'Even though we never met before... you know – weird, isn't it?' She picked up a handful of sand and let it fall through her fingertips. 'All that time, we were never really living. I just... I can't accept it. I know how I'm supposed to feel. I'm trying to feel it, to appreciate this wonderful society they've created for us and remember how lucky we are. The end justifies the means – that's what they keep telling me, but my heart just can't accept it.' Noir's young voice cracked. 'I feel so cheated.' She turned to the rainbow again. 'So many years. They told me I'm one of the lucky ones but – I feel like I've lost everything.'

'But it's still part of us,' said Yvonne. 'It doesn't matter what really happened, what really existed – it's about the memories you hold inside, and they're still real. No one can take that away.'

'You're starting to sound like Shaw: all pro-system,' Noir replied, shaking her head.

'Me? Come off it – I'm Code Black too, remember. I couldn't be pro-system if I tried.'

Troy felt like someone had punched him in the face.

'Is this real?' he asked, his voice sounding full and loud over the crackly AV feed conversation. Yvonne Willis, telling her sister she wasn't pro-system – it didn't seem to match up with her personality at all.

'Oh, it's real.' Noir leaned forward again and her white hand tapped the helmet. 'These are memories, my memories – I'm wearing a memory transmitter, my own invention. This is my sister and I on our last trip together. Before they forced her into re-Submergence and brainwashed her. We used to be the same – both of us wanted to live our own lives. But they got her. They got Vonny, and now she's one of them.'

There was silence, and Troy focused once more on the crackly voices from the AV feed.

'...Demergers.' It was Yvonne's voice. 'Like a stain, a smudge. I think I'll always feel it, even twenty years from now. I wish I'd never Code Blacked, but then again now I know what I know I wouldn't have it any other way. But I don't want anyone else to suffer like this.'

'You can never talk like that around them,' whispered Noir and Troy strained to hear. 'If the Institute find out, you'll be taken away. Oh, they'll treat you well enough – you'll be sick after all. Worthy of pity, but little else. They'll send you for counselling, try to work out how to fix you, pore over your cerebral engrams and try to find out how they can reprogram you to fit into the system again. Then they can fine tune the system – probably run a few tests on me to make sure I'm not headed the same way. No more rebellions – the system goes from strength to strength.'

'You've found them, haven't you?' said Yvonne. 'The Demergers.'

Her sister nodded.

'I want to meet them,' said Yvonne.

'I thought you would. They want to see you too.'

'They do?' Yvonne looked a little frightened but happy.

'Of course. We've cheated the system, haven't we? We defied all the statistics and despite the power of the Institute we survived. The fact that you've asked to meet them means more than you know. It shows you're right, mentally right.'

The images faded into snow and then a new, decidedly rainier image appeared on the wall: Yvonne and her sister walking together in Hyde Park under an umbrella canopy held by helper drones. After a few moments of walking, Yvonne's sister dismissed the drones, despite the fact it was still lightly raining, and Troy saw Yvonne was crying.

'I'm frightened,' Yvonne spluttered, tears mingling with the spray of rain on her cheeks. 'I didn't like them... they didn't seem like good people. I thought Demergers would be, would

221

be… different. But… they scared me. The people at the Institute, OK they're a bit boring, a bit rule abiding, but they seem like good people.'

'They've taken our *lives* away,' said Noir, smoothing fine drops of water into her hair, and Troy thought how different Noir sounded as a young woman: fresh, genuine and passionate. The old images didn't match this cold woman whose pale face kept appearing out of the darkness. 'It should be this way – society shouldn't take the easy option. We all have a duty. As parents, we all have a duty, don't we? To care for our children. It shouldn't be left to a system, it shouldn't. They've brainwashed us – that's wrong, isn't it? And we've all had the same lives, the same friends…'

'What's so wrong about that?' said Yvonne, shivering. 'Sarah, Jack, Suki… we all have the same best friends, the same parents… so we all understand each other. Sarah was like a sister to me and a sister to you.'

Noir shook her head. 'It's wrong Vonny. You know it is, you feel it too, I know you do.'

'Maybe they haven't got it quite right yet,' said Yvonne. 'But they told us, didn't they? Shaw said they're always altering minor details, enhancing the Program, making it as good as it can be.'

'What gives them the right to make a mockery of who we are?' Noir said, brushing raindrops from her hair and cheeks.

'They have a duty…'

'And what about Code Black? Have you forgotten it should have been fatal?'

Yvonne's face was now covered with a fine mist of water, but Troy could see the tears were still coming. 'There are always minor reactions. We were just unlucky, that's all, but if we just take the last chapters… we'll be just like everyone else. Prepared, happy. We could do so much good together. You've always been brighter than me.'

'Don't talk that way, Vonny.' The other girl took her arm. 'We're special. We've seen what other people haven't. They don't even understand us, those people at the Institute – we're an enigma. Neuro-integrative science says we should be dead. But the Demergers understand us. We have choices with them.'

'We had choice when –'

'No we *didn't*,' said Noir, pulling Yvonne under the shelter of a massive oak tree, a tremendous piece of vegetation with a great thick trunk and heavy canopy of green leaves. 'No choices in Submergence. They just made it look like choices.'

'But we were still *us*,' said Yvonne. 'Our thoughts were still ours.'

'But don't you just hate the idea of it all?' Noir insisted. 'Don't you want the old ways? Do you know what Shaw said when I asked about fate and chance?'

Yvonne shook her head.

'He told me people who liked the idea of fate and chance showed subtle traces of pathology when their neuroengrams and neurokinetic parametry were analysed. Dysfunctional Emergence Psychosociopathy Syndrome, DEPS, he called it. Or Demergers, to put it in our language. Really, he thinks all Demergers are sick.'

Yvonne gave another little shiver. 'But don't you think… if Shaw thinks Demergers are sick… it's dangerous, isn't it?'

Noir shook her head vigorously. 'Don't you see Vonny, that's what they want us to think. It's the brainwashing. Didn't you listen to what John said – the Institute lies about everything. Creates its own history and brands anyone who hasn't Emerged as potentially dangerous.'

Suddenly, sheets of rain cascaded around them and even the abundance of shiny leaves in the branches of the oak tree above couldn't protect them from the rush of water.

A drone hurriedly approached. 'Ladies, may I offer you an umbrella?'

They both shook their heads, laughing as the rain continued to pour down from the angry clouds above.

'There's nothing like real rain,' said Noir.

Chapter Twenty-Five

The images faded into black and Noir, the real one, let out a long sigh. 'How are you adjusting?' she asked, sounding very awake suddenly. 'Your eyes – they'll adjust a little, even in this short space of time.'

'Yes, I can see more,' Troy admitted, wondering why Daryl was so silent. He hadn't said a word or moved a muscle since they'd entered the amni-cell. The orangey lights were less glaring now and Troy could see a few more details around him: dust on the vinyl floor and the faint outline of what looked like transmitting equipment. Troy thought he might be in a sort of communication station: a room used to transmit digital signals around the world. 'Look... so you've met me. And I've met you. We're both Code Black survivors and I want to talk to you more, but I need to see my friend now. She's not used to this sort of thing and...'

'And you are?' The words hung in the air. 'What are you used to – you've been in Submergence your whole life. You know nothing of the real world.' The last words were spat out.

'That's why I came here,' said Troy, angry now. 'To find out more about the real world – and about you, find out why you escaped. Why you didn't want to complete your Submergence and what happened to you. *I* came here for answers, not to watch your memory feeds.'

'You do realise there's a reason I'm showing you my memories?'

'Why?'

'Because I want you to understand how the Institute operates. Everything *looks* like a choice, doesn't it? When they offered to re-Submerge you, they made it look like a choice, didn't they? You don't need to answer – I know they did. What did they tell you: your life will be ruined if you don't re-Submerge? Anyway, they don't give *anyone* a choice. They take you from infancy and mould your life the way they want it to be. They have control that way you see, no unfortunate human mishaps. Those of us who don't fit with the system, who Code Red or Code Black, well we become fatalities. Didn't you ever wonder why we're the only survivors? Why there are so few of us? They don't *want* us to live – we're too problematic.'

'But Yvonne –'

'Yvonne was plugged back into the system and reprogrammed. I gave up on her a long time ago. We were both going to join the Demergers – did you know that? I suppose she didn't tell you. Well, we were. Both of us were going to join.' Noir's voice was thoughtful. 'It didn't work out that way in the end. You wanted to know why I escaped? Is that what you said?'

'Yes, and –'

'I escaped because I found the Demergers, or rather they found me and unpicked the "truths" I'd believed my entire life. They exposed the lies the Institute had been feeding me. They would have re-Submerged me you know, the Institute, just like they wanted to do to you. But luckily the Demergers got to me in time.'

Blurry images appeared on the wall again.

'Another feed?' Troy felt anger rising. 'I need to see Hannah.'

'Just watch.'

The pictures showed a young Noir walking through the busy streets of London under towering black skyscrapers, the sun overhead making orange circles on the dark-glass windows. She looked incredibly youthful in comparison to the other people on the street, and seemed to realise it, pulling her red hair around her face, keeping her head bent down as she charged through the crowds. People smiled and stepped aside to let the young girl past, some looking confused by her hurry.

After a moment, Noir darted into a service alleyway, empty except for two drones hovering overhead cleaning windows. As soon as the young girl was hidden from the view of the main street, the drones began to float downwards until they were resting right by Noir's feet, just a few inches above the concrete floor. Nothing could have prepared Troy for what happened next: Noir stepped carefully onto the drones, a foot on each one, wobbling slightly as she found her balance, and was carried high into the air, powered by anti-gravs, until she was flying over the buildings of London. Then the feed faded to black.

'That's how I escaped,' said Noir. 'The Demergers arranged it all, of course. They have connections with the NEs. They can act as an intermediary. They heard about Yvonne and while we were still at the Institute and some months later I consented to their escape plan. I was living outside the Institute by then – still heavily monitored of course, still going in for tests on a regular basis. It was when I learned from the Demergers that the Institute was planning to forcibly re-Submerge me, that's when I escaped. I tried to warn Yvonne but... she was so scared of the Demergers. And of course it didn't help that I got myself an NE boyfriend when I left the Institute – it was enough to convince Yvonne I didn't know my own senses.'

'How did the Demergers contact you?' asked Troy.

'Thought the Ethernet... very hush, hush. We were their heroines, you know, Yvonne and I – still are. Emergers who beat the system, just like you. If the Institute had discovered any of our comms I'd have been re-Submerged instantly, but the Demergers were more organised than the Institute gave them credit for. It wasn't a light decision, but it was the right one. Free.' She said the last word rather sadly, as if it were an idea rather than a reality.

Suddenly Noir stood up and Troy involuntarily took a step back. Now his eyes were adjusting to the light, he could see parts of her face that weren't clear before. Her skin was still grey and shadowy but now he could discern the high cheekbones and rather pronounced jaw evident in the AV feed of Noir as a young girl. He could also see some sort of scar or raised skin on one of her cheeks.

'I take it Daryl didn't offer you any fuel – food, drink?'

Even the idea of food agitated Troy's stomach. *Hannah. I need to get to Hannah.*

'Don't worry about her,' said Noir, as though Troy had spoken out loud. 'And no – if you're wondering I can't read your thoughts. But I can see what's written all over your face.'

'I need to see her,' said Troy. 'I need to know –'

'If she's OK? Yes – she's OK. They've taken her to a secure pen, but she'll be fine. They're not nice places, but it won't kill her to wait while I take you to our information hold. I want to show you docustreams about the Institute – the real Institute.'

Troy was intrigued, but his urge to see Hannah was stronger. 'Let me see Hannah first... just so I can see that she's safe.'

'No,' said Noir simply. 'She's an Emerger, it'll do her good to experience life down here for a little while.'

'I really think –'

'I wouldn't make trouble, Troy,' said Noir, removing the helmet from her head. It swung in mid-air, swathed in shadows, from what appeared to be old-fashioned cables attached to the ceiling. 'Her life is cheap down here, so I suggest you play along. She's part of the Institute and the Institute likes to play God. It takes life and it destroys it. But we're every bit as powerful. We can destroy too – take a look beside you.' Noir's face moved towards Troy's at speed, bright white, pale eyes unblinking.

'Look.' Noir's voice was challenging. '*Look.*'

Troy looked around the room, but all he could see were waves and dark shadows. But then something made him focus on one particularly large dark shadow on the floor a foot or so away from him, which had the eerie shape of a body. He blinked and refocused, seeing a shadowy leg with a projectile weapon bound against it and then what appeared to be a lifeless hand. The shadow didn't move, and Troy realised with a jolt that it was Daryl, lying dead just inches away.

'As I said.' The voice was even colder now. 'We can create life and we can take it away too. It's not just the Institute that gets to play God. And if you're wondering, it was a thought that killed him. One of mine. The weak minded...' She tapped the helmet that dangled by her shoulder. 'This device is much more than a glorified memory projector. It's very powerful – a neural-disruptor. I based it on some designs I saw at the Institute, oh years ago now. I was a neuroscience grad in the Program. But there isn't time to talk about that. There are things, history documents, information... come with me.'

Troy's whole body went rigid. He couldn't believe the awfulness of what had just happened: Daryl, a living, breathing human being... gone, just like that. Killed. The fear came in waves as he began to realise Noir was psychotic, absolutely psychotic. She was talking about playing God – and her people were holding Hannah.

There was some movement in the darkness, a grinding, crunching sound, and a small rectangular panel rolled open at the back of the room revealing a dull square of grey light.

'A tunnel,' said Noir, her white hand gesturing towards the open panel. 'It's light inside but this room can't be lit – not properly at least. You could bring a pack of sun lights in here and the room wouldn't light up. Security, as I said. If Emergers wanted to come in here and rifle through our secret files or discover how we transmit information, it would take them months to adjust to the light. By then, we'd have destroyed everything. It'll be a relief for you to get in that tunnel, believe me – I remember what it was like not being able to see in here. Well, don't just stand there. Get inside.'

Reluctantly, Troy made his way across the room, arms stretched out in front of him, fingers feeling for any obstacles. He knew the dark shadow of Daryl lay somewhere nearby and felt nauseated by the idea of it, but worse was the thought of Hannah, alone and frightened, waiting for him to come back for her. As he got down on his knees, he could see bright light inside the tunnel and instinctively shielded his eyes, which watered and stung as the yellow glow hit them. Along the narrow floor ahead he could see the flat platform of a service droid, the sort used for pulling freight back and forth, and also lines of thin silver metal running far into the distance: service rails, just like the ones Troy had seen running around the black cylinder factory. The lines of metal, he noticed, were slightly bent where old brackets and pins had been – probably they'd been removed from another location and relocated here. *The best thing is to play along,* thought Troy. *Play along and do what this woman wants, she's clearly unstable.* But he knew he would get to Hannah and get them both out of here as soon as he was humanly able.

'Lie down on the floor of the tunnel,' said Noir, 'and the service droid will pull you along. I'll be right behind you.'

Chapter Twenty-Six

As the service droid came to a rattling stop at the end of the tunnel, Troy pulled himself up and out, blinking and struggling to focus as he was assaulted by bright light all around. He was standing on thick metal, covered in tiny hammer marks where it had been manually beaten flat, and was surrounded by a warren of tunnels and passageways.

'This is the Adjunct,' said a voice, and he turned to see the tall figure of Noir standing beside him, holding her elbows close to her ribcage. Under the harsh sheet lights that gripped the curved metal roof overhead, Noir's skin was a sickly pale colour and her eyes bright and feverish. Her red hair – the same natural red that was so shiny and thick on Yvonne – was dull and streaked with grey and she looked at least ten years older than her sister, although Troy realised that in reality they were nearly the same age. In short, she looked like an ill, unhappy and dishevelled version of Yvonne, loose skin hanging from her arms and face.

Seeing her in real light, with no weapons at her disposal, Troy thought he could physically overpower her if he needed to. But without knowing where Hannah was, he couldn't risk anything just yet and besides he was sure she would not be far from her secure drones. He would still have to play along.

Noir took a few stiff steps forward and into a narrow passageway with algae growing up the walls, gesturing for Troy to follow. He did, noticing various oval-shaped entrances dotted along the corridor, some covered with crumpled curtains, others sealed with battered sheets of corrugated metal.

'This one.' Noir moved towards a dirty brown curtain suspended over an entrance way on a piece of orange, plastic string and then ducked under it, grasping Troy with tight, strong fingers.

Pushing the curtain out of his face, Troy tried to make sense of what he was seeing. It looked like they had just stepped into a saloon, judging by the wooden bar running against one of the walls and bottles of cloudy spirit hung behind it, but bizarrely the rest of the room was covered with shelves of old-fashioned flexisheets – books, to use the antique term. It was like a cross between a very rundown library from the twentieth century and one of the disreputable drinking holes Troy had been warned about at university. Chairs rested upside-down or half leaning against tables and dozens of glasses (the dangerous kind that had lethal edges if broken) sat along the bar and on tables, white hoops of liquid residue clinging to their sides. A few dirty bowls rested here and there with dried layers of glutinous soup lining their bottoms. A wizened old barman leaned against the wooden bar, sipping on a glass of cloudy spirit and syrup.

'Clear spirit. Two.' Noir snapped her fingers at the barman and pulled a chair from the floor, dusting it off and sitting down. As she sat, Troy noticed for the first time what she was wearing: poly-armoured combat trousers and matching jacket. Against the black fabric, the scar on her cheek was even more pronounced and Troy noticed her mouth drooped slightly on the scarred cheek side as if some of the muscles had been damaged. Behind her, the scrawny barman unlocked a steel cabinet and removed, with great reverence, a glittering container of clear spirit, before pouring two very short measures into water-stained tumblers. He brought the glasses over to the table, bowing in an odd, jerky fashion as he set the drinks down.

'No charge, no charge,' he mumbled.

Noir took a delicate sip of clear spirit and smiled: a startling gesture that made Troy feel both disorientated and apprehensive. She looked much more human when she smiled, much more like she could be Yvonne Willis's sister, and he had to consciously remind himself of the slumped figure of Daryl lying dead in the amni-cell.

'This was the first place the Demergers took me,' Noir said, the smile fading. 'When I got out. It's an information bar. Makes sense doesn't it? Information is entertainment down here – at least, the sort of information they have in this place. The Demergers took me here and told me I was free. We didn't stay long. The Demergers are Emergers after all. Albeit flawed one, so they are never comfortable here amongst NEs. Amongst the real people.' She leaned back in her chair and watched the barman hurry towards them with two gloopy bowls of dumplings in thick white soup. He set them down and threw two pairs of chop-spoons on the table before bowing and hurrying away again.

Picking up the bowl and holding it to her lips, Noir said: 'And this is the exact same meal they gave me,' before taking a large slurp and setting the bowl down. She gave a little shudder as she swallowed the thick liquid. 'It tastes as bad now as it always did. The cause. That's what we talked about. That's what we always talk about down here, in this bar. Fighting for the cause. You're not eating?'

Troy reluctantly reached forward and took the bowl, taking a short draught of thick soup. It tasted salty and unhealthy, but the warmth was calming in the damp bar and as the liquid hit his stomach he realised how hungry he was. He reached for the chop-spoons and began forking dumplings into his mouth, which tasted equally as bland but at least the food was filling and energy giving. He hoped Hannah had been offered something – she must be starving by now.

'Do you have any idea what sort of life we live down here, Troy?' asked Noir. 'Those feeble Demergers who I once looked up to are simpering cowards. They talk against the Program but they have been through it. They hide amongst their Emerger brothers and sisters bitching behind their backs and meeting in secret. They are cared for up there and only come down here to pretend they are against the system. They have no idea what it is like to live around these people. I have no regrets, but... there are days I'd give anything to live above ground again. To see my sister.'

'But you can,' said Troy, surprised.

'No.' Noir shook her head. 'I'd never join that... that group of *slaves*. No matter how bad things got down here, and believe me they get bad. There are weeks, sometimes months, when our vitamin D lights breakdown and the tablet supplies run out. Most of the people down here have never seen real fruit – they don't even know it exists. We fight over corn and scraps of protein for the little nutrients they give us, but still the illnesses are rife: scurvy, colds, anaemia... things that were eradicated in the twenty-first century. We're sick people, Troy – that's the truth of it. Sick, unhappy and persecuted. And it has to stop.' She shouted the last word, banging her hang violently on the table. 'We go from plan to plan, but the Institute remains. Nothing is ever done.'

'But the Institute can help. The Emergers can help. They really want to help."

Noir ignored him. Reaching into her pocket she removed a black cylinder, holding the little tube of shiny plastic against her neck. She deployed it and sighed, dropping the spent container on the floor and rubbing her neck. The gesture unnerved Troy greatly, knowing what he did about black cylinders, but Noir seemed unchanged by the shot of whatever it was she'd just given herself.

'We're all on these things of course,' she said, nodding at the floor. 'It's a derivative of nerve gas – not good for you, but it numbs the edges. The NEs got me onto it straight away.' Troy watched her but didn't say anything. It was disturbing, he thought, that these people had given Noir, presumably only eighteen at the time, a black cylinder habit that she'd taken with her throughout her life. 'I wish they hadn't,' Noir continued. 'I should have remembered Uncle Jeffrey.' She laughed, an oddly musical sound considering the roughness of her voice.

Uncle Jeffrey. 'Did you... it was a lesson wasn't it?' said Troy, searching for the memory. 'Uncle Jeffrey. They designed him to stop us... to keep us away from cigarettes. Drugs.' Troy knew his uncle was only a computer program, but that didn't stop him feeling fondness for him. Jeffrey had always been the life and soul of the party, always played with Troy and his sister when they were children, went out of his way to in fact. As a child, Troy noticed, but never really registered, how much Jeffrey smoked. He always indulged his habit away from the children and outside the family home. Troy's Auntie Sally nagged him to stop, but generally she tolerated his bad habit good-heartedly enough and laughed when he quoted his knowledge of some old man who smoked sixty cigarettes a day and lived to be more than 120.

A day before Jeffrey's fortieth birthday, whilst playing in the garden with Troy and Troy's cousins, he'd coughed up a small amount of blood and laughed it off in his usual way. But soon the blood came virtually with every cough and in larger amounts, and by the end of the day Uncle Jeffrey had gone to lie down upstairs and slept right through dinner.

The next day, Uncle Jeffrey was diagnosed with Stage 4 lung cancer, effectively a death sentence. The doctors said surgery wasn't possible since the cancer had spread throughout his body, eating away at him from the inside. The tumour cells had spread into every organ including his brain. Despite all the advanced medical treatments the prognosis was poor. Chemo and nano therapy were poured into his veins, filling him with toxic chemicals, making him sick, causing his hair to fall out, prolonging his torture, extending his death throes.

It took him three months to die. Troy watched him deteriorate, watched his wife and children die with him. Maybe they didn't die in the same sense but they died all the same. All that was left were shells within a shell of a family. Of course, Troy had vowed never to smoke – just as the Submergence Program had wanted. Perhaps it had saved his life, but then again, it had taken away decades of it too.

'Listen, I don't know what it is you want to tell me about the Institute...' Troy tried to ignore the bloody mark on Noir's neck, suddenly noticing there were five or six less vivid marks next to it. 'But whatever it is, can we get it over with. I just want to get Hannah out of here.'

Noir nodded. 'Drink your spirit – it's not like up there.' She pointed to the ceiling. 'We don't have much of it underground. It's a rarity. We're lucky to have it.'

Troy picked up the glass warily, but knocked back the clear liquid in one go, feeling a warming numbness travelling down his throat. It didn't make him feel any less anxious about Hannah but it seemed to please Noir, who was watching him intently.

'So.' Noir snapped her fingers again and the barman came hurrying to the table with a pile of papers, flexisheets and docustream cassettes. 'This is a real newspaper for you.' She picked up an antique newspaper with real paper pages. 'We haven't had these since the fifties. Here. Take a look.'

Troy took the folded, yellowing paper and opened it out, reading an article on the front page with the headline: 'Europe Bans Total Submergence'.

'That's what they called it back then,' said Noir taking a sip of her drink. '"Total Submergence" – back when it was a new concept. Of course it caused uproar. Understandable really, when you consider the moral implications. After all, doesn't a baby have a right to experience real life, or at least become an adult and choose for itself whether to go into an artificial existence?'

Troy found himself nodding, scanning the newspaper article which talked about all the countries so far that had banned this 'new concept' of 'total Submergence'.

'It says here the military were experimenting with the technology over eighty years ago.' Troy checked the date. 'No, over 100 years ago.'

'Yes,' said Noir. 'It was all hush hush, but they were using the technology as far back as the twenty-first century. The military wanted to train super soldiers from birth with no fear or morals. It was the military who funded the initial Submergence trials. They pumped in the credits to develop the early stages, whilst denying all involvement of course.'

'Yvonne… at the Institute, she told me it was the gaming industry.'

Noir laughed and shook her head. 'It's one of the nice little tales the Institute tells to cover up its sordid history. Originally, Submergence was built to commit murder and violence, no matter what everyone at the Institute will tell you. After it was clear the military were funding Submergence on a mass scale, they tried to justify it, saying they could reduce the number of violent people in society by limiting violence to soldiers. There were plenty of protests, sabotage attempts – terrorist attacks on laboratories where the theory was being developed into a reality. Here.'

Noir flung another paper on the table and opened it out to show Troy pictures of protesters and rioters outside what the tagline claimed was a 'Psychodevelopment Institute'. Then she brought out another paper with the headline: 'UK's First Submergence Babies'.

'So quickly?' said Troy, noticing the date – ten years after the news about military experiments. The picture under the headline showed people bringing babies to what looked to be a scaled-down version of the Institute in London, amid a sea of protestors holding banners and pelting the adults with baby shoes and bottles.

It suddenly seemed so surreal. Troy was sitting having a relaxed sensible conversation with a woman who had moments ago committed murder. Troy tried to keep his defences up but his woman before him had changed from the monster he'd first met.

'Orphan babies were Submerged first,' continued her voice level and emotionless. 'Allegedly for their own good, but of course those at the Institute needed test subjects to prove the system worked. We think they were from Russia, those first test babies, but the information has been lost. Before they'd even turned out one healthy adult, parents were bringing their babies, believing the Institute offered a head start in life. They were paid of course – that sounds ridiculous now, when you hear of the sums parents pay to Submerge their babies. But it's true, the first Submerged babies were generally from very poor families. They were all guaranteed anonymity but some names leaked out, and they were persecuted, those first parents – sometimes there was violence. That was when society still had some sense about right and wrong. But then the Institute's public relation machine jumped at the chance to condemn the violence and justify their own existence. They were trying to eradicate violence from society, they said, so every extremist action by the protestors added weight to their argument. Here.' Noir flicked through the pile and found a flexisheet. 'This is about the first Code Black.'

'There was a national outcry,' Troy murmured, looking at the pictures of a child-sized coffin with thousands of mourners standing around it. '…Ray Mirkins, five years old… parents never forgive... tragic mistake say Institute, and a one-off... Doctor Frankenstein...'

'The Institute was dogged by problems and controversy,' said Noir, 'something they conveniently forget to tell new Emergers. But they kept their heads low, kept the babies coming in and after five years they turned out their first batch of Emergers and reintroduced them to their parents. The children were well-behaved, did well at school – the results you'd imagine. Gradually the duration was extended. If it worked for the short term why not use it for longer? Why not take the child through not just the terrible twos but even more of the risky period? They jumped from a five-year program to ten and then to over twenty years. The first Emergers left the Institute in a blur of publicity. They were obviously astounded by the media attention they received and full of praise for the system. Well who wouldn't be?' Noir gave a humourless laugh. 'They'd Emerged as celebrities. OK, they got a few death threats from the "extreme fringes", as the press began to call Submergence protestors, but it was clear they were assets to society. Wealthy, popular... the Institute disseminated as much information as possible about its first successes. Their personalities, their likes and dislikes, and more objective data: their IQs were all in the upper 1% of the population and their psychometric evaluations showed surprisingly well-adjusted individuals with PS scores higher than those previously recorded by anyone. In response to the claims of fixing, all the data was reconfirmed by independent laboratories. The Emergers all performed uniformly and consistently well, much to the delight of the pro-Emergence groups. So – a success, wouldn't you say?' Noir's voice was hypnotic. Troy couldn't help but be soothed by her. Despite himself, he was transfixed.

'Yes,' said Troy, noticing a flexisheet titled: 'Emergers Win Top Government Jobs' and a picture of a very young Professor Shaw beneath the headline.

'He was the first Emerger,' said Noir, following his eye line, 'as I'm sure you know. The Institute are very happy to talk about their successes. But did they mention the Emerger who was killed by a jealous work colleague? I doubt it – as I say, they tend to leave out the violent parts of the Institute's history. Anyway, the more money they received, the more the Institute's public relations machine was able to cover over any negative publicity and convince parents they were being selfish for not providing the perfect upbringing for their children. Figures were quoted about childhood accidents, drug taking, truancy, higher education up take. Of course the children within the Program had 100% attendance rates, had no accidents, took no drugs and uniformly went onto further education. They had no choice. What were a few selfish years with your child compared to the nine or ten decades of happiness you were giving to them after their Emergence?

'Gradually the demand grew so large that several other Institutes had to be developed throughout the country and then throughout the world. The tide turned further and those who had been brought up independently, "Non-Emergers" were gradually looked upon with emotions bordering on fear and suspicion. They were just too much of an unknown. People, even fellow NEs, felt that they had an unknown potential for violence and antisocial behaviour, a feeling propagated subtly by the often affluent and influential Emergers. Employers began rejecting them outright in favour of Emergers. Emergers should have helped NE's not destroyed them. Take a look at this.'

Noir flung a tablet to him across the table – the title of the loaded text read *22nd Century History*. Troy activated it with a touch and it jumped to a bookmark.

'A famous test case in 2103,' he read, 'lost the battle for NEs. Harold Defreitas was refused an interview without reason at a London City Investment Bank. He had all the relevant qualifications and had graduated top of his class. He had undergone all the psychometric examinations that they required and had passed all the bank's stringent requirements. Harold claimed his human rights had been violated because they had only interviewed Emergers. Defreitas' childhood was dissected and every dark life event, however minor, was played out to the media and the court. Eventually the judge (an Emerger himself) ruled that the bank had the right to only interview Emergers as they were proven to be more stable, honest and trustworthy in the long run.' Troy put the book down, hating himself for getting sucked into this show reel of information while Hannah was in a cell somewhere, but also fascinated by what he was learning. She was doing her own brainwashing. He knew that. He didn't know how real this information was, but he had to keep reading.

Noir nodded. 'It was a landmark case and put the nail in the coffin for the anti-Emergence front.'

Troy continued. 'In 2174 the Compulsory Emergence Act was passed by Prime Minister Albertson. Every child born from that day forth would be required to be enrolled into a socio-psychological development Program or else relocated to purpose-built "secure" dwellings on the outskirts of the cities and towns. Institute funding would be moved into government control, thereby ensuring safety and standards across the board. In a famous speech, Prime Minister Albertson stated that this move would ensure the survival of the country and that Britain would once more be great. He made the decision for the future of mankind.' Troy jabbed at the power off switch. 'So any parent who couldn't pay for Submergence had to relocate?'

'There were protests, but by then there were more Emergers than non-Emergers – brilliant, intelligent people with social and political power. Even the push into space was moving ahead at astounding speed, all credited to and fuelled by the energy, efficiency and intelligence of the Emergers. The first permanent station had been set up on Mars purely staffed by Emergers. NEs were a dying breed hunted by society and forced to hide. Everything written about NEs and worse *Demergers* – those who were Submerged but abandoned mainstream society in secret without the courage to leave their Emerger comforts – was spun to be condemning and fear inducing. Finished?' She nodded towards Troy's half-empty bowl of dumplings and got to her feet. 'You don't want to eat that slop anyway. I've got something else I'd like you to see.'

Chapter Twenty-Seven

They left the bar and weaved their way down passages and into a crowded, cave-like area full of noisy, angry people. In contrast to the Aerodome in London, there were plenty of children around, malnourished and miserable, hunting on the floor for scraps of food or sitting against the walls sobbing quietly and begging for credits. A woman pushed past them with a scrawny baby held to her chest, the baby's face blank, eyes listless.

As Troy followed Noir through the crowd and down yet another passageway, he decided he'd had enough. He couldn't leave Hannah for another minute – she must be petrified.

'Listen.' He stopped walking. 'I need to see Hannah. Now.'

Noir turned and stared at him. 'Patience, Troy. There's something else you need to see.' Her voice was soft, almost gentle.

'The only thing I need to see is Hannah. I'm not going any further.'

'Oh, I think you will,' said Noir, pulling a comms device from her waist. 'If you want to see Hannah again.'

Troy looked at the comms device and then at Noir, who was breathing quickly, the tinge of danger back in her eyes. Around them the silvery metal walls were clouded with patches of brown algae, like a creeping disease that threatened to swallow the tunnel completely. He understood what Noir was saying: do as I say or I give the go ahead for Hannah's execution. Whether she would do it or not, he had no idea, but there was no way he was taking the risk.

'Fine. Show me. But after that we go and see Hannah.'

'Whatever you want,' said Noir. 'You might change your mind about a lot of things when you see where I'm taking you.'

They continued down the tunnel, Noir's thickly treaded armoured boots pounding against the metallic floor, passing more holes covered with curtains or sheets of corrugated metal. One of the curtains wasn't quite drawn, and behind it Troy saw a skinny teenager with a shaved head sitting on a yellow-stained mattress, an even skinnier toddler in her arms. Black cylinders lay all over the floor and the girl had tell-tale red marks on her neck.

'Here,' Noir said, stopping by the only hole in the tunnel with a proper covering. The hole was sealed with a thin plastic door that had an electronic opening mechanism beside it, its rubber cover sprayed with tough-looking dirt. She tapped a few numbers into the old-fashioned code lock and the door rolled slowly open to reveal a vast, gloomy storage bay full of what looked like hundreds of open metal coffins. Inside the metal boxes lay a mixture of thinly shredded paper and strips of old clothing, and on top of the material were babies. Lots of babies – two or three to a box.

'Our abandoned young,' said Noir, stepping aside so Troy could see the room more clearly. 'Thousands of them.'

Troy stared. His eyes roamed the room quite automatically, sweeping over the still, bluish-skinned babies. Many of them were alive, he noticed after a moment: some breathing in a rapid, desperate way as if air were precious, and others taking raspy breaths into phlegm-filled lungs. Somehow, knowing there were living babies among the dead was worse than seeing a room full of corpses.

'How are they so quiet?' asked Troy, unable to keep the horror from his voice. 'None of them are crying. Why aren't they crying?'

'An old twentieth century painkiller,' said Noir. 'Heroin. Cheaper than black cylinders. It helps keep them sedated until the inevitable happens.'

Troy shook his head, unable to comprehend what he was seeing. 'This is barbaric. Totally, totally...' There were no words to describe the awfulness of what he was seeing.

'The Institute knows about this,' said Noir. 'They know, they know about all of it and they do nothing. They preach about a perfect society – perfect? A society that allows starvation to go on under its nose? That lets babies die by the hundred? She knows – Hannah. She knows all this goes on. But she ignores it, they all do. It's too uncomfortable for them, so they go on with their "ideal" society – ideal for anyone who can pay – and let the rest of us rot.'

Troy was speechless. From the moment of Emergence, he'd felt something was wrong with what the Institute was doing, but benevolently so, like a misguided parent thinking it was doing its best for its children. But this was... to let something like this go on just a few miles outside the city centre was unbelievable. Did Hannah know, really? He couldn't believe it, and yet... his heart beat hard against his ribcage, sending waves around his torso. What happened in this room, it couldn't be allowed to go on. And suddenly with a rush Troy realised everything he'd thought was important wasn't important at all. His adjustment issues, his quest for knowledge – all that could wait. It couldn't be true. His instinct was that this was wrong. Everything Emergers believed belied what he saw before him. They were all programmed to help people like this. How could they let it happen?

'I'll help you. I just struggle to believe they could let this happen. This isn't right...'

245

'I'll show you soon how you can help,' said Noir, with a victorious smile. 'And your friend too – she can help us. How long has she been at the Institure?'

'A year I think… maybe a year and a half.' As Troy spoke, he felt uneasy. Hannah? Helping Noir? He didn't like the idea of it somehow. But if it meant putting an end to what he was seeing, perhaps it was the only choice.

Noir frowned, creases appearing around her tired eyes. 'Not ideal. But not bad either – they'll have briefed her on security protocol at the very least.'

The stagnant room was becoming too much for Troy and he stepped back into the tunnel, rubbing his eyes and wishing he could rub the memory away too. He knew the image would appear in his nightmares for many years to come.

'Too much for you?' Noir called after him. 'This is our reality. Every day. And it has to stop. We have to stop it.'

'Just take me to Hannah,' said Troy.

When Troy and Noir arrived at the secure pen, Hannah was sitting on a hard, plastic seat wearing tight wrist bonds. Her head was bowed. A lacklustre air purifier sat next to her, leaking brown water onto the floor and blowing icy cold air that rearranged her sleek dark-brown hair into a wild mess. Lane stood over her holding a gun.

Hannah looked up when she heard the entrance mechanism and managed to dredge up just the hint of a smile when she saw Troy, then a wary glance as she noticed Noir standing in the doorway with a black cylinder dangling from her hand.

'What's going on Troy? Can we leave?'

'Noir wants to talk to you,' said Troy, his voice nearly breaking because now he saw Hannah he badly wanted to get her out of this place. She was so innocent and good – she didn't belong with these people. Surely she couldn't really know what went on down here? 'They want to talk to you and then… then they'll let you leave.' Troy turned to Noir, but she didn't say anything. He realised suddenly that she'd never said they could leave after Hannah provided information. 'That's right isn't it? Then you'll let Hannah leave?'

There was silence. Hannah started to cry and Troy went to her and held her, ignoring the threatening figure of Lane standing over them.

'They took my comms device and cloned my retinal and iris scans,' Hannah whispered. 'I thought they were going to kill me. They still might – I'm no use to them now they have all my data.'

'Listen.' Troy took Hannah's face in his hands. 'It'll all be fine, I promise.' He lowered his voice to a whisper. 'I'll get you out of here, but first we have to help them.'

Hannah nodded, looking up at him with her blue eyes frightened and tearful. 'I know,' she managed to say, but the words were choked.

'Take the prisoner to ward three,' Troy heard Noir say in an oddly detached voice, as if she were ordering food in a voice-automated restaurant. 'Troy. You'll come too. You can help us retrieve the right information from her.'

'Troy?' Hannah looked desperately from Troy to Noir and back again. 'What does she mean? What information?'

'They want to know about Institute Security,' said Troy. 'I've… it's not right what goes on down here, Hannah. The Institute knows about it and lets it happen. Are you telling me you didn't know? About the abandoned young, the babies left to die alone… the children starving…'

'What are you talking about?' Hannah sounded horrified. 'No one *starves* to death anywhere – this is the twenty-second century… do they? They don't, do they?'

'I've seen a whole room of babies, dead or dying. No one is helping them.'

'It's a lie Troy. She's lying to you. We accept everyone. NEs don't have to pay to have their children put into the Program anymore. Any NE can bring their baby to us and we will Submerge them for them. They will join our family and live with us in happiness. If the parents are caught by the NEs bringing their babies to us they are executed and the babies left to die, that is what you saw. It is...'

Noirs hand shot out, her lithe frame belying her power. She slapped Hannah in the face with a sickening bang and Hannah fell heavily to the floor.

Troy leapt forward but was held back by Lane, her arms wrapped around him in a vice-like grip.

Hannah sobbed on the floor her head in her hands.

Noir towered over her and leant down menacingly. 'You're going to tell me everything I want to know otherwise we will have further discussions.'

'I can't talk about Institute Security,' said Hannah. 'Please! I can't. It's treason.'

'You don't have a choice. You will tell me everything including about your precious IS,' said Noir airily, turning and stalking back towards the doorway. 'Troy – perhaps you can explain it to her.'

'Hannah, please.' Troy tried to squeeze her hand but she snatched it away. 'Cooperate. She's unstable, they all are. They'll hurt you.'

'They talk about change? But how are they going to do it?' Hannah stood up and shook her wrist bindings at Noir. 'By force? By violence? That's all they understand down here Troy – brute force. They don't want to live alongside us, they want to dominate, to have it all their way. Ask her Troy, ask her what she's going to do if I tell her what she wants to know. If I betray my family.'

Noir pushed another black cylinder into her neck, then dropped the container onto the floor. This time her pupils dilated and her chest began to rise and fall rapidly. She sucked in a deep breath and let it out. An image of the crumpled heap that was Daryl lying dead on the floor jumped into Troy's mind, and the vague semblance of solidarity he'd felt with Noir when he was looking at the baby room evaporated. The horror of seeing all those starving babies had made him forget to be even-handed, open-minded. What was it his Submergence father had said? *Two sides to every story.*

'What will I do? Is that the question?' Noir nodded rapidly. 'Is that the question? What will I do with knowledge of Institute Security protocol?'

Troy nodded uneasily, watching Noir twitch and blink.

'We're going to bring an explosive inside the Institute,' said Noir, 'and blow the whole building to pieces.'

'No!' Hannah shouted, struggling to free herself from the wrist restraints. 'You can't. Thousands of people work there – and the Submerged... there are so many of them. They'll all die. If they knock out the Core the repercussions will propagate through all the Institutes in the country. Everyone currently in the Program will Emerge prematurely – they'll all Code Black – they'll all die.' Hannah's eyes were pleading.

Noir looked troubled. 'The Submerged? Is that who you're worried about?'

'Of course!'

'How strange.' Noir looked quizzically at the spent black cylinder on the floor. 'Well... I suppose I haven't explained myself properly. You see, *you're* going to be the one bringing the bomb into the building. So really you should be worrying about your own safety. Explosives are dangerous.'

'What are you talking about?' Troy's voice had risen to a roar, and he held Hannah tightly. 'You won't touch her – do you hear me? Don't touch her!'

249

'What? No, there's no way…' Hannah struggled free of Troy and got to her feet. 'I'll never do that. Do you hear me? Never.'

Noir smiled sadly and shook her head. 'I'm sorry, Hannah. This isn't a request, and it's not something you have a choice about. Because… how can I put this nicely, *you'll* be the bomb. But don't worry. You'll die for a good cause. Not like all the thousands of us down here who die slowly every day. There's no other way.' Noir gave a tired sigh and nodded at Lane, who came forward and jabbed Troy with the gun, forcing him to let go of Hannah's shoulders. 'We've tried reasoning with the Institute – they won't listen. This is the only answer.'

'You've never reasoned with us!' Hannah shouted. 'Never. All the talks we've tried to host, all the placating laws… you've never responded to any of it. It's always all your way or nothing. We are prepared to help anyone who comes to us with an open heart. Let us go!'

Troy eyed Lane's projectile weapon. He knew what he was planning to do and his heart quickened as fear pounded through him. He wasn't made for such actions. His hand darted out and he made a grab for Lane's gun. She managed to pull it out of his reach, but in one swift move he took Lane's arm and tripped her to the floor. As Lane hit the ground, she aimed the projectile barrel at Troy's chest and held it there, gripping the weapon tightly in her tough, prosthetic fingers.

'Let Hannah go,' said Troy as firmly as he could manage. 'Let her go, I'm warning you…'

'Me?' Lane said from the floor, giving him a contemptuous look. 'Warn me as much as you like – it's the secure droids outside you should be worried about. Now get off me before I bury a bullet deep into your chest. I'm no peace-loving Emerger so I suggest you move now. I have no qualms about killing you!'

'Don't Troy.' Hannah was shaking her head. 'Don't try anything.'

Reluctantly Troy stood aside and Lane got to her feet. Hannah let herself be led out of the secure pen, through the floating passage and into the tunnel outside where scores of hanging secure drones roosted on the ceiling above. Troy followed as closely as he could.

'Let's go,' said Noir, bringing up the rear.

'Where? Where are you taking her?'

'Ward three,' said Noir. 'We're going to ward three. All of us – you're coming too.' And with a wave of her hand, she pulled out her comms device and whispered into it. A black cloud of secure drones descended slowly from the ceiling, their red lights going from dim to bright as they settled a half metre or so above the floor. There appeared to be hundreds of them, as far as the eye could see, and the noise was horrendous: a terrible, grinding buzzing sound like a million angry wasps. Everywhere Troy turned, the blank face of a drone greeted him with its red-light stare, woven tentacles dangling down ready to lash anyone to its shiny metal surface. *They're programmed to suffocate.* Troy looked desperately for Hannah, lost in a sea of blackness, and although he could catch glimpses of her between the drones, she kept bobbing in and out of view and before he knew it all the drones were moving around him, floating slowly forward and knocking him along with them.

Chapter Twenty-Eight

They travelled down a maze of corridors and open spaces until Troy was totally lost and disorientated. He tried to memorise the twists and turns of the tunnels, but he was distracted by the alarming sights he saw: two drum heads roasting a dead seagull over a fire of chemical boxes and tarred wood, swarms of children running around, many bow-legged and all clearly hungry and unhappy, pulling what food they could from rubbish piles, and countless adults walking in the waddling way Troy knew meant they were severely vitamin D deficient, shouting and fighting. Along every corridor, in every corner, more secure drones in various states of repair hung ominously like watchful security guards. Everywhere the tension was palpable.

After travelling for what felt like miles underground, they arrived at an empty storage bay full of medical equipment: old-fashioned manually adjusted beds, body-scanner drones and boxes of auto-syringes lay around the dusty, resin floor and torn open boxes of blankets and scrubs rested against the slightly curved walls. It was a huge chasm of a space and had clearly stored many kilos of equipment at one time. Tired-looking anti-grav strip devices still lined the walls, which once, Troy felt certain, had generated sheets of gravity across the room and held boxes and furniture in mid-air until they were ready to be used.

'I'm truly sorry about this,' said Noir, as Lane led Hannah towards one of the beds. 'Really. But it's for the greater good, as they say. Isn't that what the Institute says? Five deaths a year, five Code Blacks, but it's for the greater good? Their greater good of course – well this is for ours.' She gave a little laugh and reached into her pocket for another black cylinder. 'Down here we just have to watch and suffer. But now – finally, we can do something. Finally!' She clapped her hands together.

It was agony for Troy to watch Hannah look so terrified. He felt a terrible mixture of anger, remorse and guilt – this was *his* fault. Troy had known Noir was bordering on psychotic, he'd *known*. And yet he'd still let her convince him that she was fighting for a good cause, something worthwhile. When they'd visited Hannah in the secure pen his first thoughts hadn't been of overpowering Lane and escaping. No, he'd wanted Hannah to give Noir information. And now, with secure drones everywhere, there was no chance of breaking free. Every muscle in his body wanted to reach out and try to again snatch Lane's projectile, to shoot a path out of the slums, but he knew with so many drones around he didn't have a hope.

'We won't need to lash you to the bed, will we?' Noir asked Hannah, picking up one of the tentacles hanging from a secure droid and feeding it back and forth between her hands. 'They *can* be rather temperamental – the class twos.'

Troy gritted his teeth. 'You've got a hundred secure drones here – she's hardly going to run away, is she? Just… why are you doing this? What you're planning, the explosive, you can't really believe it's right.' Troy didn't want people to live like this, hungry, addicted and sick, but killing thousands of people could never be justified. He'd been programmed to believe in peace and to find violence repugnant. He had thought that it was wrong but he was beginning to believe that maybe the ends did actually justify the means. Sadly it left him weak in this situation where action could be required. There was no need for violence amongst the family of Emergers but here… And using

Hannah… he didn't want to think about Noir's plans for Hannah. Guilt coiled around his insides like a cold, oily snake.

Hannah lay back on the bed. 'Don't Troy. Or they'll kill you.'

'I don't care. I'd rather they did – use me, Noir. Use me as your explosive.'

'I'm afraid I'd rather not,' said Noir, sounding genuinely unhappy. 'Code Black survivors are heroes down here Troy. When the team hear that someone else has escaped, has survived – it's wonderful for morale. She on the other hand – she will have access to the secure areas and she's dispensable to us. Just like we are to her.'

'You're not dispensable to me,' Hannah protested. 'No one is. Everyone is equal. I… what are you doing?'

Lane went to a white cabinet that stood dusty and abandoned a few feet from where Hannah lay, and retrieved a piece of handheld equipment with a large blue screen. It looked just like the biomed scanners Troy had used at university, and Troy watched with great trepidation as Lane held it over Hannah's arm. He was poised for any sign of discomfort or pain on Hannah's part. If they hurt her, he didn't think he could stop himself from lashing out, secure drones or no secure drones.

'It might be low on power,' said Lane, using her rubber fingers to switch on the device.

Noir rolled her eyes. 'Power. Our eternal problem. It's not like up there with your solar cables. Down here we fight over a nearly spent battery.'

'No,' said Lane, sounding pleased. 'It's OK. There we go.' As the screen flashed to life Troy edged forward and saw the familiar biomed welcome screen appear on the device. He felt momentarily relieved: bio-scanners were, at least, not designed to cause harm.

'Yes, go ahead and look Troy,' said Noir as Lane swept the scanner over Hannah's forearm. 'You didn't know Lane was a medic, did you? Not a medic from your clever Program,' Noir glared at Hannah, 'but a real one who learnt about the human body from real humans and not Emerger clones.'

Troy watched Hannah's bones appear on the screen, her arteries and veins pulsating around them, and obscurely the names of elbow bones floated into his mind. He remembered labelling each and every one of them for his last exam, the exam he'd 'failed'. As the scanner moved downwards towards Hannah's hand, something surprising appeared on the screen. Inside Hannah's arm, between the ulna and the radius, rested a small metal object about the size and shape of a dog-tag.

Lane zoomed in on the object. It was a metallic disc pinned by two biosynthetic bolts to the tissue halfway between the bones of Hannah's forearm.

Hannah looked away, but Troy leaned in for a closer look.

'What *is* that?'

'Do you want to see yours?' Noir waved at Lane to hold the scanner over Troy's arm. Troy watched in disbelief as an identical metal disc showed up just above his wrist, nestling between muscle and bone.

'We all have them,' said Noir matter-of-factly. 'Institute issued – even for non-Emergers. The ones who live above the surface, anyway. They can't be removed. Look closer.'

Lane magnified the image so the metal disc almost filled the screen, her prosthetic fingers surprisingly fluent on the bio-scanner.

'What are they?' asked Troy, both fascinated and disturbed as he focused on the magnified disc. There were what appeared to be fine tubules emanating from the peripheries of the disc.

'You were a med,' said Noir, in mock surprise. 'Haven't you seen these before?'

'Never.'

'Of course not. These discs don't feature in the Submergence Program – the Institute has nothing to gain by

255

telling people too soon. They wait until we Emerge before they admit we're fitted with them and "explain" their purpose. Medical data, isn't that right?' The last comment was directed at Hannah.

'They look like neurotubules,' Troy ventured. Neurotubules were effectively small microfine tubes used for cannulated nerve fibres, feeding them nutrients and axoplasm to maintain neural function – effectively a life support for nerves and the nervous system.

'That's exactly what they are,' said Noir. 'They're linked to the nerves of your hand and also to the nerves around the blood vessels. If you try and remove it your hand dies. There is no way to get around it. Believe me we've tried.'

Troy stared at Lane's prosthetic arm.

'OK, back to the Emerger,' said Noir, and Lane put the scanner on Hannah's arm and pressed a few buttons.

'It's active,' Lane told Noir. 'Active!'

Noir looked relieved, but said: 'I knew it would be. These devices are transducers,' she told Troy. 'If you've been Submerged since birth, absorbed all the Institute's messages, Emerged successfully and continue to live a good Emerger life, they remain active. But if people commit a crime or a Demerger finally plucks the courage up to leave their cushy life, turn their backs on the system in other words, their security access codes are deactivated. It's virtually unheard of and to have someone from the Institute like you in the clutches of the wrong people, well... Yours will still be active, but not for long. As soon as they find out you've visited the slums you'll be too much of a liability.' She waved her arm at Troy. 'Mine was active for a year after I Code Blacked. They deactivated it when IS traced me to the slums. An NE sold information on me, so I knew it was only a matter of time. My access clearance was never as high as your pretty little girlfriend's here. I remember sitting with a couple of Demergers in the info bar holding a scanner over my arm and watching my transducer deactivate. That's when I knew I could never go back.' As if to demonstrate her status as an exile, Noir flipped yet another black cylinder from her pocket and deployed it into her neck.

'They're not trackers,' said Hannah, straining her neck to look at Noir. 'Troy, don't listen to her. They contain our medical data.'

'Yes, that's what the Institute told me too,' said Noir. 'They told my sister the same thing. But it's not true. Their real purpose is to bar those of us who've Demerged, who've chosen to live outside of Institute control, to bar us from sensitive places the Institute wants us to stay out of.' She turned to Troy. 'Anyone with a non-active transducer is prevented from entering or going anywhere near the Institute, and other key "security" areas without permission. That includes NEs – like your father. He was an NE, wasn't he?'

'How did you –'

'Let's just call it a lucky guess. All NEs, those within Institute control anyway, are implanted with an inactive transducer from birth. Anyone born without a transducer, like the children down here, well, they may as well be implanted with an inactive one – Institute security views it in exactly the same way. No transducer, no entry. So, perhaps you're beginning to see our dilemma.'

'None of you can get into the Institute,' said Troy. He didn't know who or what to believe anymore – everyone was as bad as each other. For the Institute to control people like this... it wasn't as wrong as blowing up thousands of people, but it wasn't right either.

'So.' Noir clapped her hands together. 'Let's start with the questions.' She went over to Hannah. 'The main entrance – we haven't got a hope there, I know that. Funny isn't it, in a society that trusts one another, that the Institute should be so well secured?'

'To stop terrorists!' Hannah shouted, raising her neck higher from the bed.

'They have an answer for everything, don't they?' said Noir. 'The Institute. So we won't be trying the main entrance. But there are other entrances, service entrances. Tell me Hannah, what's your role in the Emerger world?'

'Counsellor,' said Hananh, so quietly the word could barely be heard.

'Good.' The corner of Noir's mouth turned up. 'As a counsellor, you help set up the apartments for new Emergers, that's right isn't it? So you'll have a good knowledge of the delivery bays.'

'I'm not going to tell you anything.' Hannah bit her lip. 'I'd rather die.' She focused on the ceiling.

'Not possible,' said Noir. 'Living tissue is important. We've tried using corpses to trick the entrance mechanisms but the transducers are automatically de-activated when the flesh dies hence the network of neurotubules.' She spoke into her comms device and a tiny transporter drone, essentially a little cage on anti-gravs, floated out from the crowd of secure droids. In its cage were two objects: the helmet Noir had worn earlier when she killed Daryl and a thick metal hoop about the width of a fist.

She lifted the helmet with great reverence from the cage, shaking the cables that ran off it and were attached to a small, black battery pack sitting underneath. Next to the battery, the circular hoop was inanimate, resting on its side.

'You saw some of what this device could do back in the amni-cell,' said Noir, 'but I didn't explain how it works. It sends out an electromagnetic pulse that depolarizes the nerves and can target the unmyelinated nerve fibres that supply your pain sensations. In short, it can cause pain. Not pleasant at all. The human body can't tolerate much disruption without succumbing to unconsciousness, followed by a fairly rapid death. Don't

258

worry –' She put a hand up as Troy's neck muscles tightened and Lane reached for her projectile. 'It has another function too. As a neural accelerator. It can enhance my neural capabilities so they verge on telepathic. Not quite telepathic, but verging on it. At any rate, I can certainly control the thoughts and actions of a subject. This was probably my greatest invention before…' Noir's hand flew automatically to her neck, and seeing the red marks Troy didn't need her to finish the sentence. *She must have been brilliant,* he thought. *To have designed something like that. Brilliant. The black cylinders… they must have ruined her. If only she had re-Submerged and been a true Emerger she could have done so much.*

Noir shook the cables loose where they'd tangled and placed the helmet on her head, crouching slightly. The device hummed with power.

'Let me tell you something interesting,' said Noir, adjusting the device and turning to Troy. 'The neural accelerator won't work on you.'

'Why not?'

'Because your brain's too strong. Code Black. That's why I could invent this device, and that's why you'll be relatively immune to it. You need a strong mind to operate it too. Of course, theoretically others could use it, but I'm fairly certain it would fuse their brain cells after a few minutes. A strong mind Troy – that's what saved you. We pulled against the system, you and I. But her.' Noir glanced at Hannah. 'Her mind is soft and pliable. Like most people. The Program has laid down hard neurointegration pathways which leave her open to me. She has no deceit in her, her brain is an open book – the beauty of Emergence. That's why the system could cage her and trick her all the way through the Emergence Program. Hannah, tell me about the service entrances at the Institute. Help me.'

Troy looked at Hannah, expecting her to object, to shout, to put up a fight. But she lay totally still, her head resting on the bed, looking peaceful. And then she began to speak in a slow, dreamy voice.

'There's an entrance to the Institute used for removing laundry,' Hannah murmured, seeming not to register who she was talking to. 'It's completely automated – pods come back and forth all the time. The entrance is covered by sensors, but Emergers with active transducers are identified by the signature from their implants. I'm on the access list.'

'Perfect.' Noir removed the helmet and Hannah frowned and rubbed her forehead, seeming to have no recollection of what she'd just said. Placing the helmet on top of the battery, Noir picked up the silver hoop that lay in the bottom of the drone's cage and held it out to Troy. 'You've never seen one of these,' she said. 'No, no you don't need to answer. I know you haven't. We had the same programming, sorry, *upbringing,* remember? What do you think it is?'

The silver metal glittered under the harsh, white lights and Troy stared at it, confused. It didn't look like anything more than what he could see: simply a ring of metal. Noir's gestures told Troy the hoop was heavy, very heavy, so he guessed it was solid metal, rather than hollow, and perhaps made of platinum.

'It's a necklet,' Noir supplied. 'These were very fashionable a few decades ago. You won't remember them, they were before your time, but when I Emerged everyone used to wear them. Usually they project a flattering light up onto the face – but this one is a little bit different. Sit up.' She went to Hannah and held the device out to her. 'Sit up and put this on.'

Grudgingly Hannah took the necklet and lowered it over her head. It lay against her collar bones and Troy could tell by the way Hannah's skin went white under the hoop that it must be uncomfortable.

'Thank you,' said Noir with a smile and spoke into her comms device. 'Constrict and activate.'

The hoop made a whirring sound, then tightened until it was a snug band around Hannah's neck. 'The vintage fashion accessory you're wearing is, would you believe it, a micro explosive. It's now been activated.'

Troy couldn't stop himself. He leapt forward, arms outstretched ready to rip the device from Hannah's neck, but the cloth strap of a secure droid caught him. It wound around his stomach and slammed him back onto its hard body, knocking the wind out of him.

'I wouldn't tamper with the explosive if I were you,' said Noir, watching as Troy was reeled back by the cloth straps. 'Try to disconnect it and it will explode. Even if you did manage to detach it yourself – let's say by cutting her head off – now it's been activated it must be re-attached to another human host within five minutes, or it will self-detonate. And no, it can't be deactivated now, even by me. Another little security feature. Technology is amazing, isn't it?' Noir stared at Hannah in wonder. 'Ten years ago, to blow up a building like the Institute you'd need a block of explosives at least a metre wide. But these days they come packed into something so tiny. Amazing, just amazing. OK.' Noir nodded at Lane. 'It's time. Don't you think? All ready?'

'All set.' Lane held up her projectile.

'Shortly, we'll take Hannah to the Institute,' said Noir, seeming not to notice that the secure droid was tightening its hold on Troy. The restrainer strap was now pulling painfully against his stomach and ribcage and he knew if it got much tighter his ribs would fracture. 'She'll grant us access to the Institute's communication centre, where we will broadcast new docustreams, ones the public have never had access to before. Then we will detonate the explosives and destroy the Institute and more importantly the Core.'

'I won't help you.' Hannah shook her head. 'You can kill me, but I won't help you into the communication centre or send out *propaganda and lies* against the Institute.'

'That's what I thought you might say,' said Noir. 'It wouldn't be in your interests after all –'

'It's *wrong*.'

'So I have a deal for you. If you show us how to access the communication centre, we'll remove the explosives from you and take you out of the building with us before the bomb is detonated. We'll bring you back here, with us, back to Troy. The Institute will still be destroyed, that's unavoidable, but your life will be spared and you can join our new society, our free society.'

Troy knew his face must be pale – under the restraining bands his chest had begun to cave in, squashing his lungs. A searing pain on his right side told him one of his ribs was already broken.

'Override…' he managed to splutter as the restrainer grew tighter still and unbelievable pain shot through his chest. The hard metal of the droid was crushing his spine, turning him inside-out. He knew unconsciousness must be fast approaching, but through the occasional sharp shots of lucidness a thought occurred, a ray of hope. They were going to set Hannah free. If she co-operated with them, she'd be allowed to return to him and they could be together again. *The Institute, all those people… everyone will be killed.* True. *But Hannah and I will live. She'll live. We'll be together. All those people, children and babies dreaming their beautiful dreams of a beautiful childhood would die. His childhood and his family would die.*

He noticed other drones had begun to cluster around him like blank-faced vultures waiting to pick his bones. The room swam in and out of focus and the lights overhead turned orange, then red. 'Control tower,' Troy heard someone say, probably a woman, probably Noir. Then he blacked out.

Chapter Twenty-Nine

There was a loosening around his chest, Troy definitely felt it, and he could smell burning fibre. Then there was blackness again, but through the blackness were strange fragments of images: a hospital bed, people in the slum district staring at him, children running and prodding, lasers going off, a huge, round circular-steel door like the sort found on a bank safe – and grinding sounds as a code-pad was pressed and the metal circle swung open. Then softness below him and he could see a safety cabinet with underwater gear inside – pressure suits and face seals with mechanical gills on them – and a huge metal wheel being turned to seal the door. He felt antigravs pushing him upwards, up a metal tunnel with a ladder inside it. After that, blackness once more.

When Troy awoke he found himself on a lumpy bed, staring up at murky water. He blinked slowly, feeling confused but too tired to panic. He wasn't back at the Institute, he knew that much – this wasn't some sort of eerie déjà vu. Above him was a dome-shaped glass ceiling that separated him from the vast body of water swirling overhead, but there was nothing else up there, no secure droids or AV sensors. It wasn't a hospital or a psychiatric ward.

Troy tried to sit up but made the mistake of inhaling at the same time, triggering a white-hot pain like a laser cutting into the right side of his chest. He fought to stay conscious, pulling himself upright and scanning the room, forcing his breaths to remain shallow as he noticed Noir standing several metres away with her back to him. Troy couldn't see Hannah anywhere.

'Where is she?' Troy shook his head. 'Where *is* she?' His ribs throbbed. He got up and staggered towards Noir, who swung around, a creepy smile on her lips. 'Where's Hannah?'

Seeing he was about to speak again, Noir held up a hand to silence him. 'Hannah is being held securely while we assemble the group – the group that will escort her to the Institute. If she co-operates, you have nothing to worry about.'

There were waist-height counters running around the curved walls of the dome room, and the surface nearest Noir held Ethernet paraphernalia: goggles and gloves. On the wall, thinscreens buzzed with co-ordinates and a few metres away dangled Noir's neural accelerator, attached to a tall stand like the childhood measuring devices Troy remembered from school. Its cables suspended the helmet from the top of the stand and then ran all the way down to a silver battery that weighted the bottom.

Except for Noir the room was completely devoid of people and indeed, fairly devoid of objects save for the Ethernet devices and the lone hospital bed on wheels sitting incongruously under the highest point of the glass dome. As he glanced around the room and the ceiling, Troy noticed that stuck high up on the outside of the dome, ten metres or so above the hospital bed, was a curious bubble-shaped object that appeared to be empty, connected to the dome with a circle of metal. It looked like an escape hatch, and he observed it carefully.

'Ready to meet the bravest of the Demergers? These ones at least have the backbone to leave their little cosy nests,' Noir asked, and he quickly looked away from the ceiling.

'No – I… why are you doing this? You know it's not right.'

'Many of the Demergers are important people,' she said, looking at him inquisitively as though she couldn't quite believe he was arguing with her. 'Experts.'

'All I want to know is that Hannah will be kept safe.'

'As I said, if she co-operates you have nothing to worry about. But don't you want to know, Troy, more about life, your life? The Institute told me the same lies they told you: Code Black is a mystery, they have no idea why it happens. But that's not true. They tell us we have less choices, but in fact we have more.'

'What? What choices?'

'Meet the group and you'll find out.'

'I'm not interested.'

Noir ignored him, and instead picked up a pair of ethernet gloves. 'Comming the co-ords now,' she said, and digits flowed around the screen. 'Put these on.' She threw gloves and goggles at Troy and he nearly shouted in pain as he caught them. 'We're meeting them in VR. In a chat room to be precise.'

Sensing he didn't have any choice, Troy donned the Ethernet gear and entered virtual reality. Blackness followed. He was used to primary VR interfaces being a pale lemon colour, but apparently in the slum district yellow was just too cheerful. Catching a glimpse of something out of the corner of his eye, he turned to see Noir, or rather Noir's avatar – the virtual image she'd created for herself – hovering beside him. Her 'tar was a writhing, undulating cloud of red smoke with two black slit eyes sitting in its centre, the corners turned up in a self-satisfied way.

Since Troy had never registered with the system, he wasn't surprised to look down and see his own 'tar was standard issue: a blocky body made of white cylinders and cubes. It was seen as poor taste to adopt an overly realistic body image, so the majority of avatars or ''tars' Troy had seen in his virtual experiences were simple colour variants of the Ethernet standard issue. Some people chose thicker body cylinders or rounder face

265

areas, but the general look was the same – although Troy did remember one girl at school who'd designed herself a wolf-shaped 'tar with green fur. Years later she'd ended up in trouble with the police, Troy remembered, for illegally selling second-hand drones without a permit.

But never had Troy seen anything like the 'tar Noir was using. He marvelled at the programming behind it – it must have taken months to design a smoke 'tar that would look realistic in the millions of different Ethernet spaces.

The two 'tars waited in the main menu room, a black-walled cube that pulsated to unheard music, white spiral decorations twirling endlessly on the walls. In the centre was a spinning yellow box, indicating a comm message was waiting.

Noir smashed the box with a swirl of smoke and immediately the virtual yellow cardboard splintered and fell to pieces, allowing a map to float up into view.

'Touch the map,' Troy heard Noir command.

He hesitated, then touched it and immediately a door appeared.

'We go through.'

'This is the chat room?' Troy said, looking at the many tables spread across the vast space in front of them. It was nothing like the chat rooms he was used to, which were generally cosy and intimate and used for small conferences, virtual lectures or social purposes. But he supposed really a chat room was any space where multiple people could interact with anonymity and guessed it was a prudent security decision for a group meeting in the slum district, where everyone believed they were being constantly monitored by big brother upstairs.

'Wait!' Smoke shot out and blocked Troy's path. 'Security probe. We have to check it's safe. IS is everywhere.' Noir unleashed a white ball of light that whipped around the room at frightening speed, before returning to them and flashing green.

'All of these people are Emergers chatting about their perfect lives and we sit right in amongst them. Isn't it poetic?'

'OK, we're clear.'

They floated into the space, which was divided into a grid by hundreds of oval-shaped sealed booths. Inside the booths were tables and chairs, and varying numbers of avatars floating on the seats. Green lights outside indicated a chat was public and could be joined by anyone, amber meant an invite was required and red meant the chat was private. Where a red light was displayed, the walls of the booth were cloudy and no avatars could be seen inside – although the size of the booth itself indicated to a certain extent the size of the meeting. Troy was fascinated by the number of avatars on show, some very boring and conventional like the ones he remembered from Submergence, but most colourful and inventive. He spotted a few mythical creatures, including a black dragon and a griffin, and endless swirling, colourful artistic creations that must have taken hundreds of hours to Program.

'You visited several chat rooms during Submergence – your presence is logged, conversation can be recorded... all for the "public record" of course and anyway, what Emerger would mind such stringent security? They're all as honest as they come, aren't they? Nothing to hide. Not like us. Which is why we hide here. Open code. All honest and loving. Makes it easy to hide in plain sight. If we think someone might want to Demerge, then they are sent an invite.'

Noir's smoke avatar stopped between two of the booths where the gap was slightly larger than usual and made a gesture towards the floor. Immediately, a small cabin sprang up from the ground, causing all the neighbouring booths to move apart and creating a ripple that ran throughout the whole room far into the distance.

Suddenly, Troy found his avatar was in a sitting position, floating above a seat in front of a table. The familiar red chat

267

room action box appeared above his head, offering him invitation and query options, but he minimised it with a swift gesture and waited as other avatars appeared around the table. The more 'tars were arriving, the more the table expanded and its simulated look changed, from a cosy wooden kitchen table to a long study desk the shape and size of a lab bench, until finally it became a grand conference table inset with ruby-coloured leather.

The sound of chatter filled the air almost immediately and Troy heard fragments of very mundane, everyday conversation. *Strange,* he thought, as he listened to a discussion about football results. *I would have thought talk would be much more serious, given the nature of the meeting.* Even more curiously he heard Noir, whose avatar floated beside him, talking about seagull repellent. But as she was speaking, another voice, a duplicate of Noir's voice, whispered, 'Troy, *Troy.*'

Troy was thoroughly confused. 'Yes?'

'Don't speak to me directly. Don't look at my 'tar.' The voice was superimposed over Noir's chatter about bird traps and was difficult to disentangle. 'IS might be monitoring this discussion, so we're all running a "small talk" algorithm program. Our 'tars talk about nonsense while we have our private discussion over the top of them. Download the same program and let it take over your 'tar. It's coming now.'

Institute Security. If the room was being monitored, this could be the opportunity Troy had been waiting for. But how – how could he send a message to them? There was no way, with Noir beside him and he couldn't risk doing anything that might further jeopardise Hannah's safety.

A little blue globe descended above his 'tar, the standard "add-on" bubble, and Troy touched it reluctantly, knowing as the "small talk" program downloaded in a flurry of white ones and zeros that his chance to contact IS was lost for the time being. As the add-on downloaded he felt disorientated, as though he'd been sucked away from the table and then dropped back down onto it from mid-air. On his return there was silence and the resolution of the room was grainy and pixelated. In the now grey and white space, every 'tar was still, watching and waiting as Noir's red smoke swirled higher and higher into the air.

'Welcome Cell G.' Her voice was tinny, but without the distraction of "small talk" it was much easier to understand. 'This is the day of change. Change can be painful, change can cause chaos and disruption, but after change there is "new". That is what we must all remember. We Demergers and NEs alike, members of this cell, are dedicated to the "new". We know "new" is needed for us, and we'll do whatever it takes to get it. Today we've been met with a quite unexpected piece of good fortune and what I need from you is immediate mobilisation. We need to act now, right now. I'll tell you why. Today, a Code Black survivor joined us, bringing with him an Emerger – a girl whose transducer remains active and who has the security access protocols for the very Core itself.'

There was silence as the news was digested, then ten different applause programs thundered around the room. On the middle of the table, the familiar chat room 'log-out' button shook a little to represent the surge of mass approval and a thought occurred to Troy – everyone would have to log out of this room when the meeting finished. What if he were the last to go? He would have a few private, precious seconds to deliver a message to IS, provided he could somehow remove the 'small talk' program.

Of course, it was entirely possible Institute Security weren't monitoring the chat room at all; that they never monitored and talk of being 'watched' was just NE paranoia. But it was worth a try.

'Beside me is the Code Black survivor. His Submergence name is Troy, but here he may soon be another Demerger Dominant.'

To Troy's astonishment, every 'tar in the room bowed their heads or, if they didn't have a head, fell forward from their virtual seats in deference to him. He turned his virtual head away, embarrassed, and thought more about how he might deactivate the 'small talk' program. Would altering his 'tar settings help? No, they were purely visual. What about viruses? He could tell the simulator that his 'small talk' program was a virus and request that it be removed, but it would take too long, at least five minutes for the scan to take place. Then it hit him. Simple running. If he switched to simple running, all non-essential programs, 'add-ons' in other words, would be turned off. The function was a hangover from years ago when the Ethernet got congested at peak times and users needed to par down to less space-heavy 'tars to enter heavily used areas. Now, in the age of super Ethernet speeds, people rarely used it They simply enjoyed the millions of fun and business add-ons – accent simulators, dictation devices, 'tar colour washes, the list was endless – every time they went online, but they *could* all be deactivated instantaneously.

'Join us.' Noir addressed Troy, breaking his chain of thought, 'and you'll be a pioneer of a new society, a free society. You'll be a leader. I know you want change as much as we do – help the cell, help us destroy the Institute, demonstrate your willingness for change.'

Troy noticed that a few of the 'tars began to dissolve away, the table shrinking as they disappeared. It was clear that support even amongst the Demergers was fragile.

'You're talking about killing thousands of people,' said Troy. '*Thousands* of people. Innocent people.' More 'tars faded away and the table shrank further.

'The greatest changes in history,' said an earnest, male voice beside him, 'were precipitated by death on a mass scale. Sacrifice, but for our greater good.'

A murmur rippled around the room. *'For our greater good.'*

'You have nothing to go back to now,' said Noir. 'You're beyond re-Submergence. They won't risk it once they discover you've been to a restricted zone. And Hannah – what about her? She'll be exiled. Escaping with an NE – it's not something nice Emergers do. She'll be an enigma. And they don't keep enigmas in the system, surely you've realised that by now? Her life was already ruined before we got involved, Troy. Her choice, not yours.'

'Join us!' Voices erupted around the room.

Troy listened to the cries and felt... stirred. They really believed, these people, that what they were doing was right. And Noir was right, he couldn't go back now and nor could Hannah. So what choice did he have? *No.* Troy shook the seductive thoughts away. *No, no, no. This is wrong, it's all wrong.* But was it? Maybe he'd just been programmed by Submergence to believe it was wrong. Maybe this group were right... Troy knew his 'tar was flickering to indicate confusion. It was all too complex, too much to take in.

'Cell G, ready for mobilisation?' boomed Noir, silencing the clamour.

'Ready Demerger Dominant.'

'Excellent. The Emerger has been fitted with a necklet bomb. You will take her to the Heathrow Tunnel, and from there Gathin has arranged cleaning drones to carry you unseen to a service entrance at the Institute. The Emerger has already given us instructions about how we can get into the building using her transducer as a pass. If at any stage the Emerger doesn't co-operate, Gathin will retreat and detonate the explosive. We'll be able to force the Emerger close enough to the Institute to cause a lot of damage, but obviously this option isn't ideal. The ideal option is to get into the building and ensure total destruction by getting into the Core itself. Plus we can send out our communications direct. If she co-operates and we access the communication centre, the explosive will be removed and detonated separately. The Emerger will accompany the group back here. Cell G, is that clear?'

The two 'tars opposite Troy seemed to be talking but he didn't hear anything. Noir's shout reverberated through the synthetic environment, 'No! Enough. You play along or there are consequences. Clear?'

The mention of Hannah rang in Troy's mind like a low-battery siren on a taxi-pod and with sickening clarity he realised something he should have realised before: *Hannah will never co-operate. She'll die before she leads the group into the communication centre.* And then another thought occurred to him: Noir had said that the bomb would detonate if it was tampered with. He almost laughed hysterically. *Hannah can set the bomb off herself – and she will, of course she will. She'll set off the bomb before the group get anywhere near the Institute. She was a true Emerger. Surely they realised that she couldn't harm others and would do the right thing. Their plan was doomed to failure. Or maybe they could not understand selflessness and sacrifice. It was beyond them.*

Troy glanced at the 'log-out' button and hope began to evaporate. Even if he did get a message to IS – and it was a big if – how would they ever get here in time? As soon as Hannah got to the surface, she would most likely detonate the explosive. It would be the most logical thing to do: she'd be a good distance from both Central London and innocent people underwater. If only he could warn her, or somehow delay the mobilisation. Maybe IS could remove the explosive safely and Hannah's life, and the lives of thousands of people, would be spared.

'The Emerger must not be harmed unless necessary,' Noir continued. 'But if it's necessary, you know what to do. Time for mobilisation. You will immediately take the Emerger to the Heathrow Tunnel. Of course I don't have to warn you about the consequences of disobeying orders. You'll each visit the control tower before you leave to be fitted with the appropriate tag. Ready?'

'Ready.'

'Then let's go.'

Hands, paws and swirls of colour shot forward and hovered over the 'log-off' button in the centre of the table, and one by one avatars began to disappear. But Noir's 'tar remained beside Troy, swirling and rippling on the spot.

Patience, thought Troy. *Be patient.* Any uncomfortable facial gestures he pulled in the real world would be mirrored by his 'tar, so he tried to clear his mind, to appear impassive.

The last of the group reached forward and logged out, and now it was just Troy and Noir, alone. He waited, not watching her, and made the gesture that allowed him to access his settings – a gesture that meant his 'tar would temporarily disappear. It was a gamble and he knew it: if, after he'd chosen simple running, he exited his settings and Noir was still in the room, she would know his vanishing act was settings related and not a log-out. *Settings, operations, simple running.* He selected the function, waited just a moment, then exited the settings menu and found himself back in the chat room. A room which, to his relief, was now empty.

I don't have long. He sent off a message to a generic IS address. He hoped the AI could direct it appropriately.

'An NE group with Demerger help... they're planning to blow up the Institute. There's an Emerger with them.' Troy paused, knowing he'd already taken long. 'Send help to the underwater slums. Big glass dome.'

Troy's blocky white hand shot forward and hit the log-out button, and he prayed he'd been quick enough not to arouse suspicion. But just as the virtual world began to break up around him, he spotted something in the corner of the chat room. It looked like… a rainbow. A glimmering rainbow hidden against the far wall. Could it be a 'tar? If someone had heard, one of the Demergers, it was all over. They would waste no time mobilising and Hannah was as good as dead. *Please, please let it be nothing. Just a decoration or an Ethernet blip.* With a whoosh the virtual world disappeared and he found himself staring at the inside of his AV goggles, feeling light gloves on his hands.

Chapter Thirty

Ripping off the Ethernet equipment, Troy turned to see Noir, who eyed him curiously. He was aware his chest was heaving, but hoped his face was impassive. The pain came with every breath, but he used it to focus and compose himself.

'Are they taking Hannah now?' he asked, trying to keep his voice relaxed despite the constriction he felt at his throat. *Does she know what I was just doing? Has she guessed?*

'It won't be long. The group are coming here first to be fitted with regulators.' Noir sighed. 'Gathin is briefing them and finalising the arrangements, making sure everyone is aware of the consequences if they fail. The Demergers are weak. Despite their words they still deep down are Emergers who believe in their programming. The group have to be watched very carefully, monitored. Even the NEs can betray us. That's the way of things down here. If one of the group sees a way, a window of opportunity for themselves, they'll take it. We're naturally self-interested, that's how real people are. So we have to make sure there are sanctions, rules. Everyone will be fitted with a minor explosive – personal bombs you could call them – with detonators here in the control dome. Anyone who misbehaves will be exterminated.'

Troy couldn't help himself. '*That's* the loyalty your group have to each other?' Another point for Emergence.

Noir held up her chin, contempt in her eyes. 'As I said, natural people are self-interested Troy, it's a fact of life. But our actions today, we've agreed, are for *our* greater good. The greater good of this group. Just like the Institute's actions are for the greater good of *their* group.'

'Just the greater good of the group? What about everyone else – the thousands of other people here, underwater? Or in London?'

'Life will be better for us – for those of us who don't want to live the way the Institute tells us to,' said Noir, as if this were a rational explanation. 'That's the way society works. The stronger groups, the clever groups, force their will on those weaker. We've been weaker for a long time, but now the tide is changing.'

There was a buzz and a light illuminated the outline of an electronically sealed door a few feet away.

'The troops,' Noir said, using her comm to release the door mechanism and directing a squat, hovering drone into the centre of the room. With its oval sides and deep well in its centre, the drone reminded Troy of the old shoe-fitting robots that measured his feet as a child. But before he could wonder as to its purpose, the entrance opened and five men and women trooped into the control dome – two less, Troy noted, than the 'tars that had been present in the chat room at the end of their meeting. That meant that eight people had already pulled out.

'Where are Rayer and Jenna?' Noir asked.

A tall woman with a superior expression and short, clipped brown hair shook her head. 'They weren't convinced it would be in their interest. They've gone to hide amongst their Emergence family. We'll track them.' The voice Troy recognised: it had belonged to the rose 'tar.

'How incredibly stupid of them,' said Noir, ushering the woman forward. 'Left leg.'

The woman hesitated at first, then placed her leg, sheathed in black, armoured trousers, into the drone and waited. There was a clunking sound. She winced. 'Ouch.' Then she removed her leg, which was now fitted with a silver hoop similar to the one Hannah had been forced to wear, but somewhat thinner. The woman stared at the band for a good few seconds, before pulling her shoulders back and staring defiantly ahead.

'For *our* greater good,' she said.

A squat man with a bald head covered in patches of loose skin and washed-out blue eyes came forward and placed his leg quickly into the drone, clearly wanting to get the experience over with.

'You're not coming with us, oh great leader?' he said once the device was attached, his voice loaded with sarcasm. 'Safer here in the dome?'

'It's in my best interests,' said Noir with a smile.

'So it is,' he said. 'And as our leader of the new world, you'll serve our interests – the interests of the NEs and the Demergers. What about *him*? How do we know he'll serve our interests?' He inclined his head towards Troy.

'No one can know,' said Noir. 'All you can know is that, like me, he's a Code Black survivor, so the Institute is of no benefit to him. In the end, like everyone, he'll serve his own interests, whatever they are. Just like you will.'

The man nodded again.

Troy was aware his teeth were clenched. It was impossible to stand still and he found himself bouncing on the balls of his feet, the gritty black floor feeling slightly springy underfoot. Watching and waiting while the cell mobilised was unbearable. The control dome was silent, save for the gentle clicking of the tagging drone and the rustling restlessness of the Demergers and NEs, who were clearly anxious to leave for London.

'Troy.' Noir rested an unwelcome hand on his shoulder and he turned, the shiny white lines of her scarred cheek filling his vision. He thought fleetingly that whatever made those scars must have caused Noir considerable pain.

'You're part of something incredible,' Noir continued. 'A moment in history. Within hours, think how the world will have changed. Freedom.'

Hannah won't co-operate. Troy wondered how Noir could be so blind. *She won't go through with it. All you've really done is sentence her and your cell to death.*

'Where's Hannah?' he heard himself say. 'Where is she? I need to see her *now.*'

'That's not possible,' said Noir, unwinding her hand from his shoulder. 'Or necessary.'

Troy glanced up at the ceiling. There were no secure drones – he'd already examined the walls and the glass ceiling and they hid nothing. He glanced up again and noticed the curious thick, round-metal circle set into the glass ceiling, just big enough for a human to crawl through. Outside the circle, the air-filled glass bubble was solid and clear. *An escape hatch.* It was too high up to reach without antigrav assistance, but he held onto the image. Perhaps somehow, he could get Hannah up there so she could swim to freedom. *But then what?* Hope slid away as Troy remembered she'd still be wearing an explosive – an explosive Noir could detonate at any time.

As he bounced from one foot to the other, watching the last of the cell receive their leg tags, his gaze swept over Noir and he realised she had no weapon, or at least none that he could see. Her prized neural accelerator dangled from the stand near the Ethernet thinscreen, but she was several strides away from it. *I could break her neck,* he thought. *It would be easy. One arm around her throat and a quick pull backwards. With no one to lead them, the cell might demobilise. At the very least, it will buy us some time.* The thought sickened him. *Surely killing one person, for the greater good...* He took a sharp intake of breath that stung his ribs. Those words again: *for the greater good. He couldn't do it. It was against everything that he knew and had been taught. It was ingrained into his being.*

'I've had a thought,' Noir said, and Troy realised she'd finished tagging and had been standing, watching him. 'Tell me something Troy, have you ever thought about what you missed? When you Code Blacked? Did you ever think about the last chapters?'

'Hannah... I need to see –'

'Gathin.' She addressed the short, bald man. 'You're the socio-psychologist. Nature versus nurture. What do you say we test the Code Black survivor?' She turned to Troy. 'Gathin used to be an Institute programmer – intimately involved in the Submergence programming, too involved. He saw things that changed him, that changed his ability to believe in the "perfection" of Emergence. At the Institute they called it "over awareness". They decided he'd seen so much of the programming it had numbed him to his own upbringing, undone all their "good work". That was their take on it. Down here, we believe he saw enough of the programming to release him from the control it held over him. At any rate, he knows everything you could want to know about Submergence programming. So. Gathin. What do you think? A classic choice test for the Code Black survivor?'

Gathin's pale eyes slid over Troy with interest. 'It would be fascinating. Do you have a choice in mind?'

'Yes.' Noir walked a full circle around Troy, coming to face him again before she said: 'Here is your choice Troy. You can see Hannah. Right now. I can bring her to you before we take her to the Institute. You can even talk to her. Tell her whatever's on your mind. She may never come back you know. That's choice number one.'

279

Chapter Thirty-One

'I'll take it.' Troy was certain the other choice would hold no interest for him. To be able to see Hannah, just for a few moments... 'I don't care about choice two. Let me see Hannah.'

Gathin sucked his teeth and said: 'And choice number two is? Code Black survival and the last Submergence chapters? Am I right?'

'Exactly.' Noir stretched her arms out and studied Troy's face. 'Choice number two is this: Gathin explains to you all about the last Submergence chapters – the chapters you missed, exactly how they work, why you and I couldn't accept our new society, but how a few short programs can change our feelings entirely. He'll explain about your psychology – why you're better, stronger than the others. How you can use this to your advantage. Wouldn't you like to know Troy, why you survived when others didn't? Wouldn't you like to know the storylines that allowed Hannah to accept her fate? The storylines that turned my sister Yvonne from a Code Black survivor into a pawn of the system? Isn't it fascinating, don't you think, that a short program of experiences can create such an acceptance?'

Troy hesitated. The need to know the secrets of Emergence, to discover how these magical 'last chapters' made everything OK, was strong, and a few hours ago he had been desperate for this knowledge. Back at Yvonne's laboratory he would have given anything to understand, not just the last chapters of

Emergence but also why he'd Code Blacked. He'd been selfish then, only thinking about his own feelings and agenda. But spending time with Hannah, experiencing someone so selfless, so altruistic, a person who only thought of others, had opened his eyes. He understood now why Hannah would sacrifice herself. *The whole is greater than the individual* – wasn't that what his Submergence father had always said? He wanted to understand. He wanted to know what happened in the last chapters. He yearned for an end to his doubts so he could embrace his Emergence family.

'Or how about this?' Noir said, contempt dripping from her. 'How about you have the opportunity to make a difference? Option 3. Lane,' she shouted out, 'give him your gun.'

A stunned silence descended across the room. Lane, who was standing quietly against the wall, stood to attention her eyes confused. 'What?' she questioned.

Noir gave her a hard stare. 'I said give him your gun, now!'

Lane walked over and held her projectile weapon out to Troy. He looked at it keenly aware that every eye on the whole room was focused upon him. One of the figures moved forward as if to intervene, but he was halted by a raised hand from Noir. Her eyes bored into him.

'Take the gun Troy and shoot me,' Noir said.

Troy met her gaze but found it unreadable. The same contempt was there, but he would read nothing further.

'Go on Troy, reach out and take it then you can end me and end this whole business. It is for the greater good Troy.'

His hand quivered forward but he could not reach out. He tried to visualise himself grabbing the gun and firing at Noir. He could save so many lives. Noir was evil. He could do good. He was convinced that he could, but in the end he found he couldn't reach for it. It was too much. It was against everything that he believed in and against everything he was. He would be betraying everything he had learnt so far. He would be betraying his parents whether they were computer generated or not. They had given him his childhood and made him the man he was at this moment. They would be proud he had no doubt.

'You don't have long to decide,' said Noir. 'Do it Troy. Show us what you are made of. We have to mobilise very soon and this is your chance to save all of your precious Emerger family.'

He shook his head and stepped back. 'I'd like to see Hannah.'

Noir looked surprised and raised a dark eyebrow at Lane, who shrugged and re-holstered her weapon.

'Let's just be clear: you'd like to see the Emerger? Instead of learning about the last Submergence chapters, and instead of killing me?'

'Yes.'

'What do you make of that, Gathin? He doesn't fit the pattern. Another weak Emerger. Well, why not? Let's bring her here, see what happens.' Noir turned to Troy. 'We can mobilise immediately afterwards.'

Troy glanced at the hatch again. What was it – an emergency exit? A delivery hatch? Either way, there had to be something in the tower that would float up and connect with it – it was useless otherwise. He glanced down at the rubbery, dark floor below and saw... something. A table-sized, grey rectangle carved into the ground which must be, could *only* be an anti-grav platform. Troy was certain of it. He found himself reaching his foot forward and feeling one side of the grey rectangle through the sole of his shoe. The grey lines certainly had depth to them – enough depth to be a platform. But where were the controls? Feeling the eyes of the group on him he snatched his foot away. It didn't matter, he realised, if he found the controls for the platform or not – Hannah would still be wearing an explosive that the cell could detonate. He strained his ears for an IS force but heard nothing.

'Bring the Emerger to the control dome.' Noir's voice cut into his thoughts. She turned to Troy and added: 'You have three minutes to say your goodbyes, then we mobilise. Foolish choice, foolish. You've just thrown away a lifetime of knowledge.'

Troy held his breath as the door mechanism sounded and Hannah was led into the control dome. She was flanked by two secure drones, their straps floating menacingly close to her neck and torso, and she looked pale and tired, but held her head high. Her eyes were closed, but as the entrance shut behind her one of the drones stuck out a flexible rod and pressed a beige strap that was wound around her wrist. The strap fell away, attaching itself to the rod, and Hannah blinked and looked around.

Three minutes. It wasn't enough time to say goodbye. There would never be enough time.

Troy marvelled at the strong tilt of Hannah's chin and how unflinchingly she looked over the assembled mix of Demergers and NEs. She was scared, certainly, but the fear was secondary. Her determination to be strong overcame it. He went towards her and took her hands in his, feeling warmed by them. They stood, looking at each other. Neither said a word – there was nothing to say. No words could change the situation, make it better, and no words could sum up Troy's feelings for Hannah. He wasn't sure a lifetime would be enough to tell her how he felt. The moment seemed frozen in time and yet the three minutes passed within moments.

After their time elapsed, restrainer straps snapped pointedly at their backs and they stepped away from each other, letting their hands drift apart.

'I want to go with her,' said Troy. Seeing Hannah had been a mistake. The situation had been awful before, but now it was totally unbearable. To see her leave now... he couldn't watch and wait while it happened. 'I want to go to the Institute.'

Maybe there was a way, if he stayed with her, that he could save her, remove the explosive and detonate himself instead.

'Not possible,' said Noir, looking absently at her flashing comms device. She paused, then brought the shiny pebble closer to her face. 'It's not... that won't be...' She shook her comms device as though it were broken and then looked at it again. 'Gathin,' she said, her voice suddenly unsteady. 'Take the others in the cell... please take them down to the service tunnels and wait with them there.'

'But we need to mobilise,' said Gathin. '*Now*. We need to capitalise on this –'

'Yes, yes I know. But there's been... I have a visitor. I need to speak with the visitor first.'

With a curt nod that indicated extreme disapproval, Gathin turned towards the entrance and the rest of the cell followed. 'Be careful,' Gathin said over his shoulder as the group passed through the mechanical door. 'Don't take long or we won't be back.' The door closed tightly, and Troy could hear the group tramping over metal behind it.

An eerie silence followed, during which Noir stared in bewilderment at Troy and Hannah as if she had no idea why they were there.

'Wait,' Noir said. 'We need to wait.' She hunted in her pockets for black cylinders and found none, which seemed to unsettle her even further. Then she looked at her comms device. 'It's clear,' she whispered into the little moulded oval. Another pause, then the sounds of footsteps outside the control tower.

'*Open,*' Noir said, again her voice shaky, and slowly, the tower entrance rolled to one side revealing a person – a woman.

'Not possible,' Hannah breathed, taking a step towards Troy.

The woman was tall and healthily built, her shiny red hair glinting in the dim, blue lights that were arranged around the tunnel behind her.

Troy stared, all thoughts of IS forgotten.

'But... how did you... what are you doing here?' he said, although there were many more important questions he wanted to ask.

The woman managed a half smile when she saw Troy, but it quickly fell away as her gaze shifted to Noir.

'Hello Anya,' said the woman.

'I've asked you before,' Noir replied, 'not to use my Submergence name. My name is Noir.'

'*Yvonne.*' Troy couldn't believe what he was seeing.

Yvonne Willis walked calmly into the control dome, the door whizzing closed behind her.

'What are you doing here?' said Noir, hands delving into her pockets. 'I told you to comm me before... if you ever...'

But Yvonne wasn't paying any attention. '*Troy.*' Her kind face crumpled. 'Thank goodness you're OK. And Hannah... what are you doing here? Don't answer – I know. You're his perfect match. I think I can work it out for myself. We thought – oh Troy, we thought you'd been killed, blown to pieces. I can't tell you what a relief it was to hear you were... well, not OK, of course, but *alive.*'

'Wait.' Noir's cheek began to twitch. 'You knew he was here. How did you know?'

Yvonne turned to her sister and looked her over, from her bony, muscular legs to her pale, creased face. 'What's *happening* to you?' She swallowed hard. 'What happened? Have you been sick? You look ten years older.'

Noir flinched, pulling herself tall. 'Twenty years underground will do that to a person. Not all of us have access to sunshine all day, every day.'

'No,' said Yvonne, scrutinising Noir's face. 'It's more than that. Those red marks...'

Noir shrugged and looked away.

'Anya,' Yvonne said softly. 'I wish… if only you'd let me help you.'

'If only you'd let me help *you*. Just tell me, how did you know he was here?'

'I was in the chat room this afternoon,' said Yvonne.

Noir went whiter than ever and the twitch in her cheek doubled its speed. 'You… that was a private session. A private military session.'

'I wasn't spying,' said Yvonne. 'My sensors told me you were in the room – they didn't tell me anyone else was there. I didn't see anyone else there, as a matter of fact, not even you. The only 'tar I saw was Troy's.'

Troy felt his mouth go dry. 'You keep in contact,' he said. 'You.' He pointed to Yvonne. 'You knew your sister was down here the whole time. You're in contact with her. But you said you had no idea –'

'Yes,' said Yvonne, 'Anya and I have kept in touch since she left London. I couldn't risk telling you – all our sessions were recorded. And anyway, what different does it make? I never had any intention for the two of you to meet. I knew it would be disastrous.'

'On the contrary,' said Noir. 'Troy's presence has allowed our military campaign to move forward for the first time in decades.'

'The rainbow,' said Troy. 'You were the rainbow – in the chatroom.'

Yvonne gave a delicate little cough, clearly embarrassed. 'Yes. My 'tar here, a covert one. It's a little more inventive than the one I use back in London, but I felt it was fitting. We've been meeting in secret for years, Anya and I. I find her co-ords and then trace her and stay covert in the room. We use a similar covert chat program to the one she and her disillusioned conspirators like to play around with. Lucky, I suppose. If we hadn't kept in touch I would never have traced you here.'

'Doctor Willis,' said Hannah. 'Please, you have to help.' Her hands went to the explosive around her neck. 'They want to blow up the Institute. Thousands of people.'

Yvonne nodded and said: 'That's why I came.' She turned to her sister. 'Please, Anya. Please. This isn't who you are. You can't go through with this. Remove the explosive.'

'I can remove it, but it can't be deactivated,' said Noir, approaching the tagging drone that sat redundant in the middle of the control dome and giving it a hard kick. It squeaked and hurried underneath a counter. 'Not by me, not by anybody. If it's taken from its host, it will explode within minutes unless... it can, of course, be placed on another host. Would you like to volunteer?'

Yvonne shook her head, but not in answer to Noir's question. 'Dear, dear dear,' she said. 'Such a shame. How could things have come to this?'

'The Institute must be stopped.' Noir's eyes flicked from Yvonne to Hannah. A sweat had broken out on her forehead and she looked feverish. 'You haven't seen what it's like for us –'

'I *have* seen,' said Yvonne. 'I've seen it all, everything that goes on in the slums. They know it all, Anya. They've known for years what goes on down here. I'm part of Demerger monitoring – the touchy feely side. We're working to make it better. We are open and want to help but you suppress your people. We're brought up to care, you know that.'

For a moment, Noir was completely silent. Then her cheeks lifted into a venomous smile.

'*You*. My own sister. Traitor.' She waved her hand dismissively. 'None of it matters. You don't matter anymore. The only thing that matters is removing the Institute.'

'And then what?' Yvonne was still speaking softly, even though her face was flushed. 'We will rebuild.'

Noir laughed in an odd, screechy way that sounded like a bird. 'We're targeting the London Institute for one reason and

287

one reason only: it houses the UK's Submergence programming and communication centre. You know what it is Vonny. You underestimate what we know.' Noir snatched her comms device and pointed it towards the thinscreen on the wall. Rows and rows of black-glass cabinets appeared on the screen, inside of which the occasional glow of positronic transference interfaces fluttered like fireflies. 'Let me explain it to your young protégé here. Can you guess what we're looking at, Troy? The computerised brain of the Submergence Program. This is it. Your precious Core generates material for every Institute across the country. Each section is capable of trillions of calculations per millisecond. Integrated as they are, together they represent more computer power than is required to run the whole of the slum district. Quite literally the computerised core – the hub that runs and regulates the key Submergence Program. Several sub processors handle the precise neurointegration process, but without the core they would all fail. Of course, there are many safeguards and backup systems for this core program, but everything can be overrode with a simple explosion. Clever, isn't it?'

Noir pointed to a dark section in one of the cabinets on the projection. 'You see that section there? That's where the psycho-development personnel come to add or modify the Program. Only after intensive study of the neuro-parameters of subjects within the Program, though. Once this has been carried, data is integrated with the Post-Emergence psychometric tests and scientists and technicians are able to modify the Program. Add a section here, remove one from there. Place a bit more emphasis on a certain event or even add in new characters to introduce more personality traits. A slightly imprecise science, wouldn't you agree Yvonne?' Noir turned to smile at her. 'But it results in the "enhancement" of the total effect and a "better" quality of result. That's the intent anyway. Yvonne and I know firsthand that it doesn't always work out like that. Impressed with my level of understanding Vonny? Anything I got wrong?'

'Very clever,' Yvonne said slowly, watching the giant computerised mass on the wall. 'A pat on the back for you, well done, you've worked out how the Program is put together. And how to destroy it. I presume from your enlightenment that Gathin has found a new home with you?'

'In less than an hour's time it's going to be totally obliterated.' Noir pointed at Hannah. 'She'll be used to access the Institute and blow up the core processor.'

Yvonne stared at Hannah's neck, where the necklet had made red curves around her collarbone.

'Anya, no. Please. Please see reason. She's innocent. Everyone at the Institute is innocent.'

'You've been brainwashed, Yvonne,' said Noir, ending the projection and slipping the comms device back onto her waistband. 'The Institute have –'

'This has gone far enough.' Yvonne interrupted. 'Noir, you have to remove the explosive from this girl – please. Innocent people will be killed, you never wanted that. I know you, I know that's not what you want.'

'It's not possible, Vonny.' Noir shook her head sadly. 'I'm sorry. It's not possible now. The explosive can't be deactivated. It's… for our greater good. We have to go ahead with the plan, for the greater good, *our* greater good.'

'Take me somewhere,' said Hannah, 'far away from everyone, and I'll detonate the explosive. That way, no one will be harmed.'

'No!' Troy's voice boomed around the control dome. 'Remove the explosive from her and put it on me. If anyone is to make a sacrifice, I should be the one.'

'You're a true son of Emergence already Troy, I'm proud,' said Yvonne with a smile.

'No, Troy.' Hannah put a hand on his arm. 'You don't need to do that. Really.'

'Noir.' Troy shook Hannah's arm away. 'None of this is her fault, it was me… I brought her here, this is nothing to do with her.'

Yvonne smiled in a sad sort of way. 'Don't Troy. You don't understand – you've got so much more to learn, about yourself and… your *family*.'

'I don't care about that anymore,' said Troy. 'I don't care about any of it.'

'I think you will care.' Yvonne looked up to the ceiling as if asking for divine inspiration, but finding none, she rubbed her forehead and said: 'Look, I'm just going to have to come out with it. Your mother, Troy. She's here.'

'Here? What does that mean? Here, where?'

'*Here.*' Yvonne rubbed her forehead harder. 'Right here in this room.'

Chapter Thirty-Two

Troy stared at Yvonne, thinking that perhaps like Noir she'd now lost her mind.

'What are you talking about?'

'You're my nephew,' Yvonne told Troy. 'Which means Anya, yes.' She turned to Noir and nodded. 'He is. Troy is your son – the baby you put into Submergence more than twenty years ago.'

'Don't you *dare*,' said Noir, her face contorting, 'don't you *dare* talk about my son. They killed him. The Institute killed him.'

'He didn't die,' said Yvonne. 'It was Code Red, they told you that at the time. Tom believed us, why didn't you? Troy, Noir… *Anya* is your mother.'

Troy felt ice close around his stomach. 'I don't… she isn't.'

'It's true,' said Yvonne. 'I'm your aunt. I've been watching you since birth. Looking out for you, making sure you were taken care of. Of course the Institute takes excellent care of all its babies, but –'

'The *Institute* stole my child!' Noir shouted. 'He was killed – they killed him at birth.'

'No. That's not what happened. Troy went Code Red the moment he was placed in Submergence – that's true. And you heard the sirens, saw the lights flashing and assumed the worst. But no infant has ever gone Code Black – you know that, you saw the statistics. Code Red isn't uncommon for newborns, and we have ways of dealing with it. You knew that, you were informed.'

'I should never have given him up. He... he died. My baby.'

'No,' said Yvonne again. 'He didn't die. He grew into a fine young man.'

'It was so long ago,' said Noir faintly, looking at the floor. 'So long... Vonny, is it true? You wouldn't... it would be so cruel to make something like this up.'

'It's true. All those years... all those Code Reds... I'd spend my lunch breaks watching Troy's vital signs, waiting for the next one, knowing it was coming. But it was strange – when he went Code Black I somehow knew he'd pull through. Don't ask me how, but I knew it. I knew he'd be a survivor like us.'

'Genetics,' Noir murmured, and some of the malice had left her voice. 'My theory from the start, remember?' Her eyes were transfixed on Troy.

'Tom used to come and watch over Troy with me sometimes,' said Yvonne. 'Less so towards the end – I think it was too painful. Mac, he's called Mac now – his old name. No more NE activism, he's just a plain old worker getting on with his job.'

'Yes.' Noir tilted her head and smiled, as if reliving some old memory. 'We all did it back then, didn't we? Renamed ourselves. Took ourselves out of the hands of the system, took control back.' She laughed. 'He wasn't even an Emerger, *he* had normal parents. We were strong back then: NE until we die. Whatever happened?'

'We came to our senses,' said Yvonne, 'and grew up. And you came here.'

As Noir turned to the light, Troy noticed once again the scarred mark on her cheek. He thought of the pictures Mac had showed him of his mother. She'd had a tattoo, a pink tiger photo-imaged on her cheek.

'I saw a photo,' said Troy. 'My mother had a photo image on her cheek...' He watched the scar ripple under the light and suddenly he saw Noir's features in a different way. Under the craggy skin and tired eyes, he saw a young woman on a polar expedition with her husband.

'Anya had that image created to mark your birth,' said Yvonne. 'I remember trying to talk her out of it. It was for Tom as much as her – she wanted to commemorate their achievement, a baby, together. She cut it out when your father gave IS her whereabouts. With a laser, that's right isn't it Anya?'

Troy felt like he'd been hit by a garbage pod. It was too much, all too much. To find out your parents weren't real, and then to discover your mother... your real *mother* was...another level of deception.

'Troy, you have to understand,' Yvonne begged.

'I don't have to understand anything,' said Troy. 'Nothing makes sense. How can she be... it just can't be true. None of it matters anyway. All that matters is that I get rid of the explosive without hurting anyone.'

Hannah nodded, her face surprisingly composed and focused.

'You're staying here,' said Noir. 'You *must* stay here. Please.' She started to cry, a strange choking, strangulated noise that sounded like it had waited years to come out.

'Anya...' Troy shook his head, struggling to speak. 'Mother.' The word echoed around the control dome like a clanging bell, slightly off tune but settling to the right note somehow. In an odd way, he felt Noir was more familiar than his father had been, that pale, overweight man who was so keen for him to re-Submerge. 'Take the explosive off Hannah. Please. She's innocent, she's done nothing. I led her down here, it was all me.'

293

Noir wiped her face, but still there were no tears to accompany the noise of her sobbing.

'The explosive will go off. You know that.'

'Put it on me.'

'No Troy!' Yvonne shook her head. 'Noir, don't. He's ours. We've only just met him, he's only just met us. Give us a chance to get to know you Troy.'

'Hannah's innocent,' said Troy again. 'She doesn't deserve to make the sacrifice. She can have a normal life. Me – what choices will I have? They can't re-Submerge me now, there won't be a Program that can undo everything I've seen.'

Noir twisted her head to look at him, her movements stiff and uncertain. 'Yes. Yes, it's time to do the right thing. We have to let him, Yvonne. The right thing. My son – it's the right thing to do. He'll walk right back into the Institute and they'll welcome him. And then he'll deliver himself as a sacrifice.'

'You don't know what you're saying!' Yvonne stood between Noir and Troy. 'You're psychotic. Noir, this is your son, the son you thought was dead. All those years... you can catch up, build a new relationship. The Institute can help you.'

'The Institute! It's too late for me, Yvonne. I'm... you're right, I'm not who I was. I know I am. My mind... it's not what it was.' She lifted her comms device to her lips. 'Release,' she said and there was a light whirring sound. Troy turned to see astonishment on Hannah's face as the explosive grew bigger around her neck and dropped onto her shoulders. He went to her and lifted it up, feeling its cold weight as he held it in mid-air, then dropped it over his own head. It vibrated ever so slightly, sending warm tingles down his back.

'What are you waiting for?' he asked Noir. 'Re-constrict the explosive. Do it, or the whole slum district will be blown up.'

'Noir,' Yvonne pleaded. 'Don't do this. He's ours. I've known him for a few days, that's all. I've waited so many years to meet him.'

'Troy.' Hannah stood beside him, shaking her head. 'I wish you hadn't done that. I wish you hadn't.' She leaned in close to him, tucking her head under his chin.

'There's an escape hatch,' Troy hissed into her ear. 'Above our heads. The platform to reach it is just under us.' He stamped his foot to indicate the platform below. 'If we can get it working, we can swim. You can swim up, and I can swim down and away, and detonate the explosive underwater. Nobody will be hurt. Except me.'

Hannah glanced upwards, then down at the floor.

Troy tightened his hold on her. 'I don't know how to get it working. But it must have controls somewhere. There has to be a way.'

Hannah turned to stare at the neural accelerator helmet, hanging innocently from its stand a few metres away.

'A neural accelerator could control an anti-grav platform – I'm sure of it.'

'Hannah, no. Don't even think about it.' An image of Hannah's brain cells fusing together flashed into Troy's mind. He turned to Noir. 'Constrict it,' he shouted, feeling the vibrations grow faster and more intense. 'Now. What are you waiting for?'

Noir looked bewildered, like an old lady discovering she was alone in the street, wearing just her nightgown. 'Take the... the plan. Mobilise for the plan.' She turned in a circle, and seeing Troy again seemed to stabilise her momentarily. 'My son will go as a sacrifice. He'll lead us into the Institute and then will blow himself up, to purge society. To free us from Institute control.'

'If that's your plan,' said Troy, 'then re-constrict the explosive.' The vibrations were getting even more intense now, and his spine felt electric under its pulsations. Hannah had slipped away from him and was halfway across the dome, heading towards the neural accelerator. 'Hannah, don't!'

Too late. Hannah slid under the helmet, pushing its hard sides down around her tiny skull. There was a light hissing sound as the helmet secured itself to her head and almost immediately the floor began to rumble. She closed her eyes and frowned, and her face began to shake. The floor rumbled even harder and her eyes flew open, bloodshot and tear-filled.

'I can't do it,' she said. 'I'm trying… the platform…'

'You stupid, *stupid* Emerger!' Noir rushed towards her. 'What are you doing? What have you done?'

Crack!

A huge split appeared behind Hannah and began to spread up the glass dome, droplets of water pushing their way through and running down towards the floor.

Noir's scream was as loud as an audio wall as she began tugging the device from Hannah's head.

'I can't do it Troy.' Hannah's voice was shaking so much, she sounded like she was cutting concrete with a laser drill. 'I can't… I can't control it. I'm wrecking the dome, I can't stop it.'

Noir tore the helmet free and put it on her own head, but it was too late. The glass dome tower was fractured all over. Water was already rushing along the rapidly expanding crack and running along the floor, forming little silver paths around the grit and dirt, and then joining up to become one great sheet of water that spread at speed.

Troy felt a lightness around his neck and turned to see Yvonne lifting the buzzing explosive hoop from his shoulders.

'Yvonne, what are you doing?' Troy fought to take it back, but Yvonne's grip was strong. Without saying a word, she lowered the explosive over her own head, pushing Troy away and hurrying to where Noir sobbed and clawed at the neural accelerator. Hannah stepped out of the way and let Yvonne snatch the comms device from Noir's waist. She raised the black egg-shape to her mouth and whispered: '*Constrict*', swallowing hard as the device tightened immediately around her neck.

'Yvonne, no!' But Troy knew it was too late.

Yvonne went to the platform below the escape hatch and pressed the control. Slowly the flat, square platform began ascending towards the cracked ceiling, water running off it as the dark board left the ground.

'Vonny!' ripped the helmet off and threw it to one side, almost hitting Hannah square in the face with it. 'Wait – Vonny, no!' Noir splashed towards the platform, which was now almost two metres from the ground, and threw herself at its edge. Gripping on by her fingers, she hauled herself up as the platform sped up and rushed towards the ceiling. Gripping on by her fingers, she tried to pull herself up but she couldn't do it. Yvonne bent down and grabbed her arm furiously, attempting to lift Noir up onto the platform, but she was too heavy. With a scream that reverberated throughout the dome Noir fell. Her body hit the floor hard and was still. Yvonne looked down, pain and tears evident on her face as the platform reached the ceiling and she was erased from sight by a revolving metal aperture.

Troy and Hannah watched as the glass bubble began to rotate, the terrible grinding sound of glass against metal echoing throughout the control dome. After a few seconds, the bubble detached itself entirely from the control dome's glass dome and began floating towards the surface of the sea. Yvonne was just visible, head bowed as if in prayer.

Soon, the bubble had floated out of view, leaving them alone with the still form of Noir face down in the centre of the room.

'Yvonne will set off the explosion,' said Troy, dragging his feet through water as he hurried towards Hannah, keeping his eyes away from Noir's corpse. 'We need to –'

A force shook the control room, and the glass dome swayed and creaked like stiff seaweed in a strong current.

'I think she just did,' said Hannah.

With a terrible snapping sound, cracks appeared all over the dome, hundreds of them, from hairline fractures that leaked droplets of water, to giant angry zig-zags that ran from one side of the dome to the other.

The hard floor, now covered in water, rippled like a sheet of flexiglass bending in the wind and Hannah fell as low waves peaked and crashed everywhere.

Noir's body began to float face down in the water a ribbon of red blood spreading from her like a final testimony to her life.

Troy pulled Hannah to her feet, pain burning his ribcage. 'It's all going to collapse.'

Hannah nodded, and they looked around the control dome for something, anything, that might help them to safety. The only exit was the metal entrance, which was sealed tightly. 'The escape bubble has gone,' said Troy. 'We'll have to go back through the main entrance.'

Beside the large silver door, the Ethernet screen buzzed and faded to nothing with a crackling, popping sound and a counter fell away from the wall, depositing Ethernet goggles and gloves into the rushing water.

'There's no way to open it!' Hannah shouted. 'The comms device – it's gone. We can't get out.'

On the other side of the dome, a fragment of glass came crashing to the floor, followed by a gush of green water that splashed noisily and rushed towards them.

'We don't have long,' said Troy, taking Hannah's hand and dragging her towards the sealed exit. He banged on the solid metal as water rushed around his feet, but the door wouldn't budge.

'It's no good Troy.' Hannah was shaking her head. 'This is it for us. This was our time. I'm glad – we were part of something important. Our actions saved the lives of millions and Yvonne… Yvonne will be remembered forever.'

'No.' Troy shook his head. 'We'll get out.' He banged on the door again. 'There must be a way.'

He noticed the tagging drone Noir had kicked to one side earlier, its anti-gravs squealing under a heavy plastic counter that had fallen on top of it.

'Explosives.'

'What?'

'Nothing – just move away from the entrance. A long way away.' Troy splashed through the water towards the drone, falling onto his knees to drag the counter from its shiny top, while Hannah waded towards the centre of the dome.

The drone was a tired old thing, patched together with metal brackets and clearly repaired a few times over, but it still felt solid and heavy as he grasped hold of it and dragged it through the water towards the door.

'What are you doing?' asked Hannah. 'Is that a tagging drone? Oh my Unity, be careful!'

Troy nodded, straining to manoeuvre the heavy drone near to the doorway.

'What are you going to do with it?'

'I…' Troy gave the drone one final tug, his ribs aching, and placed it against the door. 'Not sure. But it has to have explosives in it – she was tagging their legs with them.'

Hannah nodded. 'I've heard of that before, penal tags. If they're small explosives they'll be polars. The sort they use in building works. They're volatile – it won't take much to set them off.'

Troy eyed the neural-accelerator, now lying like a broken toy, several of its cables snapped, on a water-soaked counter. The counter itself was clinging to the side of the glass dome by a single metal bolt. Hannah followed his gaze.

'No, Troy. Not a good idea.'

299

'If it's powerful enough to disrupt thoughts, it could trigger explosives too.'

Hannah shook her head. 'I'm not sure if it's possible to control it.'

'Only one way to find out.'

Chapter Thirty-Three

Troy went to the helmet and fitted it over his head, feeling a buzzing sensation as the device settled around his sandy hair. It didn't tighten, as the device Yvonne had put on him had done, and curious fizzing sounds emanated from its smooth sides. It felt overly warm above his ears, as though it had overheated, but just as Troy was about to abandon hope, tear off the helmet and try to physically beat the door down, a clean sensation rushed through his brain like cool water washing the inside of his skull. The room no longer looked solid, but full of energy fields, all moving at different speeds, some light and airy, others, like the tagging droid, a body of very dense, thick colours that barely moved at all.

Concentrate. Water rushed around Troy's calves as he struggled to focus on the tagging droid, not at all sure how to cause the explosives to go off. He tried speaking to the drone with his thoughts, telling it to detonate, but nothing happened. With the water at his thighs now and Hannah holding onto one of the counters to keep herself steady in the flow, Troy knew he didn't have long.

'Try to relax, Troy,' Hannah shouted, coughing as water caught in her mouth. 'It looks like it's based on a VR device – you know how they work, you have to keep it light, not think too much.'

Troy tried to let his mind go blank, hearing a tremendous cracking sound overhead as more of the ceiling gave way.

'It's not that easy to relax,' he shouted back, side-stepping a mammoth fragment of glass as it came crashing to the ground. He tried to make his mind go blank, to filter out all the sights and sounds around him, and to his amazement he began to feel something – like air flowing from his mind. He stared at the tagging droid, letting his thoughts drift towards it, feeling them touch the dense pool of energy and slip inside it. *Concentrate.* Another piece of glass fell from above, but suddenly Troy wasn't worried. He stopped it dead, holding it in mid-air with his thoughts while he let his other brainwaves work on the tagging drone. *I can feel the explosives, how delicate they are under the metal... just a few circuitries need to be twisted, then taken out, a spark... nearly there.* The glass over his head wobbled. *Nearly.* He could feel movement within the drone, something breaking up and a hot sensation like metal warmed by the sun, and there were creaking, cracking noises.

'Troy,' said Hannah. 'Something's happening.'

'Stand back,' Troy shouted, the shard of glass wobbling dangerously over his head now and threatening to drop down. 'Stand back.'

'I can't stand any further back.' Hannah's grip tightened on the counter, which had inched even further away from the glass sides of the dome.

With a metallic bang the drone exploded, sending fragments of plastic and metal skidding across the water-covered floor. Steam rose from the body of the drone as water flowed into it and immediately extinguished its internal fire, and twisters of black smoke spiralled into the air and vanished.

Tearing the helmet from his head, Troy waded to Hannah and grabbed her arm, pulling her towards the door which was now dented and coming away from the frame. They both tugged at the loose metal sheet, pulling with all their might to free it, and with a sound like a knife cutting marble the door finally came free, falling from its frame and splashing down into the water where it floated towards the centre of the dome like a beaten-up boat.

The water, which had started to creep and rush around the entrance as soon as the door had been blasted loose, now washed into the newly opened space: a blue-lit corridor, long and narrow like the wind-farm servicing tunnels Troy used to hang out in when he was at college. However, unlike the old servicing tunnels, this one curved down at the end, not up, and he could see metal rungs leading down into darkness. An image came back to him: ladders and a huge circular, metal entranceway. He must have been carried up the ladder earlier, when he was unconscious.

As the dark space rapidly filled with water, Troy wondered where it led and whether or not it would be sealed at the end. Water rushed around their knees, the smell of salt heavy, and there was an ominous clicking sound like a rubber suction cup being pulled from glass.

Slowly, a black cloud of secure drones dropped down from the ceiling.

'Oh my Unity,' said Hannah.

There were four of them, hovering just above the water, their red lights bright.

'Just go really slowly,' said Troy, taking Hannah's hand again. 'Stay close to me and don't make any sudden movements.'

'Maybe we should – the neural accelerator… perhaps we can shut them off?' They both turned back to see the neural accelerator lying on the counter – smashed to pieces. The shard of glass that had been hovering above it had come crashing down and cut the device in two, disembowelling its inner magnets and circuitry.

'Doesn't look like that's an option. Maybe there's another way to shut them off.'

Hannah winched as the freezing water crawled up their waists. 'No. All sentinel drones, secure drones, door watchers, all of them, they're hard wired. Impervious to external electromagnetic radiation. Tamper proof.'

'OK,' said Troy. 'So we'll just go slowly.'

'Fine with me,' said Hannah, moving forward through the water one tiny step at a time. But even gentle splashing movements seemed to alert the secure drones and the nearest one raised its straps: its preliminary warning gesture.

'Stop!' Troy shouted. 'It's the water. There's too much movement. How long can you hold your breath for?' The water was at chest height now and Troy's lower body had gone numb with the cold.

'I have no idea. We learnt to swim together remember?'

'We need to swim. If we swim underwater, the surface water won't move. But we have to swim slowly. OK? And come up slowly too – no rushing to the surface.'

'There's not going to be a surface soon,' said Hannah, watching water rise around her neck.

'Then let's go.'

Slowly, Troy and Hannah took huge intakes of breath and lowered themselves underwater, swimming forward with minimal strokes. The drones continued to float above them, seemingly uninterested in the two bodies moving cautiously below, and before long Troy and Hannah reached the ladder and were able to bring their heads up to the metre of air space that remained above them.

'What now?' asked Hannah, her dark hair plastered to her head, clothes stuck to her body. 'Whatever's at the bottom of this ladder – exit, droid loading area – whatever it is must be sealed or else the water wouldn't be rising.'

Troy nodded, flicking water from his hair. 'Didn't you see what was there when they brought you up here?'

'No – they put a de-sensing band on me. I couldn't see or hear. Didn't you see?'

'I was unconscious, but...' Troy closed his eyes and the memories came, fragmented and incomplete like the broken glass in the control dome. 'They carried me through it when I passed out. It's like... the doorway to a computer program vault. Really thick and heavy, a tough seal. They carried me past it. I remember something knocked my chest as we went through. There's a code lock on the outside, and a wheel lock on this one – our side.' He looked down into the rising water, but couldn't see the bottom of the ladder. 'It must be at least thirty metres to the bottom. It took... I'm not sure how long, they floated me up on something, but it took a long time to reach the top up here. We'd never have enough air to get down there and turn the wheel. Even if we took a few trips, the water would have filled up the space up here. No more air. It's a tight lock – it needed at least ten turns, maybe twenty.' He took some steady breaths. 'There must be a way.'

'Even if we could get it open,' said Hannah, 'the water would pour into the slum district and everyone would be drowned. We can't do it.' Bleeping sounds echoed around the corridor as the secure drones became completely submerged and went offline, their straps falling down into the water like strings of seaweed. 'It's hopeless.' Hannah sank a little deeper into the water.

'Wait – the drones have off-lined,' said Troy. 'We could swim to the surface. It can't be that far, and...'

'No,' said Hannah. 'The slums extend out for miles under the sea. We're far into them so we must be at least 300 metres down.'

Troy closed his eyes and tried to think, and a memory niggled at him. He'd seen something earlier when he'd been taken – the ladder, the huge door, children running around… but that had been outside in the slums… He fought to hold onto the thought, tilting his nose to the ceiling and blinking away water. *Carried here, on a stretcher… lifted through tunnels, tilted vertically to ascend…* They'd strapped him to a stretcher, he remembered now, and held the stretcher vertically so it could be floated on anti-gravs up the tunnel. A vertical tunnel with a ladder running up the side of it. And at the bottom of that tunnel had been…

'Hannah!' Troy said, spitting metallic-tasting water from his mouth. Drops caught in his windpipe and he coughed, salt stung his eyes. 'Listen… there are underwater suits. I think I saw them.' *Did I? It could have been a dream…* 'I think they're underneath us, at the bottom of the tunnel.' He coughed some more. 'If we can put on gills and suits, we can swim to the surface. We need to take a really deep breath Hannah, are you ready? And then we'll swim to the bottom.'

'I've got nothing better to do,' said Hannah, giving him a little smile.

'Ready?' As Troy said the word, he knew he wasn't. It was a big gamble. If they swam to the bottom and there was nothing there, by the time they swam back up again there would be no air pocket left. But then what choice did they have? Stay up here and wait until they had no air at all? It was all or nothing.

'Ready.'

'Then let's go.'

Troy sucked in his breath and Hannah did the same. They both flipped over and swam down into total darkness, reaching out to find the other one as they descended and feeling the walls for signs of a recess or container.

Soon Troy's chest was burning and he wanted nothing more than to breathe, just to breathe. Every instinct in his body told him to swim back up to the surface, but he carried on stroking the curved walls, feeling around for Hannah to make sure she was still with him. And then he found it: a smooth panel set into the wall. He grabbed Hannah's wrist and pulled her close, but she struggled, fighting to get up to the surface. No, he mouthed stupidly, knowing she couldn't hear him and he kept a tight grip on her even as she fought.

Finding the handle with his free hand, he opened the panel and groped inside, feeling soft material under his fingers and to his immense relief, a row of face seals complete with mechanical gills.

As he tugged a face seal free he felt Hannah go limp beside him, and panic nearly made him inhale. He fought against the agony in his lungs and fitted a face seal around Hannah's immobile face, watching the device auto-empty water and shaking her, willing her to take a breath. If she didn't, it was all over. There was no point putting on his face seal. He waited, his throat on fire, his eyes feeling like they were going to pop out of his head, and then gently, like a sleeping child waking up, Hannah took a little breath and opened her eyes.

The relief was overwhelming.

Fitting his own face seal and pausing for a torturous second as the device emptied of water, Troy took huge, cool gulps of air, elation flooding through him. Hannah's hands went to her face, her eyes registering confusion as she felt the hard visor that went all the way from her forehead to her chin. The facemask had fused to her skin and hair with cellulose adhesive, so even when she patted and tugged at it, the seal held fast.

'We need to get out of here,' said Troy, his voice booming back in his ears as the internal speakers clicked into action. He felt to check there was a wireless transmitter on the side of the device, but there was no need: he could see Hannah heard him loud and clear, and she nodded to affirm.

They swam up the tunnel and along, through the now inactive tentacles of the restrainer drones, back towards the wrecked control dome which they could see was now just a

307

jagged circle of glass teeth like a cracked eggshell. But as Troy tried to swim through the blown-up entrance way, past the loose metal doors, he was repelled by a sharp, electric field. Pain burned through his fingers, which had been outstretched as he'd swum forward, and hot, angry tingles ran up his palms and into his forearms. His ribs throbbed as he bounced to the floor.

'What was that?' said Hannah, looking on. 'Troy, your hands – they're black. What happened?'

Troy swam upright. 'I don't know. Some sort of electric field. The entrance has been electrified somehow – can you hear it buzzing?' They were both silent and a low, erratic crackling sound could be heard like water drops on a hot frying pan. Hannah nodded and swam towards the entrance.

'Hannah – stop!'

It was too late. The field threw her backwards, and she landed a few feet away from Troy, her hands black and raw.

Troy helped her float upright. 'Look,' he said, pointing towards the exploded shell of the tagging drone. A torn battery, flashing with silver sparks, lay in the metal carcass, which in turn had been washed against the metal doorway, turning the whole frame electric.

'Hannah, we can't go through this way,' said Troy. 'And there's no other way out. We need to head back down and unscrew the sealed exit at the bottom of the tunnel. The one that leads back into the slums.'

'But the water…' Hannah shook her head, hair floating around in loose tendrils. 'It will go through into the slums. Everyone will drown.'

'There must be other sealed doorways down there, safety valves. An evacuation procedure…'

'Come off it, Troy. It's the slums. It's amazing these suits were here, but safety valves – they'd cost thousands to maintain. No one in the slums would waste the money.'

'There *must* be. Even in a slum district, there must be some sort of procedure.'

'No.' Hannah looked certain. 'It's not like that down here. It's so disorganised. Maybe we should just stay here and wait for the rescue teams to come.'

As she spoke Troy's battery alarm began to bleep. Above them the tunnel shuddered and the walls began to creak.

'Our gills,' said Hannah. 'They need power points to charge them. Mine's on critical battery already. Look – yours is too, I can see it flashing.'

Troy saw the flashing battery signs inside both visors. 'We have to open the door down there. It's the only way.' But Troy knew he couldn't really do it. They were NEs but they were people and they could be saved. He couldn't trade their lives for his life any more than he could have shot Noir in cold blood. He grabbed Hannah's hand and they swam back down the tunnel. When they reached the huge, round steel door that separated the tunnel from the rest of the slum district, his survival instinct suddenly kicked in, and Troy took the wheel and began to turn.

'Troy… I don't think… really, what if…?'

'Hannah, it's our only chance.' He stopped turning the wheel. 'The people down here, they don't do anything for anyone, you said so yourself. I don't want to do this, but if they were in my position, every single one of them would do the same thing.' But he knew he was lying and the resolve just wasn't there.

'I wouldn't,' said Hannah, crossing her arms and turning away. 'And it really doesn't matter what *they* would do, it's what *you* do that's important.'

Troy went back to the wheel but made no motion to turn it. Probably he never would have been able to – it was just a gesture. With a sigh, he floated away from it and towards Hannah and holding her hand they floated up to the curved roof of the tunnel. A small air bubble remained in a slight outpouching of the tunnel.

'Things were going too well,' he said. 'It was all too easy. So… this is how it's to end? Ironic that I am a true Emerger after all at the very end. A sacrifice for the greater good?'

'For the greater good.' Hannah took a deep breath, appearing to savour it. Both their visors were glowing with the emergency battery sign so they took them off, taking deep gulps of the stale air which was rapidly diminishing around them. Troy pulled her close to him as they stared down into the rising tide of water. They dropped the gills, watching them float away, their lights dimming and disappearing as they drifted away down the tunnel.

Images flashed through Troy's mind, almost all of them from Submergence: his parents, his school, some of the experiences he'd had with women – synthetic women as it now transpired. Funny to think that until now all his successes and failures with the opposite sex had been dependant on a computer program and whether the Institute decided he needed to have his heart broken or his ego boosted. But Hannah was real: his time with her had been the real thing, and it warmed him in the freezing water to think that he'd been allowed a glimpse of real love before the end.

As the water flowed around them and he felt the cool bones of Hannah's delicate hand in his, all his bitterness, all the anger and hurt and humiliation, the feelings of hatred he'd had towards the system, and Yvonne for a time, and his hatred of Noir and the Demergers, it all evaporated. He wasn't angry about anything anymore. The system had tried to give him the best outcome, but due to a fluke of circumstances that appeared to be genetic by all accounts, he'd exited the Submergence Program early and gone his own way. The Institute had given him a wonderful childhood, loving parents and formative experiences that kept him safe from harm. And the Demergers – they were misguided, but that didn't mean he had to hate them. Given the chance he would have tried to help them and bring them back into the fold.

He wondered what life would have been like if he'd been brought up by Anya – or Noir as she'd called herself. Very different. Would Noir have joined the Demergers if her child hadn't been put into Submergence? Probably. And she'd have taken her baby with her, down to the slum district to fight out an existence amid cylinder heads and troubled individuals scratching a selfish existence together. Troy probably wouldn't even have made it to his twenty-first birthday.

Beside him, Hannah held his face in her hands and gazed into his face. She smiled and Troy thought she'd never looked more beautiful despite the wet hair plastered to her face. He wished he could save her – she didn't deserve this.

There were ominous creaking, groaning sounds all around them as the tunnel began to twist and buckle.

'So – we'll either be crushed to death or drown,' said Troy. 'Which do you fancy?'

'Neither.'

As they sat in silence, waiting to die, they took comfort in the touch of each other's bodies. Silence was the only communication they needed.

Chapter Thirty-Four

Hannah broke the silence, 'I can't believe Noir was your biological mother.'

'I never had any thoughts about what she'd be,' he said, treading water but tiring. His ribs ached and his lungs throbbed. 'There wasn't time to think about it. Everything happened so quickly – I didn't expect to meet her so soon. But I do realise how lucky I am. How things could have turned out if she'd brought me up.'

'There are so many people who aren't so lucky,' said Hannah, leaning forward and kissing him briefly on the lips. 'Imagine the impact a mother like that could have had on you. If you'd been with her from a young age, imagine the damage she could have done.' She sounded strangely calm and rehearsed.

'I'm sorry she died, but Yvonne – that's the real tragedy.'

'She died saving thousands of people,' said Hannah.

'Just like we are going to do.' Troy leaned forward and kissed her, and as he did a rush of colours swirled around him.

A tremor rumbled through the tunnel walls and the water suddenly surged up obliterating the air pocket.

'Hannah?' Troy managed to say before they were both submerged. They looked at each other in the water, their hair flowing about them in the current.

His lungs began to burn and he realised the end was close. The murky water was all around him and flooding his consciousness. He suddenly felt at peace as the water around them stilled and gained a brilliant clarity. The blue light filtering from below danced around him, illuminating him in a beautiful ballet. It felt achingly familiar.

He pulled Hannah towards him. Hannah's small face, eyes wide and bright, lips tilted towards him for their final kiss, began to fade under a rainbow of swirls. He reached out but all he could feel was air instead of water. Then her face disappeared completely and he was surrounded by a soft yellow light. And there was no water, just a feeling warmth and weight around his legs and chest.

'Hannah?' He reached out for her again, but his hands felt nothing, not even a cool breeze against his fingers. His eyelids fluttered and with a start he realised they were closed and he was watching orangey yellow snow. They fluttered some more and Troy wrenched them open, feeling some sort of lightening around his forehead, a pressure being released.

There was an expanse of milky coffee-coloured ceiling just a few feet away, and with a jolt of motion sickness he realised he was lying down and wasn't vertical at all. There was no water, no Thames, no Hannah. He put a hand to his forehead and felt a small grove running around it.

'What's happening?' he said. 'What's *happening?*'

'Hello Troy,' said a voice. 'Welcome to your Emergence.'

A wave of disorientation hit Troy so hard that if he hadn't been lying down, he would have fallen over. He felt like he'd walked into a brick wall. There were lights all around, bright, white lights, and they made his eyes water and his vision blur.

'Hannah. *Hannah.*' He still reached for her, even though common sense told him she wasn't there. A few faces swam into view: kind, smiling faces, some pink, some brown. He couldn't tell yet whether they were men or women. But everything felt intensely *real.*

'Where am I?' he croaked, and was alarmed at how loud his voice sounded.

A face leaned in. It was familiar.

'Congratulations Troy, you made it through.'

'Who… *Yvonne?*' Troy reached towards the face in front of him.

'No,' the face said, smiling away and clasped his hands in hers. 'No, not Yvonne. My name's Susan. It's OK, you've come through just fine.' Around him he heard similar phrases being echoed by cheery individuals, and murmurings and stirrings from every corner. *You've come through fine.*

'Welcome to this new world we have made for you,' said Susan. 'We have given you all that we can until now. Thank us not, but help us build a better society.'

Troy sat bolt upright, a hysterical laugh escaping his throat.

'My… my Emergence? *My* Emergence.' He frowned at Susan. 'I've seen you before – you were helping the other Emerger, Alan.'

'The computerised me.' Susan smiled. 'They drop it into the Program so I'm not such a shock to you.'

'No. *No.* I don't believe it. I just don't believe it.' He was laughing loudly now, looking around the room and seeing other Emergers sitting up, smiling, embracing their counsellors. 'It's just… I feel like… like….this is, *this* is my Emergence? None of it was real? Yvonne? She survived? And Hannah? Where is she?'

'Survived is one way to put it,' said Susan, with a knowing smile. 'You could say Yvonne is eternal, she can never die. She was a computer program, a rather brilliant one. You'll remember her forever and always, as we all do, as our greatest hero and greatest teacher. There's a shrine to the Yvonne Program here in the building. We often go and have some reflection time, to remind ourselves of all that we can achieve when human beings are at their best. And the people in the slums – well there's even better news there. The slums don't exist here Troy. They were a computer program too. A program designed to teach you what happens when societies fragment along monetary lines and to guard against such a rift happening in our society.'

'So what does that mean?' Troy found himself smiling at the other Emergers, many of whom were looking around the room, taking in their new location and new brothers and sisters, while others were focused on their counsellor, asking incessant questions as he was. 'That everyone is an Emerger?' His face fell. 'And Hannah? Is she a computer program?'

'One question at a time,' said Susan. 'Everyone in this society is given an Emergence upbringing. No one can be let down by their parents – everyone has an equal shot at life. Isn't it wonderful?'

'Wonderful,' Troy said, 'but what about Hannah?' He wasn't sure he wanted to know the answer. 'Was she a computer program too?'

Susan smiled again. 'As if we'd be so cruel. No, she's real. Very real as a matter of fact. But she's not your counsellor, she's your Emergence partner. Everyone has them. Some are just friends, whereas some lucky few find a love match, just as you learned during your last Submergence chapters.'

'So where is she?'

Chapter Thirty-Five

The group was shepherded into the lecture theatre looking confused and bewildered, all newly Emerged, all still in their cotton pyjamas. The man on the podium spoke, his voice loud and authoritative.

'Welcome new Emergers. My name is Professor Chen. I'm much less stuffy and obnoxious than Professor Shaw, whom you've all met and didn't like very much.' He paused for a moment, smiling. Everyone smiled back and a few people laughed. 'Today is the most important day of your lives, your Emergence day. Confused? I'm sure. Scared? Just a little. I can tell you I was confused and scared when I sat in your position twenty-three years ago. Let me explain what has happened. You would have already worked out that you were still within the Program when we fooled you into thinking you had Emerged prematurely.

'Early on, when the first subjects went through the Program, we found an unacceptably high rate of Demergence phenomenon. People were just not accepting the beauty of the Program and we were getting far too many post-Emergence psycho-social problems. After extensive research we found that the problem was not within the Program itself but in the way people behaved and interacted after they Emerged.'

Looking around, Troy noticed that everyone in the room, just like him, was hanging on every word Professor Chen said.

He was a good orator and it was also clear he'd given this talk many times before.

Chen strode from the lectern to stand in the centre of the floor. 'So we had to do something. We inserted the premature Emergence scenario to give you all a controlled taster of what you are experiencing now. We usually refer to it as your pseudo-Emergence. We let you ask all the questions you wanted to ask and also get a taster of why the Program works. We let you see the dark side of humanity without risk and now you are free. What you do now is up to you. We have given you the building blocks for your life, how you live it is up to you. We have I hope, like good parents, instilled you with morals and ethics and virtues to be a good member of society.

'Please bear with me just a little bit longer. You have all completed the first years of your university courses. If you wish, and I strongly recommend you do, you can pick up where you left off, none of you actually failed. To be melodramatic, it is your destiny. So what happens now, you ask? Well, you will stay within these grounds for four days during which time you will interact with each other, get to know your new family. Accommodation is organised for you on the outskirts of the city – not inside the building, no, we want to give you a taste of the real world. You'll be sharing your accommodation with your new Submergence family and I can tell you – you'll make some lifelong friends while you're living there. I will leave all the precise logistics for your counsellor to discuss.' There were some excited murmurings within the audience as people began speculating where they would be placed and with whom.

'Look around you my friends,' Chen continued, ignoring the restlessness with practised ease. 'Each of you shares a common past and I hope we can all forge a common future. We are all brothers and sisters. Congratulations again. Happy Emergence Day!' He began clapping, initially alone, but it wasn't long before the entire room joined in, everyone clapping

317

vigorously, some cheering too. Troy looked at their faces. The majority were beaming with joy, obviously enthralled by the chance for a new beginning. Others looked confused and fearful, although not unhappily so. When Troy looked again to the front of the auditorium the Professor had gone.

'So, Troy.' Susan pulled a fresh flexisheet from the box under her desk and began tapping it with a large silver stylus. 'This stylus is no good.' She tapped again on the sheet, smiling as a line appeared. 'Ah, there we go. It's working now. So, you've decided to sign up for medical work?'

'Not work. Training.' Troy watched her tap shorthand onto the flexisheet. She must be, he thought, the only counsellor in the entire building to still use the old flexisheet note system instead of auto-dictation, but she said she preferred to make notes by hand – apparently she remembered everything better that way. 'Five training shifts a week at Guys.

'Good, good,' said Susan, continuing to make notes.

'It looks like the Program picked well for me,' said Troy. 'But I'm not sure yet. I'll need a few years I think.' The interview room was eerily familiar and Troy thought back to his career counselling sessions in Submergence. Maybe they based that room on this one, or vice versa.

'Of course, very sensible,' said Susan, looking up from the sheet. 'The system can only measure so much. Mind you, your Emergence and pseudo-Emergence – Emergence phases one and two – were uneventful. There's no reason to suspect the Program hasn't matched you up correctly. We've been monitoring your neurokinetic activity since birth after all – in theory we know what we're doing.'

'I know.' Troy smiled. 'And I'm grateful.'

'Remember we can help with more than just careers,' said Susan. 'Monitoring your neurokinetics tells us so much about you, not just your vocation. We know what you like and what

318

you don't like, how you're likely to react in certain situations... the whole ball of string. And now you've Emerged, well – the data we have on you is almost perfect I would say.'

'Really?' asked Troy. 'You carry on taking data once we've Emerged?' He was unperturbed. The whole idea of being monitored was old news now, he'd gotten thoroughly used to the idea and understood the logic of it.

'Of course,' said Susan. 'It's very valuable. In the post-Emergence world we can *completely* distinguish the individual's likes and dislikes from their behaviour. If they go bowling every week, for example, they obviously like bowling. It's a bit harder to determine absolutes within the parameters of the Program as everyone does the same activities, hence the negligible percentage of career matches that don't work out. But the post-Emergence data gives us certainties – 100% certainties. Would you like to know the news about your love match?' Susan didn't wait for an answer. 'It's 100% now.'

Troy wasn't sure what to say about that. It was hard to get excited about the possibility of a relationship with someone you'd never met.

They chatted for a while about the future and then Troy said:

'So tell me – did I feature in Hannah's dreams too?'

'It depends on her personality.' Susan rifled through a pile of flexisheets. 'It's most likely you didn't. She doesn't have such heightened sensitivity to visual stimuli, so I imagine they might decide that meeting you in the flesh, talking to you in person, would be enough for her.'

'But she had the same experiences... before we met?'

Susan waved a 'telling off' finger at him. 'Now, now. It's bad manners to snoop into someone else's final chapters, you know that. But I can tell you that female subjects generally have the same experiences only with the gender reversed. Just like

319

she would have met versions of your girlfriends, only for her they would have been boyfriends.'

'Right.' He realised that he had clenched his fists and had to consciously relax his forearm to release his fingers. He forced a smile. 'But it wasn't me.' He hesitated, struggling to keep his voice light. 'It wasn't me she fell in love with. It was just an image of me, just like I fell in love with an image of her.'

'Yes Troy, it was your image, and I'm sure you've guessed that the face and body of the Hannah you knew was taken from her holo-image. Even the voice you heard, her voice, is identical to the real Hannah, as was yours to her. We do try and inject some of your personality traits into the sim but it has to be within the constraints of the Program.'

It was still so hard to take in. Hannah existed – well, at least someone who looked and sounded like her. But he had fallen in love with the person, not just the body and the face. What if the real Hannah wasn't the person he'd loved? He'd loved a virtual reality personality – a person generated by a vast computer. Who he loved was just digital code, an endless string of ones and zeros again.

He calmed himself and looked into the counsellor's eyes, searching for any sign of understanding, any realisation as to how anxious he felt. All he found there was genuine excitement and happiness. He struggled to maintain his disgruntlement but lost, his anger crumbling away.

'So am I supposed to marry her?'

'No Troy, don't be ridiculous. You will meet her very soon and after you leave here you will be free to meet up or not as you please. You've already shared so much. That is part of the beauty of it all. We are proud that our matching results in a 93% marriage rate.'

The Institute gates swung open and Troy walked through them, his meagre bag of belongings slung over his shoulder.

320

Five white taxi pods sat waiting, their doors wide open, and as he made his way towards them, a young woman with sleek, dark hair and blue eyes set in a delicate face was climbing into the first. Something made her hesitate, and, glancing over her shoulder, dark hair swinging aside, her eyes met Troy's. With a hesitant smile of recognition she turned towards him, and he returned her growing smile with a grin of his own.

He paused for a moment, then started walking towards Hannah, realising in the same instant that it was the first true decision he had ever made.

Epilogue

Extract from *Emergence - The History of a New Beginning* by Professor Albert Harris. Copyright – Virtua Publishing House, 2430

One of the major issues with the whole Emergence phenomenon was that of parents and the function of parenthood. How could parents possibly interact with their offspring after so much time apart? What possible link could there be between them, since parent and child had never met and the parents had been absent during the formative years. These questions and concerns caused considerable problems for the forefathers of modern Emergence theory. Early attempts to reintroduce parents to their Emergent offspring caused major psychological morbidity to both parties.

In the late twentieth century and early twenty-first century foetal medicine took major leaps forward. The gestational age to which a (then termed) 'test-tube' baby could be kept alive ex-utero increased, while the gestational age at which babies could survive after premature delivery decreased. Inevitably, it was soon possible for mothers to be removed from the equation. Mankind could now take a sperm and ovum and make a human being without the need for a human womb.

Early Emergence theory, pioneered by Dr Evesham and explained in depth in his original paper 'Better Man For A Better Mankind', stated that the genetic component of an individual was unchangeable and that was why the necessity to alter the environmental factor was paramount. Now the final part of the puzzle could also be altered. By enhancing the genetics we could ensure that the offspring were optimised and would thus receive the maximal benefit from the system which we placed them in.

Naturally, in order to maintain genetic diversity cloning was prohibited, but it is the author's view that this was a fundamental mistake and is the source of much of the Demergence which, although greatly reduced, is still present in limited pockets of our society today.

Still, the genetically manufactured model of Emergence is close to perfection and has eradicated almost all the earlier problems with the system that was associated with parents. One can only hope that in the future the lottery of genetics will be eradicated entirely in favour of one standard, proven genetic code that offers good health and more importantly a stable mindset in every individual in our society.